THE
SAVAGE
QUEEN

BOOKS BY ASHLEY METZLER

THE AISLING TRILOGY

The Mortal Queen

THE SAVAGE QUEEN

ASHLEY METZLER

SECOND SKY

Published by Second Sky in 2025

An imprint of Storyfire Ltd.
Carmelite House
50 Victoria Embankment
London EC4Y 0DZ

www.secondskybooks.com

The authorised representative in the EEA is Hachette Ireland
8 Castlecourt Centre
Dublin 15 D15 XTP3
Ireland
(email: info@hbgi.ie)

First published as *Aisling: A Spell Unbinding* by Atmosphere Press in 2022.

ISBN: 978-1-83618-414-0
eBook ISBN: 978-1-83618-413-3

To the forests and their flowers and all the legends they hide.

THE ISLES OF
RINN DUÍN

ROKTLING

THE ASHILD SEA

THE ASHILD SEA

ANNWYN

KINBREGGAN

TILREN

AITHIRN

THE ASHILD SEA

N W E S

BOOK 1 RECAP

Bound by both her duty to her clann and all the Isles of Rinn Dúin, Aisling is handfasted to one of the twelve fae sovereigns: she, a fragile symbol of peace between mortals and fair folk.

Aisling is spun into the fae king's world of bygone beasts and primal magic, where mankind's perspective on centuries-old racial feuds is challenged each day Aisling tastes the alluring, savage world views of her lord: the nightmare muse of grisly fireside tales and blood-soaked legends. Wicked philosophies that awaken a creature in Aisling she realizes is not so different from the enemy king she's now eternally tethered to.

Aisling discovers she can wield magic in the form of violet fire. An ability the realm once believed impossible for a mortal thanks to the consequences of Ina, Lir's mother and one of the twelve original Sidhe sovereigns. Ina forsook her mountain kingdom of Iod to save Bres, Lir's father and the original Sidhe king of the greenwood, during an unnamed war. As a result, the gods damned Ina's kingdom of Iod, dooming them to a legacy of mortality and breeding humankind.

Gradually, Lir teaches Aisling to summon her magic the Sidhe call *draiocht*—a sentient, primeval beast that resides in oneself. Aisling relishes this newfound power despite the Unseelie and Sidhe's anger: the fair folk believe Aisling's magic is an ill omen. So, Aisling, Lir, and his knights pursue the Unseelie amidst the feywilds to quell increasing unrest. But it isn't until Lir confronts Balor, the king of the fomorians, that he discovers Danu, the empress of the dryads, has envisioned the finality of the war between the mortals and fair folk: the Sidhe will lose and mankind will triumph.

Among the more prominent Unseelie Aisling encounters while traversing the feywilds, is Racat. A large, sinuous beast that refers to Aisling as his "friend".

Eventually, a second union is requested by the counsel of mortals to better solidify the peace between fair folk and mankind. Dagfin, the mortal Roktan prince, and Peitho, the Sidhe princess of Niltaor, are to be wed. It's at this union, Lir, driven mad by Danu's prophecies, betrays the treaty between mortals and fae in an ambush of Unseelie and Sidhe alike.

Aisling takes Lir's betrayal of their union as an opportunity to flee from both the shackles of her past as well as her political marriage to Lir. Aisling escapes in pursuit of answers, wondering who she is and why she can wield the *draiocht*. She also races for the curse breaker: the remedy to Ina's crimes Dagfin believes rests at Lofgren's Rise.

Additionally, Dagfin owes the magic a debt because he betrayed his union to Peitho, fighting and fleeing with Aisling. Dagfin is also known as a *Faerak*: a hunter and slayer of Unseelie beasts for mankind.

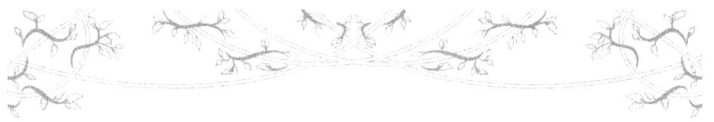

BEFORE

INA

The Sidhe queen knew it would storm the day she chased death.

She knew the skies would crack with brilliant light as the *dragún* slithered through the silver linn—the first droplets poured across the earth by the cauldron of the Forge.

Yet Ina also knew Racat wouldn't escape. Not this time.

The Sidhe queen dove into the Linn of Wanting and swam toward the beast. She bore no blades nor skills with said weapons, for the gods and the Forge had only ever gifted her with the sight and something else. Something Ina hid like a dark jewel in a trove of beasts. Something she treasured. So, while the other twelve Sidhe sovereigns partook in the Wild Hunt and stalked the three *dragúns* with their axes, spears, bows, and knives, Ina only bore her ability to see into the realm of morrow if she wished to capture a *dragún* for herself and claim victory.

The *dragún* cackled beneath the lake's surface, watching as Ina summoned the *draiocht* to breathe where there was no air. Vulnerable to the wrath of the Forge-cast beast before her.

"Your fellow sovereigns have tried their hand with chains, blades, snares, and tricks. Yet none have ever followed me into Forge-brewed waters without a single weapon on their person. So, tell me, Ina of Iod, are you foolish or mad?"

He approached her, a sinuous shape, inky hair floating around its colossal head as it sparkled, even now, beneath the tempest's roar above.

"I've come to strike a deal with you, Racat!" she cried, summoning a cloud of bubbles as she spoke.

Racat defeated the distance between them. Ina didn't flinch nor hesitate even as the *dragún* brought himself nose to nose with the Sidhe queen. A behemoth, obsidian beast annealed with glistering scales, a mane of feral black, and two pointed antlers that dug into its temples.

"What deal could be of any appeal to me?"

"Power."

Racat laughed louder this time, its cadence vibrating through the lake and electrifying the storm swirling in great winds above.

"I am power."

"And yet, you could be more. More than a prize in the hunt. More than a beast in the wild. You could leave these waters and walk amongst the Sidhe of this realm. You could rule."

The *dragún* considered Ina more closely, narrowing its eyes.

Ina swallowed, steeling herself and balling her hands into fists at her sides. Braids of silver unraveled from their beads and clouded around her face as the *dragún* sniffed her.

"You claim to wield such power?" it asked.

"The gods gifted me no blades. Instead, they offered me both sight and a treasure like no other."

"What treasure?"

"A rare and powerful weapon."

Racat scoffed, "All power is me, and I am all power. There is no weapon powerful enough to be of any significance to me that I'm not already aware of."

"You don't know it because I've hidden it away," Ina said. "I can bind you to it, link you so that one day, you might embolden your might and live through my treasure."

"Impossible."

"Is it?" Ina challenged. The *dragún* hesitated, its scaly body moving more slowly in the undercurrents as it weighed the Sidhe queen's words.

"I've foreseen it. Everything will come to pass *if* you agree to my costs."

The *dragún* snapped its jaws, quickening Ina's heart.

"At what cost?"

"You serve Iod and Annwyn. You bless both kingdoms with your might."

"Enslaved to the fae? Shackled, imprisoned, and boasted like a hunt?" The *dragún*'s expression flashed with outrage, great fangs lengthening as it bared its teeth.

"No, as comrades. As partners. As allies," Ina assured the *dragún*.

"There's never been such an alliance."

Ina held her breath, heart thrashing inside.

"Then let us be the first."

Racat smiled, eyes glittering violet.

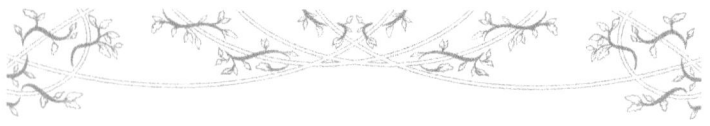

CHAPTER I

AISLING

"Aisling," the wind called.

Aisling was a child once more, racing through the woods.

"Come now, Aisling!" Starn shouted from behind. "You'll have to run faster than that if you ever dream of escaping us!"

Aisling's lungs burned, and her feet were scraped raw, but still, she cut through the trees a few paces ahead of her brothers and Dagfin.

"Come face our wrath, you cowardly beast!" Annind shrieked with giddy delight.

"We'll wear your hide on our back as we return triumphantly to the people!"

"The five princes of the North: Monster Slayers!" Dagfin chimed, his voice closer than the rest, gaining on Aisling's heels. Their games an excuse for Aisling to slip past Tilrish gates and coax her brothers into chasing her.

Aisling broke through the trees and skidded onto Hannelore's shores, Dagfin on her heels. So, without another thought, she leaped into the linn and swam to its center. Starn, Iarbonel, Fergus, Annind, and Dagfin all stopped short, reluctant to wet themselves before the hour was up and Castle Neimedh's supper bell rang. Before Nemed would discover they'd again slipped past Tilren's guards and indulged their childhood for an afternoon. Before Aisling knew the world was a fae one. That monsters lurked both in the wild and in oneself.

"*Aisling,*" an unembodied voice called again, this time closer.

Her brothers and Dagfin were already far away, trudging up the stony shores. Dagfin glanced over his shoulder to see if she'd followed.

"*Aisling,*" the wind growled.

Panic seized Aisling, gripping her legs and pulling her under. The world turned wet and blue, deep, and immeasurably vast. Aisling squirmed, searching for the rippling surface above when a dark mass caught her eye. Her body fell limp with fear.

It approached—its sinuous shape caressed by the undercurrents of Hannelore. A scaly beast cloaked by the cold cavity of the loch. Eyes shimmering with the reflection of a dying sun up above.

"You may call me friend."

Aisling screamed, suddenly unable to move her arms or legs. She was held in place, a prisoner of the loch until the surface crashed atop her head and released her. But once she emerged, she was alone and grown. A woman now. Her brothers and Dagfin were gone, and Hannelore was a distant childhood memory. A memory slipping through her fingers like wisps of ash.

"*Aisling.*" Now, the wind bore the same deep, seductive lilt as Lir. His voice achingly familiar. Her name on his lips was a spell: a cruel enchantment sinking its teeth into her heart.

She spun, wiping away the hair stuck to her forehead.

Rain descended like strings of glittering pearls, flooding the glen. Great willows caged the black pond, lapping at her waist, eyeing her as she swiveled, searching for him. His voice slithered through the blades of grass, the wet earth, and the mossy bodies of slumbering stones.

A wolf stalked forth from the surrounding forest. It padded closer, licking its fangs and narrowing its sage eyes.

Aisling called for the *draiocht*, but her fire didn't work the same way in dreams—his or hers, she couldn't tell. The perpetual showers extinguished her flames, cloaking her hands in smoke.

"A heart for a heart."

She cursed the wolf, turning from it to trudge through the pond, clawing at the algae floating atop, only to come face to face with a more formidable beast—the *same* beast in another form.

"*Aisling*," Lir whispered, smiling down at her. His voice echoed throughout the glen as if spoken directly into her mind.

His breath slipped between her lips. The cord between them knotted fiercely. But never did his mouth meet hers. Instead, the pain of an "almost touch" jolted her awake. It wrenched her from her dreams as it always did—Lir's voice dissolving into another's.

CHAPTER II

AISLING

"Aisling!" Dagfin shouted.

Aisling woke swathed in vines of emerald. Dagfin tore them off her body, bloodying his hands on thorns like teeth.

Aisling lurched forward, summoning the *draiocht*, her magic, without another thought. Her hands flickered with violet fire, withering the lianas to dust as she clawed them away, as well as, unfortunately, her feathered bed and the embroidered canopy now black with her influence.

Dagfin lunged for a nearby tapestry, ripping it from its mantle and pinning Aisling to the ash-ridden bed. Her fire bristled, suffocated by the throw's threads and the weight of Dagfin atop her.

He held her down, waiting for the last glimmers of the *draiocht* to vanish from her violet eyes.

"Is it gone?" Dagfin asked, meeting her gaze for the first time. His heart was hammering against her own. The sensation of his body pressed against her was strange. As firm as she'd imagined: the sharpness of his form, the muscles he'd developed in adulthood. The smell of him steeped in ocean air and starry nights.

"It's gone," she replied, more breathless than she'd realized.

Indeed, the *draiocht* had sunk back into its primeval cavern, awaiting its next summons.

Dagfin lingered atop her, eventually straightening and settling his boots on the creaking floors. The abrupt absence of him leaving her cold.

He wore Roktan blue today, the Roktan crest embroidered onto the front of his jacket in bronze thread: a fist holding a gleaming star. A riff off the symbol of mortal man. His shirt beneath was neatly pressed, the laces unwoven and left to dangle down his chest where a belt was strapped horizontally. Knives and sharp things buckled to its front. The only non-obviously destructive element was a flask of worn use.

"He's found me," Aisling said. "Even here, Lir's found me."

Dagfin cringed at the sound of the fae king's name on her lips, surveying the destruction. Vines, branches, the forest that slithered through Roktling, into his castle, the port inside Castle Roktling's monolith, and onto his father's ship, the *Starling*. All for her. Finding her private cabin and cradling her in the way only Lir's power could, even despite distance.

And at the briefest of shudders from a remaining vine, Dagfin flicked his wrist. Like a sparrow, his throwing knife cut across the cabin, stabbing the forest's thread till its sap bled atop the creaking floorboards.

"It won't happen again."

"It will *always* happen again. It will never stop, Fin. And I won't run from him for the rest of my life." Aisling gathered a fistful of ash. "Lir will stop at nothing till he gets what he wants. Running or hiding will do nothing but encourage a beast who enjoys a chase."

"It's a good thing then that I hunt such beasts."

"You cannot win this fight, Fin. A fae king isn't another Unseelie you can bring back on your shoulders."

Dagfin scowled. "Give me a reason."

Because there was an invisible cord knotting, snapping, angrily tearing at her core to return to the fae king. Because she and Lir would spiral into eternity before they never saw one another again. Because the Forge fated them.

But she could never say those words aloud.

Dagfin took her silence as answer enough, shaking his head in disbelief. "So that's it? We've run this far only for you to surrender to him once more?"

"We continue as we have," Aisling said. "Until I find what it is I want."

Dagfin fell silent, electricity brewing in his stormy eyes, muddled and shadowed—the ghost of how she once remembered them.

"And what is it you want, Aisling?"

Aisling opened her mouth to reply, but no words left her lips. The answer evaded her, swarmed amid her mind in a hive of everything left unanswered. Who she was. Why she was. What she was.

But before Aisling could make sense of her thoughts, Fergus burst through the door. His expression slackened at the destruction left in Aisling's wake, and the tension was still thick between his sister and the Roktan prince. But this was far from the first time they'd discovered Aisling lit with feral flame or cloaked in soot.

"By the Forge," Fergus cursed, appraising the damage. Both fear and the faintest hint of disgust flickered across his expression.

"What is it, Fergus?" Dagfin snapped, tearing his eyes from Aisling. Fergus stammered. Nerves brought about by the shadows creeping at the edges of Dagfin's posture. Indeed, everyone knew not to provoke the *Faerak* after there was mention of the fae king. Especially if it came from Aisling's lips, and such a temper could only mean he'd heard Lir's name all too recently.

"Starn's ordered every crew member to gather on deck," Fergus managed. "We're set to sail come dawn."

Dagfin nodded, clenching and unclenching his fists. A tell-tale sign of his efforts to stifle the frustration churning within.

"We'll just be a moment."

Fergus made as if to protest, thinking better of it and ushering himself out without another word.

Aisling dusted her skirts—a simple linen gown Gilrel would've scoffed at. Rags compared to the beetle-encrusted necklines, the spider-web bodices, the fitted skirts of puckering petals she'd donned in Annwyn.

Her conversation with Dagfin was fortunately interrupted and, if Aisling had a say in it, would be left that way. So, she rose from the destruction to follow Fergus from her cabin, caring little for her garment's singed edges. After all, only deceit would bring Dagfin solace. And Aisling was more than capable of lying, but not to Dagfin.

"Here," he said as she brushed past him, handing her a folded bundle of soft wool. Aisling carefully unfurled its fabric. It was a cloak of midnight blue. Thousands of silver stars scattered across its folds, delicately sewn into constellations Roktling's seafarers sought for guidance when lost amid the sea. Fiacha's Southern star, the Sunless Throne, the Goblet of Dreams, Odhran and the Weight of the Night. Odhran, forced to glare upon the sands of time until the last grain was spent, and all of evening's kingdom would crush him flat.

The cloak twinkled in the pillar of soft morning light spilling from her cabin window.

"You needed a new one."

The fact that she'd burned the last three went unsaid yet acknowledged by the flitting of their eyes to the ashen debris.

Aisling said not a word. "Thank you" felt insufficient, and anything else, any other emotion, seized her by the throat and turned her tongue to stone. So, she wrapped it around herself and lifted the hood instead, watching as it brushed the cabin floors around her boots.

Dagfin studied her closely, forcing Aisling to wonder what he saw. For before him stood what he'd sworn by *Faerak* law to hunt. His old childhood playmate, now the sort of creature he slaughtered.

"Go on without me," she told Dagfin, unable to bear the silence any longer. "I'll meet you on deck in a moment."

He exhaled, running a hand through his tousle of hair. She knew he wanted to warn her of her brother's temper, Starn's loathing for being left waiting. But he said nothing instead. Either because he'd never convinced Aisling to do something she wasn't already inclined to do, or because he'd grown weary from their travels. Exhaustion riddled the nuances of his appearance. The red around his eyes, the slackening of his shoulders when he and Aisling were alone, the tired dimness of his boyish smile.

At last, he nodded, vanishing out her cabin door without another word.

Aisling wasted not a moment.

If she took too long, one of her brothers would come looking for her, or worse, Starn himself would break down her door. So, she turned her back from the mirror on her vanity, removed her leather gloves, and flipped her palms face up, appraising them for the first time since she'd used her fires. She hoped that perhaps this time, the pain was no more than a figment of her imagination.

Bloodied and blistered, the agony mocked her. Her skin peeled like the skin of a snake, burned by her fires and devoured by the hot teeth of the *draiocht*.

Aisling allowed herself a brief sob. For the most persistent tears to flee before they forced the rest out. Then she inhaled, wiped her face with the backs of her hands, and slowly slipped the gloves back on. The tender wounds protested as though baiting her to scream from the tops of her lungs. Instead, she ground her jaw and wished for dust.

The *draiocht* laughed. "*Only monsters prefer to endure the night than concede to morning.*"

CHAPTER III

AISLING

Dagfin was right.

Aisling needed a new cloak, but not for the cold. Aisling no longer looked entirely human, nor did she look thoroughly fae, but rather something in between. Her eyes were larger, the violet of their irises less human, and her features sharper. Something uncanny about the way her body moved.

She'd overheard the tales spilled around goblets of foaming mead, whispered beneath moonlight showers, and shared between lovers. In some tellings, the northern princess traded to the fae king as a symbol of peace between mortals and fair folk was a victim; her soul was sucked from her chest by a single kiss from the barbarian lord. In others, she'd bargained her soul, lost her soul, willfully gave her soul, stolen something she had no business meddling with. But no matter the version, all the stories ended similarly: the northern princess was no longer mortal. She was something else. Something no king nor queen nor commoner had ever witnessed before. She no longer belonged to iron but to the Forge and its bygone magic the Sidhe called *draiocht*.

And while Feradach selected the crew aboard the *Starling* for their discretion, Starn thought it best to hide Aisling's face lest the potent truth of the rumors inspire fear in those around her. Lest they discover the full extent of her abilities.

But even with her face shrouded in the shadow of Dagfin's cloak, the *Starling*'s idle chatter fell silent as the sun rose over the Ashild. Gleaming through the cave in which their ship bobbed. All eyes pinned on Aisling.

Starn stood at the forefront of the ship, anchored to the port. The whole crew turned to heed his words: seasoned seafarers hardened by salt-ridden winds, the prideful gleam of the sun, and the memory of shipwrecks. Their mortal hatred for the Aos Sí reflected in every glance they offered Aisling. In the tightening of their fists around their iron swords, daggers, and belts whenever she appeared. Their faithless prayers to the gods they didn't believe in. Aisling, the queen of those who buried their comrades deep below the surface. Where mortal man's fire and iron were obsolete.

And even as the crew's attention wavered at Aisling's arrival, her eldest brother continued speaking.

Aisling kept to the side, hip pressed against the boat's edge.

Mortals wreaked of mortality, a stench Aisling had never understood nor detected until she was reunited with her clann, with humans, after months of living with the fae. After she'd changed body, mind, and soul, their smell wasn't what made her keep her distance. It was what hung limply from the mainmast like a gory chandelier.

A white stag peered down at the *Starling*, forced to watch mortal life till it wasted away on iron chains. The firelight from inside Castle Roktling's monolith port gilding its corpse. Indeed, none had bothered to clean its hide of blood nor exchange its eyes for glass orbs. Instead, they left it to rot

—a declaration of their hatred for the fae world. For the war waged for centuries between their races. For Lir and the forest he was the heart of.

"Did you hear me, Aisling?" Starn asked, waking Aisling from her reverie. Now, the crew glared at her without shame. Most oppressive, her eldest brother's crow-like gaze seared into her skin. The image of their father flickering across Aisling's vision and replacing Starn's face for a fraction of a heartbeat.

"There is to be no music, no shouting, no sound other than a whisper while atop the deck. Not until we reach Fjall-norr," Iarbonel, her second eldest brother, reiterated to spare his sister Starn's wrath.

Indeed, their path to Lofgren's Rise would be perilous, the threat of Unseelie ever present until they reached land northwest.

"This is no normal voyage," Starn continued. "We don't only mean to reach Fjallnorr, but to outrace those who pursue us. In which case, our efficiency is of the utmost importance."

Every sovereign or subject, mortal or fae, was forge-bent on hunting Aisling down. She the enemy's bride, a runaway queen, a traitor, and a sorceress. The first of her kind. And if they couldn't reach Aisling first, they'd take the curse breaker rumored to rest atop Lofgren's Rise in Fjallnorr country. A name that'd been written in tapestries of stars by the Lady. A weapon to cure the faults of Ina and the dooming of her kingdom to mortality. The mistake that bred humankind.

"This is your last opportunity to forgo this journey, and if you so choose, do so now."

The *Starling* groaned, the ocean slapping against its round belly and the sails billowing restlessly, eager to set sail. But none of the crew uttered a word. The quiet between them was thick and oily. Willing themselves not a glance in Aisling's direction.

Starn smiled, turning on his heel to begin undocking the ship. The rest of the crew interpreted his departure as their dismissal. All had chosen to continue on the *Starling*.

These rare mortal men who knew of the Unseelie were either brave or foolish. For Aisling had come face to face with such archaic beasts herself. The trow, the Cú Scáth, the fomorians, the dryads. Aisling knew the depths of their hunger. Their thirst for mortal blood and the marrow from human bones.

The crew finished loading the vessel with barreled and packaged goods. Dagfin and Starn had selected a craft already scheduled to travel west and to Lofgren's Rise in the name of commerce. Otherwise, a lone ship setting sail from Castle Roktling would breed suspicion and prying eyes Aisling, Dagfin, nor her brothers welcomed.

Each crewmate did their part to untether the *Starling* from its port, deep inside the monolith on which Castle Roktling sat. Indeed, the fortress bore the burden of facing the sea's wrath for all eternity—an iron bastion carved by mortal hands and delicately balanced on the bones of stone giants.

The only way to enter Castle Roktling was through its monolith and via ship, sailing directly into the colossal heart of stone until their vessel reached a glimmering port of sapphire, bronze, and iron, traced by murals of celestial maps and staircases spiraling upwards. But today, the *Starling* sailed out of the monolith and into Roktan harbors.

Aisling hid further inside her cloak as they emerged from the cave, the *Starling*'s bone-white sails shimmering beneath an overcast sky as its oakwood body pushed against the foaming waves. Outside the monolith's belly, Aisling could set eyes on Roktling land once more. Its city towns trailing down the black cliffs, dissolving into ports spilling over with blue sails.

A lump grew in Aisling's throat, impossible to swallow. Her eyes pricked with heat, for the last time she'd left Roktling, she'd counted the breaths it took for Dagfin's face to disappear behind the veil of mist perpetually shrouding his coastal kingdom. But that day, such mist hung more thickly. Grief, a rich shade of gray for the passing of a child destined to be king: Dagfin's older brother.

Today, Dagfin stood before the bowsprit, his back to Roktling and the anglers casting their nets where boats didn't bob, hauling in shimmering scales. The taverns, shops, and homes decorated with seashells and made of stone, save for the frames of their doors, forged in iron. A repellent against the fair folk should they pillage their land.

Aisling knew the sight of Dagfin's kingdom took hold of his heart and squeezed. It made him want to run, to fight, to forget. And in many ways, Aisling should never have been surprised by his becoming a *Faerak*: hunters of the Unseelie, preying upon beasts bold enough to violate mortal boundaries.

Some of the common folk paused to watch the *Starling* disembark. Bidding farewell to the monolith's shadow in favor of the open sea and the storm clouds approaching from the west.

But where Roktling was a kingdom of joyous people, today and all the days since Lir's betrayal, they mourned the brief treaty that'd offered them peace, even if for a short while. A respite against the ever-present threat of Sidhe or Unseelie, now gone.

Seeing nothing but silver on the horizon, Aisling's brows knit.

She longed for the forest. For the smell of rain and mud and wet leaves. For the croaking of insects and the babbling of creeks. But the vines that'd crawled through the *Starling* and held her were nothing compared to the elms that bent over and plucked her from the earth like a weed. A pale comparison to the puddles that deepened to swallow her whole. The forest intent on delivering Aisling back to her fae lord. The thorns, the stinging nettle, the poison ivy, and the wolves that nipped at her heels the further from the forest she ran, all inspired by Lir's hunt for Aisling.

Alas, the water was salvation. A refuge where the forest couldn't reach them. Couldn't take what it believed belonged to them,

"Do you think Nemed is out there?" Aisling asked as her brothers, Iarbonel, Fergus, and Annind, joined her at the ship's side.

"You mean to ask if he survived?" Annind looked to shore, his eyes searching the faces of those waving their vessel goodbye as if their father might be standing amongst them. The fire hand of the North, high king to all the Isles of Rinn Dúin, potentially, at last, slayed by the fae king's ambush. The day Lir had betrayed the treaty, driven mad by Danu's prophecy and unable to accept fae defeat or slaughter. A fact for which Aisling couldn't blame him.

Nevertheless, his choice left destruction in its wake and lost him Aisling. He, yet another who'd kept Aisling in the dark.

"Aye, he survived," Iarbonel assured Aisling to comfort her. Assuming Aisling's query was born out of concern. Aisling wasn't certain whether she cared if Nemed's iron bones rotted in Unseelie pits or on fae stakes. He who'd burned the forest and delighted in its ashes. He who'd lied to her all her life and kept the truth hidden, obscure, and

Aisling powerless. All her clann, complicit. His only saving grace was his unexpected rejoicing at the magic Aisling had stolen back after centuries of an unbreakable curse.

"Father always survives."

"Perhaps this time is different," Aisling said.

"I've learned never to underestimate Father," Fergus chimed. "Rest assured, he's searching for the curse breaker as we speak."

"Or searching for Aisling herself." Iarbonel rested his elbows along the vessel's edge. "I can't imagine the... *changes* Aisling has undergone wouldn't weigh heavily on his mind and motivations. You all heard him celebrate Aisling and that she'd done what no mortal has been capable of before: she stole back the *draiocht*."

"No." Annind shook his head. "That very well may be. But he won't search for her like every other forge-forsaken creature on this plane. He'll wait till she goes to him."

"Go to him?" Aisling scoffed, batting away the memory of his glistening eyes the first time he'd witnessed Aisling wield the *draiocht*.

"You're his daughter, Aisling," Annind said. "Nothing will ever change that." His coal-black eyes met her glare. "You'll never be alone so long as your túath breathes an iron breath. For blood of iron may rust but will never break like a spell. I promise you that."

Aisling held her brother's stare even as he reached for her gloved hand and held it. Hesitating before he touched her.

Aisling had witnessed the horror, the grief, the confusion flashing across her brothers' expressions each time she summoned violet flame. The disgust they hid from her. The contempt all humankind had shown her since she'd sacrificed everything for their sake kindled unique rage within her.

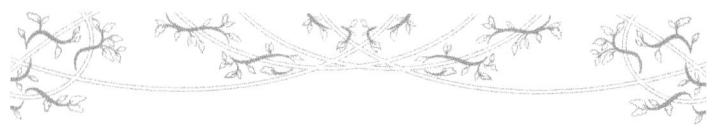

CHAPTER IV

AISLING

Aisling rose from the black pond the same way she'd emerged from Annwyn's aqueducts. Clawing toward the surface and the glimmer of light from above.

Water transcended time and space. Became a passage for those who belonged elsewhere, even in dreams and visions.

"*Aisling.*" Lir called her name from the shadows in the surrounding forest, nothing more than a calm wind threading through her ears. Aisling turned to find him, meeting his eyes where he lay in the grass.

She approached him this time, ascending from the pond until she reached the blades of green, stretching herself out to lay beside him. As though Aisling and the fae king had returned to the feywilds, sleeping during the day and prowling at starlight. The rain descended toward the earth like stars made of honey, dripping from the sky.

His gaze was feline—more glorious than the rain that dappled his face in the storm's most precious jewels.

"You shouldn't trust a promise, Aisling." He spoke to her, his voice thrumming through her core and pricking her skin.

"Yet I should trust yours?"

"You and I are different."

"Aye, as you've told me countless times before, I am no longer as mortal as I once was. No longer belong to their world but rather with the Sidhe."

"You misunderstand me: you belong nowhere other than with me."

Aisling felt her heart splinter, forcing herself to tear her eyes from his. But the pain of it, his proximity, their cord, their fated string, knotting between them, fraying, pulling, tugging at her heart, snapped the dream into oblivion.

Aisling woke to the ghosts in the walls. The "adjusting" of cottages, inns, taverns, or ships built by man's hands. Fae things didn't creak. Their bones didn't click nor groan. They *breathed*. Grew alongside the life breath of the wild.

"It can't happen again," Starn hissed, his voice traveling beneath Aisling's door and into her quarters. "There cannot be any more fires. Every mortal man, fae, and fiend is hunting her."

"Feradach is just as intent on obtaining the curse breaker as any other sovereign. Like every man aboard the *Starling*, he personally recruited trusted seafarers of Roktling. To enlist any man with a loose tongue would be to set our competitors upon us."

"Aye, your father has done his part, but if you think they're immune to the fear of her, then we've already lost this race to the fae king."

"You've never shied away from a battle with the fae, Starn; why start now?"

Galad. Aisling's mind spun at the memory of her eldest

brother's crimes. Her chest hollowed for her Sidhe friend. Rage bleeding across her tongue.

Starn scoffed. "As much as I'd enjoy nothing more than to bathe in the blood of my fae conquests, you know good and well, that isn't what this is about."

"What's it all about then, Starn?" Dagfin's tone dropped deathly low. "Why help Aisling?"

"She's my sister."

"Is she?" Dagfin challenged, and the question cut through Aisling's heart. "Is that still how you see her?"

Aisling held her breath, both eager for and dreading her brother's response, but it never came. The silence clawed at the *Starling*'s walls, the grinding of bone on wood vibrating through Aisling's core. So instead of replying, Starn changed the subject.

"If you're ever to rule the North alongside me, to be a Roktan king, you cannot continue to be so lenient."

"I won't try to control her."

"Your impulsivity, stubbornness, and heart have always gotten the best of you. But it can't as a ruler, Fin. A sacrificial heart will only ever yield death in a world like this."

"You may want nothing more than to sit on your father's throne, Starn, but I can't imagine anything more soul-sucking than standing behind a fleet instead of fighting with it. Nothing more hopeless than ordering those to do what I can do myself. Making choices that cost a part of my soul, even if for the greater good. You want authority, Starn. Leadership. And you're good at it. Made for it even. Able to make the hard choices without bowing to the cost of them. Nemed's favored child. But I can't and won't subject Aisling to it."

Starn exhaled, frustration potent in his breath.

"You can't outrun your blood nor your duty."

Silence swelled between them until Aisling wondered if

they'd left and she'd missed the sound of boots on floor-boards. Now it was Dagfin's turn to redirect the conversation.

"I'll ensure there are no more 'outbursts' when it comes to Aisling," Dagfin conceded, his voice rough with lack of sleep.

"This crew may be aware of what she is, but they don't need reminding of why they despise the fae."

"If I could take more Ocras, it would be—"

"Ocras?" Starn repeated. "Do you have any Ocras left?"

"Enough," Dagfin replied without hesitation.

"Fin, don't exchange one demon for another. If—"

"Enough with your lectures. This isn't the same. The Ocras will be the difference between what keeps us alive and what doesn't."

Starn exhaled.

"Let me stand guard tonight," her brother offered. Indeed, the brothers began their journey rotating their night watch of Aisling but slowly, Dagfin took on each of their shifts. This despite most, mortal or fae, wanted Aisling dead. "You can't continue this way, Fin."

"I'm fine," he assured, but Aisling wasn't convinced, and she didn't believe Starn was either.

At last, footsteps beat against the *Starling*'s floors, fading as they turned down the corridor. It was only a handful of seconds later that Aisling's door clicked open.

"You're awake," Dagfin said, relief sweeping his expression. His hair was unruly, and his eyes dark-washed with familiar exhaustion. He closed the door behind him.

"Are you alright?" he asked.

Aisling nodded her head in place of a lie, concealing her hands between the folds of wool.

She shoved the fresh memory of Starn's words to the side, boiling her blood till she felt like a kettle whistling with heat.

"Good. Nightmares enjoy the open sea." And although Aisling knew he spoke of Lir, unable to utter his name aloud, Aisling only thought of herself.

"Is that what I am?" she asked sincerely. "A nightmare?"

But Dagfin hesitated, searching for the words as he paused beside her bed. Was she a demon? A monster cast by the blood of the Forge? The questions lingered between them. None knew what she was nor would be. None knew what enchantments had bespelled her being. Only Lofgren's Rise bore any hope of answering those questions. Questions which branded Aisling's mind and fought for attention every hour of the day.

"You're Aisling," he said. He crouched beside where she lay and ran his fingers through her tangled tresses. She'd taught Dagfin how to braid hair when they were children. When she needed to pin back her mane to better run through Tilren's alleys. When he'd called her name repeatedly, searching for her. And rarely, if ever, did he find her lest she wished for him to.

"Do you remember the tale of Odhran and the Weight of the Night?" he asked.

Aisling closed her eyes, remembering but feigning ignorance so he'd tell it again.

"Odhran was forged in a cauldron of churning sun, destined to heat our realm come summer solstice and vanish at the autumn equinox. But when Nefae, maiden of stars, perished after a duel with Lora, mistress of midnight, the night dripped from the sky, threatening to flood the entire realm in evening. So, Odhran ignored his destiny and his making, catching the night sky before it dissolved entirely and swung it onto his shoulders. The sun called Odhran home every summer, the voice vanishing come autumn, but

Odhran couldn't move lest the night collapse. Forced to carry the weight of the night till the end of time.

"Some believe he found his way home, solved the burden of the night sky, and returned. Others believe he's still there, watching us from up above. But even if he cannot return, legend has it his constellation lights a path home for those weary and lost: a true passage home."

If Aisling never opened her eyes, she could pretend they were hiding beneath her covers in Castle Neimedh as children, whispering stories till dawn arrived on the golden chariot. But this peace, this taste of a home, was something she could never return to. Even if she followed Odhran's constellation.

"You need to rest," she replied, catching his hand and holding it against her face.

His expression muddled the moment their skin met. Shoulders slackening. Eyes flickering despite the dark circles haloing his eyes like fog. Since the day of the ambush, Aisling couldn't remember the last time he'd slept more than a handful of hours.

"I'll be good as new by morning."

"Fin, let my brothers stand guard. Or allow me to—"

"No." The word spun silence into the air, string unspooling from its bobbin. His body went rigid, forcing himself to pull away.

"You don't trust them." These were words Aisling knew neither she nor Dagfin wished to speak into existence but bred flames of suspicion, nevertheless.

"Do you?"

Aisling considered. The image of Galad's branding flashed across her mind's eye against her own volition. She thought of how her brothers' eyes betrayed them—flecked with fear and lack of recognition for their only sister.

"Truthfully, no. Yet not one of my brothers has ever laid a hand on me nor threatened me with a weapon. And yet you have."

Dagfin hung his head. Indeed, Dagfin had used an iron bolo to quiet Aisling's flames and detain her, scalding her skin and rendering her diminished of all power and strength. A betrayal, a necessity, her salvation, all in one.

"Ash, I—"

"Promise me you'll never wield iron against me again."

Dagfin met her eyes.

"I promise," he said, watching her with the churning of the Ashild behind his lashes. No more than a whisper.

CHAPTER V

AISLING

Time devoured their passage bite by bite. It swallowed days, grinding their bones till Aisling paced her cabin restlessly, glaring out at the ever-expanding horizon, the endless sea that tasted of the patience Aisling cared little to practice. The sooner they arrived at Lofgren's Rise, the closer she came to discovering what she was. *Who* she was and what would become of her. Every day, every hour, every breath before then, would be torture to her impatient soul.

"You need to eat," Fergus would say, bringing Aisling plate after plate of dried bread, cheeses, fruits, and salted meats. But no matter its form, Aisling felt compelled by the *draiocht* to vomit her meal.

"Here, take this, it will help." Annind offered his sister medicine for the sea sickness. An anecdote for the perpetual swing of the ship beneath their boots. But it scarcely alleviated her symptoms. She expelled meal after meal over the side of the ship, thinning her flesh and paling her complexion. But Aisling knew well by now her sickness had nothing to do with the rocking of the ship. Aisling hadn't been able to keep down her meals for weeks. Some strange tinkering of the *draiocht* as her blood thickened like the Aos Sí. It was only now, in close quarters, that anyone had noticed.

Thunder cracked across the sky, heralding the arrival of an impending storm. An ill-timed cloudburst considering the mighty crags that rose from the sloshing sea to surround the *Starling*. The first appearance of anything other than salt water, rising from the depths like the black spine of a beast.

Aisling raced from her cabin and onto the main deck, eager to understand. She'd faithlessly prayed and begged to forge-forsaken gods for anything other than never-ending waves. Anything other than the stench of fish, salt, and the bitter beating the *Starling* endured from pearl-tipped waves.

At last, there it was: jagged rocks, shards of ships, and the ruinous remains of marble statues whittled into the image of man, fractured but glaring at their ship from behind the veil of ocean mist. Hundreds of them, and as though frozen in time, they held weapons above their heads, faces contorted with rage or fear. Some statues climbed up the rocks, bodies half submerged in the sea. Some reached for the *Starling*. Some decapitated, amputated, chipped, crumbling, but all watching. All still as death. A city of ruins and ghosts hid amidst the Ashild.

A chill crept up the nape of Aisling's neck, her hands growing cold as she gripped the boat's edge.

"What is this place?" Aisling whispered to Annind, standing by the bowsprit beside her. His eyes narrowed, ebony hair curling in the fog and falling across his forehead.

"I don't know," he answered honestly, frightening Aisling. For it was rare for Annind to be left unknowing.

Aisling glanced over her shoulder at Starn and Dagfin at the mainmast, both staring at their map in disbelief. They both gestured to the helm, considering how to avoid what they were sailing into. The Roktan seafarers scattered across the ship and to their stations. But the rocks multiplied, hundreds appearing as the mist parted, surrounding them from every angle. The *Starling* trapped between the ocean's stone teeth.

"This wasn't supposed to be here," Annind said, clearing his throat. "There was a text in father's library back in Castle Neimedh. The details elude me, but I remember the mention of land materializing and vanishing without rhyme or reason. Mortal men transforming, lost to sea but found as stone."

Aisling swallowed, pointing at the marble statues. "These were once mortal men?"

Annind nodded his head, refusing to meet her eyes.

"What could do this?" Aisling pressed.

"*Murúch*." One of the crewmates moved to stand on the other side of Aisling. His doublet torn at the fringes, his tunic stained in sweat and salt. Skin as dark and rich as autumn's last leaves, he was perhaps only a few years Starn's senior. A ruthless sort of beauty.

"Unseelie donning the guise of beautiful maidens where the ocean falls most silent," he continued.

Aisling turned to find the crewmate watching her. Eyes of brilliant amber, lined in coal and reflecting the gold star nailed to his left ear. He unlatched a crossbow from his back, readying it with an iron-dipped quarrel.

Aisling was familiar with this crewmate, often watching him ready the sails before they left, studying the map at odd hours, hushed conversations with Dagfin below deck, and overseeing the crew when they went about their hourly duties.

"Aisling, this is Killian." Annind introduced them, eyes still locked on the statues glaring back and voice brittle with anticipation.

Killian smiled, offering Aisling his free hand.

Aisling considered his calloused fingers but ignored the gesture. There was something Aisling recognized in the curve of his expression and the glint in his eyes. Something hungry. Something predatory. The chains of iron beads and teeth wrapped around his throat, the knotted tattoos across his chest, visible only by the unlacing of his blouse. The iron belt chains, the iron rings. Something Aisling found she despised.

"You should make an effort to be more friendly, faerie." Killian's smile widened, at last lowering his hand. "Perhaps the others wouldn't deem you an ill omen for sailing." He propped his crossbow at the ready, glaring through its sight.

Faerie. Danu had prophesied humankind would refer to the Sidhe this way eventually. Yet Aisling hadn't anticipated that fate would unravel so swiftly.

"You'd be wise to follow their example and keep your distance," Aisling replied.

"You'll find you prefer it when I'm near, faerie. Especially with signs of potential murúch close by."

"Shh," Annind warned them, but they continued their conversation. The rest of the crew drew their cutlasses and daggers and readied the cannons.

"I quite like these murúch," Aisling said. "They seem to prey upon the weaknesses of man, of which there are many." Aisling's eyes flicked to the surrounding statues—all of which were male.

He laughed at that. "No one knows anything about the murúch, much less lived to tell the tale of experiencing one."

Aisling opened her mouth to bite back but was stopped short. Her stomach catapulted into her throat. Realization dawning.

Aisling spun on her heel, taking in the sight of the crew

eyeing the crags, the marble statues, and the all-too-still waters with lethal poise. Trained seafarers, either fond of sailor songs or having seen enough demons themselves to never turn their back on a silent sea nor ignore the strange. Sailors, among those few mortals, who understood the differences between Sidhe and Unseelie best.

Starn and Dagfin stood at the helm, exchanging glances with Fergus and Iarbonel positioned below the mainmast. Their muscles taut, their hands shifting to their weapons, their foreheads dappled in sweat.

Dagfin, at last, fixed his eyes on Aisling's own.

Men. All of them. All save for Aisling.

A song rose from the currents, as soft and sweet as a drowning. It grew louder, a woman's voice humming, then crooning a dreadful curse into the salt-ridden air. The melody, one of loneliness and shipwrecks. Of lungs filled with water and a mother's, a lover's, a goddess's honeyed lullaby.

Aisling recognized the sound, its allure less potent the first time she had heard it, a meager whisper compared to the choir that thickened the air with a smell Aisling now recognized.

Lust.

At the fifth note, Dagfin shifted his attention from Aisling. An enchantment taking root.

"No," Aisling breathed.

The Roktan prince searched for the source of the music, every step nearing the boat's edge. Weapons lowering, cannons left unmanned, shoulders slackening, as the melody rippled from one crewmate to the next. Killian's crossbow tapped his knees, lips parting as though drained of conscious thought. Only a man's desire left behind.

"By the Forge," Aisling cursed.

Once the murúch had sung that first note, it was already too late.

Aisling leaped from the forecastle, starting for a bundle of rope at Fergus's feet below the mainmast.

"Ash!" Annind sluggishly reached for her. She was too quick, already untangling the pile of rope as her fingers soaked her gloves with blood. Her burnt palms ripe with blisters from conjuring the *draiocht* a few days prior.

How had they been so stupid? So foolish to set sail without the proper precautions when such dangers abounded?

Aisling tied Fergus's wrists, then Iarbonel's, making quick work of her knots before she strapped them to the mainmast.

"What are you doing?!" Iarbonel's face contorted, the eyes he shared with their mother narrowing in a cruelty her brother didn't harbor when fully himself.

"Aisling?!" He struggled against her, but his movements were sloppy, weaker than normal.

"Trust me," she whispered, but the look in both Fergus's or Iarbonel's expressions told her they didn't and hadn't since the day they'd discovered what she'd become.

Aisling bit down as she worked, ignoring the agony of her blistered hands. Sprinting to her brothers first for, if truth be told, she bore little pity for a crew she knew despised her. Her only motivation for preserving their lives, the potential for a delayed arrival to Fjallnorr. As well as whatever humanity she still clung to.

So, she bounded toward Annind, snatching his hands.

"Clever, faerie," Killian said as Aisling left him to defend himself against the murúch, his lids growing heavy, eyes losing and gaining focus, warring with the *draiocht* tangling its fingers around his heart.

"How'd you figure it out?" he asked, his speech slurring, his body stiff, fighting for agency as he dipped his hand into his breast pocket.

"As I said before, the weaknesses of man are many."

Aisling left Killian untied, refusing to waste another moment tethering a stranger instead of finding Dagfin, already moving to the edge of the *Starling*. The same dreamy expression he'd awarded her each time she'd woken him in the dead of night to sneak past Tilrish guards written across his face.

"Fin!" Aisling shouted, smacking into him and nearly toppling him over the side of the ship. Hardly able to catch her breath from weeks of running and lack of nutrition. Lungs burning in her chest.

"Ash?" He turned to her, a brief flash of sobriety quickly muddled into whatever charms the murúch threaded into a man's heart.

"It's not real, Fin," she hissed, knotting his wrists again and again.

"What do you mean?" he asked, as though the mass choir of celestial voices wasn't staining the fog with magic, thick enough to gulp.

"It's Unseelie, Fin! Their voices steeped in magic, meant to either drown you or turn you to stone. You have to wake up!"

"Unseelie?" Dagfin's brows pinched, watching Aisling closely.

And once she'd knotted his wrists again and again, Aisling left him, setting to work on Starn's hands. Starn scowled at her, jerking his arms away from his sister, as though repulsed by her touch alone. Nevertheless, Aisling continued, blood spilling from her gloves in creeks of red and dying the sleeves of her linen dress.

A splash ruptured on the other side of the boat. Aisling swiveled. Three men leaped off the ship as though their lovers waited on the rocks dressed in their deepest, most heartfelt desires.

"Ada?" a crewmate mumbled, an older man, strong for his years, climbing over the edge of the *Starling*. "Ada!" He dove from the side of the ship, crashing into the foaming waters below.

"Lucia," another man groaned, following the older mortal's lead.

Aisling shook her head in disbelief. She hadn't had time to tether them each to the mainmast. Couldn't have woven them each together while her palms screamed with pain.

Even Annind, Iarbonel, and Fergus challenged her knots, pulling until Aisling feared they'd break their wrists to escape. Their eyes glazed over, focused on the crags now scraping the edges of the *Starling*.

"That's your voice, Aisling," Dagfin said, peering over the edge of the *Starling* once more, searching the mist for something he'd never find, his hands still bound and the rope pulling at the mainmast. "I can hear you," he said. The strain of his voice ripped Aisling's heart in two.

"You're out there," he drawled on, his *Faerak* determination taking hold of his posture.

Wrists bound, Dagfin awkwardly drew a dagger from his belt and began sawing at the rope tied around his wrists, clearly having been tethered before in his years as a *Faerak* and well-versed in releasing himself.

Aisling blanched, glaring at the iron knife held backward and making easy work of her knots, unable to grab it herself without searing off her own hands. Such was the curse and weakness of magic. So, Aisling yanked Dagfin's jacket, forcing him to face her.

"Enough Dagfin, I'm right here!" Aisling screamed, knotting her fists in his shirt. He shrugged her off, snapping the last cord of the rope and releasing himself. He shoved her against the ship's edge with the iron knife still tightly clasped in his hands. His attention flickering between Aisling in his path and the rocks around them, the statues. Willing to do anything if it meant diving into a sea where the murúch's anthem rose as their lust for flesh heated the air.

Aisling pressed her palm against his chest, pushing him away from the edge. Wincing at the sheer pain of the pressure on her wounds. The wild splashing of sailors leaping overboard driving Aisling mad.

"Dagfin!"

Dagfin leaned toward her. Those stormy eyes appraised her every feature as though calculating whether Aisling was real or a figment of his imagination as the murúch bespelled him to believe. But Aisling saw the moment she became not real, not imaginary, but a dream just within reach. The tormented longing splintering the softness of his heart.

His need was made heady with the murúch's song, still entranced by their witchery. Only now, their tricks were twisted by Dagfin's yearning, unaccustomed to women being aboard ships built for men. Dagfin's pining made bold, unashamed, and starving.

Aisling tangled her fingers in his shirt, doing her best to restrain him.

"What will it take to keep you from leaping overboard, Fin?" Aisling asked, more to herself than him, heart pounding inside her chest.

"I don't know that I can help it," he growled, wrenching his eyes shut as he clawed for clarity. His hand moving to untangle Aisling's fingers from his shirt so he could race to his death at the murúch's command. Aisling shook her head.

He'd cut her rope and her strength was no match for a *Faerak's*. So, Aisling leaned forward and grazed his lips with her own, pulse fluttering as he fought the murúch's song. He resisted the undying urge to give in to their magic in favor of tasting her.

And then something snapped in his expression. A familiar glint of sanity.

Dagfin stilled, a battle waging in his mind. Such was the magic of more chaotic Unseelie: enchantments of possession, of manipulation, of soul-consuming consequences.

Aisling held her breath. A strange guilt tugging at her conscience the moment his hands moved of their own accord, finding her waist and pressing her against him.

Dagfin's hands slowly slid up, finding her neck and tilting her head up so her eyes met his own.

"Kiss me," Aisling said, the memory of Lir and the kiss they'd shared burning her lips against her own volition. Haunting her even now. Yet this was necessary. This kiss for Dagfin, a means to save his life. To prevent him from leaping overboard. A justification she repeated again and again in her mind.

Dagfin shuddered, moving his thigh between both her legs and raising it so they fit together.

Aisling's stomach knotted, brows drawing together. The murúch's song growing louder. The chaos around them, spinning faster.

Dagfin lunged forward, pressing his lips to Aisling's, opening her mouth with his own. Tasting her as though she might vanish whilst inside the tight ring of his arms. She, a charm whispered between lovers, gone as fleetingly as it'd been spoken, making bloody his heart.

He weaved his fingers through her dark tresses. He appeared to relish the torment. The world tilted on the axis of the *Starling* as he became familiar with the shape of her mouth. Explored the curves of her body for the first time. The heat of his breath, burning her lips like the fires of salvation.

"Dagfin," she said, straining for breath each time his mouth left hers. Unsure whether his name on her lips was designed to stop him or ensure he never pulled away.

Her heart thrashed against his own, her abdomen coiling hotly, pushing him back as her dress now dripped with blood. Pain and pleasure weaving artfully together. He'd always been physically stronger than her, they all were, but now that he was a *Faerak*, his grip bound her to the edge of the ship.

It was Starn who broke their kiss. Climbing up the ship's edge and stealing Aisling's attention.

Aisling reached for her brother with every ounce of strength she still harbored but she was a breath too far. Dagfin holding her in place. The edge of her brother's coat slipping between her fingers.

"Starn!" Aisling screamed.

A blur of color flashed across the ship. Aisling blinked, processing the speed with which Killian grappled Starn to the floor. A flying comet, pummeling the high prince to the deck of the *Starling* so hard, Aisling believed the ship might crack in half. The sheer momentum pried Aisling and Dagfin apart at last.

Killian pinned Starn down, the backs of his palms scarlet with gore. Starn struggled beneath his grip, still dazed by the murúch's enchantment as Killian retrieved a dagger from his breast pocket. Dipping its tip in the pouch at his belt, Killian began his strange practice, carving a knot into Starn's palms as he'd done his own. Aisling gaped, studying the sight of her brother writhing in pain. A sense of reluctant satisfaction accompanying it. But the moment Killian's blade lifted, the fog in Starn's expression lifted, the cruel edge of his severity returning in full force.

Somehow, Killian had broken the enchantment.

Killian rose to his feet, wiping the sweat from his brow before finding Dagfin.

Dagfin was a harder catch. So, Killian hurled the dagger at Aisling.

Aisling raised her arms, instinctively reaching for the *draiocht*. But it was unnecessary.

Without hesitation, Dagfin moved, catching the blade and throwing it back. Unwilling for anything, or anyone, to stop him from obtaining what desires the magic made potent. The desires Aisling had twisted with a single kiss.

The two fought hand to hand, dealing ghastly blows while their crewmates continued to dive overboard, those quick enough to reach the crags shifting to stone before Aisling's eyes. The others disappeared beneath the surface. Their last bubbling breaths were all that was left in their wake.

"Steer the ship!" Starn screamed, to anyone who would listen, as the edges of the *Starling* splintered with each scrape against the crags.

Starn ran for the other crewmates, slamming his fists into their jaws so hard, they collapsed unconscious. The charm cleaved. His knuckles bruised and split by the third strike.

But any longer and the *Starling* would be without a crew. Without a ship. Without the means to race to Lofgren's Rise.

Aisling swallowed, stripping her gloves from her hands. She closed her eyes, preparing to call the *draiocht*.

And perhaps the murúch smelled her potent magic. Perhaps they felt it sparking in the air around them. All the same, they poked their heads from the water, from behind their stone statues, breaking their song to shriek at a decibel high enough to shatter their eardrums.

The Unseelie were stripped of all gowns, coat, or chemise, nude and in the image of lovely mortal females. Their lithe bodies were half mist, half material, as pale as bone and slick with the sea. Hair the material of windswept clouds, glittering in the fog like snowcaps and shimmering fae wings. Mouths agape and filled with teeth designed to scrape flesh from bone.

"*Skalla!*" they screeched. "*Thief*" in the fae language Rún.

Aisling fell to her knees, pressing her palms against her ears and bloodying her hair.

She whispered to herself, doing her best to focus on the *draiocht*.

I wish to summon the fire.

"Enough, Aisling!" Starn shouted from across the deck, swiping another sailor's legs and sending him smacking into the floorboards, preventing him from leaping to his death.

Aisling whipped her head in his direction, searching for a reason.

"There's no other way!" she shouted back, face streaked in tears and warm crimson.

"Do not wield your magic, Aisling!" he commanded, freezing Aisling with the black ice of his eyes. And then it occurred to Aisling how much her brother loathed and was repulsed by her magic. To condemn the *draiocht* even when it was their salvation.

Aisling looked around and saw only chaos.

The *Starling*'s crew wailed for their lives, flailing amidst the rapids, having woken too late from the murúch's enchantments. Hordes of murúch swarming both rock and sea. Dagfin pinned to the deck, screaming as Killian carved another rune into the center of his chest. And worst of all, the *Starling* barreling into the crags with no man, no soul at the helm to guide it onward.

"The *Starling*, Starn! We will die if this isn't ended!" Aisling yelled, straining to find her voice amidst the discord.

Starn ran toward her, knocking down crewmate after crewmate, each clamoring to die.

"Let me end it!" she shouted.

He glared at her for a moment too long. Loathing personified, a high prince orbited by the screams of the dying and the song of lust and hunger. Every second a second lost to eternity, forever gone and hurtling them toward death.

At last, he shook his head.

"No," Starn spoke, and Aisling's heart shriveled. "There are mortal men in the water still. Wield your magic and they die, Aisling!"

Aisling watched as sailor after sailor turned to stone, joining the civilization of skeletons buried in the ocean's dark bed or crag statues already lost to the Ashild. Relics for the murúch to brandish for the centuries to come. But indeed, many men still splashed about the waters, fighting to climb aboard. Digging their nails into the wooden boards and peeling skin from the tips of their fingers. The *Starling* careening toward the jagged crags like a dying star.

"Aisling!" Dagfin shouted, at last awakened, reality hitting as he covered the bloody rune Killian had carved into his chest. Slowly he staggered to his feet, wearily making his way to the helm. The murúch dragged the men clawing up the side of the ship back into the ocean's frigid embrace, returning them to the sea. Some of those Unseelie were even determined to make it aboard the *Starling*, to claim the ship for their own. All of them destined to die lest Aisling intervene.

So, Aisling wrenched her eyes shut and bundled her fists.

"STOP, AISLING!" Starn roared, racing toward her with violent intent. He, on the precipice of sealing their death in the tales chronicled by ocean-gleaned stars.

Come, Aisling called to the *draiocht*. Inhaling as it cackled and crawled from its ancient lair to greet her and explode from her palms.

There was quiet.

A steady inhale before the exhale.

Before the water exploded with violet fire.

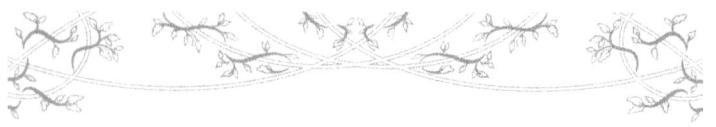

CHAPTER VI

AISLING

When sung together, the screams of man and beast are the same. Steeped in terror, pain, and cold desperation. Scratching at Aisling's mind long after they'd bled into something else entirely. Silence.

"HOW COULD YOU?!" Starn yelled, his voice crooked with pure rage. He started toward her, quickly held back by Dagfin.

Aisling forced herself to meet his eyes. To study their glassy, bloodshot orbs, glaring at her with such hate. For at this moment, he didn't behold his sister. The child he'd watched learn to walk, the girl who'd embroidered his coats, or danced with him at midwinter, tossing their heads back in laughter. No. Today that woman was dead. She, nothing more than a demon, dressed in his sister's skin.

"How could you?!" he repeated, face stained in scarlet, sweat, and salt. Aisling stood still, hands hanging limply at her sides. The patter of her blood dripping against the deck at the cost of her *draiocht* was too loud. Ringing inside her head as every crew member still alive watched her with equal loathing. Iarbonel, Fergus, and Annind incapable of glancing in her direction much less meeting her eyes.

"I saved all your lives," Aisling said, at last, her temples pulsing with pain. "If it weren't for me—"

"Saved us?!" A crew member interrupted, every letter sour with his poison. His weathered face contorted in both anger and disbelief. "You brought this upon us! Summoned devils with your magic! You all saw it. The way she raced onto the deck the moment the crags appeared," he spat, waving his arms as if to frighten a wild beast away. "She's nothing more than a faerie!"

At the word, Aisling's posture sharpened. She narrowed her focus on the crewman, the sole subject of her attention. Unrivaled loathing blackening her gut, for the bend of his brows, the knotting of his broken nose, the balling of his fists, and the horror all the crew harbored, mirrored a potent memory. Mimicked the day she'd returned from months amongst the Aos Sí, after sacrificing *everything* for mankind. Everything despite their lifelong lies. Her kind, her clann, her túath, her family had rewarded her loyalty with suspicion, disgust, and fear.

"You would all be dead." She spoke evenly, her voice melding with the sky still groaning with the impending tempest. And at the sound of her voice, smooth and lithe, the whole *Starling* shared a collective shudder.

"Every one of you would be rotting at the bottom of the sea or hardened to stone had I not intervened. You should be grateful."

Starn took a single step toward her before Dagfin held him back once more.

"You disobeyed me. Disregarded my orders."

"They were foolish ones."

"That isn't for you to decide." His tone grew deathly low,

rage eclipsing his fear. "You are to stifle every ounce of your magic. To suffocate whatever compels you to this madness."

The backs of Aisling's eyes burned, a solitary tear scalding her cheek as it fell.

"You fear what you cannot understand," she said. "You exercise your blood-given power to day's end but when it is a power that surpasses your own, one you cannot understand, you fear it."

Starn's lips pressed into a thin, white line. Iarbonel, Fergus, and Annind held their breath as their eldest brother released a humorless laugh. One that echoed across the Ashild. The electricity both webbing across the sky and knitting between the siblings.

"Power, little Sister, is meant for those born to wield it. Those of steadfast courage." He gestured at Dagfin. "Wisdom." Iarbonel. "Heart." Fergus. "Intelligence." Annind. "And unrivaled strength." Starn. Her eldest brother straightened as he spoke. "You were a spoilt princess who refused discipline, indulged temptation, and surrendered to wistful fancies. That is why you were not made to be king, Aisling. Why whatever power you bear is a forge-forsaken mistake. For all you were made for was to be traded."

A hush fell over the sea. The crest of every wave craning their frothy heads to behold Aisling. The same way the trees refused to turn their backs on the wolf who disemboweled its prey. The gore that attracted the reluctant eye rather than deter it.

"You will obey me," her brother continued. The beat of every crewman's heart thrashed inside Aisling's ears like frightened hares. The smell of their mortal sweat, their rotten breath, sickened her. Doing her best to focus on the burns on her palms, sewing threads of agony beneath her flesh.

"I will not," she said, biting her tongue till it bled.

"You will," Starn said. "Because I am your king."

"You're close," Lir whispered over the thunder of the waterfall and the downpour, rising from the natural pool to meet her in knee-deep waters. Raining as it always did in these dreams. "I can feel you." He circled her, stopping to whisper in her ear from behind.

Heat slithered up Aisling's spine.

"What is it you hide from me?" Aisling asked, turning her head to catch the nuances of his expression.

"It wouldn't be hidden if I told you." A truth, for the Sidhe couldn't lie.

"Prevent me from discovering what I need and I'll—"

"Kill me?" he asked.

Aisling hesitated, cursing herself for it internally.

"You're free to try but it isn't as simple to kill a *caera* as one might believe. You can take my word for it." Indeed, Lir was bound by his need to kill Aisling as well as his need to protect her. To choose to ensure the crimes of his mother weren't repeated, or to choose not to fail his second *caera* the way he believed he had his first. Narisea, the mother of his late son. Both passed centuries before Aisling was born. And Ina, his mother—one of the original twelve Sidhe sovereigns gifted with sight, who forsook the mountain kingdom of Iod in her attempts to prevent Lir's father, Bres, from meeting his end. The gods punished all her kingdom for it, making them the first mortals known to the realm.

"Why do you still hunt me?"

Lir's expression softened. "Because I have no choice."

"Because you made a promise?"

By the blood of the Forge, I vow to you the first taste of my blood, the first cut of my heart, and the last words from my lips.

A heart for a heart.

"You and I are bound by the Forge, by fate, by need." His eyes fixed on her own. "Describe it however you like. Your soul speaks to my own."

The fae king moved to stand beside her, their arms mere breaths from touching. Yet his touch was exactly what would toss her back to reality and out of their dreams. She, forced to smell him, feel him, look at him, but never touch him lest their phantom world vanish like mist blown by the wind.

"Do you believe what we both covet rests at Lofgren's Rise?"

Lir considered for a moment, eyeing the waterfall with renewed interest.

"Yes."

"And should they conflict? Should whatever we find at Lofgren's Rise destroy either of our ambitions at the cost of the other?"

Lir slipped his hands into his pockets.

"The mortals, your father, cannot find the curse breaker," he said, moving to stand beside her. "The gods took it and do not take kindly to being taken from. What the mortals have lost shall stay lost, so I'll stop at nothing to ensure the fire hand never obtains the curse breaker for himself. And if that means preventing you from finding the truth of what you are, then so be it."

Aisling felt the rage before she saw it. Anger traveled through her bones and opened a door for the *draiocht* to burst through. Clambering from its abyss and lighting the fae king in flames of radiant amethyst.

Aisling staggered back, satisfaction and horror warring within her. Impressed with herself and at once heart-stricken at the sight of Lir wrapped in flame. The fair folk's only weakness other than iron.

"Well done, little thief." Lir appraised himself, assessing the licks of violet encasing him. Unharmed, hardly phased, seemingly immune to her fire in his world of dreams. "You never cease to impress me."

"I lost control."

"Control, Aisling, is a word meant to bridle your strength. To ensure you never fulfill your potential." Lir stepped closer, the natural world crawling toward Aisling from the surrounding forest and clawing up her boots, her skirts, and her cloak, knotting themselves in her hair.

Lir tilted his head down, his breath sinking between her lips. "Don't let them domesticate you, Aisling. Don't let them starve your wolf. Bare your teeth and refuse to be leashed."

And just before their lips came together, reality dipped its hand into their pool of dreams and yanked her out.

CHAPTER VII

DAGFIN

If the Sidhe never existed, Dagfin would've ruled Roktling alongside Aisling. A thought that haunted the Roktan prince throughout day and night alike.

Aisling was fearless, unafraid of pursuing whatever it was she wanted. Dagfin needed her resolve, her courage, and maybe then, had everything worked out differently, he could've accepted the crown with Aisling by his side.

And now, after the murúch, Dagfin would be forever possessed by regret. Regret that he hadn't harbored the courage to kiss Aisling of his own accord, and regret that the murúch had forced the act. Nevertheless, he was enraptured by the taste of her. The feeling of her in his arms.

Dagfin pressed the heels of his palms into his eyes.

A knock sounded at the door.

"Come in," Dagfin said.

Killian stepped into his quarters. Dagfin's room was flush with dark blue velvet, bronze embroidered stars, hanging lanterns, and Centari rugs from the mortal kingdoms in the south. A half-finished chess match was strewn across his bed while maps, quills, and three compasses were tossed about the desk at which he sat.

"How many?" Dagfin asked, reaching for a quill and parchment.

"Fifteen dead and twenty-five alive."

Dagfin's chest constricted, a weight pressing down on his shoulders. He forced himself to record the numbers, every pen stroke carving their deaths into the fabric of reality. Before they'd been written, Dagfin could shove away the truth. But when it glared at him from the parchment, the ink wet and winking, he could no longer deny what'd occurred.

"Feradach will understand," Killian assured. He moved toward Dagfin's desk, throwing himself into a wingback chair. "In times like these, death on the high seas is inevitable."

"My father's reaction is the last thing that concerns me."

"Then it's the faerie."

Dagfin's mood darkened at the name.

"Don't call her that."

"It's what she is," Killian continued, opening the pouch strapped to his bandolier and pouring the powder into a flask. The smell of it, of volcanic rock and charred edges, flared Dagfin's nostrils and quickened the pace of his heart. Ocras. "As I understand it, your memories of her are only just that now: memories."

"Nemed paid you for your services in protecting his sons. That's where your experience lies. As for the rest, you know nothing save for beast and mortal, but nothing in between."

"Because there's no such thing. We all saw what she did out there."

"Are you suggesting mortals are not capable of mass violence?"

"Not with magic," Killian said, leaning forward in his

chair. "Magic makes the violence too easy. Disconnects its wielder to the crime for they don't feel the sensation of a blade against flesh."

The sound of the Roktan crew burning alive screeched inside Dagfin's mind, scratching at the flesh of his conscience. Dagfin shook the memory away. Now, the whole *Starling* treated her like a disease, scorning her when she was within earshot and avoiding standing too close. Their memories of the murúch and Aisling hanging heavily overhead, rotting and vegetating in the salt-ridden air. Weeping for their lost brethren when anger temporarily dissolved into sorrow.

Still, although they hadn't truly known what they'd signed up for, there was no turning back. Not when they were this near to Fjallnorr.

"She had no choice. The *Starling* was careening toward the rocks and the murúch were multiplying. Those of us that still live wouldn't have made it out alive had she not intervened."

"We could've found another way. One with less ruthless measures."

"I agree, yet I can't judge Aisling for, at the very least, making a choice. What action did any of the rest of us make other than succumbing to the murúch?"

"There was still time," Killian said.

"She did what she believed she had to. Whether or not it's what I would've chosen is irrelevant."

Killian exhaled, shaking his head.

"And that's the difference they'll chronicle in the legends when tales of you and her are spoken around fires. You and I are heroes, Dagfin. Don't justify the crimes of your villain because you're capable of love and she is not. You'll never change her, Fin. No matter how much you might want to."

AISLING

"Tell me, has the *draiocht* always burned you this way?" Killian asked, stepping into her cabin. Aisling knew it was Killian without turning. She could smell the iron strapped to his narrow waist, his sweat, and the mortal blood crusting the backs of his hands.

"You've got a sharp eye." Aisling glanced at him over her shoulder, willing herself not to wince while she bandaged her hands with linen. "Is that why you became a *Faerak*?"

Killian paused, turning her words over in his mind.

"It appears I'm not the only one with a sharp eye."

"It takes less than vigilance to determine the iron at your hips is made to carve fae bones and the fangs around your neck were wrenched from their screaming mouths."

Killian lifted his hands in mock surrender.

"I mean you no harm, faerie."

"I couldn't say the same." Aisling turned to face him, clenching her fists at her sides. Her blood was hot, near scalding, as it bled through the linen and dripped onto the floors. Killian's attention drifted from Aisling's scowl to her hands, then the crimson puddling around her boots.

"Your wounds will become infected if not treated."

"I'm not concerned," Aisling bit. "I heal more quickly now."

"Like the Aos Sí themselves," Killian conjectured.

Aisling was reluctant to respond, wishing for the *Faerak* to leave her chambers so that the hate pooling in her gut would abate and the stench of his iron would seize the prickling in her nostrils.

"I can treat your hands if you let me."

"Did Dagfin send you?"

Killian nodded his head in response.

"Then tell Dagfin he can come to help me himself if he so wishes."

"The Roktan prince has had his hands full dealing with your... *massacre*. So, he sent me in his stead. You can trust me," Killian said. But by the cruel edge of his smile, Aisling knew trusting this *Faerak* was a death sentence.

Aisling scoffed. "Trust a *Faerak*?"

"You trust Dagfin," Killian argued, stepping toward her like a child afraid to frighten a doe.

"Dagfin," Aisling said between clenched teeth, "is no *Faerak*."

"No?"

"No," Aisling maintained, gripping her hands tighter. "He's a prince who despises his crown and will stop at nothing to flee from it. Even if he must flee into the chomps of a beast."

"We all have our reasons, faerie," Killian said. "But we're all *Faerak* nevertheless."

Aisling batted away the memory of Dagfin's iron bolo wrapped around her at his union several weeks ago. Suffocating her. The pain he'd inflicted knowingly. How even he, the one she'd trusted above all others, had kept so much hidden from her.

"And," Killian continued, "it was Dagfin who asked me to treat your hands. Of course, he warned me you might bite if I tried, but I'm no stranger to the occasional temperamental beast." Killian chuckled, clearly amused with himself.

Aisling wondered if Dagfin knew the source of her injuries. He either assumed her burnt palms were a result of tying ropes or he knew the truth: that each time she summoned her violet flame, the *draiocht* burned her in return. A cost that tore flesh from her very bones. Healing only to render such agony all over again the next time she called its name. Power at the cost of pain.

"Very well," Aisling conceded. "I'll allow you to treat me in exchange for a vulnerability of your own."

Killian's brows pinched, studying her expression. At last, he nodded his head.

"What are the symbols you painted onto your own hands, Starn, and Dagfin's chest? The powder you dipped your dagger into? I saw how it broke the murúchs' enchantments."

Hesitation flashed across Killian's amber eyes. Hesitation and thick suspicion. But he kept his promise, exhaling a long breath before speaking.

"Tell me, faerie, do you believe a mere mortal could face a forge-blessed beast and live to tell the tale?" He didn't wait for Aisling's reply. "No, the gods made certain that mankind's curse purged our lungs of the *draiocht* and made us weaker, our life spans shorter than both Seelie and Unseelie. So that if ever we were to stand and fight against them, we'd fail. Our only salvation, flame and iron.

"But it was a *Faerak* centuries ago that discovered all curses have their weak points. Loopholes if you will. So, we made use of them."

Aisling laughed. "You wish to fool the gods?"

"We don't 'wish', faerie. We have and will continue to damn the gods by taking back what is rightfully ours. As you yourself have done."

Aisling bit her tongue, the blood in her palms bubbling with heat.

"The *Faerak* discovered that the minerals present where the kingdom of Iod, Ina's mountain kingdom, existed before she'd cursed them all, bore power unique to mortals. Our ancestors' magic. And when reintroduced to our blood, we're capable of miraculous feats. Capable of slaughtering the very Unseelie who'd slaughter us instead. It's called Ocras."

Aisling's mind spun and throbbed at the temples.

"You wield the *draiocht* as well then?" she asked, her voice higher in pitch than she'd anticipated.

"No," he said, and Aisling's heart dropped. A part of her hoped she wasn't the only mortal in the world capable of harnessing the *draiocht*. "We imbue ourselves with trace amounts of magic that strengthen our bones, make keener our eyes, shrewder our minds. Powerful mortals. But we cannot wield magic as the Aos Sí do. Nor as you do."

"And the symbols?" Aisling asked, gesturing to the backs of Killian's hands.

"They're runes, similar to those on your fae friends," he said, appraising his own. Immediately, the image of Lir, bare-chested, in the feywild's hot springs sprung to her mind, remembering the interlace and the illustrations painted onto his skin. "A way to channel Iod's minerals in a certain direction. For example, these are protection runes. Symbols that ward off enchantments and charms."

"To break the murúch's power."

"Aye," Killian said. "To destroy the murúch's hold."

Aisling sat down at her vanity, her mind continuing to swirl. There was no need to further question the *Faerak*'s honesty. She'd seen it herself. The way Starn's and Dagfin's eyes had regained their lucidity the moment Killian had carved their flesh and reunited Iod's minerals with their blood.

"How much of this are the mortals aware of?"

Killian considered her, seemingly taken aback by her questions.

"I sometimes forget how sheltered you were, faerie. I've heard the tales: the daughter of iron and fire locked behind her father's walls, eager for release until it came in the form of sacrifice."

A sadistic smile broke across his face, the first signs of a beard lining a mouth of pearly white teeth. Killian spoke of Aisling as though she were another woman, from another time, dead and gone.

"The mortals know *almost* everything. They bear a vague if not simple understanding of Seelie, Unseelie, and even *Faerak*: They believe Seelie and Unseelie are one and the same, sometimes nothing more than myth or tales from the mouths of fools. The royal clanns control how much and what they know, selecting what they consider necessary information from the Forbidden Lore. Most of the history of Ina and her curse is sealed behind túath doors."

Aisling gritted her teeth. The memory of her own túath's lies revealed throughout her time in Annwyn reignited embers of fury. How painstakingly slow she'd discovered the truth. How all had deceived her. Her clann, her family, the Sidhe. How all made certain she was weak and easily controlled. A lesson she'd learned at the expense of what little remained of her innocence.

"You have your answers now, faerie," Killian said, waking Aisling from her bitter reverie. "Now it's time to hold up your end of the bargain."

Aisling picked up the brush on her vanity and began unraveling her tangled tresses. Blood slickening her grip.

"My wounds will heal on their own by morning."

Killian's expression narrowed.

"We made a deal, faerie. And a promise."

Aisling smiled.

"You, a human, aren't weak because the gods made you so. You're weak because you refuse to do what you must."

Aisling turned from him, preferring her reflection to the stench of his iron.

"Betrayal. Broken promises. All food for the powerful, *Faerak*," she said, as he stormed out the door.

CHAPTER VIII

AISLING

Ice gripped the *Starling* like a heart wronged.

The further north they sailed, the tighter the cold squeezed. Until at last, land was in sight. A behemoth of spear-sharp mountains, snow-dusted pines, and black sands.

Fjallnorr.

Aisling raced to the main deck for the first time since the murúch, bracing herself against the cold. The remaining crew eyed her more heavily now, their hatred hardening the air until Aisling found it difficult to swallow.

She'd saved them all. If it weren't for her, for the choice laid upon her hands and hers alone, every one of them would be dead.

"You should eat." Dagfin's voice materialized beside her, drinking from a flask of what Aisling could only assume was doused with *Faerak* Ocras. "Once we leave the ship, food and drink are not guaranteed."

Aisling shifted in place.

"I'm full," she lied.

In truth, she'd barely eaten in weeks. Hadn't felt satisfied since she'd left the Sidhe. And by the expression on Dagfin's face, Aisling knew he, at the very least, suspected her mortal food aversion. But there was more written across his expression, his posture, his demeanor that gave Aisling reason for pause.

The dark rings beneath his eyes had vanished. He stood straighter. His movements were sharper. His eyes brighter.

Not only was this the first time Aisling had stepped on the main deck since the murúch, but it was also the first time she and Dagfin had spoken. Aisling was holed up in her quarters and Dagfin was healing from the runes Killian had engraved in his heart, busy dealing with Aisling's aftermath. And even when he'd come to knock on her chamber doors, Aisling feigned sleep. She couldn't confront Dagfin after what she'd done. Couldn't allow him to see the darkness that'd grown inside her since she'd left Tilren's walls. The darkness in all its glory. And more than anything, she was frightened of his judgment.

"Ash—" he began before Aisling interjected.

"I'm alright, Fin," she said, meeting his eyes. The memory of his mouth on her own, the taste of him, setting murders of silver-eyed ravens loose in her belly. Made her pulse quicken alongside his own. She'd known Dagfin all her life but never in that capacity. There'd been a time she'd prepared herself for a life with Dagfin before she'd been traded to the fae, and she'd found she looked forward to it. To eventually consummate their marriage. But now that a single kiss had occurred, the energy between them had shifted.

"I meant to say, I don't regret anything."

Aisling's heart stuttered, forcing herself not to dither.

"It was the murú—" Aisling started but now it was Dagfin's turn to interrupt her.

"I know you don't believe that," he said, glaring deeper than just her eyes. "I despise myself not only for what the murúch did to my father's crew but because it was they who encouraged you to do what I should've had the courage to do with my own free will. A moment stolen and compelled by the murúch instead."

The wind cut across both their faces, howling against the *Starling*'s sails. The sheet of ice crawled atop the Ashild, splintering as their ship cut toward Fjallnorr. The crew shouted orders for the anchor to be loosened and dropped into the surrounding coast.

"We're here," Aisling blurted, cursing herself for it. The shift in topic, tightening Dagfin's expression. "I should prepare my things." Aisling turned to flee, for the last time, to her private cabin.

Dagfin caught her forearm, holding her in place. Not with his grip but with his breath, burning down her neck as he spoke.

"I regret how that kiss occurred and I'll damn the murúch for it. Yet I'll count every breath for the hope of another, praying to the godsforsaken Forge the first wasn't the last."

Aisling hesitated. She'd be lying if she said she hadn't enjoyed their kiss. If a part of her hadn't waited all her life for him to muster the courage to do it. Yet more than any other feeling brewing inside her chest was guilt. Guilt it'd occurred at all? Guilt the murúch had compelled it? Or guilt because of the fate-forged cord knotting between her and the fae king? Aisling wasn't certain. Only that she loved Dagfin and always had. What shape that love took, she wasn't certain nor did she wish to explore it. It was too tender, too fragile, too dangerous to meddle with lest she drop it and it shatter.

~

Silently, Aisling rejoiced the settling of her boots on Fjallnorr's black sands. Shards of frozen obsidian glass were the threshold to the northernmost land in this plain or the next. She wore a thick, gray, wool dress, a leather belt settled loosely at her hips, gloves, Dagfin's Roktan cloak, and a cape made of rabbits' hides. A crown of ebony braids, like a circlet, twisted around her head before the rest of her tresses spilled down her furs.

Her brothers wore leathers like those they'd donned on hunting excursions with Nemed. Only now, iron graced their every belt loop while silver hides draped across their shoulders.

Dagfin and Killian dressed similarly, although their garments were more form-fitting, traced in weapons with their flasks of Ocras tightly belted to their chests. Minerals from the kingdom of Iod, Aisling now understood.

They each, alongside the few crew members brave enough to accompany them ashore, stared down the ice-ridden forest. A fortress of glass needles, snow, and shadows who shivered alongside them. Cold, quiet, and waiting.

They'd had the option of docking their ship on Fjallnorr's ports closer to its capital Heill, but none thought it wise to announce their arrival to this country's king; a man near as bloodthirsty and feral as the fae themselves. One who'd be just as hungry for a curse breaker hidden in his land. So instead, they'd sailed to a barren edge of the continent where nothing but wilderness grew.

The trees whispered to one another, appraising Aisling and her group. They knew her name, of course, growing more excited the longer they looked. Aisling didn't mind. She'd starved for the forest, even one layered in frost. Lir's heart-beat beating in the northern wind at the sight of it.

"Lofgren's Rise is just past this forest." Dagfin was the first to speak, his voice somehow lighter, richer than it'd been the past several months.

"Is there any way around it?" Iarbonel asked, shifting.

"The only path is through." Killian flipped a quarrel between his fingers.

The crew exchanged terrified expressions and thick gulps, longingly glaring at the *Starling* bobbing off the coast behind them. Indeed, what lay between here and there was more than just winter and evergreens. It was the dens of Unseelie and the Sidhe themselves. It was only a matter of time before the journey forced them to forgo their man-made shelter in exchange for the wild.

"And what about the fae king?" Fergus glanced at Aisling without thinking.

Indeed, Aisling could feel Lir. The growl of his heart as he searched for her own.

"He'll come for me," Aisling said, starting to the tree line. "It cannot be avoided, and he cannot be outrun."

The forest was loud.

The wolves howled, the wind whistled, and the carpet of leaves crunched beneath their boots. Every pine and birch snapped their spines, doubling over and laying their spindly limbs across the frozen earth.

"*Skalla*," they whispered, heaving arctic temperatures through their primordial lungs.

"What's happening?" Fergus asked, eyes wide and darting left and right.

Everyone except for Aisling drew their weapons as the wolves stepped out of the shadows and bared their teeth, padding toward Starn and Dagfin at the front of their party. They snapped their wet chomps, licking their gums as their muzzles wrinkled ferociously.

"*Skalla.*"

"By the bloody Forge," Starn cursed, swinging his longsword in threat. The wolves cared little for his blade, trudging nearer with increased need. At a certain point during their journey thus far, they'd been chased by a pack of wolves. Yet now, because they did not flee from the forest, the wolves approached their guests.

"Stay back!" Starn lunged for the nearest, almost severing its ear from its head, but the hound moved deftly to the side.

"Enough," Aisling said, pushing through the crew and her brothers to get to the front. The forest fluttered, branches swaying, needles rustling at the sound of her voice.

Starn hesitated, daring a glance at his little sister approaching from behind. His nose scrunched in annoyance, watching Aisling with the same contempt he'd allotted her the past several weeks; as though she was the curse incarnate, having damned all mankind.

"Ash." Dagfin caught her arm.

Iarbonel, Fergus, and Annind spectated from behind, eyes wide as young moons. Unfamiliar with this feral realm of sorcery.

"Move another step, Aisling, and you'll regret it," Starn bit. "Lest they bite off your arm and you delay our journey further."

In response, the wolves barked at her eldest brother, saliva spraying across the quilts of snow beneath them.

Annind frowned. Brow arching as it always did when he was weighing two possibilities.

"Wait," Annind said, glancing between Aisling and the forest. "Let her go."

Starn paused in surprise, swiftly regaining his hateful posture. Annind's hand on his arm, he watched as Aisling continued past him, perhaps wishing to choke her in iron rather than allow her another step forward.

The forest's bones tightened the further into their woodland she walked. And as Aisling came into view, parting the folds of her brothers and the crew, the wolves focused, lifting their heads to sniff the *draiocht* snickering from Aisling's abyss.

"Ash," Dagfin called again but Aisling ignored him.

The wolves hushed their barking to mere guttural growling, appraising Aisling with all the lethality of the wood around them. Indeed, Aisling could smell their hunger, their fear, their fury, overridden by their desire to obey. To obey the forest? Lir? She wasn't certain. Nevertheless, the moment Aisling neared, they bowed their heads, noses to the ice, making way for Aisling to pass. The forest exhaling her name.

"Incredible," Annind said, breathless.

Fergus clutched his dagger. "What's happening?!"

"They demanded their queen enter first," Annind said, shaking his head in disbelief.

"Queen?" Starn spat the word like fire on his tongue, eyeing Aisling sharply. "The natural world isn't capable of rules, authority, or order. They live in anarchy."

"Yes," Annind said as they one by one followed Aisling into the forest. "Nevertheless, they understand dominance. And they understand power."

Starn hissed something beneath his breath, both refusing to sheath his longsword as he passed and spitting at the wolves' paws. They snapped at him in response, cursing his stench of ash and iron.

The forest groaned, memorizing each of their faces as they entered its agrestal bastion. For it would be centuries before any one of them was forgotten, a piece of them forever stolen by the woodland.

CHAPTER IX

AISLING

Aisling emerged from a puddle of rain on the forest floor, lifting herself from the earth and onto her two feet. Lir already stood waiting, leaning against the trunk of a willow. And as soon as she appeared, his eyes flashed a more vibrant shade of green.

"Are you just a dream?" Aisling asked, pulling apart the willow's hanging branches, a veil of flowering leaves. "Or are you real?"

"This time or every time?"

"Every time."

Lir considered her, his dark lashes beading with moisture from the cloudburst around them.

"Real," he said, his voice warming her abdomen.

"So, you've magicked your way into my mind."

Lir smirked. "It's not I who's magicked their way into someone's mind."

"Then who?"

Lir's expression grew more satisfied.

"I searched for a way to you. Any way I could touch you,

feel you, be near you," he said. "And had you not wanted the same, I never could've stepped into your dreams the way I have."

Aisling ignored the silver-eyed ravens taking flight inside her abdomen. The heat creeping beneath her cheeks.

"You're capable of a great many things, Aisling. In time, you'll cast spells, enchantments, wield the *draiocht* to the cusp of your own limits."

"I don't understand."

"I think you do."

"You think you know everything."

He smiled at that, a razor-sharp grin that tilted the earth.

"I know what I want," he replied, angling his head down to meet her eyes. They spoke a pace away from one another, shielded by the arms of the willow but steeped in the storm all the same.

"And what if you can't have it?"

Slowly, Lir closed the distance between them till they stood but a breath's width away. As with every time, as though he yearned for her touch as she did his. Against her own volition, craved it. The smell of him, the taste of his proximity, tightening the cord between them and pulling till Aisling believed she might surrender what self-control she still hoarded.

"A lesson you'll learn in our eternity together, *ellwyn*, is that I always get what I want."

Aisling held her breath.

"*Ellwyn?*"

Lir opened his mouth to reply but was interrupted by a noise. An image perhaps? Aisling wasn't certain. Only that it caught his eye. Something shifting in the periphery.

Aisling followed his line of sight but saw nothing, the beat of her heart racing alongside his own. His eyes widened with a strange sort of panic Aisling had only ever seen when the fae king believed himself outside control.

"Wake up," he said, his voice rougher now, laced with urgency. "Wake up, Aisling."

Aisling staggered back as he reached out for her. Never had they touched before. Always, just before their bodies met, Aisling was snapped back into reality. Until now.

Lir caught her wrist, the sensation of his skin atop her own, burning where they touched.

Their gaze connected, Lir both equally perplexed and shocked, eyes large and questioning. But it was too late. Aisling was already spiraling back, falling upwards, and out of her dreams.

Aisling woke to a sword at her throat.

An impossibly large man dressed in blood-matted furs stood above her. He was perhaps a decade younger than her father. Dark stains streaked across his face, smeared by sweat, dirt, and snowstorms. A torch in one hand and his blade in the other. The stench of his iron was thick and putrid.

Aisling paled, her tongue turning to ash in her mouth.

The man brought a finger to his lips.

"Sshh," he said, lest she scream.

The others all lay sound asleep. Fergus snoring, Iarbonel hidden beneath his furs and cloak, Annind still curled beside the dying fire, and Starn, dagger in hand, passed out at the base of a nearby tree. The rest of the crew that'd accompanied them were equally as unconscious.

The stranger's men tiptoed through their camp, silently, deftly. Slitting throat by throat before their victims bore the wherewithal to scream. Death smoking their camp alongside the dying fire.

There were perhaps ten of them, maybe twelve, sifting through their camp while their horses waited behind a thick grove of trees, Aisling realized, peering into the darkness. Her eyes more capable of adjusting to the night ever since she'd changed.

Aisling swallowed, searching for Dagfin and Killian. Last Aisling remembered, it was two of the younger crewmates' shift to keep watch but Aisling knew better than to believe Dagfin would ever rest if there was potential danger nearby.

"Get up," the man ordered Aisling, his voice a mere whisper in the midnight winds. A strange accent inflecting his voice.

Aisling did as she was told, the tip of his blade still at her throat, cautiously uncurling herself. The man watched her closely, narrowing his eyes to better see past the shadow of Dagfin's cloak veiling her features.

"Who are you?" he asked, deathly low.

But it wasn't Aisling's face that surrendered her identity. It was her brothers' weapons, their Neimedh tartans, their embroidered fists clutching the ruby-red flame of mortality. The stranger's men fiddled with her brothers' things and signaled to their leader. Four Tilrish princes and their sister, the not-so-mortal queen of Annwyn.

The stranger's brows rose.

"Could it be?" Without further hesitation, he tore the hood from her head and held the torch beside her face. Gilded by the firelight, Aisling scowled at him, her violet eyes glittering amidst the darkness with the primeval, forge-touched magic she knew he searched for. Wished to see before confirming it was, indeed, she in his presence.

"You weren't so difficult to find." The stranger smiled,

cocking his head in gesture. His men obeyed, tossing him chains of iron.

"Let's see if iron affects you the same way it does them," he said.

Aisling clenched her jaw. She knew what was to come. He'd bind her with iron like a wild beast, smothering the *draiocht* to strip her of all her power.

Aisling considered summoning her flames. There was little her captor could do against fire with nothing more than a sword. But his men bore weapons of all make and size, brandishing them beside her unassuming brothers' throats, her clann—whether or not she felt such blood thinning, it gave her reason for pause. To summon her *draiocht* would be to risk their lives, either by the blades of their enemies or her uncontrolled flames. Starn's voice ricocheted in her mind. "*How could you?!*" The harrowed expressions the crew all shared after Aisling had single-handedly sacrificed their comrades to spare the *Starling* and those who remained aboard were an unwanted memory. The weight of her guilt a burden.

Aisling swallowed the *draiocht*.

Dagfin and Killian were still nowhere to be found. So, Aisling dug her nails into her palms as the stranger wrapped her in his iron chains, tugging on them like a leash. The iron clawed beneath Aisling's nails and sunk into her teeth. So potent, Aisling could taste it on her tongue; blood and rust and dirt whose acid blistered her senses. She shook her head, fighting the dizziness.

"Tell me, do you have fangs as well? Pointed ears?" The stranger moved to part her hair, Aisling readying herself to bite off his finger. But before she bore the opportunity, a dagger whistled past them both.

Faces splattered in blood, Aisling flinched, focusing on

her captor's screams. His hand was nailed to the nearby pine by the body of a knife. Her chest tightened at the sudden violence.

Starn, Iarbonel, Fergus, Annind, and those left alive jolted awake at the abrupt commotion. Blades were already pressed against many of their necks; others were free to leap to their feet or swift enough to bat their captors away. Starn included.

The high prince whacked his assailant's blade to the right, plunging his dagger into his thigh with his left hand. The man screamed, falling backward as Starn bolted for Iarbonel, wrestling another stranger atop the ice. With a wicked elbow to the temple, their enemy flew to the side, disoriented and clutching his head.

Crossbow bolts whipped through the camp, striking he who detained Fergus straight through the jaw and nailing Annind's opponent in the eye till the tip of the bolt sprouted on the other side of his skull.

The horses whinnied madly, pulling at the tethers binding them to the nearby trees.

But it was Dagfin who watched from the shadows as Aisling's captor plucked the knife from his hand. The fleshy sound of it echoed into the surrounding woodland as Dagfin slid behind him, quiet as a falling star, and poised his blade beneath her captor's chin.

"Who are you?" her captor growled at Dagfin. The rest of his men paused, recognition dawning that their leader was at blade point. And should he somehow escape Dagfin's hold, Killian stood at the camp's periphery, crossbow aimed for release.

"I might ask you the same," Dagfin said, the levity in his voice prickling Aisling's nerves.

"Ah." The stranger laughed, still clutching his punctured

hand. "You're a *Faerak*. I'd smell that Ocras anywhere. Especially in such potent doses."

Dagfin pressed the tip of his blade till the stranger's throat beaded crimson.

"*Faeraks* slaughter beasts by the dozens but do they slaughter mortal men as well? Those they've sworn to protect from monsters like *her*?" The stranger tilted his head at Aisling, still bound in chains of iron.

There was a flash of conflicted emotion darting across Dagfin's expression, but it was gone before Aisling could understand it.

"Give me your name," Dagfin demanded, growing more impatient.

"Should I say I'm the chieftain of Fjallnorr, Sigewulf IX, and first among equals: would that suffice to spare my life?" The stranger grinned crookedly, a smile that forewarned deceit.

Dagfin hesitated, his grip on the dagger shifting.

"Perhaps it'll only justify your death," Starn said, wiping sweat from his brow with the back of his sleeve. "Considering you've just attempted to murder four Tilrish princes."

"You don't include your sister?" the stranger asked. "Or do you not consider her blood anymore?"

Starn worked his jaw, deigning to turn in Aisling's direction.

"Enough," Dagfin fumed. "If we're to believe you're the chieftain of Fjallnorr, what is it you want with Aisling?"

"If I am Sigewulf, isn't it each of you who should be answering to me? Considering you've trespassed on my land, avoided my ports, and wandered through my forests. You're fortunate I didn't immediately slit each of your throats while you slept."

Fergus gulped, surveying the dead for the first time, limply strewn across the forest floor.

Killian released a grim laugh. "Perhaps you would've, had you not anticipated two *Faeraks* in their company. So now, with only the trees to bear witness—land you know as well as the Fjallnorrians is no land of man's—it's a blade that decides sovereignship. And right now, chieftain or not, you're in no position of power."

The supposed chieftain of Fjallnorr nodded his head, digesting Killian's words, the tip of his bolt, and the edge of Dagfin's dagger. Each of his men was paralyzed into submission until their leader was freed. Expressions hidden behind bleeding streaks of paint.

"Free her," Sigewulf commanded his men. They hesitated, glaring at their leader for a second too long, forcing him to repeat himself. "Free her!"

Two men rushed to unlock and unwrap Aisling's shackles.

The relief as soon as the iron was lifted was euphoric. Every morsel of bodily strength returned to Aisling in a single breath as the chains fell away and onto the cold dirt. The *draiocht* gasping for air, after nearly drowning in a magicless cavern.

Aisling cracked her neck from side to side, baring her teeth at the chieftain with renewed rage. He wasn't the first man of royal blood to either bind her or attempt to, but Aisling would ensure he was the last.

Before she could think more of it, Aisling traced a circle in the air and summoned a halo of fire above Sigewulf's head. A dangling threat should he not comply. Starn shifted but this time said nothing, grinding his frustration between his teeth.

"Ash," Dagfin warned, but Aisling ignored him.

"What is it you want with me?" she asked, studying the beads of sweat glistening atop Sigewulf's forehead with the threat of her flames. For the first time, Sigewulf's face went slack with apprehension. He swallowed, the muscles in his throat bobbing. A mighty chieftain made fearful in her presence.

Aisling's lips curled, unable to resist the satisfaction such fear bred.

"What does any man want with something coveted, rare, and valuable?" he asked in return, watching every nuance of her expression. "He wants to claim it for himself."

With swift ease, Dagfin shoved Sigewulf into the body of a pine, tearing apart Aisling's enchantment. His strength alarming.

Dagfin poised the dagger's tip beneath the chieftain's chin, pointing it as though he'd shove it past his mouth and into his skull.

"Come now, *Faerak*. You can't condemn me for the sins we share."

"Give me one reason not to plunge this blade up your throat."

"Other than your vows to protect man from beast?" the chieftain taunted. "For one, you might find me useful in locating the curse breaker."

Silence rippled throughout the camp, nothing but the chuckling midnight trees interrupting each of their thoughts. Mention of the curse breaker was risky, especially from the mouth of a chieftain, king, or laird. Indeed, every man or fae alive was in pursuit of the curse breaker once its existence was spoken into the northern winds at the last fae and mortal union. To name it again was to declare oneself a competitor.

"I know these lands blind, how the trees shift and move, how the night stretches at odd hours, stealing from the daylight. How the mountains will play tricks on your mind."

Iarbonel visibly shuddered, exchanging nervous glances with Fergus.

"You need me," Sigewulf said.

Dagfin shifted, weighing the chieftain's words while Sigewulf's men awaited the release of their leader. Their white-blonde hair dyed gold by the light of their torches.

A branch snapped in the distance. Perhaps ice cracking or soil upturned.

Dagfin and Killian tensed at once, searching the dark around them. Panicked, the horses bucked, grabbing their tethers with their teeth.

"Do you have more men out there?" Starn asked.

Sigewulf shook his head. "No, Fjallnorr kin travel in small groups."

"For forge's sake," Annind blurted, shifting his body so his back faced the camp and not the surrounding forest.

"Aisling," Dagfin said, releasing Sigewulf. "Step away from the trees."

Indeed, Aisling stood at the lip of their camp, tiptoeing the line between firelight and shadow. Slowly, Aisling moved to stand beside Dagfin, shoulder to shoulder.

Not another sound was made. Somehow worse than a growl or roar. The quiet mocked them and licked its lips.

"Some more of your friends?" Starn asked Aisling, tightening his grip around the haft of his blade now slick with sweat.

Aisling glared at him. The words eluded her. For she couldn't smell nor feel a single animal save the chief of Fjallnorr's frenzied mares. No wolves, nor foxes, nor hares, nor birds, nor snakes. As though the forest were suddenly empty. A fathomless abyss made of spindly bones.

But then it laughed, teeth clicking as it cleared its throat of dirt.

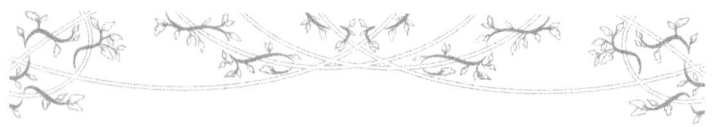

CHAPTER X

AISLING

In the mountains of Fjallnorr, death was frostbitten, relentless, and inevitable.

Cloaked by webs of silver frost, this Unseelie tore through the earth and its carpet of leaves.

It stood on two creaking legs, wrapped in ivory roots and thorns. A decaying corpse still clad in forge-welded armor. Its grave possessed by the forest of ice in which it lay.

Aisling stared it down, balling her hands into fists at her sides.

It tilted its skull to the side, curious, before dissolving into frenzied laughter once more. Worms, beetles, and dirt skittered from its eye sockets as it appraised their party.

"*Fear gorta,*" Sigewulf exhaled, staggering back.

Aisling silently repeated its name, but she already knew its kind.

Unseelie. "*Dealing with the Unseelie is complex. They're not a single race. They're many with various lords, chiefs, matriarchs, and leaders. Ranging from pure beast to conscious, intelligent creatures. All chaotic, archaic, opposed to order and governed solely by hunger and need.*" Lir taught her this what felt like a lifetime ago. And since then, Aisling had become familiar with multiple breeds of Unseelie. Some tales claiming even Aisling herself was Unseelie.

Aisling's pulse raced but she swallowed her fear and reached for her *draiocht.*

The fear gorta unlatched an obsidian greataxe from its back. Ice creeping down the weapon as its rotten bones gripped the haft. It spun the blade between its crimson stained fingers, narrowing its eyes on Aisling.

"*Skalla,*" it wheezed. Aisling lost her breath, staggering back. But then its attention shifted to Dagfin and stayed.

An arrow shot across the expanse.

The reed stuck into the fear gorta's head, juddering still from the impact. But the creature was unfazed, turning to find Annind, poised with a bow in hand.

The Unseelie reeled back his arm before releasing his greataxe. It flew, winding toward Annind. The blade cut across Annind's chest despite his attempts to dodge the onslaught, dying the snow beneath him red while he rolled in the dirt.

"Annind!" Iarbonel shouted.

The axe continued on, circling their camp like death's raven. Slicing the Roktan crew members one by one, Fjall-norrians, leaving their bodies dismembered in its wake before returning to its master like a hound on a chain.

Aisling ground her teeth, ignoring her earlier concerns and unleashing wicked wildfire at the fiend. Concentrating all her power on the demon and not their camp nor on one another. Fortunately, the fire found its target, igniting the skeleton like a torch in a dungeon of trees. The Unseelie cringed, bracing itself against the heat, devouring its ancient skeleton spark by spark.

Killian unloaded his quiver of bolts on the fear gorta, he and Aisling watching with horror as the fear gorta ripped them from its body and extinguished Aisling's flames. Frost splintering from its mouth, its sockets bleeding ice and smothering every lick of fire till it trudged forward in smoke and ice. But it wasn't the cold that snuffed Aisling's fire: it was something that tasted like magic. Like plums and shadows and bubbling cauldrons. Some sorcery this Unseelie wielded to dampen Aisling's might or that of any other for that matter.

It towered over Aisling, glaring down at her with an unholy grin. Aisling hesitated, too afraid to feel the pain of her burnt and blistered palms dripping on the snow below her boots.

Dagfin lunged for her, pushing her out of the fear gorta's path. It dove for the earth, pinning Sigewulf standing behind Aisling instead.

It crouched atop the chieftain, maw opened wide as it delved into his flesh and tore him apart piece by piece. The sound of tearing skin horrific enough to make Aisling's ears bleed.

The mighty chieftain of Fjallnorr felled by a single Unseelie.

A second passed and his life was gone.

Aisling's stomach churned, nausea inspired by sheer horror.

After months in the feywilds with Lir and his knights, she'd not garnered an understanding of what it meant to be mortal in the woods. To be vulnerable. A candle-lit flame snuffed without a passing thought. The wilderness was no place for man. Even the mightiest among them.

But there was no time to dwell on his death lest more be dealt. Aisling called upon the *draiocht* again, spilling violet across the beast. At last, it turned from its meal, hunched and cackling, fixing its absent gaze on Aisling. Winter's glass spider-webbed over her flames with ease. Powerful, arcane magic, resisting Aisling's own.

Aisling hissed; her *draíocht* snuffed by another.

It lifted its greataxe from the ground, readying it to strike as four more men swung their blades. Iron bouncing off its impenetrable bones. The clinking of its metal a death decree to all who stood before it. For indeed, it swiped at them with ease, harvesting their lives for its forest of ice.

At last, it found Dagfin amidst the chaos, picking up its feet to race toward him.

Why Dagfin? Aisling thought to herself, starting toward the Roktan prince. But she wasn't quick enough. The fear gorta moved like a shadow, here one moment and gone the next, whipping through the camp with unmatched speed.

Aisling braced herself for Dagfin and the Unseelie's collision, but it never came.

Instead, Aisling beheld in horror as Dagfin not only punched through the demon's chest but pulled out its heart. A rotted, slimy, black coal tangled in maggots, beetles, and thorns.

The fiend exhaled one last breath. Its body shriveling to a pile of ash atop the snow. Bones, age-old, prepared to return to the soil from whence they came.

Dagfin watched as the ashen heart slipped through his fingers like the sands of time. Joining its grave beneath the ice for the final time.

They ripped through the pines, scraping their faces on blade birches, howling aspens, and poison pines, all clawing for

Aisling as they fled. Popping roots from the earth to caress their Fjallnorrian mares, stolen from dead men.

"We'll never survive this," Fergus said, voice veiled by the frozen waterfall outside the cave. A shallow hollow of refuge from the winter winds, the Unseelie, and the forest. Their mares restlessly snorting just inside the cave's threshold.

"It's only the beginning," Aisling said, and all knew it to be truth. The Unseelie wouldn't stop for common man, much less for the sons of the fire hand, for Aisling, and for some reason, Dagfin. The Unseelie would stalk their mortal party, hunt them, and in the same breath a beast was vanquished, another would rise.

Aisling's brothers, even Dagfin and Killian, weren't accustomed to voyages such as this. And in many ways, neither was Aisling. She bore experience traversing the wilds, yet then, she hadn't run from the demons, rather hunted them alongside Lir. Her place in the food chain lowered several ranks without him. Made vulnerable to beasts of prey. At least, Aisling thought to herself, for now.

"We'll find safe haven here for the next several days," Starn said, glaring out at the forest lying in wait. Anxiously anticipating their return to its embrace. "We'll regain our energy."

"There's no time," Aisling interjected, binding her burnt hands with strips of her wool dress. Dagfin watching every loop of fabric as she worked. Bringing his flask to his lips as though it offered mortal absolution.

Iarbonel shook his head. "Ash, we can only move so quickly and survive. Annind can scarcely ride a horse in his condition."

Annind reclined against the cave wall, his fear gorta wounds bound by linen and leather. The bleeding was, at last, trickling to a stop. Still, Annind was pale and soaked in sweat, a wisp of his usual self.

"I've done it before," Aisling said.

"With the Aos Sí," Killian conjectured, crossing his arms and leaning against the cave wall. "We aren't like the Aos Sí, faerie. The Unseelie don't cower at our feet, the wilderness doesn't mind us, and our wounds don't heal by the light of tomorrow."

All eyes drifted to Aisling's hands, burned again and again by her fires. Already healing as all fae healed.

"Do you believe the Sidhe will slow their pace for us? That the other mortal sovereigns—those still alive and not tending to their destroyed kingdoms—will wait for us?" They each stared at her, mortal features either dancing in shadow or gilded by firelight.

She'd seen how effortlessly the chieftain of Fjallnorr had been slaughtered. How humankind was outmatched in a race against everything Other, a competition where a loss was met with death. Death, who nipped at their human heels. And if the same happened to Dagfin—if Dagfin, as strong as he was with his *Faerak* Ocras, was snuffed as swiftly and abruptly as Sigewulf... Aisling burned the end of her thought. "We will lose this race if we don't continue on."

Starn spoke not a word, seething silently as he kept his eyes pinned on woodland shadows.

"What does it matter to you?" Fergus countered, expression bent with frustration. "You care not for the curse breaker. Your ends are yours alone and us your pawns."

Aisling closed her eyes, doing her best to quell her most base urges, come awake after months with the fae king now impossible to put back to sleep.

"You speak to *me* of *pawns*?" she said, meeting Fergus's eyes. Bloodstained fingers twitching.

Iarbonel stood from where he sat.

"Enough," Iarbonel said. "Enough arguing. We may not survive this regardless, but we seal our death if we cannot keep from biting at one another's throats."

They each fell silent, weighing Iarbonel's words. So, Aisling used this as her excuse, taking her leave to breathe outside the cave. Away from Killian's iron, left by the fire to smoke the cave in its putrid stench.

Starn eyed her every step, ensuring she knew she was being surveyed.

Aisling climbed up the mouth of the cave and sat atop it, avoiding the ice and nestling herself amidst the frigid stone. A reprieve from what simmered beneath her flesh and, at times, drove her mad.

She rested her head, quietly listening to the moaning of mating insects, the rustling of trees, the songs of star-filled skies, or the cracking of ice in the wind. A melody Aisling had craved over the last several months, her thirst for it, at last, slaked. Allowing herself a moment to indulge in the feywild's savage embrace.

"You never did fear anything," Dagfin said, startling her. "Even when you should've. So, I'm not certain why it still surprises me you choose to taunt danger and bait yourself to the wilds. You shouldn't be out here alone."

"You speak as though you don't understand what it means to be imprisoned." He sat beside her, shoulder to shoulder. "To live a life sheltered and gray, only to taste magic and find anything else suddenly insufficient."

Aisling didn't care to glance at Dagfin for fear her heart would splinter at what she found. Every glance they shared pricked her lips and twisted her heart.

"I was never kept in the dark," he said. "Never lied to, and never traded."

Aisling smiled bitterly. "Perhaps, but you've always been caged by the Roktan crown and the legacy it implies."

He shifted then, watching her in the pale light of the moon.

"It's not mine to take."

"If your brother could've chosen one person to take his place, it would've been you. Feradach knows this, I know this. You need not feel guilty for taking what is rightfully yours."

He swallowed, glaring up at the constellations above, "I wish it was as easy for me as it is for you. As children you followed shadows, endured nights put to bed without dinner, and gritted your teeth through the lashings you knew would come. Doing as you liked regardless. And now, you set the world on your heels."

"You say it as though it's a virtue. My impulses, my rebellion is more vice. More need," she corrected. "Lest my soul collapse like a dying fire."

Dagfin ground his teeth. "You speak of survival at the cost of embracing this wildness inside you, whatever it is that makes you like *them*, but all I see are hands burned again and again, a body thinning, anger bounding from within. There is power in you, Aisling. As children I saw it in your spirit and now it's taken a more literal form. But it isn't wise to let it unravel, lest you find yourself plunging toward your own destruction, falling too fast to stop."

Aisling crossed her arms, allowing the wind to brush her cheeks. The forest coaxing her calm.

So Dagfin knew her wounds were a product of summoning the *draiocht*. It was a relief to no longer hide it from him. To no longer endure the pain, endure the fear of whatever was happening to her, but to also no longer bear the burden of hiding it from the Roktan prince.

"Is it self-control you boast in the daylight, when by shadow you relish in your own form of power?"

Dagfin did a double take, staring at Aisling despite the dark.

"What do you—"

"I know about the Ocras. Killian told me some and I connected the rest."

Dagfin focused on the distance, still as a hunter.

"You're addicted to it, aren't you?" Aisling continued. "That's how you healed from Killian's runes so quickly. How you ripped the fear gorta's heart from his chest. You start and you cannot stop. Why, the flask is perpetually at your lips. Why is that?"

Dagfin turned his head, unable to look her in the eyes.

"Because you crave it as much as I do. Power gives us some semblance of control, Dagfin. And without control we become controlled by another. Someone brave and ruthless enough to take what's theirs. So, it isn't virtue, Dagfin. It's need. As much my own as yours."

He shut his eyes, leaning his head against the rock. Aisling wasn't certain if he didn't know what to say or didn't care to say anything at all. Only that he never spoke again, taking her hand and lacing his fingers through Aisling's before kissing her cheek. As soft as a coastal breeze, laced with the roar of crashing waves beyond. Aisling's cheeks bled crimson. She wasn't certain what to think of it. But before she could decide, he fell asleep by her side.

Now, Aisling was alone with the wilderness. Hour by hour, waiting, listening, at long last speaking to the forest as it'd longed to speak with her. Finding in herself the voice Lir had coaxed to life.

CHAPTER XI

AISLING

Aisling crashed against stone, washed ashore by her dream's black sea. She dragged herself to her feet, at once searching for Lir through the veil of thunderhead tears. But where he usually appeared without warning, without word, without summons, he was nowhere to be found.

Against her own volition, Aisling's spirits fell. She found herself searching the forest, twirling in a shifting kingdom, calling his name with no response. Aisling couldn't remember the last time he hadn't visited her dreams, forcing her to wonder if they'd always been just that. Dreams. Or, if this were an ill omen. The beginning of something strange afoot.

The woodland chuckled, amused by her search, so Aisling ignored it, traveling deeper into the forest. But even after hours, after peering behind every maple, yew, and cypress, after speaking his name like a spell, he was nowhere to be seen. Suddenly endlessly far. Gone and alive only in her memory.

After several days, their mares refused to run, eating snow and licking ice whenever their riders would allow it.

Annind grew weaker by the hour, forced to share a horse with Iarbonel. His wounds fought infection but refused to close entirely. And every day spent on horseback, traversing the ice-ridden landscape, trees sheathed in glass, he spoke a little less. Kept to himself beside their brittle fires and braced against the cold.

This deep in the forest, the branches knotted their fingers overhead like fae interlace, shielding them from the brunt of both snowstorms and highland winds. Aisling found logs, wrapped their ends in linen and spare furs, burning fire after fire to give them a beacon in the shadows. To warm them when teeth began to chatter, and eyelashes sharpened with frost. And while Aisling found she could go days without food, what little she managed, the others struggled to keep their appetite at bay.

Dagfin and Killian scoured the periphery of their camp, but were only fortunate to find a single hare to split between the six of them. Hunger carving their features till they scarcely bore any resemblance to the day they'd first set foot in the Fjallnorrian wilds.

So, Aisling bid the wolves that visited her in the dead of night, when everyone else slept, to hunt hares, foxes, pheasant, deer, and any other creature with a beating heart for their party. To sustain them. Yet Starn refused every offering and so, the others did as well.

"Where are you going?" Starn asked, unable to mask the venom in his voice. He caught Aisling's arm just before she was able to slip between the trees, her mare beside her.

"The horses are hungry," she said. "There's a creek not

far from here so I was hoping to find some sort of vegetation by its shore." Indeed, the wolves and the owls whispered this to Aisling when they believed none others listening.

Starn considered her, weighing her words as though she spoke in riddles.

At last, he nodded his head.

"Killian," Starn ordered, and the *Faerak* at once stood from where he sat beside the camp.

Aisling's brow furrowed. "Scared I'll set the wood aflame?" And by the expression on Starn's face, he might've been. She despised his suspicion. His watchful glares, his paranoid glances. Loathed the self-righteous tilt of his head each time she spoke until Aisling wondered if it was just his gestures she despised or him as well. The prospect of burning his tongue from his mouth, more reasonable by the day.

"I'll go with her," Dagfin piped, flipping his dagger into his belt.

Aisling ground her teeth but said nothing, preferring Dagfin to Killian and recognizing this wasn't a battle she cared to fight. Nor that she found it worth her while. So, she conceded to Dagfin's company as she ventured further into the forest.

"His distrust for me grows by the hour," she said, aware that Starn eyed her from their camp as both she and Dagfin faded between the trees.

"He feels responsible for all of us." Dagfin unstoppered his flask and gulped several mouthfuls.

"So why has he come? Why risk his own life and those of our brothers—yours—to help a sister he hardly tolerates much less trusts?"

Dagfin's expression narrowed in thought.

"Starn always has his own agenda. One he'd rather take

to his grave than share with anyone other than himself, Fergus, Iarbonel, or Annind."

"He hardly needs to share it, for his motivations to be clear. His actions make it obvious."

Dagfin turned to her. "What do you mean?"

"He's in pursuit of the curse breaker for our father."

And Aisling knew the moment she spoke the words aloud and Dagfin didn't immediately deny them that she was right. That Dagfin knew as well.

Aisling hadn't heard a whisper of the fire hand, nor a sign. Starn's ambition and need for approval was the only suggestion Nemed was still alive after Lir's ambush.

With two legs of iron, the great fire hand of the North could scarcely ride, much less venture through the wilderness in pursuit of myths and legends. Nevertheless, Aisling had seen the potent longing in his eyes when he'd beheld Aisling's flames for the first time. The emotion in his voice when he spoke of stealing back what he believed was rightfully humankind's.

All this time, Aisling was glancing over her shoulder afraid of her competitors, while one of her greatest adversaries slept around the same fire. Drank from the same flasks. Rode at their side. Killian brought along to protect this rival, forged with the same blood that once flowed freely through Aisling's veins.

"Did he tell you?" Aisling asked, holding her breath.

Dagfin looked straight ahead, eyes pinned to the approaching creek babbling to the stones.

"No," Dagfin said. "But he didn't have to."

Against her own volition, Aisling's heart ached, punctured inside her chest and bled out slowly. She cursed herself for it. For having hoped for anything else. For *wanting* to believe Starn had come along for her. The memory of a doll he'd whittled for her ninth birthday, flashing across her mind's eye. A memory that felt stolen. Taken from a girl that no longer existed and planted inside Aisling's mind.

So, Aisling shoved away the sadness, replacing it with something else. Something grim, cold, and unforgiving. The *draiocht* purring at the taste of it.

"And you?" Aisling asked. "What was your plan?"

Dagfin reacted viscerally, whipping his head in her direction. Anger, frustration, and guilt making crooked the curve of his mouth. A mouth Aisling could still feel pressing against her own near as tangibly as she'd felt it aboard the *Starling*. The memory, dipping her stomach.

"To be by your side like I should've always been. Perhaps then, you would've never wed *him*."

Aisling cringed at the venom in Dagfin's last word. But she was never given a chance to respond.

The wintertide birds whistled for Aisling to turn around. She listened, peering between the branches, finding a figure nestled between the glass oaks. One who already studied them in return.

Aisling's boots froze in place. Their mare panicked, yanking at the reins to be released.

She sat upon a throne—an old, gnarled, winterkill oak, bowing atop the snow. Its branches moving, slithering, forming, and reforming long after they'd molded a seat from its body. Fawning over she who sat upon it, absently glaring at the glittering loom before her.

The Lady.

"There is a lady who wastes away in a cave, century after century, weaving. Every thread a thread of fate. There are some who believe that once these threads are placed upon the

spindle, woven and knotted together, there are none who can undo its tapestry." Lir had spoken such words just moments before he'd betrayed the treaty between man and fae. Had vowed to claw that very tapestry apart till nothing but shreds remained, refusing to concede to Danu, the empress of the dryad's, prophecies. To make certain the Sidhe vanquished mankind.

Every hair on Aisling's body stood and stiffened the moment the Lady turned to face them both. Her horse eager to flee far from this place.

And although the Lady's eyes were hidden by an enormous ivory spider pinned to the bridge of her nose, Aisling felt the weight of her gaze. Smelled the magic in the air: of the earth, of forgotten, forbidden spells, and frostbitten nights of yore. Her robes spilling around the loom as she worked, shimmering, arctic white, seemingly threaded with the silk of concentrated starlight. Trees stretching, craning, for the Lady to weave their branches into her blinding loom.

"You blunt my shears," she said abruptly. A voice that spilled and flowed, guzzled by the ears of those who listened.

Dagfin shifted, one hand instinctively reaching for Aisling's own, while the other wandered to his daggers.

"And you." She tilted her head at Dagfin. "You knot my threads."

"You're the Lady." Aisling exhaled, both afraid and in awe. The *draiocht* within her inclining its head to better taste her magic-sweet aura.

"I am," she said, skin of polished obsidian stroked by the branches of loving trees. "I've come to warn you, Aisling."

Aisling blinked, curiosity compelling her to take a single step forward. Dagfin held her hand tight, falling into step beside her.

"I braid your thread again and again, but it always frays,

snaps, hardens against my shears. I cannot compel your thread, manipulate it, weave it, so I've come to speak with you instead. To prevent you from lacing the way I expect your thread will."

Her fingers moved swiftly across the loom, strings of pure, radiant light.

"I don't understand."

"It's not for you to understand, Aisling."

"Then speak, Lady, and enough with your riddles," Dagfin chimed, his posture shifting from prince to *Faerak*.

The Lady's fingers tensed at the loom, snapping a string. Her nostrils flared at the smell of Ocras on his breath. A potent warning.

"You and I, *Faerak*, want the same," she said, the spider atop her face twitching as she continued her work on the loom. "For this violet thread not to indulge a hand of thorns, lest she find herself forever tangled in a greenwood, slaked only by strength and power."

Aisling felt the electricity of Dagfin's temper before she saw it. The heavy, open sea storms thundering in his eyes.

"A hand of thorns," Aisling repeated. "You reference Lir."

Dagfin frowned at the mention of his name.

"The dark lord of the greenwood, the white stag, the Sidhe king, your *caera*. Aye. Every breath nearer to one another, every touch closer, will only ever herald desolation in both this realm and the next."

Aisling's eyes pricked with heat.

Dagfin's attention darted between Aisling and the Lady.

"*Caera*?" he asked.

"Woven together by my threads of fate, dipped in the Forge, and made potent by blood. I created the first threads but from then on, they take a life of their own. Growing, traveling, choosing what they will until it is entirely outside my control. My only duty to the loom."

Aisling dared not glance at Dagfin, bracing against the cool edge of the woodland breeze.

"Stay away from the Sidhe king, Aisling," she commanded, fanning embers of rage in Aisling's chest.

Dagfin rolled his shoulders back, cracking his neck side to side, teeth bared. "You did this. You bound her to the fae king."

The Lady laughed, the sound of it shattering the ice clinging to every branch till it showered in knife sharp blades around them all.

"No, *Faerak*. You did."

Dagfin didn't hesitate.

The insinuation he'd bound Aisling to Lir because of his complicity in trading her to the fae striking a furious chord.

He threw his dagger, its iron cutting toward the Lady with unparalleled accuracy. But the Lady didn't flinch. Instead, she smiled, watching as the surrounding trees intercepted the knife and slammed it into the earth, knocking Aisling, Dagfin, and their mare off their feet.

Aisling cursed beneath her breath. Trees of all shape and form were under the sovereignty of Lir, so what magic did the Lady boast that snuffed that of others?

"What say you, Aisling? Heed me and prosper. Disobey me and breed ruin."

The pines thrashed violently, roots rising from the earth as the Lady sat still as the moon, orbited by the crystal limbs of the winter woodland.

Aisling found her footing and glared at the Lady in return. Arrogant, she sat straight before her tapestry, twisting threads and pulling at their bodies with her slender fingers. Each thread, one of fate. A life controlled, dictated, spun, and put to use. A life stolen. A life lost. As Aisling's own had once been: used by kings and discarded when necessary. Only for the Sidhe to call her "thief" and the mortals to whisper "traitor" behind her back.

Aisling shook her head, ignoring the angry turning of her stomach. The heat pricking her fingertips. Danu had foreseen a similar fate between Aisling and Lir. And warned them both of its outcome.

Yet Aisling found she cared little for either the Lady's or Danu's visions. They were manipulations. For what was seen had not yet come to pass.

This was never about Aisling and Lir. Whether she and the fae king were near, far, together, or apart was irrelevant. This was rather another means of manipulation. For the Lady was accustomed to snipping, threading, and weaving her threads, grown frustrated with one that refused to comply with her work. To be sown, pulled, and cut into strict order. A fact that rippled through Aisling with incomparable satisfaction.

Aisling lifted her chin.

Screaming, the mare reared. The wind howled through the trees and danced with Aisling's hair till it fanned around her, as though submerged beneath the water. Inky black and alive. Her eyes glistening a shade brighter.

"Disobey me and breed ruin!" the Lady said, this time louder.

Aisling gritted her teeth. "I say ruin."

The spider atop the Lady's face bled black, shuddering with the Lady's rage. The world upturned, folding the Lady in a pocket of the Other, and leaving devastation in its wake.

The strings of her loom, awakened like serpents, darted at Aisling and Dagfin, tangling around their ankles and dragging them into oblivion. A fathomless abyss of white light, shimmering with eternal intention.

Aisling raised the *draiocht*, but the strings weren't made of linen. No, they were rather braided by mystical light. Immune to her fires. Cackling at Aisling's and Dagfin's efforts to snip their strings with the *Faerak*'s blades. Ripping the flesh of their joints raw as it pulled them under and into the Lady's abyss of blinding light.

Until frost crawled down the cords, freezing each string solid, then bursting into thousands of jagged shards like stars. The Lady shrieked, a sound like glass cracking and echoing into eternity. The world blurring as the Lady vanished and both Aisling and Dagfin were freed.

But Aisling and Dagfin didn't find salvation.

Hands of ice rose from the snow. The hands clasped both their wrists and lifted them to their knees so that when they met his eyes, they already bowed to a fae king.

CHAPTER XII

AISLING

"A Sidhe queen should never be on her knees," the fae king said, padding closer, hands of ice rising from the earth like the limbs of the dead and shoving Aisling onto her feet. His fae accent both familiar and heart-wrenching. "Lest her king demand it. And I don't see Lir anywhere in sight." He grinned.

Silver eyes sparkled the same hue as his waist-length hair, braided through and crowned by an obsidian circlet. Two curving horns sprouting from its metal. The same vicious and glaciated edge reflected in the hard angles of his armor.

A sled pulled by wolves sat behind him.

"They'll write legends about you, you know?" he said, a pace away from Aisling—held captive by the hands of ice. Shackling her wrists, her ankles, and binding her to the earth. This close, Aisling could see his pointed ears bedizened with crystals. His fangs flashing when he spoke. "You're remarkable."

But before either Aisling or Dagfin could say a word, ice

speared through the earth and toward them. Impaling their consciousness till the world fell black.

Lost in a pool of ink with neither an up nor down, Aisling swam in the dark. And if it weren't for Lir's absence, she would've found comfort in the dark. Warm, whole, and absolute.

Aisling woke in a room made of glass. No, not glass. Ice. An ornamental, four-poster bed cradling her as she slept, swathing her in great, snowy-white pelts that smelled of leather and bitter winter winds.

She jolted upright, noticing for the first time she wore a new gown. Aisling blanched, her stomach dropping, hoping the gown had been magicked onto her when she was unconscious.

A dress with sheets of secret-thin gossamer spun around her figure, spread over the bed and sweeping the frigid floors with their great length while silver bear claws held the most essential pieces together. A headdress made in the same fabric was pinned to her temples and billowed down her back.

The Roktan cloak Dagfin had gifted her, on the other hand, was draped across her bed, alongside her old woolen and tattered dress.

Aisling didn't waste time. She leaped onto her feet and scoured the room. A chamber resplendent enough for a Seelie queen albeit bone-chillingly cold.

Arched mirrors speared for the barreled ceiling. Aisling

was reflected a thousand times over. One of hundreds spinning like a top at the center of the room. Roaring bears, smiling badgers, and timid foxes carved around each mirror, polished in silver even as they bared their fangs.

Otherwise, the room was empty. No door, no windows, no Dagfin, no escape. A shred of panic increased the pace of her heart as she swiveled.

Aisling approached the nearest mirror, pressing her palm against its glass.

She was thinner, gaunter than she'd last seen. Her hair unbrushed and sprinkled with specks of ice like uncut jewels. But it was the largeness of her eyes and the elegant stroke of her every movement that unsettled her most of all. Even since the *Starling*, Aisling's appearance had greatly changed. When she was fully human, Aisling was lovely. Now, she was *otherworldly*. Fierce and powerful, branded by the feral insignia of the Forge.

Aisling's eyes glazed with tears. Happy tears, for her reflection was one she'd craved. Her reflection was someone who mattered, someone capable, someone worthy, someone feared. A predator and not prey.

Overcome with emotion, with joy, violet fire flickered from her fingertips and blackened the mirror. The smell of burning flesh smoking the room.

Aisling shuddered, leaping back as frost overtook her brittle fire and ran up her fingers, her arms, clawing for her neck. A similar dulling sensation, gnawing at her *draiocht*, to when she'd confronted the fear gorta or tried to burn the Lady's threads.

The *draiocht* exploded larger, sucking the wind from Aisling's lungs but melting whatever ice still threatened to sink into her bones.

Aisling glared at the mirror with renewed suspicion,

hardly surprised when it rippled, and a white bear lumbered through.

"What is that smell?" he asked, referencing the stench of burning flesh and inhaling deeply. "It's... delightful."

Aisling balled her hands into fists, obscuring her burned palms from his sight.

Animals born in magic-concentrated land, such as Sidhe kingdoms, were as sentient and intelligent as the fae themselves. In fact, her chambermaid in Annwyn was a small and mighty pine marten Aisling hardly let herself recognize she missed.

"Who are you?"

"Forgive the intrusion, *mo Lúra*," he said, the baritone of his voice rattling the frozen roses hanging from the chandeliers above. "I am Greum. I've come to escort you to my lord."

"Where is Dagfin?"

"You mean the *Faerak* prince?" The bear tilted his head to the side. "Don't fret, *Skalla*. He's in good company. I dare say I don't think we've ever... *housed* so many princes beneath his lordship's palace."

Aisling hesitated, studying the bear's expression.

So, this fae king had caught her brothers as well.

"This is *his* palace then," she said, lifting her chin even as the behemoth of the bear straightened onto his hind legs and stared down at her. Its miraculous armor clinking as it moved, engraved in blade-sharp snowflakes and thorns.

Greum laughed. "Everything the ice touches is his palace. His domain. So long as your breath mists from your lips, you are subject to my lord."

"I am subject to no lord."

The bear laughed again, falling back onto all fours and shaking the ground. Aisling kept her balance, grasping at one of the bed posts.

"If it weren't against my lord's wishes I'd have the flesh torn from your bones by now."

"Only after I make ash from your hide."

Greum grinned. "Your threats amuse me. Usually thieves aren't so reckless."

"I'm no thief."

"You stole the *draiocht*."

"It was given."

He scoffed. "Thieves are usually liars, I'll give you that."

"And usually beasts are not so long-winded." Aisling crossed her arms.

"Even so, you'll find your fires carry little weight while in his lordship's presence. You may be strange, *Skalla*, but you're young yet. Your powers are a flicker in comparison to the ages-old strength of his lordship."

"Take me to your lordship then."

"Very well, *mo Lúra*." Greum bowed his head in mock respect. "Follow me."

The bear heaved his massive form, turning to the mirrors once more. Without hesitation, he stepped through a rippling, shimmering surface till he disappeared entirely. Leaving Aisling glaring at her own distorted reflection.

Aisling swallowed the stone in her throat.

Closing both eyes, she reached for the mirror. Her first hand sunk through, then the next, whatever lay on the other side impossibly colder than her chamber.

Aisling focused, gathering the courage to plunge through the mirror and through to the other side.

≈

DAGFIN

Thank the Forge for Ocras. Otherwise, Dagfin would've woken to find his bones frozen.

The *Faerak*'s eyes flickered open, appraising his new surroundings for the first time. He lay in a chamber of stone, blocked off from the open courtyard beyond by bars that rose from the earth in jagged, thin pillars of ice. A prison cell, Dagfin realized.

"Aisling," he said absentmindedly, at once searching his surroundings for her. But she was nowhere in sight.

"Where are we?" a voice groaned from behind.

Starn, Iarbonel, and Killian were unfurling from the ground, rubbing their eyes and holding their heads. Fergus and Annind, however, had yet to wake, lips turning blue.

"You're in Oighir," a stranger replied.

Dagfin's skin prickled, spinning on his heel to find several wolves stalking toward their cell. From where Dagfin stood, he estimated there were thirty or so cells, wrapped around the periphery of the courtyard. A flagstone expanse dusted in snow and boasting a large fountain at its center. Its statues depicted a bear and a stag mid-battle, water frozen and glistening in ribbons of ice.

Beyond, sharp towers jutted at the blizzard skies and floating bridges—like blown glass—connected turrets, flying buttresses, and battlements wrapped in thick quilts of skull ivy. Verandas and their staircases braced against the heart of winter, each and everything twinkling with a lustrous glow that emanated from the bulbs of brambles of eyebright, glittering like bundles of stars around the castle.

"Oighir," Dagfin repeated. He'd heard of this keep before. The druids farther north spoke of such a kingdom, offering sacrifices to both the ruler of this bastion and the forest that encased it to keep from starving or freezing at the cost of the cold. A fae domain, ruled by the son of Winter who sat on a throne of frostbite.

"Where is Aisling?!" he said, louder than he'd intended.

The wolves grinned.

"The bride of the forest is... well taken care of."

Dagfin's nostrils flared. "If she's harmed—"

"Our lord would never mistreat a fellow sovereign."

"Yet you dare to imprison mortal princes?!" Starn interjected, reaching for the bars to better glare at the snickering wolves. "This is a direct offense to mankind."

"Last we heard, the *Damh Bán* made it so offenses can be commonplace once more, if not enjoyed," the nearest wolf said. *Damh Bán*. They were referring to Lir.

Another wolf nodded, licking its fangs in response.

"Release us!" Starn yelled.

"Or what, mortal prince?" The wolves crept forward till they stood a few paces from their cell.

Killian moved to grab his crossbow only to find it gone from his back. In a panic, the *Faerak* searched his bandolier, his belt, his boots, realizing to his own horror all his weapons had been stripped off his person. None of the others were an exception, including Dagfin.

The wolves dissolved into a frenzy of laughter.

"You'll remain here until our lord summons you," the first said, coming up for air.

"We won't survive a summons in this cold," Iarbonel said, gesturing to Fergus and Annind, still lying unconscious atop the stone, the youngest of the brothers weary after their days journeying in such harsh climates, not to mention Annind's injuries from the fear gorta. "We need fire and heat."

The wolves exchanged glances. "So weak, so frail, so ill-equipped for the natural world. You claim us perversities of nature, but it is man that is a blight in both this realm and the next. You weren't made for this world, unable to withstand even its seasons. You're a curse to punish a Sidhe queen and nothing more."

"Even so, I wager your lord won't be too satisfied with two fewer princes once he summons us," Dagfin said, focusing on the largest wolf at the front of their pack.

The beast frowned, ears falling flat against his head as he considered.

"My lord would relish a mortal death, especially if said death is reaped from the Neimedh Clann."

"Even if such a death comes at the cost of any and all leverage?" Dagfin took hold of the prison cell bars. "If your lord wanted us dead, we would've been by now."

At this, the wolf snarled, wrinkling its muzzle.

"Frigg, perhaps the human has a point—"

"Enough!" the center wolf, Frigg, barked at the canine behind him, silencing any others who considered speaking. "Bring them a handful of torches, whatever scraps from the kitchens, and no more."

The rest of the wolves bounded for a large wooden threshold, the door groaning open at the sign of their presence and closing behind them as they exited the courtyard. Frigg lingered long enough to snarl and snap at Dagfin before chasing after the others.

"You think they'll return?" Iarbonel asked, shrugging off his jacket to place over Annind, pale as the blizzard weaving around them.

"If they value self-preservation, then yes," Dagfin said, scouring the courtyard for a way out, for a weapon, for any and all options. He'd been imprisoned before on his *Faerak* missions—a banshee's den in the Hills of Hidris, a bocanach's lair further south, a kelpie's nest in Aithirn's shallows—and he'd learned there was always a means of escape no matter how formidable the prison.

Starn shook his head, pacing back and forth in their cell. "At the first opportunity, we flee from here and return to Tilren."

"What of the faerie?" Killian asked, instinctively glancing at Dagfin.

"She'll fare fine on her own." Starn's words inspired silence, nothing except the howling of the wind and the brush of evergreens swaying to interrupt the dense quiet.

"You can't be serious," Dagfin said at last. "You'd forsake your sister?"

"You were right, Fin. She hasn't been my sister for some time, nor the Aisling you remember. Her actions aboard the *Starling* are proof enough of that."

Dagfin's shoulders grew taut, anger rising in his gut. Starn had always been cut-throat, impatient, and frustrated when ignored. But Dagfin had never realized the darkness of Starn's vices until it was channeled at Aisling.

"She's changed, as we all have these past several years," Dagfin said. "And she's given us all a second chance when we scarcely deserved it."

"It's better for her if we part ways," Iarbonel chimed, the kind curves of his face speaking both doubt and guilt.

Dagfin's brow knit, understanding dawning.

"Your charade to help her expired more quickly than even I assumed it would," he said bitterly. A sentiment that struck Iarbonel the hardest, his shoulders slumping forward in shame.

"It's not personal." Killian stepped beside Dagfin to peer outside the bars himself. "I met you each in Roktling at the behest of Nemed, paid to keep you all safe on the journey ahead. Continuing to accompany the faerie is counterproductive. She's a beacon for the darkest shadows in the wood."

Dagfin scowled. "How did Nemed know of our whereabouts?"

Immediately, Iarbonel averted his eyes, so it was Starn who spoke.

"I had Feradach impart a message to Nemed once we reached Roktling."

Dagfin reeled, his temper rising with each new word.

"My father?"

Starn nodded his head. "Aye."

"Did Feradach know the contents of your message?" Dagfin held his breath, praying a silent prayer to the Forge that his father hadn't betrayed him or, at the very least, withheld information.

"I have no way of knowing but it's possible. Regardless, I told Nemed our whereabouts and that's when, instead of ordering us back to Tilren, he requested a favor: pursue the curse breaker in his stead."

"And at that point in time, I was ordered to Roktling, paid in full," Killian said.

"Of course, he believed Aisling would guide us directly to it, but it's swiftly been made clear she'll only slow us down. Especially since she's made more enemies whilst away than just her own kind." Starn crossed his arms. "Not to mention, she can't be trusted. I was willing to entertain her until the *Starling*. Not anymore."

Dagfin's muscles ached from his anger, cording in his arms, back, and neck. Starn stood straight, doing his best to convince them all he was certain of his decision. But Dagfin saw past the veneer, through to the aching guilt and grief inherent within his choice. As though he mourned the memory of a sister he believed no longer existed, while his doubt that she may still be alive cannibalized him with guilt. And somehow, that made Starn's crimes worse; he realized it was a cruel choice but made it regardless.

"All that being said, it's best we return to Tilren our first opportunity. Annind won't survive a trek to the tip of Lofgren's Rise, and as it currently stands, nor will Fergus. If Aisling goes with us home, she'll only seal their fate. Father will send his, as well as the other mortal sovereigns' fleets, in our stead. Aisling nor any other Sidhe will stand a chance against four mortal armies."

All eyes shifted, setting on the two youngest Neimedh brothers lying unconscious and blue on the stone floors.

"I won't leave Aisling," Dagfin said finally. More a vow than a statement.

"If the hopes of eventually bedding the faerie is what's stopping you, then get it done with and the wisdom in Starn's words will be made much clearer." Killian leaned against the bars. "Although I warn you, the act may be pleasant, but the aftermath of such intimacy with either Seelie or Unseelie is only ever written in curses."

Dagfin didn't hesitate. He swung his fist at Killian, striking him in the jaw so hard, the sound ricocheted off the walls of the courtyard.

The other *Faerak* slapped against the floor, rising with a hand rubbing his red jaw.

"Where was this strength against the murúch?" Killian kicked Dagfin in the chest, spinning on his dominant heel to return the punch in the jaw.

Dagfin dodged the kick but braced against the speed of the punch, blinking through the blinding pain searing through his temples and into his ears.

"Or were the murúch another excuse to try and bed

her?" Killian flashed a smug smile, thwacked off his face with the edge of Dagfin's boot.

The other *Faerak* blew into the bars before crumpling to the stone, blood spilling from his cracked lip.

"Stop this!" Starn yelled. "Look at where we are. Neither of you will be of any use escaping if you can hardly stand. Aisling can come along if she wishes. If not, she can rot for all I care."

Dagfin and Killian glared at one another, measuring whether another strike was worth their time.

A snicker erupted just outside their cell.

Each turned to find the pack of wolves spectating their display, mouths split wide, and teeth bared in laughter.

Frigg stepped forward.

"His lordship demands your presence, princes."

CHAPTER XIII

AISLING

Aisling stepped onto a floating bridge of solid ice. It glittered in the soft light cast by frozen flower bulbs. The pollen at their center imbued with an ivory radiance.

Fae light. An alternative to fire, which the Aos Sí all despised and feared. Their only weakness other than iron. But in Annwyn, such fae light was warm and golden. Here, it was only cold.

Beneath the bridge were thickets of eyebright. A forest of twinkling light, tangling beneath the walkway and powdered in fog.

Yet it was what lay ahead that captured Aisling's attention and held it. A platform cut from the same ice as all else, crowned by an imperial staircase with a glimmering, sharp dais atop it. Eight colossal columns carved in the image of bears lined the room, each one hunched and carrying the weight of the ornamental ceilings polished with ice. Ice, a bed for the frozen hands that grew from the rafters to claw for the dais below.

Aisling followed Greum over the bridge, carefully placing each step lest she slip.

The bear escorted her up one side of the imperial staircase till she stood before a throne. An ornate seat seemingly carved from snow as resplendent as diamonds and surrounded by bowing pines, white with frost.

Several other Sidhe, plated in artful armor, stood around the throne. Their eyes as silver as their lord's, sharp and upturned, with irises as pale as pearls. A fierceness far outweighing even the wolves that prowled around the base of the throne in defense of he who sat atop it.

The fae king.

Striking, primeval, and inhumanly lovely.

Silver hair sparkling, his greatsword, once sheathed at his waist, now jutted from his throne, watching as Aisling came into view. The fae king crossed his legs and leaned lithely to the side till his head rested in one slender, tattooed hand.

"I could gaze upon you for a lifetime, *mo Lúra*." His voice filled the room despite the softness of it. The inherent calm he instilled in a chamber full of feral, forge-brewed creatures. "Wintertide compliments you."

"You're Delbaeth," Aisling said, ignoring the heavy glares of every Aos Sí and beast in the room. "One of the twelve Sidhe sovereigns."

Indeed, Delbaeth, as Aisling had learned during her time amongst the Aos Sí, was the Sidhe king of ice. Son of Winter, they called him. A greatsword as tall as himself, gifted to him by the Forge, now displayed at the back of his throne.

"No," he said, amused. "Delbaeth was my father. My name is Fionn. And yours is Aisling."

A chill crept up Aisling's spine at the sound of her name on his lips. She considered him, glancing about the room and meeting the eyes of the others for the first time. Something between curiosity and fear flickering across their other-worldly expressions.

"Where are Dagfin and my brothers?" Aisling asked, ignoring his introductions. She bore little patience for those who stood in her way and a fae king, one with as much reason to either wish harm on Aisling or want the curse breaker as much as anyone else, would stop Aisling or deter her from achieving her ends entirely. Indeed, Aisling knew not what the inter-relations between the Aos Sí were like. Gilrel had mentioned conflict between the courts in passing but never divulged more than a handful of details. A fact which Aisling now cursed.

"How about an exchange, *mo Lúra*?" Fionn smiled, the edges of his lips curling gently. "I'll return your brothers and the *Faerak* in exchange for Lir's whereabouts."

Aisling shook her head.

"You ask for information I cannot give. I bear no knowledge of Lir's whereabouts."

The Sidhe, Greum, and the wolves all shifted. As though the mere mention of Lir's name was enough to inspire unease amongst even his own kind.

"What a privilege you wield: to draw upon Sidhe strength while encumbered by only one of our weaknesses. For here you stand, lying between your teeth."

The ease of his posture stiffened with frustration. A deadly, lethal sort of poise that made frigid the breath they shared.

Aisling steeled herself, praying to the godsforsaken Forge none saw her swallow before speaking.

"It's no lie. I've not laid eyes on him since he betrayed the union between man and Aos Sí. A fact of which I'm sure you're well aware."

Fionn stood from his throne, his Sidhe guards rigid as he

swept down the stairs. He wore no shirt, no tunic, no blouse. Only a translucent robe of sparkling black, exposing his muscled abdomen and arms painted with fae markings. His trousers belted at his hips.

Aisling's breath caught in her throat as he approached, the vast height of him quickly becoming more apparent. He smelled of frost. Of wet wood and rivers frozen by winter's overzealous touch.

At last, he slowed to a halt, tilting his head to meet her.

"Bring them in," he said, but not to Aisling. The wolves nodded their heads, exiting briefly through the arched doorways on either side of the chamber.

Aisling clenched her jaw. A torrent of emotion whirling violently within her at the prospect of her brothers having been harmed. Hoping Dagfin was safe.

Starn, Iarbonel, Fergus, and Annind limped into the room, shoved roughly about by the wolves that escorted them.

Annind winced, his complexion somehow paler than it'd been the last time Aisling saw him. Hands and ankles shackled with chains of enchanted ice.

They oriented themselves as they emerged from whatever dungeons the fae king no doubt kept them in, finding Aisling standing before Fionn. The difference was obvious. While they'd been imprisoned, Aisling wore a gown as lustrous as an opal and had been given a private audience with the fae king.

Starn's expression was all fire, twisted with rage and frustration. Indeed, Starn was accustomed to being the respected sibling: the one amongst them acclaimed, admired, and gifted luxury whilst Aisling was nothing more than a pawn designed to be slid across a board by the hands of lairds, chieftains, and kings. But not in the fae world.

None of Aisling's brothers reached for her. None shouted her name nor fretted over her well-being. They only hung their heads and sneered, enduring the moment.

Instinctively, Aisling stepped past Fionn, starting for her brothers, but the fae king caught her wrist and pulled her back.

"Not so fast, *mo Lúra*. We had a deal."

Aisling jerked her arm, but it was no use. The fae king was seemingly made of Oxheim stone and as powerful as the crags it built.

For a fragment of a second, Aisling considered summoning the *draiocht*. But not only did Greum's voice echo inside her mind that her power would be futile here, she also knew it unwise to be so reckless in the face of her captor. Not to mention, she felt the same witchery that'd dulled her magic in the presence of the fear gorta strangling her *draiocht* even now. A pale comparison to her *draiocht*'s usual might. She was trapped in this ice fortress and at the mercy of its lord. Dread seeped beneath her flesh at the thought. She did her best to stifle the panic fluttering inside her chest. They were outnumbered, overpowered, and caught when vulnerable. If she wished to free herself and Dagfin, then she must be cunning.

And as if reading her thoughts, Fionn continued, "I heard what you did aboard the mortal ship. Burning alive handfuls of mortals to save the breath of those you cherish most. Both attractive and impressive. You're ruthless, powerful, and great, Aisling. Everything necessary to be queen. But if you even so much as conjure a spark whilst in my presence, you'll suffer the consequences."

Aisling seethed, rolling her neck from side to side to keep her anger at bay. But it was Dagfin and Killian being shoved into the throne room that diverted her temper.

Starn scowled at the sight of both *Faeraks*, stripped of their weapons.

Dagfin's eyes were circled with blue, and his posture slumped. The ghost of the warrior he'd been not long ago. Still, tempests brewed behind his dark lashes, sparking with renewed electricity the moment he recognized Aisling, held by Fionn.

"Aisling—" he said without thinking, quickly struck in the gut by the butt of a sword from a nearby Sidhe.

Aisling dug her nails into her palms.

"So hostile, Your Lordship. Is this how you treat all your guests?" Aisling asked.

Fionn's expression brightened, seemingly eager to banter with Aisling. "The *Faerak* has been... troublesome. But once we deprived him of his Ocras, he became vastly more manageable."

There was silence as Dagfin collected himself, rising from the shimmering floors with blood dripping from his bottom lip.

"You care for the *Faerak*, don't you?" Fionn said abruptly. "You composed yourself quite well until he entered. I'd wondered which one of all these princes you preferred."

Aisling could feel his pale eyes studying her, stripping her of all and anything he could glean. A tingle of frost electrifying her nerves each time his eyes fixed upon her own.

"Although I'll admit, I hadn't expected this." Fionn licked his lips. "What would the *Damh Bán* say?"

"Do you intend to insult a foreign queen? To hold her and her escorts prisoner?"

"You see, Aisling," he said, using her name as though he'd known her all his age-old life. "You might be a prisoner but a cherished one. I've always had a bad habit of wanting whatever is Lir's. Every oak, every ash, yew, and elm must eventually succumb to winter. As should his bride."

Aisling reeled, unprepared for the words that left his lips. The cracking of the shackles around Dagfin's wrists echoing inside the chamber as he struggled to free himself.

"Release me so that we might fight hand to hand," Dagfin spat between clenched teeth. "Then we'll see who the bloody Forge blesses, fae."

"Fae?" He clicked his tongue in disapproval. "Your prejudices have grown stale. Indeed, if the mortals ever wish to survive Danu, they'll need to rely on every Sidhe they damned the past several centuries."

Aisling whipped her head toward the fae lord.

"Danu?"

Empress of dryads—Aisling had met her once before. A seer like Lir's mother Ina, who foresaw the end to the war between mortals and fair folk. Who gleaned the fair folk's doom, spiraling Lir into madness. An Unseelie of immeasurable power and with a legion of followers.

"I thought you knew," he said, returning his attention to Aisling. The glimmer in his eyes punctuated with the intensity of a bird of prey, appraising its catch. "The Unseelie need a formidable sovereign, capable of protecting their interests and their realm. A task Lir ignored for the sake of Annwyn and the Seelie at large and suffered because of."

Aisling's eyes narrowed. The *draiocht* stirring to the taste of her annoyance. Aisling couldn't explain it, but she could hardly bear to hear Lir spoken of in such a way. As though she'd burn any who spoke ill of him. A right she alone felt entitled to.

Nevertheless, the fomorians had disavowed Lir as their king when Aisling and his knights had traversed the feywilds, claiming a need for a new leader. Just before Lir slaughtered all dissenters who spoke of such treasonous intentions.

"Yet his forsaking of the peace treaty between mortals and Sidhe re-established himself as king. Lord of both Seelie and Unseelie. I saw the fomorians, beasts, ghouls, and Leshy ride into battle at his command, ambushing what the mortals believed was another union of peace."

Fionn laughed beneath his breath, stepping closer to Aisling.

"Yet, there are those still unconvinced. Still bitter their king turned their back on the Unseelie. Those who support someone else. Someone new. Someone capable of changing the course of Danu's prophecies."

Aisling's brows knotted.

"Danu herself."

Fionn nodded his head. "Precisely. You didn't think Lir was immune to usurpers, did you? It was inevitable. Lir is passionate, obsessive, powerful, and ruthless. I'm only surprised it took this long for those who both fear and despise him to wish him dethroned."

Aisling bristled, the subject of Lir on this fae king's tongue breeding fire beneath her skin. But she knew better than to react. So, she ignored his taunting.

"And I suppose you intend to support Danu?"

Fionn tilted his head to the side.

"I intend to do what I believe Lir cannot. Regain Sidhe authority over the feywilds, in this continent and every continent, every court, every kingdom, every realm. And if that means ending Danu myself, then so be it."

"You're a fool to even consider challenging Lir. He'll tear your court limb from limb before he ever surrenders even a morsel of his power to another."

Fionn stepped nearer still, his breath cold and biting,

traveling through Aisling's hair till it billowed on a phantom wind. The hairs on her arms standing to attention.

"Perhaps. But not if I have you."

He reached to stroke her cheek.

"Don't touch her!" Dagfin shouted, shattering the chains of ice with pure force. Quicker than Aisling could blink, he rose, stole a dagger from a nearby sentinel, and threw it at the fae king's chest.

Fionn caught Dagfin's dagger, freezing it solid and crushing it between his fingers. A sharp crack followed by the shatter of glass.

Three more sentinels grappled Dagfin to the floor with a blade at his throat. The wolves snapping mere inches from his face.

"Impressive," the fae king said, "for a mortal. The Ocras still courses deep in your veins, emboldened by natural heroism. Although, I'd suggest going lightly on the Ocras from now on, *Faerak*. Magic always takes all that it gives. As I'm sure you're already experiencing."

"Let them go," Aisling said, eyeing Dagfin and ignoring her brothers. Starn, Iarbonel, Fergus, Annind, and Killian, unable to move, speak, or flinch without a response from the fair folk around them.

Greum circled them, a low rumble vibrating through his core.

"How quickly and often you forget our deal: Lir's whereabouts, for your kin's freedom."

"I told you, I know not where he is, and even if I did, you'd have to pry it from my lips."

"As much as I'd love to explore your lips, *mo Lúra*, let's make another deal."

Aisling hesitated, glancing at Dagfin, Killian, and her brothers. Annind was weak and conditions such as this would only kill him more quickly. Imprisonment was death for her youngest brother. The snapping of her heartstrings worsening the resentment she already felt for her clann. She should leave them. Give them time to recognize how they'd wronged her. Continued to wrong her. Make them rue every last disgusted glance. But try as she might, she couldn't bring herself to forsake them. To abandon the last vestiges of who she was before Annwyn. Before Lir.

"What are your terms?" She forced out the words.

Fionn's mouth split into a devious smile as he leaned forward to whisper in her ear.

"Your escorts' freedom in exchange for our true binding."

A *true binding*? Aisling assumed he meant a union. A marriage.

A marriage to the fae was a sacred event where souls were bound and knotted in a tapestry woven with fate's threads.

Aisling staggered back a step, tearing herself from his touch.

"You have until the end of *Samhain* to agree."

CHAPTER XIV

AISLING

Samhain was a festival of death.

That's what Aisling's chambermaids told her when she still lived in Tilren. Nothing more than legends, myths, and tales to scare off children. Greum, however, described it differently.

"His lordship enjoys celebrating this blessed period, when the gods feel closer to waking than any other time of the year. Tonight marks the beginning of *Samhain* and it concludes with the lunar month."

"A month?" Aisling asked, at once frustrated. "My youngest brother doesn't have that sort of time. He'll die before then. And Dagfin—"

"Let me ease your concerns; his lordship has given them each proper accommodations and even a healer in the case of the wounded one. That is, until the end of *Samhain*. Then it is up to you to decide whether you wish to strike a deal with his lordship or not."

Aisling exhaled, relieved they were no longer being kept in the dungeons.

Aisling followed closely behind the bear. Watching as it carried its great body through the misty corridors of glittering opal. Every alcove, balcony, and arcade glaring out at a frost-ridden forest. A family of snow-capped mountains huffing in the distance. This was the world from Fionn's palace: *Oighir*, Greum had called it. A land like a jewelry box, tipped over and spilling a trove of crystals, diamonds, and stars. Punctuated only by the tips of evergreens and spindly birches.

"During *Samhain*, the veil between here and the Otherworld thins," Aisling conjectured. To the mortals, the Otherworld was death and the land beyond the living. To the Aos Sí, however, the Otherworld was the beginning of all things as well as the end. A supernatural, primordial realm of unencumbered magic.

"Aye, the spirits will fancy themselves more mischievous, and once they catch wind of your scent, they'll not hesitate to explore their interest in you. It isn't often a mortal steals from their plane and lives to tell the tale."

Aisling shuddered so Greum laughed in response, the icicles spearing toward them from above quivering.

"I too feared *Samhain* as a cub, but with time I grew to cherish it. Praying the same spirits that spilled the Forge's tonic in each Sidhe kingdom and blessed me with speech would also damn the mortals that burned our forests."

"And damned they are," Aisling said. Cursed by Ina.

Greum glanced at Aisling over his shoulder.

Against her own volition, Aisling smiled. She found she quite liked Greum. A beast that reminded her of one far smaller yet equally, if not more, deadly.

The bear, at last, paused before a great threshold. An obsidian door etched with fae markings and laced with garlands bubbling over with cranberries sugared by the frost.

"I leave you here, *Skalla*."

Aisling nodded her head in thanks, returning her attention to the door the moment it peeled open by a phantom hand.

Cautiously, Aisling stepped into the room.

Inside, it smelled of leather and wine. An enormous cylindrical chamber filled with mirrors. The ceiling spiraled into a glass turret above, layered by balconies and narrow floors bustling with what Aisling could only imagine were gowns. Thousands upon thousands of dresses, cloaks, tunics, and gúnas made of furs, wools, feathers, silks, chiffons, brocade, and tweeds flocked by cardinals.

And at the center of the chamber sat a table spilling over with fae foods. Roasted mushrooms, fragrant beef stews, plum puddings, ripe and ruby raspberries, buttered pastries, and a broiled boar's head sitting at the center, tusks and all.

At once, the spices and herbs transported Aisling back to Annwyn. Cinnamon, candy cardamom, juniper berries, warm nettle, milk thistle. Her heart aching and stomach growling, desperately starving for anything she could keep down. Yet, despite her curiosity, these foods were forbidden to Aisling. There were enough tales that forewarned mortals from partaking in the same feasts as the fae.

So, although Aisling's mouth watered, she kept her composure, finding Fionn's eyes from across the chamber. Her belly fluttered, eager to unravel the fae lord's intentions and free herself from Oighir.

"When was the last time you ate, *mo Lúra?*" he asked, plucking a fae raspberry and popping it into his mouth. Aisling resisted the urge to whimper, imagining and tasting the sugar on her own tongue.

"Greum assures me Dagfin and my brothers are well taken care of." Aisling ignored Fionn's question. "Is this true?"

"See for yourself." Fionn waved his hand and the mirrors surrounding the room rippled, transforming their reflection into the image of Annind. He lay in a pile of blankets like clouds, cared for by an old, gray rabbit. Starn paced his quarters while Fergus, Iarbonel, and Killian feasted on a small mortal banquet, and Dagfin argued with the guards outside his door.

Aisling swallowed, relief a luxury she wasn't prepared to let herself indulge just yet.

"How do I know this isn't trickery?"

Fionn strode closer. "You can see for yourself this evening. They'll attend my masquerade celebrating the inception of *Samhain* like all others."

Aisling released a breath of relief. Watching as the image of Dagfin dissolved too soon and her reflection returned.

"I ask again," Fionn continued. "When was the last time you ate?"

"Yesterday," Aisling said, clearing her throat.

"Mortal food, I assume. And did it go well with you?"

Aisling slid further into the room, called to the wealth of the feast.

"Do you make a habit of asking questions you already know the answers to?" This considering Aisling was thin and sharp, lacking proper nourishment.

Fionn licked his fangs, amused.

"Only when I enjoy the answers. Come and indulge, Aisling. For it is only Sidhe meals that will satisfy you from now on. All else, your body will repel."

But Aisling didn't move. She stood stock-still, resisting the temptation to bite and partake in a fae meal. One she'd managed to resist since she'd first stepped foot in Castle Annwyn.

"Go ahead, take a bite."

Aisling felt her fingers twitch without her consent.

This was unwise. After everything, Aisling knew better than to trust a soul other than her own, yet it wasn't trust or faith that propelled her nearer to the table. It was mad and urgent hunger.

Aisling reached for a sweet roll, still warm.

She brought it to her lips, the hair across her body standing to attention the moment she sank her teeth into its bread. Her stomach heating, the *draiocht* licking its lips deep within its abyss and glowing a brighter tinge of black. And, at least, from the first bite, she wasn't charmed. Not bespelled. Not cursed or blistering or vomiting or drunk.

She was satisfied.

Fionn was right.

Aisling reached for another roll and then another. Filling her belly for the first time in weeks with forge-sent foods.

Fionn leaned over the table, placing both his hands on the edge.

"And your *draiocht*. It burns you."

Aisling tore her attention from the table, considering the fae lord more closely.

Aisling hadn't summoned the *draiocht* before him. Not yet. So how had he known she suffered from the very power she called upon?

"I watched you through my mirrors in your bedchamber. When you accidentally burnt your own reflection. Mirrors are gateways, Aisling. Especially during the period of *Samhain*."

Aisling resisted the urge to shiver, steadying the goblet of water in her hands.

"I suspect the *draiocht* resists you when you're far from Forge magic. Seelie, Unseelie, the feywilds, whatever form it takes or essence it imbues. You must be near it to inspire your *draiocht*, lest it burn what humanity remains."

Aisling had considered that possibility. She often harbored suspicions but never spoke them aloud nor explored them in the privacy of her own mind. But Fionn's theory was one she'd toyed with on occasion and seemed likely enough. A prospect that revived a glimmer of hope in Aisling. After all, Fionn had been right about the fae food. Maybe, Aisling allowed herself to hope, she might not be doomed to smite herself whenever she conjured magic.

"Let's see for ourselves," Aisling said and summoned the *draiocht*.

A flicker of panic flashed across Fionn's expression, swiftly vanishing as violet fire sprouted from Aisling's fingertips. The flames grew hungry and eager but painful all the same, stinging Aisling as they sizzled and blistered her flesh once more.

Aisling bit down at the *draiocht*, commanding it back into its abyss and hissing in pain.

Fionn's lips bent with disappointment yet nothing in comparison to the gray of Aisling's disillusioned, frustrated spirit. Hope killed by reality. Yet Aisling couldn't bear the disappointment. So, it evolved into rage.

"Enough of this," Aisling growled, her patience growing thin. "Every moment I waste here, tiptoeing around the sensibilities of a temperamental fae king, I jeopardize my chances of reaching Lofgren's Rise before all others. A risk I cannot and will not afford. So enough of these games."

They stood at opposing ends of the feast, watching one another over the pale glow of the frozen buds creeping up every wall.

"There are no others," he said.

Aisling's brow furrowed.

"Everyone is—"

"Dead," he interjected coolly, tossing a strand of silver over his shoulder. "Or they will be soon enough. You see, the other Sidhe sovereigns are either too afraid of Lir to attempt to take the curse breaker for themselves, too reliant on him to do it for them, or eager to let me do the dirty work in their stead. And as for the mortals, I can't imagine any will get far. This is a game, Aisling. One that outmatches all and any mortal. Beasts, spells, a forest divided between your *caera* and Danu. These are matters for the divine. Even your *Faerak* friends will not stand a chance if they continue on the same trajectory."

Aisling's eyes watered, desperately clawing at the sadness and the anxiety looming around her like a dark cloud.

"You're impatient for what lies ahead, I understand, Aisling," Fionn continued. "But consider this not me delaying you, rather expediting your journey."

Aisling set down the goblet, her interest piqued.

"Let me guess, you wish for me to betray Lir and help you obtain the curse breaker in exchange for your aid reaching Lofgren's Rise?"

Fionn slowly moved around the curve of the table, approaching Aisling. So, Aisling, coyly, continued moving, studying the way his throat bobbed at the sign of a chase.

"I wish for you and me to be bound together. To make this realm our own. You've been foreseen, Aisling. By Ina, by Danu, by the Lady. I bear no doubt the future is written in the shadow of whatever your birth has presaged. Together, we can shape it. Shape your destiny till none dare challenge our sovereignship. Not your father, not Danu, not Lir."

"A true binding. You mean a union?" Aisling asked.

"Of sorts."

If Fionn wanted a union with Aisling, it would never succeed. She and Fionn weren't *caera* while Aisling and Lir were. In which case, if Fionn pursued a union, Aisling and the son of Winter would be forced by magic's hand to fight to the death. It would never come to that, of course. But teasing the possibility could be a means of biding her time till she sorted through her next steps.

"Is it your mirrors that tell you all this? That whisper the words I wish to hear?"

"They've shown me what unravels in the present time, this is true. But I know what truths speak to you because they speak to me as well. Aisling, you and I are the same. Controlled all our lives, imprisoned."

"A fae king claims to understand weakness? Helplessness?" The very words burned a fire in Aisling's gut, reigniting past fury into new flame.

"At the beginning of all things, when the twelve kingdoms were split by the Forge, the gods made one last creation, more precious to them than either land or sky, Seelie or Unseelie. Three *dragúns*."

"*Dragún?*" Aisling repeated.

"Rún for dragons," Fionn explained. "The *dragún* of immortality, the *dragún* of power, and the *dragún* of prosperity. Legend has it, any Sidhe sovereign capable of taming such beasts or dominating them would be blessed with its strength and ability. So, naturally, the Wild Hunt ensued. A trail of blood, destruction, disease, and war left in its wake. The only Sidhe sovereign to obtain a *dragún*? Ina."

Lir's mother.

Fionn was near enough that he could touch her, but refrained, pouring himself a chalice of Sidhe wine instead as he continued to pursue her around the curve of the table.

"The other two *dragúns* were never caught, so the original twelve Sidhe sovereigns battled over Racat instead. The *dragún* of power."

Aisling froze.

Racat.

The *draíocht* inside her stirred.

She knew this beast. Had come face to face with it in the cloak of darkness, unable to see beyond the glimmering of its eyes as it prowled toward her in Annwyn's aqueducts. After Danu had tossed her forward in time. A monster said to live in Annwyn's gorge and travel in the waterways beneath the earth.

"*You may call me friend.*"

Its voice slithered inside her mind.

"You've heard of this *dragún*?" Fionn asked, watching her behind the brim of his chalice.

Aisling masked her emotions and shook her head, careful to conceal all that Fionn didn't already know thanks to his mirrors.

"I assume Ina didn't manage to keep Racat? This considering she would've adopted Racat's power and blessed Iod, a strength that never would've allowed for Iod to crumble and the curse to take hold," Aisling said, eager to avoid his question.

"Yes and no. She won the Wild Hunt thanks to Racat but lost regardless. Her efforts to keep Bres alive rendered whatever victory she'd managed obsolete. A mistake—a *failure* that even Racat's blessing couldn't remedy." Fionn's tone was bitter, Bres's name on his lips like poison.

"So, Bres's life was threatened after the Wild Hunt? What war was ensuing in the aftermath of Ina's victory?"

"One of envy," Fionn said, pressing his lips into a firm line. He wished to elaborate no further, that much was evident, leaving Aisling to assume the other fae sovereigns were envious of Ina's victory and Racat.

So, this was how it'd happened.

The war that defeated Bres, Lir's father, was one Aisling had heard of before. Yet never had any divulged the reason for inter-conflict between the fair folk.

Now it was clear. This was the period where Ina forsook her own mountain kingdom of Iod to save Bres, failing and dooming her people as a result. Cursing them and stripping them of their *immortality*, *power*, and *prosperity* to damn them as mortal.

All this, from a war bred by envy and a hunt for dragons.

"What happened to Racat?"

Fionn took another sip.

"Ina gifted the beast to her son for safekeeping. That is, until the time came for the *dragún* to make a choice of its own."

Aisling paused.

Lir was the most powerful Sidhe sovereign in this realm or the next. Born of two original Sidhe sovereigns but also imbued with the power and blessing of Racat.

Aisling's mind spun. Fionn had told her more than anyone else ever had. As far as she knew, not a secret was left unturned nor withheld from her.

"Lir came to power and instilled obedience in every other Sidhe kingdom and Unseelie race to prevent another Wild Hunt or ensuing war. His punishment for Oighir? Lir ensured Oighir is only ever powerful when the frost arrives and chills the earth. Only when winter is nigh can I flex my strength, imprisoned by the edge of the northernmost continents. Exiled lest we be powerless. And so, I'll cling to whatever power the Forge gives me if it means avenging my father's death. Another casualty of the *dragún* war."

Fionn handed Aisling his chalice, at last, catching her.

Aisling considered it, repeating the warnings in her mind. She'd only ever known Sidhe wine to be dangerous, lethal, and incompatible with mortal tongues. Yet, if she could eat their foods perhaps... perhaps one drink wouldn't hurt.

Aisling accepted the goblet and brought it to her lips. The same euphoric wave rippled through her, encouraging the *draiocht* within to writhe and hum a gleeful tune.

"Lir instills obedience but wouldn't have punished a member of the Sidhe without cause. So, tell me what you've chosen to exclude from your tales. Why would Lir punish Oighir?"

"You're cunning." Fionn licked his fangs, considering Aisling before speaking. "Bres and Ina weren't the only ones to break their vows to the Forge; vows promising never to love another Sidhe sovereign."

"Delbaeth," Aisling conjectured. Fionn's father.

Fionn's expression tightened as he set down his chalice. The perfection of its rounded edge now corrupted by a single crack.

"Aye, my father. But that's enough about politics and history. You shall soon see why you and I are cut by the same shears."

Aisling nodded, keeping to herself the Lady's words.

"*You blunt my shears.*" Aisling's fate was outside the Lady's control and all others for that matter.

"Come, select a gown to be delivered back to your quarters for this evening. I've commissioned every seamstress and tailor in Oighir to craft a dress for you." Fionn gestured at his horde of dazzling gowns. "It'll be an evening you won't soon forget."

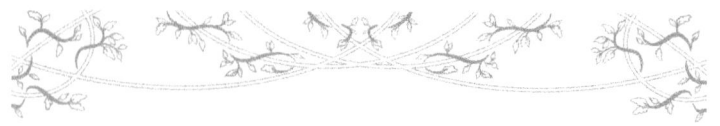

CHAPTER XV

AISLING

Fionn's lips were cold. At the slightest touch, they nearly froze Aisling's hand, numbing her palms to the pain of her most recent burns.

Aisling shivered. He watched her closely as he looped her arm through his, eyes lined with sparkling white dust. A foil to the bear headdress he now wore with teeth exchanged for shards of ice. The same moon-white shade as his robes, his cross-collar shirt, his embroidered trousers, or the satin ribbon tied around his waist.

He, a pale crystal glimmering in a palace whittled from winter. Burning too brightly to look directly in the eyes.

"Shall we, *mo Lúra?*" Fionn asked, gesturing to the gargantuan mirror before them, lined with sculptures of bears as large as Greum and Sidhe knights, all brightened by fae light.

Aisling clenched her jaw but nodded all the same.

"How does it work?"

Fionn held his palm before the mirror.

"Every mirror is linked to the *draiocht*. So, you must first ask the *draiocht* to enter and only if it allows, will it grant you access."

"Has it ever stopped you from entering or leaving?"

"Rarely. Only when I use the mirrors as a looking glass instead of a gateway. A window instead of a door. The *draiocht* can be unpredictable and, at times, even harbor an agenda of its own. That's why it's important you master it, Aisling."

Fionn closed his eyes, moving his lips as though speaking a silent spell. And perhaps he was. The mirror turned to liquid as they passed through. Aisling felt cold, then soaked, as though she were submerging herself in water. Her body shuddered of its own volition, tasting Fionn's magic-ripe influence: a deep freeze, crushed wolfberries, and freshly thawed rapids.

They appeared atop another imperial staircase, washed over by both music and light. This chamber was large, exploding with snowdrops, frozen lilies, and virgin-pale gypsophila. Another throne sat here as well, embedded with Fionn's longsword just like the last.

Each stairwell twisted toward a ballroom of impossible size and make: rib-vaulted ceilings paneled in silver stained glass so the evening stars could peer down at their celebration, mimicking the sheen of the petrified dew clinging to every salt-rock surface, the chandeliers like upside down trees iced over and made everlasting, all multiplied a hundred times over by the mirror standing at the center of the dance floor and the fair folk that slipped in and out of it, traveling from all across Oighir to attend Fionn's masquerade.

Aisling inhaled sharply, struck by the sound of fae music. The melodies whisking her to Annwyn once more. The *Snaidhm*. The wild, provocative, emotional melodies braided together till Aisling felt most alive. Instruments mortals bore no names for, breathing to life the voice of all that didn't sing or speak or weep. The trees, the rivers, a snowstorm, an ocean's tempest. Sounds Lir had opened Aisling's ears to.

But the moment Aisling and Fionn appeared at the top of the imperial staircase, the ballroom stilled. Every Aos Sí in attendance, pausing their dance and craning their elegant necks to see for themselves: the bride of the forest linked arm in arm with the son of Winter. Among them and amidst the crush of guests was Starn, Iarbonel, Fergus, Dagfin, and Killian. Annind was nowhere to be seen.

Aisling swallowed her concern. Despite this, Fionn studied her every nuance. The way her eyes brightened or dimmed, the tension in her shoulders, the pursing of her lips.

So, Aisling swept down the staircase at his side. Her gown an intricate masterpiece of silver thorns and cape sleeves that dusted the foggy floors, trimmed with white furs. The skirts billowing at her waist, expanding into a blizzard and clouding around both her legs and slippers.

Fionn escorted Aisling down the final step, waiting till the music resumed to speak with her.

Aisling released her arm from Fionn's hold, adjusting the mask that sat atop the bridge of her nose. The top half of a bear's head, made entirely of verglas.

"So the spirits of *Samhain* won't remember your face," Fionn had said when he'd gifted her the mask outside her chambers. The counterpart to his headdress, Aisling had quickly realized. But it wasn't only Aisling who wore a mask. The whole of Fionn's court wore one as well, beasts of all shape and form pinned atop their fae features.

"Enjoy the inception of *Samhain*, Aisling," he said, bowing his head. "I'll call upon you shortly."

And with that, he disappeared into the crush of his court,

Greum lumbering shortly behind. The Sidhe's attention bobbed between Fionn and Aisling, skeptical eyes narrowing behind their masks. For Aisling, the fire hand's daughter, the not-so-mortal queen of Annwyn, the bride of the forest, was clearly no ill-cared for prisoner and not yet dead.

"Ash." Starn navigated through the crowd lithely till he stood at her side. Her other brothers, Killian, and Dagfin, were interspersed throughout the ballroom, eyed by every Sidhe guard and armored beast.

They each wore new clothing. Garments from Oighir, obvious by their style and make: luxurious robes, cross-collared shirts, and a ribbon around their waists. Masks made in the image of forest beasts: Starn's a lion, Dagfin's a raven, Iarbonel's a badger, Fergus's a rabbit, and Killian's a fox.

"We leave tonight," he said with no further introduction. Aisling couldn't see his eyes well, but she saw the curve of his mouth well enough. The distaste he tried and failed to conceal. Indeed, the image of his younger sister, arm in arm with another fae king, one who'd imprisoned him easily and effortlessly, while he stood in a room filled with hundreds of Sidhe, was enough to heat all their father's fires in this life-time and the next. But he composed himself, as every mortal soldier was trained to do in the face of battle, and swallowed his loathing.

"Where's Annind?" Aisling asked, feigning flippancy considering an armored boar glared at her across the room, its mace already at the ready. As though thirsting for an excuse to flay her alive.

"He's being cared for as we speak in a palace room, enjoying every mortal food and tea the kitchens have available."

Aisling glanced at Fionn across the room. He spoke with a group of trooping fae, elegantly interacting with his subjects. He was clever, Aisling was quickly realizing. She shouldn't have surrendered her feelings so recklessly. Inquiring about her brothers' and Dagfin's whereabouts had informed Fionn that the most efficient way of buying Aisling's affections, trust, and allegiance was through her companions' good treatment. Meaning, all and any information Fionn had gleaned from Aisling thus far, he'd used to his advantage. A fact she both admired and damned all at once.

"It reeks here of cattle and overripe fruit." Starn wrinkled his nose, ensuring no Sidhe accidentally brushed against his shoulders. Aisling didn't need him to elaborate further. She knew Starn spoke of the bipedal animals woven into Sidhe culture and court life. Yet they didn't smell the way Starn described them. To Aisling, they smelled wild.

"I'll be sure to tell father exactly where to find this abomination. He'll burn it to the ground along with every Aos Sí and their beasts gallivanting inside," Starn said, and now he did grin. "And I'll be glad to be gone from this place before this feral occasion is done with."

"How do you intend to escape?" Aisling asked. "And what of Annind?"

"There are five entrances to this ballroom. Iarbonel, Fergus, Dagfin, and I have each studied where each door leads. See that one? To the left of the main entrance?"

Aisling nodded her head. A smaller threshold guarded by two white bears near as large as Greum.

"That one leads straight to the palace courtyards. One need only navigate through a series of gardens before leaping over the wall and finding freedom once more."

"And the guards?"

"Killian's been dousing those bears' flasks with twisted honey: sap from a petrifying plant, harvested by the *Faerak* for use on those Unseelie they wish to keep alive. He found it in Annind's healer's satchel, mostly used as an anesthetic. Dim-witted hare," Starn spat, crossing his arms.

Aisling shook her head.

"Annind is too injured to slip through guarded passages, navigate through labyrinths, or scale castle walls. He'll not survive the trip home without proper care."

"You've been away from your clann too long, Aisling. Annind would rather die a free man than live amongst the fae."

Aisling worked her jaw.

"Watch your tongue. You speak ill of nightmares while still asleep."

At this, they both glanced around the room. Indeed, every member of the Sidhe whispered amongst one another when they believed themselves out of earshot. Glancing at Aisling and Starn with potent hatred. Children of iron.

"We leave tonight, Aisling. Father will send the mortal fleets to Lofgren's Rise in our stead."

"And those mortal sovereigns who've already attempted and failed?" Sigewulf's death flashed in Aisling's mind.

"They'll try again, this time with more men. None will stand a chance against iron in so great numbers. Prepare yourself for the signal."

"Why the sudden hurry, brother?" Aisling stole a goblet of fae wine from a passing badger's serving plate. A gesture that didn't go unnoticed by Starn, who eyed the chalice of fae wine as though it were poison. And to him, it was. "Shouldn't it be I rushing you onwards? After all, you've accompanied *me*."

Starn's laugh was without humor as he forced the next words from his lips.

"I only care for your best interests, little Sister."

Aisling glanced up at her eldest sibling, studying the

familiar scar along his jaw. One he'd collected chasing Aisling through the woods and to Hannelore's Linn when they were children. The wound that had ultimately outed them and their adventures to Nemed.

"I used to look up to you," Aisling said. "I believed you painted the sun with flame and pinned it to the sky with an iron arrow."

Starn's eyes were dark as coal, harboring all the severity of their mother Clodagh and all the authority of the fire hand.

"If only I'd realized then you were and always will be a boy too eager to sit on an iron chair far too large for himself. Too obsessed with proving himself to an elusive father to ever develop an identity outside his thirst for validation."

Starn worked his jaw, his crow-dark hair falling across his eyes, simmering and balling his hands into fists. A gesture that didn't escape the Sidhe or the bestial guards' notice.

"When were you planning on informing me that the only reason you chose to accompany me was to steal the curse breaker for yourself? To deliver both I and whatever lies at Lofgren's Rise back to Castle Neimedh as the triumphant high prince worthy of his father's crown?"

Starn reeled, eyes wide and glazed with hateful tears.

"I never—"

"You still believe me so stupid, so naive as to think your aid was anything other than self-serving?" Aisling scoffed. "As soon as I negotiate your freedom with the fae lord, return home before you truly suffer the consequences of something far too large for you. You're not equipped for this, and you'll kill yourself as well as our brothers in your attempts to prove yourself."

Starn leaned forward, teeth grinding in his fury.

"I warned you of ordering me—"

Aisling stepped toward him. "And I warn you now, brother," she hissed, relishing the way Starn flinched. "If any of you stand in my way, I shall not hesitate to do what I must."

Starn froze, glaring at Aisling as the ballroom continued to spin and the guards shifted, weapons in hand. But he said nothing.

"Is everything alright?" Killian said, approaching from behind and positioning himself between Starn and Aisling. A shoulder between them to protect the high prince.

Dagfin joined shortly after, quickly keen to the tension circuiting between them.

"I was just telling Starn that I've chosen to continue on my own. As soon as we're freed from here, you're all free to return home."

"What? You're not planning on agreeing to Fionn's terms, are you?" Dagfin focused his attention solely on Aisling. The sheen of disappointment that washed over his features heart-wrenching.

Mercifully, Aisling didn't have time to respond. She wouldn't and couldn't agree to Fionn's terms, but she'd find a way to free them and once she did, the choice to return to either Tilren or Roktling was a choice of life or death for the mortal princes.

The lights of the ballroom dimmed, the music increased in tempo, and the wind burst through the floor-to-ceiling windows, gripping the ballroom with ice that bit beneath the flesh.

The Sidhe laughed, watching as hundreds of translucent, wispy creatures tore into the ballroom like comets made of storm clouds. They ran between the skirts of the Sidhe, brushed against the chandeliers, singing, and tossing midnight stars between one another until the night sky was brought inside, hovering above all their heads.

Spirits from the Otherworld heralding the beginning of *Samhain*.

The room grew plump with enchantment.

Aisling could feel the thinning of the veil between their mortal realm and that of the Other. For the world began to glow with the soft luster of a dream, the wicked whimsy of the spirits bending reality and shaping it to their will. Indeed, they moved and danced like sylphs, bore the wildness of the dryads, and the eternal, primeval aura of the celestial; the endings of the past made real in the present. Long-since passed Sidhe soldiers sparring with their ghostly swords mid-air, racing on stags, and dancing with their lovers.

If this was the beginning of *Samhain*, Aisling looked forward to its middle and end. Wondered what the forest would look like disrobed and unmasked as the realm of witchery that it truly was.

Fionn approached Aisling amidst the chaos and offered his arm once more. Greum and Frigg shortly behind.

"Join me?" he asked her after nodding in greeting to Starn and Killian. Eyes lingering a moment too long on Dagfin.

Aisling nodded her head in silent agreement. So, Frigg snapped his chomps at Dagfin before his lordship turned, Aisling on his arm.

Against her own volition, Aisling glanced at the Roktan prince over her shoulder.

"Ash, wait—"

Aisling hesitated, holding the *Faerak*'s eyes before forcing herself to look away.

It's better this way, she assured herself. Dagfin was safer in Roktling, and Aisling couldn't live with herself if anything happened to him during her pursuit. She'd seen how quickly the chieftain of Fjallnorr had been felled by a single, passing Unseelie. The mightiest among men not fit for the pursuits of the fae. So, despite the tearing of her heart, she willed every step apart from him. Her heart aching at the intensity of his stare as she walked away.

Fionn and Greum led her to the front of the imperial staircase.

From here, the whole ballroom was laid before them both. And with one snap of the fae king's fingers, everyone in the hall dissolved into silence—even the spirits—holding their breath to discover, at last, what their lord whispered into the Forge.

"Tonight, fate will continue its course," Fionn said. "Tonight, with the blessing of the Forge, Aisling and I will be truly bonded."

Aisling stiffened but said not a word, refusing the temptation to find Dagfin through the folds of spectators. The Roktan prince's expression was perhaps one of the only images capable of convincing her to step away from the ledge she now peered over.

"This will be a promise for the future that the son of Winter and his sorceress shall lead the Seelie, the Unseelie, and the mortals too," he continued. "And so, I call upon the Lady to sever the threads that lie between Aisling and the king of the greenwood."

Aisling staggered back a step, knocked off balance in her shock.

"What?" she managed, but he ignored her.

"*Rlaoim ont a Lhuire, tar anoir*," he said in Rún.

Greum translated, "I summon you, Lady, to do your bidding."

Aisling paled, her breathing heavy. Fionn had rescued

Aisling and Dagfin from the Lady, his scheming swift and meddling if now he called upon her, Aisling realized.

No, no, no. This wasn't happening.

"You've tricked me," Aisling seethed, watching as Fionn turned to her coolly. "You claimed this was merely a celebration. No union nor deal had yet to be agreed upon and there was never a mention of an *unbinding*."

Fionn's lips cut into a knife-sharp smile. "Come now, Aisling. You didn't really think I'd risk your neck on a union knowing we aren't *caera*? No, I only ever said *binding*. To have the Lady rip the threads between you and Lir and tie them anew with you and me. Besides I grow impatient."

"We had a deal! I had till the end of *Samhain* to release the mortal princes in exchange for whatever it is you covet!"

"Your mortal princes will be released once we're united, Aisling. No sooner or later."

Aisling's tongue turned to ash. Her mind spun till she believed she might vomit. But it wasn't only her mind that spun. The room tilted on its axis, every star the spirits had gathered whirling madly as light broke across the room and the Lady appeared, dressed in a star-bright gown of countless radiant threads. Spiraling around her like the rays of a star exploding just before it collided with the Earth.

The Lady stood before them, the spirits hovering around her in a cloud of ages-old ghosts come to see the unraveling of the morrow.

She smiled. "Aisling, I didn't believe I'd see you again so soon."

Fionn waved his hand flippantly and ice grew from the ballroom floors, seizing Aisling's wrists and squeezing till she couldn't move. Her mask clattered against the floor as Aisling screamed for the *draiocht*, but it was frozen inside the abyss. Snuffed and cold, unable to produce the fires she needed.

But this was beyond the weakness she'd felt the past several weeks. Beyond the burning of her palms. This was the same witchery she'd tasted against the fear gorta when it'd snuffed her fires.

This was the Lady's and Fionn's magic, dampening her might with their own trickery. Finding a way to strangle her *draiocht*. Both having tasted her arrival on winter winds the moment she'd step foot on Fjallnorrian sands.

From the corner of her eye, Aisling saw Dagfin struggling forward, held back by Killian, Starn, Fergus, and Iarbonel.

"Hold still, Aisling," the Lady continued, producing a glimmering blade of starlight from thin air. She inhaled deeply, as though savoring the *draiocht* she breathed, producing such powerful magic. The taste of liquid evening skies bleeding across Aisling's tongue at the arrival of the Lady's *draiocht*. "*Samhain* couldn't have come soon enough. You see, Aisling, the stars have aligned. The Otherworld is thin, renewing my strength and inspiring my influence in this realm. With it, enough power to do what I couldn't the last time I saw you."

"No," Aisling said, struggling against Fionn's ice, Oighir's Sidhe court witnessing the spectacle with a combination of fear, confusion, and awe. With a satisfying feeling of finality for the thief to at last be stolen from.

"Don't look so afraid, *mo Lúra*," Fionn whispered in her ear. "The pain will be temporary but the life we'll live together, mighty and everlasting."

The Lady approached, the spirits cackling behind her.

"The gods will rejoice that the omen is broken and destruction, desolation, death, circumvented."

"Yet you commit a death today!" Aisling screamed, hot tears streaming down her face as she fought against Fionn's ice, clawing at the *draiocht*. For the tearing of her binding with Lir, the thread that made them *caera*, was a death.

Wake up.

Wake up.

Wake up! she screamed at the *draiocht*.

"You cannot unbind two *caeras* without committing a form of destruction of your own," Aisling pleaded. Aisling wasn't certain why the very marrow in her bones frosted over with dread at the mention of destroying her bond with Lir. As though her very soul would hollow without the cord between she and the Sidhe king pulling her back to him. She hated him, rivalled him, fought against him and yet her body shuddered at the thought of an unbinding. She couldn't— wouldn't let this happen whether it was their fated bond speaking, or something else.

"The death of one is always necessary to prevent the death of many. But you will live, Aisling, if not the same as you once were."

The spirits rose and danced wildly, celebrating the Lady's every word as she lifted the blade above her head. White light cracked, magic swelled inside the room, till the pressure of it threatened to burst Aisling's, her brothers', Dagfin's, and Killian's ears. As though they'd suddenly been drowned in the Forge itself, lungs filled with bubbling sorcery.

"By the Forge, I vow to shear this thread," she spoke, and her voice echoed into the millennia. "To bleed a harbinger of chaos until prosperity reigns triumphant."

The world held its breath.

"By the Forge, I vow to you an unbinding."

The Lady swung her sword in a blinding arc.

Aisling saw herself scream, saw Fionn brighten, witnessed Dagfin thrashing against her brothers and Killian who held him. Saw the Lady's blade cut through the air and toward her heart.

Yet the slushy sound of a blade finally puncturing flesh wasn't Aisling's own.

It was rather the tip of an axe jutting from the very place the Lady's heart should be.

The Lady's eyes glazed over in the heartbeats before she shattered into thousands of stars. Every spirit shrieking as it flew out the ballroom windows and into the godsforsaken night.

Leaving a battle-ready knight standing in her place.

Lir.

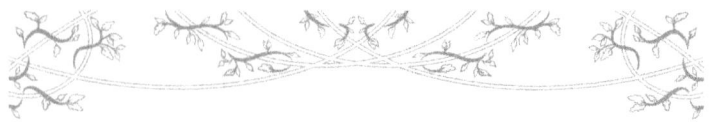

CHAPTER XVI

AISLING

"Cold, *ellwyn?*" Lir's voice echoed through the ballroom, finding Aisling's heart and impaling it where the Lady's sword hadn't.

He stood taller than Aisling remembered him, forest green eyes searching Aisling's own, ripping apart her soul, and promising both violence and mischief. Aisling's chest hitched, her eyes glassy as she processed his presence, half wondering if he were still a dream come to haunt her when she needed him most. Realizing now, when her heart lifted at the sight of him, she'd found relief in salvation from the dark lord of the forest. Relief and terror, her hunter a few paces away at long last. He who she'd fled from, feared, anticipated like an arrow to the heart.

The room stood petrified, unmoving, as Lir stalked forth. Every step echoing into eternity while the realm held its breath. His axes glimmered beneath Fionn's fae light, he alone, a forge-brewed demon delivering day's death. A woodland's every ruthless promise. A glittering nightmare more inhumanly gorgeous than any vision Aisling could conjure.

"Aren't you?" Aisling said with whatever breath remained.

"My kind rarely grows cold," he continued. "I've forgotten how weak humans can be."

"Weak?" Aisling repeated. "It's weak to complain of it."

"Perhaps fragile is a better word then?" he said, the corners of his lips curling.

Aisling couldn't help herself. Her mouth moved of its own accord, splitting into a smile herself. The same conversation they'd shared the first time they'd met, ringing inside her heart and ravaging her whole. "The most valuable things are."

Lir smiled a devastating smile, framed by dimples Aisling had desperately tried to forget.

It was then Aisling noticed the other armored Sidhe behind him. Fae knights dressed for a bloodbath.

Galad.

Gilrel.

Filverel.

Peitho.

The backs of Aisling's eyes pricked, bleeding her heart and clouding the room with Annwyn's perfume. Of forest festivals, of herb-lit pipes, bluebell castle corridors, of heady music, and barefoot dances.

They were each clad in hunting leathers and armor, each appraising Aisling in turn. Gilrel spinning her small blade between her paws, itching to be unleashed. Galad and Filverel tight-lipped behind their king, expressions resolved for bloodletting. And Peitho, hair dripping like the rays of a liquid sun, tossed the strands from her face, freeing her vision but also exposing the right side of her face.

She whose beauty was poetry personified, every nuance

pieced together thoughtfully; now, her face was the host of great scars. Burn trails.

Aisling's stomach dipped. She'd almost forgotten. Aisling had nearly burned Peitho alive in her efforts to save Dagfin after their union had gone awry.

A snow-soft laugh sounded behind Aisling as Fionn stepped forward, seemingly maintaining his calm, if it weren't for the ice crawling up the sides of the hall and jutting into icicles like thorns.

"Well done, brother." Fionn clapped, the only sound in an otherwise silent room. "What wicked heroism."

Brother.

Aisling's heart stuttered. The air in the room suddenly thinner than it'd been before. But the moment and the word were quickly gone. A piece of the recent past as Lir approached.

"Heroism?" Lir padded closer, nimbly spinning one of his axes between his fingers. "Is that what you call what I'm here to do? To rip your heart from your chest and stake it before Oighir?"

Fionn laughed again, but this time it wasn't as convincing.

"By Sidhe law, you've entered on diplomatic authority but if you don't leave now, you'll wish you had."

Oighir, indeed, listened intently. Every guest staring at both Fionn and Lir, approaching an inevitable collision. The bestial guards moving through the crowds, eager to make themselves known before Lir tried anything on their lord. This in addition to nine or so foxes, Aisling counted, crouched in the upper arcade, prepared to let their reeds fly.

"My court will not hesitate to descend upon you."

"Do you make a habit of offering your people to the wolves in place of yourself?"

"Oighir and I are one. Of all Sidhe, you should understand that, Lir. Or did you inherit our mother's flippancy for her own kind?"

Our mother.

Aisling's stomach lurched.

But it was Lir's expression that sparkled with bloodthirst. His fangs, at last, visible at the edge of his feral grin. Galad, Gilrel, and Filverel twitched behind him, expressions hungry to satiate their tempers.

The guards reached the lip of Sidhe and beastly spectators, awaiting their sovereign's command. Fionn need only give them the word and the whole ballroom would descend into chaos.

Aisling glanced at Dagfin, her brothers, and Killian standing to her right. They each found her stare and held it, perhaps waiting for the precise moment to flee Oighir while all were still distracted.

"Then fight for them in their stead," Lir said, pausing but a few paces from where Aisling still stood frozen, captured by Fionn's ice. Her stomach knotting and the cord between she and her fae king, pulling.

"Are you challenging me to a duel, *Damh Bán*?" Fionn scoffed, stepping directly behind Aisling till there was scarcely more than ice between them. And at the gesture, a muscle flashed across Lir's jaw.

Fionn swept Aisling's hair to the side, leaving her neck exposed. Aisling held her breath.

"You see, *mo Lúra*?" He bent lower, whispering in her ear and chilling her flesh with frost. "He considers you a possession, a trophy, a treasure to be won, collected, and hoarded. Not the partner, not the *equal* you and I bear the potential to be."

Lir squeezed the haft of his axes, near crushing them beneath the strength of his grip.

"If you're afraid, Fionn, just say so."

Fionn straightened, frustration lining the curve of his mouth. He feared Lir; that much was clear. But there was also undiluted envy blistering the black of his irises till it bled across the entirety of his posture.

Fionn raised his hand above his head.

"*Reacht*," he said in Rún.

At the word, his blade unsheathed itself from his throne atop the dais and shot into his hand. A translucent, glass-like blade, taller than himself.

"Now, now, brother, you're in my court. Perhaps in Annwyn, sovereigns would duel to the death but in Oighir, we prefer something far more entertaining."

"Speak it then," Lir said, eyes tracing where Fionn touched Aisling.

"A test of your valor, of the lengths you'll go to prove yourself to your *caera*." Fionn chuckled to himself, waving his sword as he spoke. "How far would you go to preserve your binding?"

Lir considered for a moment, Gilrel, Galad, Filverel, and Peitho weighing the son of Winter's words alongside their sovereign.

"The rules are simple: Only you may take part, lest you grant another the right to take your place, and in that case, you cannot re-enter the test. Secondly, you're forbidden to wield your magic during the first two tests.

"It would be three rounds, brother. A single loss would signal the loss of the test at large. And when you lose, I'll carve out your heart with your own axe, presaging the forever Aisling will stay here with me in Oighir."

Aisling grimaced in horror, jerking her head in Fionn's

direction. Cursing the *draiocht* for abandoning her now. Lir never let his axes out of his sight. The idea of Fionn wielding them, much less using them to harm Lir, was unthinkable.

Lir tilted his head back, his easy arrogance spellbinding.

"Your games are as tedious as ever, brother. I'd prefer to end this here and now, blade against blade," Lir said.

"A duel against me is a duel against Oighir," Fionn argued.

"All the more fun." Lir glanced around the room. There must've been hundreds, if not more Sidhe and their bipedal beasts spectating the interaction. And yet, Aisling knew as well as Lir it wouldn't be a challenge for the Sidhe king of the greenwood to fell them all, one by one.

"I don't think you're in a position to be slaughtering your own people, Lir. Especially when Danu offers a far more... forgiving alternative to your rule. Besides, do you really want to give the Sidhe another reason to question your loyalties?"

Lir flexed his jaw, considering. So Fionn hadn't been lying about Danu's attempts to usurp Lir nor the legions she'd amassed to betray him. All because Lir had bound himself to Aisling in an effort to quell tensions between mortals and fair folk. A treaty that had ended in violence regardless.

"Should I win this test of yours, Aisling is mine," Lir said.

Aisling bristled, souring at the thought of belonging to anyone. But given the current circumstances, she stifled her objections for another day. Hopefully, one where she was free from Oighir and Fionn's mischief. Lir may be her direct competition for Lofgren's Rise, but as it currently stood, he was a necessary means to an end to escape Oighir. And as for the frenzied pace of her heart, the heating of her skin, or the cord that jerked her toward him, Aisling despised it. Wished she could burn all her feelings for they made her weak. Made her want to return to him despite knowing her greatest chances were forged alone.

"Agreed." Fionn grinned, releasing Aisling from his touch.

Lir met Aisling's eyes briefly. And at the gesture, Aisling's heart raced a pace quicker. Lir's mischief always a step ahead of all others.

Both Fionn and Lir approached, all of the realm and its spirits holding their breath. The fae sentinels of Oighir and Lir's knights tensing in response.

Reluctantly, both kings reached forth and took hold of the other's forearm.

"By the Forge," they said in unison. "I vow it."

Aisling could feel the magic of their *draiocht* and the deal it sealed. It popped her ears with the shifting pressure, the smell of its plum-like fragrance weaving a noose around each of their throats, tightening should they betray their promise. Fae deals, bargains, and vows weren't to be taken lightly. They were met with either utmost triumph or complete death.

The ice Fionn had conjured to keep Aisling in place, dissolved and puddled atop the ballroom floors, at last releasing Aisling. Lir moved toward her, but Fionn stepped between them. A newfound pain, wrapping around her neck and forcing a gasp from her lips.

Aisling reached for her throat, finding to her horror a collar of crystal shards.

"What is this?!" she asked, desperately clawing at the contraption in hopes it might shatter, break, tear, and release her.

"Our deal's manifestation. Should Lir win the tests, then the collar will shatter. Should he not, well, consider it a gift to commemorate our true binding. One you'll look fondly over in the eternity to come. This way, even if Lir tries to take you from me after the tests have been lost, he cannot. The collar threads you to Oighir."

Aisling gaped, beyond outraged, maddened, furious, her *draiocht* kindling despite Fionn's and the Lady's dulling spells. This was no deal's manifestation. This was Fionn's way of claiming Aisling as his own. His way of boasting to Lir that, for now, Aisling was Winter's possession.

A muscle flashed across Lir's jaw, his hands white-knuckled on his axes. The glimmer of his expression violent the longer he appraised the collar. His deal with his brother made real around Aisling's throat and the stakes raised.

Fionn turned from Lir, retreating to Aisling.

"I'm nothing if not a gracious host, so you're free to stay in Oighir throughout the duration of the tests, brother. Three days' time. But should you be found speaking or lurking around the not-so-mortal queen, I'll interpret that as a forfeit and that you're surrendering to an execution."

Fionn grazed Aisling's cheek with his knuckle and frost crawled up her skin.

"Let's see how much she's worth to you, brother."

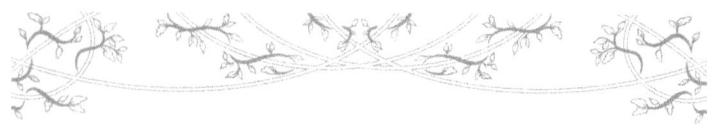

CHAPTER XVII

LIR

The Sidhe king of the greenwood grew a wych elm in the cloister his room overlooked.

The badgers passing by screamed, racing for the nearest escape as Castle Oighir's stone crumbled at the base of Lir's tree and tossed debris.

Lir took another bite of apple, amused. Just as he'd suspected, his *draiocht* had grown more powerful.

"*Was that necessary?*" Filverel said in Rún from behind.

"No, but I enjoyed it," Lir replied, switching tongues effortlessly as if both were his mother tongue. A product of the ages.

Filverel sighed, pouring himself a glass of Sidhe wine from a decanter before reclining in a chair draped with silver furs.

"You're reckless when you become obsessive."

"*Fionn could use some redecorating,*" Lir said, gesturing to the newly grown tree. An emerald in a drawer of pearls and glassy crystals.

Indeed, Lir's chamber was all ivory and silver. Plush

velvets, animal skins, shimmering snowflakes dangling from the ceilings overtaken by roots wrapped in ice, and a fireplace polished with frost.

Lir disliked Oighir and Fjallnorr as a whole. It was endless cold, frigid, and stiff. A land where lakes didn't ripple, trees didn't dance, and beasts hid in hollows or slumbered all together.

"Remind me then, why we're here. We could be halfway to Lofgren's Rise by now, one of our competitors stalled by your brother." Filverel set his chalice down. His moonstone eyes studying the glacial embrace of Lir's quarters with disdain. "And that's excluding the reckless gamble you made of your axes."

"*I made a vow the night of our union*," Lir said, tossing his apple idly with one hand and slipping the other into his pocket.

"This is one vow I'd be grateful for you to break, considering the consequences of keeping it far outweigh those of breaking it."

"I won't live another day apart from her."

"Because she's the key to complete authority over the realm? Because her proximity strengthens your *draiocht*? Because she's a tool and a weapon to be wielded? There are other ways of establishing monopoly, Lir. Racat, for one, is at our disposal. Danu fears the *dragún* and humankind will quiver in his presence. And if it's a queen you want, Peitho is more than willing. We—you don't need Aisling."

Lir met Filverel's eyes but didn't respond. The brush of morning winds, cooling the heat wrapping around Lir's heart in violet fire, bound to someday burn it entirely.

Filverel exhaled, resisting the urge to spew his objections, of which he had many.

"Fionn's tests begin tomorrow evening," Lir said, glad to

change the subject. "And knowing Fionn, he'll spare no opportunity to spill my blood nor humiliate the greenwood."

"Considering Oighir's tradition of such tests, it's possible he'll design it in the same breath as his father, Delbaeth." Filverel took another sip of wine. "Fionn declined a duel in favor of a test for a reason."

"Because he knew a loss dealt by my hands was both inevitable and obvious?" Lir asked, the image of a fox.

"In part. But he also wishes to make a spectacle and correct the past."

Lir leaned a shoulder against the wall, crossing his legs at his ankles as he continued to bite his apple.

"A wish in vain. The court of the greenwood will best Oighir once more."

"You're overly confident. You shouldn't underestimate Fionn."

"Underestimate? I've valued his worth and find it lacking."

Lir rested his head against the wall, turning to look out the window. Down below, Aisling and a great armored bear emerged and passed through the cloister.

Lir paused, his body moving to face the window against his own volition. Heart thrashing till he bore half a mind to rip it from his chest to stop its intolerable aching.

Aisling was a forbidden spell. A prayer cast from the lips of the truly desperate, those ignorant to the weight of such shadowed magic. A spell Lir found himself unable to resist, considering it again and again, wondering if this time, he might bear the courage to cast it himself. To feel the supple curves of her dark femininity and memorize them.

Lir brushed his knuckles against his lips, apple still in hand. Even now, he tasted her. Felt her lips against his own, her body in his arms. A memory rich enough to relive again and again even after having cast it out each time it bloomed.

And the collar glimmering around her throat burned Lir's bones till his thoughts for Fionn's punishment grew more creative by the hour.

Filverel shifted, waking Lir from his reverie.

"Whatever you do, Lir, whilst we're in Oighir don't seek her out. Heed Fionn's rules lest this all be in vain."

Yet still, Fionn's voice was a distant whisper as Lir followed Aisling from the cloister with his eyes, studying her shadow as it disappeared through another corridor.

AISLING

Aisling stood in a forest made of stars.

The branches clicked together, chiming like the bells laced through the branches in Annwyn. But there was no music. No foxes fixing tea nor the joyous weeping of willows. Only silence and the shape of a woman approaching.

The Lady.

Aisling paled, her body cold, numb, immoveable. Locked in place as though by invisible shackles.

"Aisling, you disappoint me," she said as her face illuminated beneath the stars. "It could have been done with. Your wounds already healing."

Aisling fought to move, finding, to her horror, her entire being bespelled. Save her tongue.

"You died. Reaped by Lir's axe."

The Lady cackled. "I am no fleshling. Tear apart my bones and rip my skin, my spirit lives in all, reborn again and again till time meets its end."

Now, she stood before her, reaching out and grabbing Aisling's throat. She squeezed. Aisling struggled for breath. Face purpling.

"You will pay for this, Aisling. I will stop at nothing to rip you and your Sidhe king apart if it means every last star must fall and the loom must break."

Aisling sipped on a tea brewed with crushed moonflower petals, doused in cinnamon and nutmeg, and boiled in fae milk. It warmed her soul, but nothing could defrost the arctic aura of Fionn's company nor the hours of restless sleep, haunted by the Lady herself.

The fae lord sat across from her at the dining table. Dwarven hares serving spiced porridge, broiled meats, and cardamom buns, forming a feast atop their table.

"Eat, *mo Lúra*."

"I've already told you: if you wish to purchase a morsel of my compliance, then show me to the Roktan prince." Aisling needed to know Fionn's good treatment hadn't ended the moment his deal with Lir was struck. The moment the collar around her neck had been sealed and forged around her throat.

"Again, you ignore your own blood, deign not to mention your brothers. Why is that?"

Aisling pressed her mouth into a thin line, setting her teacup down in response. She'd made her conditions clear.

Fionn exhaled, exasperated. "Your prince is well cared for I assure you as I've already proved at my masquerade."

"Show me."

A cord snaked around Fionn's neck, visible just beneath the silk collar.

"I'll have him brought to you at the first test, if it pleases you. As proof of my kindness."

Aisling cleared her throat, content with his response. The first test was tomorrow evening and if Dagfin was present, alive, and well, the rest of her stay at Oighir would be easier to stomach. Especially considering the vast luxury of her stay, all provided by Fionn himself as well as his personal servants.

"You needn't be so difficult with me, *mo Lúra*. I'm here to give you everything you've ever wanted, all that you desire, and anything you need."

"Then tell me, what is it you forgot to tell me the other night?"

"You reference my relationship with Lir."

"Aye, you're brothers after all."

Fionn considered, pressing the back of his middle and index finger to his lips.

"It's a lengthy, tedious tale for another time."

"We have time now," Aisling insisted, taking another sip of her tea. "Especially if you're intent on giving me everything and anything I covet."

Fionn smiled, but it never met his eyes. At last, he lowered his hand, gripping the arms of his chair.

"Before Bres, Ina loved Delbaeth. My father. In that age, the concept of *caeras* wasn't yet revealed, and so Ina and Delbaeth bore a child together."

"You," Aisling conjectured, glaring at the fae lord in a new light.

Fionn nodded his head.

"Despite this child, Ina succumbed to the allure of Bres during the start of the Wild Hunt: enemies at first, then traitorous lovers. A betrayal to Delbaeth and the rare son they'd forged together. So Delbaeth challenged Bres to a test. The winner would surrender their affections and accept Ina's choice whichever and whoever that may be."

"I'm guessing Bres won."

"No," Fionn said, wincing as though a bitter taste had just graced his tongue. "Bres cheated."

Aisling swallowed a hot gulp of tea.

"Nevertheless, it hardly mattered. Ina ran away with Bres and met hers and her kingdom's demise because of it."

A war bred of envy, Aisling realized. But not because of the dragons. Because of love.

Fionn stood from his chair. Aisling watched as he approached, circling the table before holding out his hand in offer.

"Come, let me better acquaint you with Oighir."

Coyly, Aisling accepted his hand, recognizing any opportunity to better explore the castle was an opportunity to better familiarize herself with her prison. One she'd burn if it weren't for whatever icy shackles Fionn had wrapped around her *draiocht*, quelling what might she bore. A question she hoarded, awaiting the most advantageous time to ask.

Fionn led her from the dining hall and into an arcade that wrapped around several turrets nestled beside clouds as thick as cotton.

Down below, the open areas of the castle bustled. Servants scurrying to prepare for Fionn's test, sentinels posted at every entrance, and music plucked distantly by woodland bards.

"Together, you and I could rule the realm from Oighir," he said. "You'll be gifted wealth, opulence, power, and eternal affection." Fionn brushed her shoulder with his own as they walked, prickling every one of Aisling's nerves. "We'd descend the realm into everlasting winter."

Fionn waved his hand elegantly, and at the gesture, snow

descended from the heavens in glittering flurries. Every bear statue roaring from their perches like gargoyles, every spindly turret, every silver sky bridge, every garland bleeding scarlet berries, became sugared and sparkling.

Fionn was trying to impress Aisling: this much she knew. And had she never met Lir, had never lived in Annwyn, perhaps this would've impressed her. But Aisling had already tasted Annwyn's grisly, blood-soaked magic, its adventure, smelt the herbs of the forest, and bruised her feet dancing at a *Snaidhm*. Had felt fear, anger, joy, and pleasure. Had cried, laughed, danced, and reveled whilst a part of the fae king's world: one glimmering, green, and savage. One she couldn't forget so easily.

And as though summoned, Lir appeared around the corner.

From where Fionn and Aisling stood high up on an outdoor walkway, they peered down into a courtyard traced by cypresses and boasting a statue of Fionn reclined in his throne.

Gilrel, Galad, Filverel, and Peitho were with the Sidhe king of the greenwood.

Weapons in hand, they were sparring. Dealing brutal blows against one another as each lithely navigated their duel.

Lir, himself, was an armed shadow cutting through his opponents with wicked accuracy. Every movement was made with the next in mind, felling adversary after adversary as he'd done for centuries prior, leaving a bloody trail in his wake. Eventually, the courtyard was a portrait of defeat, Lir the sole victor, twirling his blades in his hands.

Aisling inhaled sharply, her knees suddenly weak. He wore no coat, no jacket, and no blouse despite the arctic air. Instead, he was sweating and bare-chested, his broad shoulders boasting every chiseled muscle in his back, his arms, and his narrow waist. Fae markings mocked Aisling's attention as she studied them each as well, committing the wolf at his shoulder to memory, the runes along his forearms, the interlace where his trousers hung low—

Aisling flicked her eyes away but it hardly mattered. Lir had already caught her staring, grinning up at her from where he twirled his axes down below. Their eyes meeting, attention pulled by the intangible cord between them till they were drawn together once more. The falling snow, the music, the world dissolving and blurring in their periphery.

"Aisling." Aisling wasn't certain how many times Fionn had spoken her name before his voice, at last, tore her from her stupor.

"Let's not waste our time lingering," he said, his voice dripping with malice.

"They're training, aren't they?" Aisling ignored him, asking her question instead. "For the tests?"

Fionn exhaled. "It appears that way."

"Have you given them any indication as to the format of the tests?"

Fionn licked his lips. "The night before the first two tests, I gift a clue. It's up to the discretion of the player to either successfully deduce the contents of the first two tests or fail. The last test, my challenger enters blind. Otherwise, they're given no further information."

"What was the clue for the first test?"

Fionn spoke it, although reluctantly. "*Cruachan.*"

Cruachan. The word meant nothing to Aisling. It sounded western, but otherwise, it was useless information.

"Does every test require physical combat?"

"No," Fionn said, quickly losing patience. "But enough questions, let's continue on."

Fionn wrapped his arm around Aisling's waist, pulling her close until she fell into step beside him. A gentle nudge, encouraging her away from the overlook.

At his touch, Lir's eyes flared. The mischievous arrogance of his knife-sharp smile swiftly became more dangerous, laced with brutal intent.

Lir made certain Aisling was watching before he spun on his heel and threw an axe at the statue of Fionn. The blade cut through stone, severing the head from the rest of the sculpture. It thwacked and split against the cobbles, rolling away with a gathering of foxes chasing after it in horror.

Aisling didn't turn to see Fionn's reaction. She felt it in the way his hand hardened against her waist.

Lir, on the other hand, turned to meet Aisling's eyes, not a word except for a wicked quick wink.

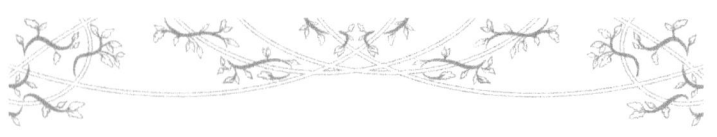

CHAPTER XIII

DAGFIN

Dagfin was starving. Not for food or drink. Only Ocras.

His body was slowing, screaming at the *Faerak* to feed it what it craved and yet, what was left of his supply was stripped from his person when they were first captured by Fionn.

And times like these, when the hunger was at its worst, was when Dagfin remembered her voice.

"You don't want this, prince. It may look glamorous, heroic even, but the gauntlet of the *Faerak* is a curse."

It had looked heroic. That day, the sound of Roktling was deafening. The screams of undiluted joy when the myths of werewolves on the periphery of their coastal kingdom were, at long last, ended by the heroine crowned by scars and riding into Roktling on an ivory mare. The corpse of some nightmarish beast slung over the rump of her mount.

"If I wanted glamor or heroism, I'd accept the Roktan

crown today. I want to make a difference. I want to fight," he'd said, biting back tears. Praying this strange woman saw him as a man and not a boy running from his legacy.

"Join your father's fleets then," she'd said, counting the coin Feradach had paid her before spinning on her heel to leave. "Forge knows they'll need every pair of hands they can get."

Dagfin ran to catch up with her, grabbing her jacket. It flashed open, revealing a bandolier shimmering with powder-filled bottles.

The *Faerak* ripped her jacket from Dagfin's grasp. Nostrils flaring in annoyance.

"If you weren't a prince, you wouldn't still be standing before me."

"Take me with you."

The *Faerak*'s expression muddled, considering Dagfin more closely this time. As though she hadn't anticipated another attempt on the Roktan prince's behalf to flee his crown.

"The life of a *Faerak* is one chasing ghosts. Nightmares the world hardly knows are anything more than either myth or legend yet terrorize them all the same. We live coin to coin, on the brink of death, for blood and hushed victory. What you saw as I entered Roktling this morning, isn't common, prince. This isn't a life anyone asks for. Especially someone like you."

"Neither is the one I run from."

The *Faerak* tilted her head to the side.

"The late prince died and so you have a duty to inherit what he could not. I'd be doing an injustice to all of Roktling to encourage you to become a *Faerak*."

Dagfin flinched at the mention of his eldest brother.

Adair was born to rule, not Dagfin. Dagfin preferred

fighting invisible beasts in the forest at Aisling's side. Not learning politics nor enduring endless lectures. And when Adair had fallen ill and collapsed, had passed on to the Other, Dagfin was no more suited for the crown than before his brother left him. Abandoned him to inherit his ghost. Something that was never his to begin with.

"If you don't take me with you, I'll find another way to circumvent my legacy. I'll run, I'll disappear, I'll—"

"Enough, prince."

"No!" Dagfin shouted. "I'll not waste a life Adair couldn't live, ruling from a throne. I do not wish: I *will* make a difference with my own two hands. Fighting that which threatens humankind in the periphery whether I die trying or live to make my life worth anything."

Silence was thick, scoffed at by the echoes of Dagfin's voice still ricocheting off Roktling's bronze walls.

At last, the *Faerak* shifted, crossing her arms.

"I'll take you with me on one condition, prince."

"Anything."

"You vow that when the day comes, you'll inherit your crown. Vow to me, to Feradach, to Roktling."

Dagfin paled, unable to swallow the stone lodged in his throat. He opened his mouth to argue, to scream, to curse death and its greedy hands for taking what was never theirs to begin with.

Instead, he closed his eyes and nodded.

The *Faerak* inhaled deeply before turning on her heel for the doors.

"Once I have approval from Feradach, we'll begin your training. And you'll have your first taste of Ocras."

∼

Dagfin shook his head, batting away the memories.

Unwanted thoughts heralded by the smell of the arena in which they stood. A colossal structure supported by statues carved in the likeness of hands, cradling the stadium even as winter encased them in glass.

The roar of spectators thrummed through his core. Thousands of bipedal beasts and fair folk alike, shouting from the rafters with their fists in the air.

As honored guests, Dagfin, Starn, Iarbonel, Fergus, and Killian stood next to Fionn's royal box. All save for Annind still recovering in his private chambers somewhere in the pits of Oighir.

Dagfin desperately tried to focus on the fae king at the center of the arena, twirling his axes between his hands. Yet Dagfin couldn't help the way his eyes kept darting to Aisling, sitting beside Fionn. A space surrounded by Sidhe guards, plush with silver furs. That armored bear lingering at Aisling's side.

She gripped the arms of her throne, eyes pinned to Lir. Her mouth pressed into a thin white line. Concern riddled across the tense arch of her shoulders. And at the sight of it, Dagfin's chest tightened.

"Keep your focus, Fin," Killian whispered beside him.

Starn nodded in agreement. "Any hint of disaster and our opportunity to flee is nigh."

"I already told you: I'm not leaving without Aisling."

"She made her loyalties clear the last time we spoke with her. She wishes to go forward alone."

Starn cleared his throat. "Aye, you may not have a choice."

"I never had a choice to begin with," Dagfin replied. "There was never a possibility of me leaving without her."

Starn opened his mouth to speak, but before he could

utter a word, Dagfin moved through the fair folk and to Fionn's royal box.

Even without his Ocras, even despite its absence gnawing at his bones, he moved nimbly.

Yet as soon as he bypassed the sentinels, Fionn's bear rose on its hind legs, blocking Dagfin just before he was to reach Aisling.

"Now, now, little human. Where are we off to in such a hurry?"

"It's quite alright, Greum," Aisling said, standing from her seat. "Fionn promised me an audience with the *Faerak*."

Greum exchanged glances with Fionn. The son of Winter clenched his jaw but nodded in approval, nevertheless. His need to appease Aisling overruling his immeasurable annoyance. Yet Dagfin couldn't care less he was making an enemy of a fae lord. So long as he spoke with Aisling.

Greum lumbered to the side and Aisling sprung forth, wrapping Dagfin in her arms.

"Fin."

She smelled of lavender and holy gardens. Was the vision of dreams that left the heart broken come morning; a silver gown made of glittering chainmail wrapped around her elegant form, and the soft curls of midnight black braided away from her face in intricate patterns. The crystal collar gleaming around her throat.

"I'm alright," he said, eager to mask the roughness in his voice. His strength rendered brittle without the Ocras as she embraced him. So, he took the opportunity and whispered in her ear.

"We need to speak. Alone."

He needed her to tell her he'd never leave her. If she chose to continue alone and wished for him to go home, she'd have to banish him herself.

Aisling pulled away, resolve flashing in her violet eyes. She couldn't respond now. Not for the sentinels that surrounded them, Greum, and the son of Winter listening keenly to their every exchange. And not for the pounding of the earth that unbalanced them both.

Aisling's attention whipped to the arena, returning to Lir at its center.

The first test was beginning.

CHAPTER XIX

AISLING

A roar rippled through the arena.

Aisling sat back down in her throne, pulling Dagfin along so he stood beside her. And if either Fionn or Greum had any protests, they didn't voice them. Right now, she found comfort in her friend's presence, but more so in knowing he was alright. That he was safe and well cared for even in Oighir. In a land that feared his blood near as much as they loathed it.

"Herein begins the first of three tests. An Oighir tradition of deciding the rightful hand of all and anything contested," Greum shouted before the arena. "In this case, Lir, king of the greenwood, challenges Your Lordship, Fionn, son of Winter, for his *caera*, the not-so-mortal queen of Annwyn!" Greum's audience stomped, clapped, and screamed from the tops of their lungs. Chanting Fionn's name.

"Should the *Damh Bán* lose, however, Fionn will carve out his heart with his own axe."

Somehow, the spectators' excitement increased, bleeding

the realm till Aisling believed the veil thinned by *Samhain* might tear.

"Let the tests begin!"

Aisling shuddered, stomach knotting fiercely.

Lir still stood at the center of the stadium, completely composed. He gave one glance to his right where his knights watched from the side. They nodded in encouragement. Peitho shouted something Aisling couldn't hear, while Galad crossed his arms, staring at the mighty archway shrouded in shadow that Lir faced.

Then he gave his last glance to Aisling, smiling knowingly.

Aisling crossed her legs, her body jittery with anxiety and trembling.

The roars that'd erupted earlier resurfaced. At first a guttural growl then a fully-fledged cry, this one more like a bird than whatever had sounded before.

Aisling held her breath.

What appeared from the shadows was nothing Aisling had ever heard of much less seen.

A colossal, three-headed beast lumbered forth. One head like a hawk, one a wolf, and the last a serpent, hissing madly at the bright contrast it experienced after having emerged from the dark. Its back legs belonged to the bird, its front paws to the wolf, and its tail to the serpent.

Aisling turned to Fionn, smirking in his throne beside her.

"What is that?!"

His eyes shifted lazily to her, but it was Dagfin who replied.

"*Ellén Trechend.* Centuries ago, it's said the Aos Sí that hail from a land called Cruachan in the West, tore open a hole in the veil between this realm and the Other on the eve of *Samhain*, ushering in the Ellén Trechend. One of the beasts made by the gods to guard the Forge during the Old Age."

Aisling's breathing was short, her lungs small as she beheld it. Growling, screeching, hissing.

"You can't possibly mean for Lir to slaughter this beast?!" Aisling said to Fionn, louder than she'd anticipated, palms growing slick even as she dug her nails into the arms of her throne.

"You should thank me," he said, resting his head on his fist. His beaded headdress clicking as he did so. "This will prove what you're worth to him. Isn't that what you want?"

Aisling seethed at the winter king. Indeed, it was what Aisling wanted. Beyond her loathing of Lir, and in the depths of her most guilty desires, she *wanted* him to want her. Wanted him to need her. And never had she ever believed he truly could or ever would outside his own self-serving motives. Nevertheless, this demon was anything but reassuring. It smelled of ancient caverns in the wild and of logs broken at the end of the fire when the tales became more lawless.

Filverel and Galad noticeably tensed, Peitho gripped the bar at the periphery of the pitch, and Gilrel gestured a silent prayer to the Forge as Lir stalked forth.

The Ellén Trechend struck first, its serpent's head snapping for the fae king.

Lir stepped to the side easily, assessing the creature as though he bore all the time in the world.

The wolf, salivating onto the pitch in great globs, snarled, its muzzle wrinkling, peeling back to reveal a collection of blade-sharp teeth. So, the hawk head screeched before pecking at Lir with its beak.

This time Lir rolled to the side, gathering to his feet once more.

"Why hasn't he struck yet?" Aisling asked, to no one in particular. Voicing her anxiety aloud.

"He's a hunter," Dagfin replied first.

Aisling glared up at the Roktan prince. His jawline was sharp, clenching his teeth as he assessed the duel for himself. "He bides his time, is patient, studying his opponent before pouncing."

Indeed, Lir paced before the creature, watching how it moved, when it was most provoked, and when he neared, which areas of its body it instinctively protected.

And although this reassured Aisling, she still cursed the small eternity before Lir at last swiped at the serpent's eyes when it lunged for him.

The movement was so quick, Aisling almost missed it. Evidence of the onslaught provided in the form of carnage sprayed into the surrounding audience, steaming in the wintry air.

The serpent reeled, baring its fangs, but the second attack was met similarly, forcing the hawk at the right to drive for Lir even as the serpent still recovered.

Lir struck for the hawk as well, but this time, the beast expected it, jutting its beak out first so its more vulnerable flesh was out of reach.

Lir dove out of the way, rolling onto his feet, and striking the center wolf that bit for his head.

The wolf howled as Lir's axe plunged into its skull.

Dagfin cursed beneath his breath.

"What is it?" Aisling asked.

"The bones of forged-brewed creatures are said to be near impenetrable. It doesn't surprise me his axes broke bone but releasing the blades might be a more difficult battle."

And just as Dagfin said, Lir struggled to release his axe from the wolf.

The Ellén Trechend roared, lifting onto its hind legs as Lir pulled for his axe. Yet it didn't come free, taking the fae king with it. He was flung through the air, hand gripping the axe.

Aisling stood from her chair, reaching for the banister. Sweat beading her brow.

Fionn clapped. "This is more entertaining than I initially presumed."

Aisling shot him a scowl over her shoulder, but Fionn's smile only brightened.

The crowd boomed. Lir, at last, finding his footing atop the wolf's head even as the hound threw its head from side to side, desperate to toss Lir off. An opportunity arising when the wolf slumped against the ground. Yet Lir stood astride, at last releasing his axe from the beast's skull.

"Why didn't he leap off?!" Aisling asked.

"He will." Dagfin joined her at the railing. "But like I said, he's biding his time. Every attack from either the hawk or serpent has been reckless, their eagerness to strike making them sloppy. He's using that against them."

This time, Lir didn't plunge his axe into the wolf's skull again. He waited, watching as the hawk and the serpent lunged for him atop the wolf. Beak and fangs first, they struck the wolf head instead, blood spewing and a pained whimper erupting, loud enough to rupture Aisling's ear drums. Lir leaped off the monster in the same breath, several stories above the ground. Too high for a normal Sidhe, impossible for a mortal.

Aisling wrenched her eyes shut on instinct, her heart in her throat. Peeking only at the sound of mass cheers and Gilrel's hollering from the side. Lir landed like a feline, absorbing the impact with more rolls than usual before springing to his feet, both blades in hand, now soaked with blood.

The wolf's head was felled by its other two heads. Both the snake and hawk turned to Lir, furious, but the weight of the wolf dragging against the snow made them slow and sluggish. Unable to reach Lir as he raced to the other end of the arena where Aisling and Fionn sat. The beast followed him, nipping at his heels and roaring with increased need.

Lir slid before the box and leaped onto the railing. Fionn's guards immediately started forward, weapons poised to strike.

"There's still a test to be won, Lir," Fionn scolded from his chair, eyes shooting to the monster approaching. "The beast won't hurt a soul outside the arena but it definitely won't hesitate to kill you even if your back is turned."

"Lir, what are you doing?!" Aisling shouted, staggering back a few paces.

Lir ignored Fionn, crouching on the railing and finding Aisling's eyes.

"I need a kiss for good luck."

Aisling shook her head, baffled, the monster picking up speed and defeating the distance between it and Lir.

"Don't be a fool, brother," Fionn chimed.

"Are you mad?!" Aisling asked, heart in her throat.

"So claim the legends," he said, as calm as if he were anywhere else but the arena.

"You don't have time for this!"

"So kiss me quick." Lir grinned, pushing his hair away from his forehead and out of glittering eyes. His dimples framing the wicked edge of his smile.

Aisling glanced at the beast a few breaths behind Lir. The two heads preparing their maws to bite down and tear apart the Sidhe king. So, Aisling lunged forward and rose on her tiptoes, finding Lir's mouth and pressing it to her own. Behind her, Aisling could feel both Fionn and Dagfin bristling, the world shaking violently either by the creature a few paces from crushing Lir to death or their kiss, she was uncertain. Only that he tasted of woodland secrets, of ragged breaths between lovers, and ink-black nights. Her body thrummed with heat and need despite the tightening of the collar at her throat. Immediately, Lir noticed the strain at her neck and released a quiet, instinctual groan against her lips, seemingly forcing himself to pull away a beat before death, turning and throwing his blades in one clean sweep.

The edge of his axes punctured both the serpent and hawk, blinding the serpent entirely while leaving only one eye seeing in the hawk. So, Lir leaped down from the railing and sliced at the serpent's throat while it writhed, leaning close enough to the ground. The hawk, however, still stood rather strong, biting at Lir without pause.

He struck the beast in the skull but this time, Lir didn't let the monster reel. Made vulnerable, he held the behemoth down with all the strength of a Sidhe king as it made sense of the pain, the chaos, Lir roaring as he did so, moving his left blade swiftly so as not to lose his hold. The second axe sliced into the hawk's second eye, blinding the final beast before Lir wrenched both blades from its body and hammered them down into the hawk's skull.

There was quiet.

A silence so thick, every snowflake falling from the gray-clad skies descended more slowly, rummaging through the muck of anticipation.

Aisling's pulse pounded in her ears. Rushed at her throat. Her body cold and rigid, bracing the banister for dear life. Until, at last, the light faded from the hawk's eyes.

Lir had won.

Fionn stood slowly from his throne, arranging his robes as Lir approached their box. The spectators still shouting, shaking the entire arena with their excitement. The body of the Ellén Trechend now blanketed in a layer of snow.

And despite the first test being over, Aisling's hands couldn't release the railing. The intangible cord between she and Lir growing taut the nearer he drew. Her stomach flipping and her lips burning where the memory of his mouth against her own lingered. He was arrogance personified, blood-splattered and sweat glistened, flipping his blades back into the sheathes at his back.

"Well done, brother." Fionn clapped. "You had us on the edge of our seats."

"I had to ensure Aisling was paying attention." Lir's grin widened, roguish and punctuated by knee-weakening fangs.

Dagfin shifted beside Aisling, but Fionn found the fae king's comments less than amusing.

"Let's see how well she pays attention when you meet your end. There are still two tests left."

"And the clue for the next?"

Fionn smiled.

"*Nimhe.*"

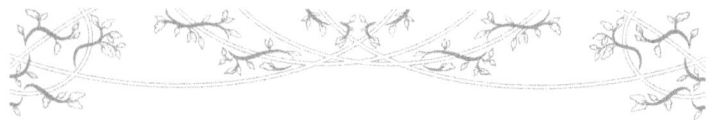

CHAPTER XX

AISLING

It snowed inside Fionn's bedroom. This, despite the glass dome overhead, allowing the stars to spill into his ice-polished chambers. A room of pale hagwood carved with snowflakes, bears, and interlacing thorns. Floors draped in fluffy furs, and his four-poster bed blanketed in velvets, silks, and the hide of some Unseelie Aisling preferred to be ignorant of.

"His lordship will be here shortly," Greum said, disappearing back through the mirror from which they'd entered.

Aisling walked further into the room.

Aisling was alone with her thoughts after the hours of chaos that ensued Lir's first victory. Her own heart still twisted and sore from the exertion of spectating his win. And if this was merely Fionn's first test, Aisling dreaded knowing both the second and the third were yet to come.

A familiar ripple sounded behind Aisling. She turned, expecting to find Fionn but instead meeting the eyes of a particularly small dwarven hare carrying a tray of bulb-shaped bottles. Aisling did a double take considering them more closely even as the hare's paws trembled.

The creature stuttered, at last, managing to speak.

"Apologies, *mo Lúra*, I thought his lordship was here, but I see I'm mistaken so I'll just—"

"No!" Aisling said, biting her tongue lest she sound overeager. Those bottles were significant, Aisling knew. "Were you delivering something for his lordship?" Aisling gestured to the tray.

The hare nodded her head, eyes narrowing in the same breath.

"You're more than welcome to leave it here until he arrives."

"I really shouldn't leave this unattended without his lordship's approval."

"Greum informed me Fionn would be here any moment," Aisling reassured her. Still, the hare seemed unconvinced.

"I'll return later." The hare spun on her heel, facing the mirror once more.

"Very well, I'll do my best to convince Fionn you bore good intentions."

The hare paused.

"He despises when those around him aren't punctual, but his temper is no match for me," Aisling continued, arching her brows to feign sincerity.

The creature's whiskers fluttered, attention darting between the tray and the not-so-mortal queen.

"I suppose it's the lesser of two evils."

Aisling internally rejoiced, doing her best to mask her interest.

The hare set the tray down beside Fionn's bed before

hopping off, offering one last glance before she disappeared through the mirror.

Immediately, Aisling wandered toward the tray. Atop it were seven bottles. One forest emerald, one bone-white and frothing, one rare violet, one blue and foaming, one lusty crimson with the consistency of cream, one clear and still, and one pink as peonies. Each swirling as though recently ladled from a bubbling cauldron.

Beneath each one, words were written on parchment in Rún.

Aisling cursed herself for not understanding, swearing she'd commit to learning the divine language at a later time.

A ripple sounded behind her.

Aisling swiftly sat on Fionn's bed, heart racing as the son of Winter materialized from the other side of the mirror.

"You're here early."

"You summoned me."

Fionn shrugged, approaching. "I didn't imagine you'd come so willingly."

"Why wouldn't I?" Aisling said, smoothing her words into mulled wine.

"You're my—" he hesitated for the first time, tripping on his own thoughts.

"Prisoner?"

He frowned, the jeweled collar around Aisling's throat sparkling as though in triumph.

"I don't want you to be. I want you to choose to be here of your own free will."

"Yet this collar speaks otherwise, as well as my inability to wield my *draiocht*."

Fionn stood before where she sat on the bed, impossibly tall and dressed in the same silver as his hair.

"The collar is a product of the deal struck between Lir

and me. As for your *draíocht*, I haven't shackled it. Merely dulled it."

Aisling blinked before checking the abyss within where her *draíocht* lived in the shadows. Still, it was frozen, locked inside its cavern and waiting to break loose. Chilled to the bone.

"It's been frozen, unable to either be woken or be wielded," Aisling insisted, hand at her heart as though pawing for a sign of the *draíocht*'s life.

"The moment I sensed you stepping onto Fjallnorrian land, I coaxed it asleep for the time being."

"You were responsible for the fear gorta?" Aisling asked, a shudder creeping up her spine. Remembering the way the fear gorta had dulled her magic.

"It would've attacked regardless, but I used its hunger to my advantage."

Aisling swallowed her anger, realizing an outburst against a captor who wanted her compliance was both unwise and uncunning. She'd find a way out of his spells and collar alike in due time.

"How is it you can steal my *draíocht* so?" Aisling asked, clearing her throat.

"As much as I'd love to boast such power as to limit your own, *mo Lúra*, I cannot steal your *draíocht*. Not without aid from a greater magic source of which, currently, I have none. I merely put it to sleep for the time being. For obvious reasons."

"A magic source like Racat?"

Fionn smiled bitterly.

"Aye, like Racat."

"Yet whatever spell you've cast to daze my *draíocht*, the Lady has used as well."

Fionn met Aisling's eyes, silver orbs twinkling with interest. Aisling damned the words, for clearly Fionn hadn't known this.

"The Lady wields many spells. Far more powerful than my own. She's been watching you far longer than you've known her name. Every step toward Fjallnorr is a step closer to the Lady. Her urgency to prevent you from reaching Lofgren's Rise, increasing by the hour."

Aisling bit her bottom lip. She hadn't realized the full extent of the Lady's ambitions. The Lady hadn't lied; she'd stop at nothing to tear Aisling and Lir apart. Yet Aisling needed Lir to escape Oighir.

"So why is it that my magic cannot awaken if you boast no such power? Surely your sleeping spell could be shattered with enough inspiration."

Fionn sat beside her, closer to the tray of potions than Aisling. Still, Aisling was merely an arm's length away from grabbing the potion parchment and pocketing it.

"Oighir and the north of Fjallnorr are potent with ice magic. It's possible, your *draiocht* is still young, not yet challenged with such witchery and so frozen until truly needed. The more powerful you become at my side, the easier it'll be to summon your power even despite the cold and sleep alike."

"I can't say I'm not disappointed," Aisling said. She heightened her voice, doing her best to sound melancholy despite the running of her heart. If Fionn would just lean a few inches closer, she could grab the parchment atop the tray of potions without him knowing.

"I'd hoped the silence of my *draiocht* was a result of a greater power and not the weakness of my own."

"Not weakness. Youth. With time, I can teach you how to surpass such limitations. With time, you'll grow alongside me."

Aisling cleared her throat.

"Lir taught me how to summon my *draiocht* to begin with."

Fionn reacted viscerally to the sound of Lir's name. Nostrils flaring.

"Then your teachings have been insufficient."

The memory of Sakaala flashed across Aisling's memory. The merrow's lawless, lusty magic, a potent influence, in what Aisling found, was powerful magic indeed.

"I'm open to your influence," she said, leaning a hair closer. Lengthening the curve of her neck and holding Fionn's gaze the way Sakaala had done with Lir.

Fionn, still rigid from overhearing his brother's name, appraised Aisling anew. His eyes darting across her expression.

"Then truly bind with me. Here and now," he said, his voice deepening as his shoulders relaxed and he mirrored her posture. Those words rang in the air between them. *A true binding*. If it wasn't a union, Aisling wasn't certain what it was nor what it meant. How two souls could weave their fate threads into the Lady's tapestry of their own will.

"How is that done exactly?" Aisling asked.

"It's better demonstrated than explained." Fionn cupped her jaw, leaning closer. "And I can demonstrate now."

"I said 'open' to your influence not 'committed'. You'll have to convince me to engage in any demonstrations," Aisling said. "At least until the tests are done with." Aisling blinked away the rage inspired by the memory of Fionn's deception: how he and the Lady had ensnared her and almost severed the bond between she and Lir without her consent. Nevertheless, rage, anger, vengeful thoughts would only get her so far. Fionn responded to Aisling most when she was coy and eager to participate in his games.

"Is that not what I've done these past several days?"

"If you believe that effort enough, then you've lost the battle before it's begun."

Aisling placed her hand beside where Fionn sat, forcing herself to lean closer. Nevertheless, she still wasn't quite near enough to snag the parchment.

"What will it take to convince you then?" He moved further into her, the tip of his nose near brushing hers as he tilted his head down. His chest rising and falling in great breaths.

"It wouldn't be a true victory if I merely gave you the answers, Your Lordship."

"Call me Fionn."

"Very well, Fionn, you've a great task ahead of you." Aisling inched closer, her lips almost brushing against his. Enveloped in his perfume of northern spices, of wintertide mornings, and frozen lakes.

He closed his eyes, tracing her arm with his fingertips, her shoulder, finding her neck, and pulling in for the kiss.

Their lips met and Aisling's stomach tossed. Sickened by the cold strangeness of it. When she'd kissed Lir, it'd been realm-shattering. When she'd kissed Dagfin, it'd felt soft, familiar, and kind. Kissing Fionn was uncomfortable. Wholeheartedly wrong. Frigid and stiff. Yet if escaping this prison meant continuing her venture toward Lofgren's Rise, she found she'd do anything. Including paying the cost of a meager kiss. One without feeling and untethered by heartstrings. A cantrip easily dealt when desperate.

The kiss did the trick. Aisling pushed far enough into Fionn's embrace to reach and snatch the parchment behind him, slowly drawing it into the folds of her skirt while Fionn was distracted.

At last, it was well hidden, and Aisling tore herself from Fionn, hardly able to endure another moment.

Fionn blinked, registering the sharp contrast with a confused expression.

"I'm exhausted," Aisling said, leaping to her feet and moving toward the mirror.

"You can rest here," Fionn said, gesturing to his bed. His silver hair dangling across his flushed face.

Aisling felt a bout of nausea churn inside her stomach, but she stifled it, baring her teeth in a grin instead.

"No, no, it's best I take my leave and allow you a respite as well."

Aisling placed her fingertips against the mirror, ready to dive into it before Fionn noticed the parchment was missing.

"Wait. Aisling."

Aisling cursed her name.

"Thank you," he said, his voice painfully genuine. "You won't regret giving me the chance to prove myself or Oighir's worth. The entire realm will be better for it."

Aisling didn't look back before she dove into the mirror. Swallowing all that'd just unraveled, darting through Castle Oighir and back to her chambers.

The journey back to her rooms was longer than Aisling expected. This, in part, because she'd materialized outside the wrong mirror, on the opposite side of Oighir than she'd intended.

Aisling sped down the corridors, avoiding meeting any of the servants' or guards' lingering glares. Aisling had never traversed these passages alone. She'd always been accompanied by either Greum, Frigg, or Fionn himself, and so, her solitude was enough to draw suspicion.

Aisling lifted her chin, feigning confidence as she rushed across bridges, down spiraling staircases, and to the east wing where her rooms were nestled.

That was, until someone or something grabbed Aisling.

Aisling stifled the urge to scream, squirming against her captor. A hand over her mouth and another wrapped around her waist, pressing the back of her body against the firm edge of someone much taller than herself.

Then Aisling smelled him. Wet leaves, rain-steeped earth, cypress needles, and smoke.

Aisling's stomach dropped. Her mind emptied as she beheld him, a fireside tale brought to life before her. The past they'd lived together now more dream than reality. Seeing him from afar had been startling enough but so close, held by him, near wrenched Aisling's heart from her chest.

"Ssshh," Lir whispered against her ear, his breath hot against her skin. Aisling could've rolled her eyes back at the pure pleasure of it. The sound of his voice, thick and rough, thrumming through her core.

A Sidhe sentinel passed by then, gaze focused ahead and uninterested in the shadowy alcove Lir had drawn them both into.

"You've gathered suspicion traversing the castle alone," Lir said once they were out of ear shot.

Aisling wrenched herself free from his grip, turning to face him. But even as she made to build the distance between them, Lir brought her closer, keeping her in the shadows.

Aisling's heart hammered against her chest. Unable to swallow, to blink for the blinding light of his verdant gaze studying her. No memory, no dream, no vision, did the fae king justice. Lir was otherworldly defined, the dark hue of his windswept hair dyed by hands of midnight. The magic aura of him, blending seamlessly with her own and defrosting the cold that gripped her *draiocht*, morsel by morsel. As violently lovely as he was elegant and wild. His touch burning through Aisling's flesh.

"You can't be here—*I* shouldn't be here," Aisling whispered, her breathing uneven. "If anyone discovers we've spoken, much less—"

"Much less what, *ellwyn*?" He grinned, a beam capable of unraveling Aisling where she stood, forgoing reason in favor of whatever pleasure the glint in his eyes promised. The memory of their kiss at the arena heating the air between them. And the fear he'd ask for another, more frightening to Aisling than any other beast.

"Why do you call me that?"

"*Ellwyn*?"

Aisling nodded.

"After we reach Lofgren's Rise, return with me to Annwyn and I'll show you."

Aisling bristled, shaking her head.

"You're risking everything! Fionn will dissolve the test and you'll have forfeited a victory if he discovers you've spoken with me."

Yet despite the tone of her voice, Lir's eyes flashed brilliantly, his smile descending into something far more wolfish.

"So, you want me to win. Perhaps I already have then."

Aisling bristled.

"You're the key to my prison and no more."

"All I'm hearing is that I'm your salvation, *ellwyn*."

"Once I've escaped Oighir, I continue on my own, lest you smite my chances of discovering the answers I need."

Lir's attention darted to the right, something catching his eye.

Without hesitation, Lir pulled Aisling against him once more, sinking further into the shadows. A group of more sentinels rushed past, their armor clinking together as they shouted to one another in Rún.

Lir pressed his hands flat against her abdomen, curling his fingers into the fabric of her dress the tighter he held her.

"Don't move," he said against her ear. Aisling heated, her heart in her throat even as seven or so boars gathered just outside their alcove. They babbled back and forth in Rún, but by the tone and cadence of their voices, Aisling knew they were arguing over which direction she'd wandered.

"Fionn asked them to trail you back to your quarters," Lir translated as quiet as a wolf in the wood. Aisling's body moved of its own accord tilting toward the deep curve of the fae king's voice. Lir stiffened in surprise, swiftly recovering and pulling her closer still.

The boars squabbled back and forth until one paused, doing a double take at their shadowy alcove.

"Hold your breath, *ellwyn*," Lir commanded. Aisling hesitated before the boar stalked a pace closer, eyes narrowing in suspicion. Then the pressure of the air shifted, Aisling's ears popped, and magic filled the air.

The boar drew his mace, moving closer still. So, Aisling held her breath as the boar met her eyes. There was a moment of pause, a stilling of everything as Lir's arms hardened around her, the firm edge of his chest scarcely rising or falling so as not to be discovered. A foil to the thudding of Aisling's heart, the heating of her flesh, or the murder of silver-eyed ravens taking flight in her stomach. Until, at last, the boar withdrew, turning back to his partner.

"*There's no one*," he said.

Lir had glamoured them. What the boar saw, Aisling knew not. Only that Lir had somehow cloaked their presence.

And even after they'd passed, Lir continued stepping

back, drawing them both into a new room entirely. A chamber clouded in steam till Aisling could scarcely see her own hand raised before her. They were in a public bathing chamber, snug against a wall decorated in polished pebbles, lest they fall into the baths to their left. The taste of winter-berry soaps dappled her tongue.

"What are you doing?!" she asked, trying to look past Lir and further into the bathing chamber. It was futile. The steam was a dense veil, obscuring any and all vision.

"I needed to see you," he said, releasing her and dipping his head to look into her eyes.

"You'll see me this evening at the second test."

His eyes narrowed, searching Aisling for something. The intensity of his eyes, his undiluted attention, curling her toes.

"It isn't enough. The thread that binds us needs more. Will always need more. My *draiocht* responds to your own, Aisling."

"That's what this is about? Power?"

"What else is there?"

Aisling ground her teeth, pushing Lir back. He gave in to her touch, as though weak to it. And yet, he drove her mad, speaking words that magicked her heart, only to stake it with his true intentions. The fae king wasn't capable of whatever he made Aisling feel. Despite everything Aisling had misunderstood, ignored, was lied to about, the fae king was still the nightmare muse of blood-soaked legends. The villain she was taught to fear all her life. His only role in Aisling's life would only ever be a pursuit of strength and might.

Aisling bit down the darkening of her heart, pulling from her skirts the parchment she'd stolen from Fionn's chamber.

"Here," she said, offering it to Lir. "For tonight's test."

Her aid, offered in the name of escape and nothing more. *Nothing more*, she repeated to herself.

Lir accepted the paper, unfolding it and reading its contents.

"Where did you find this?" he asked, considering her with a combination of confusion and amazement.

"In Fionn's chamber."

Immediately, whatever joy the contents had aroused in him burnt to a crisp the moment Aisling spoke the words.

"He gave it to you?"

Aisling tore her eyes away. "How I obtained it isn't important, only that you have it now."

Yet Lir's suspicion was growing, evolving into anger and, if Aisling was seeing correctly, potent jealousy. Lir wasn't accustomed to not having what he wanted.

"It's important to me."

"Whatever happens between Fionn and I hardly affects whatever bond you and I bear—or the power you wish to reap from it." Aisling's words were bitterer than she'd anticipated, cursing the emotion in her voice.

Lir's expression narrowed, his jaw sharpening the harder he ground it. And when his eyes drifted to the collar at Aisling's throat, he paused, the world stilling in anticipation of his rage.

"What happened between the two of you?"

"We kissed," Aisling said, both syllables bleeding the steam that circled the chamber till Aisling smelled violence, then saw it in Lir's eyes. A glint of blood rage and white fury that frightened Aisling even now. Sent chills racing down her spine. "A currency you're familiar with exchanging."

"You feel something for the son of Winter?"

"You mean your brother? One you deigned to mention much less any other information?"

Aisling wasn't certain why this felt like a betrayal. Lir had never divulged Fionn was his brother, but the topic had never arisen and so he'd never bore the opportunity. Yet, Lir didn't owe Aisling anything other than their union and the treaty it symbolized. One he betrayed as a result of Danu's visions. And no kiss, or even two, could change that.

Lir focused. "That wasn't an answer."

"Are you jealous?" Aisling smiled despite herself, moving closer to him.

"Do you want me to be?" he asked.

Aisling squinted, chest to chest with the fae king. Ignoring the dipping of her stomach, the tilting of the world as they shared one another's breath. "Now who isn't answering?"

Lir's attention shot to Aisling's mouth. His chest rising and falling a pace quicker the longer his attention lingered.

"We don't have time for this," Aisling said, aware of the shouting of the guards outside the baths and then the alcove. If anyone found them, they'd both be doomed, and the boars earlier had been a close enough call.

Aisling pushed past Lir. "You can explain everything to me another time. When we have it. Right now, every second you're near to me, is a second we risk the entire test."

Lir followed her with his eyes.

"Win or lose," he said, just before she turned the corner. "Fionn has sealed his own death."

CHAPTER XXI

LIR

Poison was sweet.

"The first taste blesses the tongue and the second, curses it." Filverel read over the parchment, passing it to Galad to see for himself.

Bláth.

Aitil.

Kalfak.

Recta.

Neantóg.

Nimhe.

Fola.

"Six of these are most likely poison while only one is harmless. My guess is *Nimhe*. Identify that one from whatever spread Fionn offers, and the second victory is yours."

Lir reclined on his bed, sorting through the fury in his heart. He hated the way Aisling inspired such rage within him. Burned his blood with her spells without ever needing to summon her *draiocht*.

"Are we certain we can trust this list?" Peitho asked, braiding her hair by Lir's chamber window.

"Aisling wants to escape Oighir more than anyone. Fionn delays her voyage to Lofgren's Rise every breath he imprisons her here," Gilrel said.

"She could burn down this castle if she wished," Peitho argued. "Yet she hasn't. Perhaps her loyalties have shifted."

Lir wrenched his eyes shut. He'd traveled as quickly as possible, blazed through the realm to find Aisling before she forgot him or betrayed him once more. And yet, perhaps he wasn't quick enough—the thought daggering his chest and breeding new rage.

"Her loyalties may have changed," Filverel added. "But she couldn't burn down Oighir. In time, it's possible, but for now, I suspect her magic is dulled by Fionn's own."

At those words, Lir cocked his head to his advisor. He'd wondered the same, questioned why Aisling hadn't used her *draiocht* before. Until he realized Aisling wasn't aware her power was more formidable while in Lir's presence. Together, their *draiocht* inspired the other's; a result of being *caera* or Danu's prophecies, Lir wasn't certain. Only that together, they were enough to bring the world to its knees till kingdom come.

"Enough speculation," Lir said, unfurling to his feet. "We allot the queen of Annwyn the benefit of the doubt until she's proven otherwise. As we would any other subject of Annwyn."

They exchanged glances.

Peitho cleared her throat, arching a brow knowingly.

"How did she say she obtained this parchment anyways?"

Lir's entire body tensed and the vines he'd grown in his rage crept down the walls with renewed vengeance.

"Tonight, I'll win the second test. And tomorrow morning, after the third test, Aisling will be one of us once more."

Lir stalked from the room without another word, his knights staring after him.

Lir enjoyed an audience.

And today, the crowd was larger than when he'd slayed the Ellén Trechend. A sea of Sidhe from Oighir crowding into Fionn's colossal throne room whether they be birds pressed against the vaulted ceilings, perched on pillars; or Sidhe craning for a glance at Lir and the table set before him. Even Aisling's brothers, the Tilrish princes and their new *Faerak* friend, stood amidst the hordes, watching.

"Ignore the onlookers and focus on the task at hand," Filverel said, eyeing the table himself.

"What fun is a victory if others aren't around to bask in my glory?"

Filverel exhaled. "Concentrate, Lir. Lest this hunt for your *caera* end in a bloodbath."

"I never assumed it would end any other way."

Filverel snorted, starting toward Galad and Peitho standing in the periphery. He paused.

"Where's Gilrel?" Filverel asked.

Lir searched the crowds for the pine marten. She was nowhere to be found. Not amidst the crush of spectators, atop the rafters, nor among his own kind.

Just then, Fionn walked into the chamber, escorted by Greum, Frigg, and Aisling at his side.

The sight of Aisling was always enough to steal the breath from Lir's lungs and today was no different.

Her cloak draped over her head and swept the floors. Lir did his best to refocus his attention, but it was futile, her violet eyes meeting his own and stirring something feral inside. So, Lir couldn't help the trajectory of his attention as it drifted to Aisling's arm linked in Fionn's own. A shadow taking root inside him at the sight of it, inspiring the doubts his knights had spoken earlier.

Aisling and Fionn stood before two thrones, glaring out at Oighir's court before taking their seats. The vision of them atop the dais together, enough to rip apart any guises Lir had managed since arriving in Fjallnorr.

Perhaps Filverel and Peitho were right, he thought to himself. Both dread and violence strangled his every thought, damning himself for the twisting of his core regardless and the pleasure her dagger elicited each time it struck him in the heart.

But just before Aisling bent to take her seat, she removed her cloak.

She wore an emerald gown. The hue of Annwyn's forests personified in the rich silk that spilled down her body, pinned at her curves by viridescent beetles Lir found he envied. Insects that tied her braids at the end, interspersed between loose, wild waves in Annwyn fashion. The folds of her gown lengthening, moving, shifting like flora come spring.

Lir cleared his throat.

This was a declaration of her loyalty. A glimmer of hope written in the fabric of her gown; Aisling hadn't strayed nor aligned herself with Fionn even if hers and Lir's motivations were at odds. An end to Lir's knights' speculations.

But the glory that was Aisling was rapidly eclipsed by Fionn's presence. The ice crawling up Lir's boots at the son of Winter's audience.

Lir hardened, shaking his head as though it could shake out the image of her. To forget Aisling was in the same room. And yet, he knew before he'd tried, the effort was futile.

"Before you is a collection of seven tinctures made with the herbs local to the seven continents," Greum said. "The Isles of Rinn Dúin, Centar, Bethel, Lilina, Fjallnorr, Shuilan, and Rolum. Each gifted by the twelve fae sovereigns before the Wild Hunt."

A dwarven hare stepped down the dais with a tray in hand. Atop it were the seven tinctures Greum spoke of, nimbly set before Lir on the table.

"For the second test, the king of the greenwood is to dip the tip of an ivory arrow in only one tincture. Six are poison save for one. He must shoot his target, and should the target survive, Lir proceeds to the third and final test. Should the target die an instant death, he loses."

"Easy enough," Lir said as another dwarven hare laid both a single reed and bow before him. Lir tested the weight of both, studying the frozen tip of the arrow, its shaft slick and slender, and its fletching made of owl feathers cut to perfection. The bow was a longbow, carved from the trunks of felled or rotted junipers. The soul of the tree whittled into the longbow still beating like a heart without a body, drumming through Lir's fingers and caressing his spirit.

All of Annwyn's knights were trained with a variety of weaponry before they came of age. Only then would they select their preferred weapon. A blade bound to their soul and eventually used to determine the bond of their *caera*. So, while Lir was always destined to choose the axes gifted to Bres by both the Forge and the gods, he'd trained with weapons of all make and size before. Including the longbow.

"Then let's begin," Fionn said with a devious smile. The son of Winter snapped his fingers and six or so Sidhe sentinels escorted a shackled creature into the room.

Aisling stood from her chair. She saw past the folds of spectators from her seat atop the dais. But it wasn't until the creature emerged from the crush that Lir gleaned who or what it was with his own eyes.

Gilrel, head bowed and ashamed, stopped before the staircase of the dais. A wolf on either side.

"Your target," Fionn said, every syllable stifling laughter.

Lir scowled. If he guessed the wrong tincture, not only would it mean losing Aisling to Fionn, but it would also ensure Gilrel's death. A poison arrow was fatal. Especially for a creature as small as the pine marten.

"Let's begin, shall we?" And at the wave of Fionn's hands, the wolves left Gilrel alone, Lir's target. Lir rolled back his shoulders, channeling his frustration into the task at hand.

The seven bottles glittered, singing a different melody desperate to appeal to Lir's ears.

Lir unstoppered the emerald brew and brought it to his nose, lured by its color. The room grew silent, all eyes fixed on the Sidhe king as he considered the first tincture. Aisling, still standing, was lowered to her seat by the gentle press of Fionn's hand on her arm. The sight of his brother touching her seizing Lir's chest in a shadowed grip.

Lir blinked, doing his best to ignore his temper and failing. Grisly thoughts clawing at the walls of his mind despite needing to concentrate on the test.

Initially, the emerald bottle smelled of a paste left behind by silk slugs and harvested to soothe wing wounds. But the scent shifted, transforming into something far sweeter. More like custard and stewed peaches.

Poison was sweet, Lir reminded himself.

Lir set the bottle down and tried three more.

The crimson tincture smelled of yule pudding, the white tincture of sugared teas, and the blue of burning nettle boiled in a pot of maple sap. All sickeningly sweet and overwhelming to the senses.

So, Lir's hand drifted to both the violet and clear tincture.

The violet bottle reminded Lir of dusk. Of the forest earth cooling come evening, heralded by the lavender haze of an approaching night. The clear bottle was far more grotesque, the same consistency as troll saliva and equally as nauseating in smell. Lir's brow furrowed. Neither smelled particularly sweet and to decide beyond doubt which was the sweeter of the two would mean tasting both. A costly gamble.

Nevertheless, Lir needed to make a choice. One was Nimhe, the other poison.

He smelled them both several times, a bottle in each hand. His audience stood still, studying his expression. The room so quiet, one could hear a snowflake's descent.

Lir's eyes wandered, inevitably finding Aisling's own.

His throat grew thick.

She held his gaze, violet eyes sinking their fangs into his heart. The shade of heartbreak, of venomous kisses. Of dreams and visions.

Lir took his reed and dipped its tip into the violet brew.

It glistered brilliantly, dripping as Lir nocked the arrow and pulled back the string.

He closed one eye.

Gilrel's whiskers twitched. She nodded once at Lir before wrenching her eyes shut. A gesture of trust, of faith in Lir's aim. Yet, the last thing Lir was concerned with was his aim. It was only the tincture at the tip of his reed that bred doubt.

Lir inhaled. Steadied the violent beating of his heart and soothed his nerves. Imitating the brush of a woodland wind in his lungs: slow and patient. Eyes wandering to Fionn.

He could strike his brother now. And in that case, he'd pray he'd chosen the wrong tincture. That poison saturated his arrow and slipped into Fionn's heart. Yet an arrow to the heart was a death far from slaking Lir's thirst for violence after the kiss Fionn shared with Aisling.

A vein snaked around Lir's neck.

Fionn's assassination would mean a bloodbath whilst in Oighir's den. Nevertheless, Lir couldn't help weighing the satisfaction of his brother's demise with the rational choice. The one Filverel hoped for, burning through Lir's back with his oppressive stare. Two badgers stood at each entrance to the hall, foxes crouched in the rafters, prepared to let their arrows fly, and several wolves stalked through the folds of Sidhe, eager to wet their fangs. Nevertheless, if Lir chose violence over reason, an escape was still possible so long as he reached Aisling the moment the reed sunk into Fionn's chest. And if he didn't... Lir's gaze slipped to the collar gripping Aisling's throat.

Lir exhaled, a breath that rattled through the leaves, through the moss-covered earth, through the warm rivers south of here.

The string released from Lir's fingertips and the arrow shot forth.

It dove like a sparrow, nailing Gilrel in the shoulder.

The pine marten gritted her teeth, taking the blow valiantly. Swallowing the agony. The sight of his knight bracing against a pain he'd inflicted deepened Lir's hatred for Fionn.

The room hushed, all eyes focused on the pine marten. Aisling sat on the edge of her seat, nails digging into the arms of her chair as the anticipation built. Gilrel either wounded or poisoned.

Gilrel swayed on her paws, sorting through the pain. Till at last, she straightened, swallowed, and stood tall.

Alive.

A second victory.

CHAPTER XXII

AISLING

Goldenrod glories tangled themselves in Aisling's hair, curling around her face, her throat, her arms, traveling beneath the sheets of her bed and hugging her body. Gently, mischievously lingering where her bare flesh touched the midnight breeze.

Aisling opened her eyes, springing awake before she was pressed against her bed, a hand covering her mouth and an axe to her throat.

"Shh," Lir said, leaning over and pinning her. "The bear is just outside those mirrors."

Aisling squirmed as the flowers grew larger, gripping her curves. She inhaled sharply, meeting Lir's eyes fully for the first time. They shone with the same reflective sheen as the bloodthirsty, skulking beneath the judgment of the moon.

"I want to take you somewhere," he purred.

Gradually, both he and the goldenrods released her.

"How did you get in here?" Aisling jolted upright.

"I slipped through a mirror."

"Must you be so reckless? You threaten everything by visiting me." Aisling stood from her bed.

A chemise sewn by brownies spilled around her ankles and onto the moonstone floors the moment she rose to her feet. Detailed with floral lace and dappled in pinprick small crystals like tears, it hugged her body before unraveling from her hips in silky waves that made endless her legs. Near translucent and shimmering with the wet sheen of sleet.

Lir's eyes smoldered, seemingly forcing himself to meet her gaze.

"I should visit you more often at this hour."

The tops of Aisling's ears burned crimson, yet she refused to cover herself—an omission Lir affected her. One she wasn't quick to surrender despite the fluttering inside her chest.

"You should be more cautious."

"It's more fun this way." He smiled, a rogue of shadows already backing toward the window, his hand outstretched. Slender fingers coiled in fae designs Aisling had memorized what felt like a lifetime ago. His shirt was unlaced and rolled up to his elbows, while his axes remained strapped against his back. Hair damp and curling around his ears.

Aisling hesitated for only a moment, finally placing her hand in his, skin burning from a magic entirely different from her own. The taste of something forbidden staining her tongue and whetting her appetite.

He moved through a mirror, gently pulling Aisling after him. They both plunged through the passage, finding themselves atop one of Oighir's rooftops.

Fjallnorr's breath was cruel and unforgiving, biting Aisling's skin and freezing her veins. More formidable than it'd been within the embrace of the woodland or aboard the *Starling*.

Lir glanced at her sidelong, pausing at the trembling of her shoulders. If Aisling were mortal, the weather would've been intolerable, but now, her fae blood burned from within, enough to keep her alive. Still the cold bit, taking advantage of what mortal flesh still remained.

Lir's fingers twitched at his sides and a cloak of giant orchid petals bloomed, draping around Aisling's shoulders and warming her instantly. The inside of the petals velvet smooth and soft.

Aisling avoided Lir's eyes, adjusting the petals instead, as she followed him onward.

Atop Castle Oighir, it felt as though they were balancing on the tip of a summit, dancing with the wind. Their hair floating as though submerged in water, breathed to life by the dark gale.

"If it were possible, Oighir seems even larger from here," Aisling said, avoiding Lir's eyes even as they studied her in her periphery.

Lir didn't respond.

Instead, he led her from rooftop to rooftop, leaping from one to the other, using the statues of roaring bears to prevent a plummet toward an inevitable death below. Aisling's stomach fluttered, her knees weak, as she glared at the drop. The ice slick and ruthless beneath her slippers.

So, Lir grew tufts of grass and rubbery buds with each of his footsteps, melting the snow lying beneath to assist Aisling and prevent her from slipping.

They traversed a labyrinth of slumbering turrets, towers, flying buttresses, and bridges, slanted roofs, and statues atop Oighir's glacial walls, twinkling beneath a blanket of stars.

Lir leapt atop one of the castle's various gabled roofs, catching Aisling's waist as she jumped behind him. Hands lingering even as he found a place to rest, leaning his back against a bell-tower and glaring down at the world far below. Arms crossed.

Monk's moss, roaming roses, and ivy spread from the fae king and grew new life atop the castle despite winter's oppressive chill. As though the forest were a droplet, dripped by the Forge where the fae king stood and rippled outward.

Aisling approached, feeling the same as the first night she'd met him. As though she were running straight for the edge of a crag, bracing for the inevitable plummet. The cord between them straightening, pulling, aching with either pain or pleasure. Aisling could no longer tell the difference.

"From the top of Annwyn's eldest ash, one can collect the stars from the night sky. Or, at the least, that's how it felt as a child when I'd first learned to fly and Crann Bethadh's tallest branch was the furthest I'd dare venture."

Aisling considered the realm of jewels overhead. As though thousands of spiders had spun their webs with threads of moonlight, dappled in gems of dew and smiling at all those who dared to change their stars.

"I can't imagine you afraid of anything, even as a child."

"Fear is natural, Aisling. It's the wisdom of a fox torn between fleeing from the hunter or leaping from the brambles for the hare."

Aisling breathed a laugh. "Is this the wisdom that compelled you to betray the peace our union symbolized? To pursue the curse breaker? To prevent Danu from ever usurping you, dare as she might?"

Lir faced her. His attention spellbinding. Making wild her heart till she prayed he couldn't glean its thrashing. The edge of his lips and the tips of his fangs mesmerizing.

"So Fionn spilled more than just his motivations. Or his affections."

"Aye, your brother made certain he tore apart any and all

veils that might lead me back to you. A work the Lady admired, considering she too warns me to keep my distance from you."

Lir's eyes glittered.

"You wouldn't be so attracted to me if I were more transparent, *ellwyn*."

Fire seeped beneath Aisling's cheeks, so she bit her tongue, resisting the sort of cunning warfare Aisling was aware the fae king preferred—knew knocked her off balance.

"I despise you," she said, eyes prickling with heat. The emotion bubbling to the surface and muddling her voice now that they were at long last alone, hidden, safe, and outside the realm of dreams for the first time since she'd run from him.

"Never," she continued, "never will you or any other leave me to rot in the dark again."

Lir shifted, adopting the lethal poise that struck gods' fear in all that lived and breathed.

"And yet," he replied, his voice deepening, "if you truly despised me, right now you'd be by my brother's side or searching for the princeling. Instead, you're here with me." He stepped closer, the air no longer cold but stiflingly hot. "The dark, *ellwyn*, is magic incarnate. When the beasts of the feywild are most alive. A realm ruled by desire and crowned by feral indulgence. The dark is whole, rich, all-encompassing. The dark is *feared*. You and I weren't made for the light, *ellwyn*. You were left to rot perhaps but seized the shadows and wore them like a hide on your back until you became the feared, and now, the dark is yours to rule. *Ours* to rule."

Aisling shook her head, the fists at her sides growing numb with cold, or something else, she wasn't certain.

"You wish to own me."

Lir scoffed as though the prospect was ridiculous. "I wish for you to be *mine*. The two are very different."

"You think I'm not aware your plans are made in the same image as your brother's? That you intend to use me to not only obtain the curse breaker but to end all and any threats against your sovereignship? I am not a tool nor a weapon nor an ill-omen. I am my own."

Lir appraised her, silent before at last speaking.

"Is that what you think? That I believe you a tool?"

"Give me another reason for the absence of your fury?! Why neither you nor your knights have placed my head on a pike for treason? For fleeing from their king? Why else would you come for me when even my túath never did?"

Lir's expression twisted, his anger at last seeping through.

"You wouldn't survive my fury," he said, moving closer till their chests were but a breath from touching. Till Aisling tilted her head entirely back, glaring up and into his eyes.

The forest he'd grown atop the cathedral rose and spread with increased need.

"So where is my wisdom, fae king? And why do I no longer fear you?"

"You should."

Lir pressed his hands against the wall on either side of her. She could see the rise and fall of his chest, the movement of his throat as he swallowed, and feel the heat of his breath. Roses and five-pointed leaves grew around the wall, creeping into her hair and around her throat. Her arms, her waist, doing what Aisling—just for a moment, a sinful heartbeat—wished Lir did with his hands. Binding her to the wall possessively, as though his prey might flee should he blink.

Aisling closed her eyes, doing her best to banish his spells.

Stay away from the Sidhe king, Aisling.

"You and I were forged for one another," he said, a breathless whisper scalding her cheeks. "When together, our *draiocht* grows, spills over the brim of the goblet others sanction to limit our power. To control us." He lowered one hand, knotting his fingers through Aisling's. "But when apart, we grow weak, half of the soul we were forged to become."

"*A love unmatched, a reckless ruinous love capable of destroying kingdoms and plaguing the earth. A harbinger of great upheaval and certain death.*" Danu's words at the Isle of Mirrors slithered into Aisling's mind and around her heart.

His vines gripped her more tightly.

"Try summoning your flames," he said.

"I cannot. Fionn's magic dulls my own and I'm not yet powerful enough to withstand it."

"You're as powerful as you believe yourself to be, Aisling. Whether you were locked inside an iron fortress, traded to the Sidhe, or captured by Fionn, you have always been powerful enough. You only need want it enough."

A stone grew in Aisling's throat, impossible to swallow.

"I want it more than anything."

"Then summon your *draiocht*."

Lir lifted their hands, fingers still laced, and parted them. His palm a few inches from her own.

Aisling focused.

In the caverns of her *draiocht*, she searched for that familiar beast. To her surprise it moved, slithered to its threshold and glared up at her. Ice cracking and splintering as it defrosted the sleep Fionn had witched inside her. Comforted by the proximity of Lir's own *draiocht*, the thread between them braiding tightly. Humming alive.

His magic was like a wolf, hungry and snarling, excited by the scent of her own. Nuzzling her fury awake and burning through the ice.

So, Aisling summoned it.

Burn, she commanded.

The *draiocht* rose, bursting upwards and into her lungs. Pain was the first taste and then euphoria. The coursing, the purling, the surge of magic through one's bones as it crackled and brightened, spilling over and ready to be brandished like a blade.

A soft, radiant fire billowed around her hand. Small, just more than a match's heat, but it was more than she'd been capable of before either the fear gorta or since stepping foot in Oighir. Illuminating Lir's hand, still poised before her own, in violet light. His *draiocht* tangling itself through her own, strengthening her fires by his mere proximity.

Aisling braced herself for the pain. For the agony of her flesh burning against her fires. But it never came. Her hands were whole. Unbloodied and unmarred by her own magic.

Aisling exhaled, in awe her skin no longer burned.

Still, Fionn's collar around her throat squeezed, urging Aisling to stifle her magic lest it truly choke her. A reminder Aisling was still imprisoned by Fionn in Oighir lest Lir win his tests. And by the flaring of Lir's expression, Aisling knew he saw the collar squeeze too. His temper swiftly quelled by Aisling's relieved laugh that she'd been able to summon fire at all without blistering or burning. Because of him.

Aisling swallowed. The intimacy of their *draiocht* humming, vibrating, growing together, toe curling.

Fionn was wrong. It wasn't Seelie, Unseelie, or even Forge territory that renewed Aisling's *draiocht* and made her strong. It was Lir. Together, their power mutually awakened, but when apart, their magic wilted. Fate cackled, spinning their thread and tightening the noose. Bound by the Forge to either create or destroy. Either way, magnificent together.

"Why is it like this?" Aisling asked, her voice uneven.

"I don't know," Lir said. "There are no legends nor myths that chronicle a similar pairing. I felt this... *bond*," he said, brows knotting as though dissatisfied with that title, "the night of our union when you touched my axes for the first time. The feeling grew over our time together, then wreaked havoc on my soul when you disappeared." He paused again before continuing. "When I thought you died and the bond severed... my *draiocht* forever changed."

He gazed down at her, sage eyes purpled by her fires.

Aisling shivered.

"Do you know what a true binding is?" Lir asked, every word slow, as though he were sifting through his mind for a coherent thought.

"The union of two *caeras*," Aisling replied breathlessly.

"No, not a binding. A *true* binding."

Fionn had been the first to speak its name. But at the time, Aisling had assumed he'd been referencing a marriage, only possible between two souls chosen by the Forge to be tethered for eternity.

"Two souls can truly bind without being *caeras*. A way of knotting oneself with another and carving it into the Lady's constellations. But for two *caeras* to *truly* bind..." Lir exhaled against her neck, unable to find the words given the moment. The heat of his breath spine-chilling.

"At the *Snaidhm*," he continued at last, "we were intended to be celebrating our true binding."

Aisling paused. "A consummation."

Lir met Aisling's gaze.

Aisling's eyes darted back and forth, processing the fae king's words, desperately collecting the thoughts whirring inside her mind. Her cheeks flushed and hot, and her tongue thick inside her mouth.

"For whatever reason the gods intend, our *draiocht* is

weak when apart and powerful together. And if we truly bind... unstoppable."

"It isn't the same for other *caera*? When they truly bind?" Aisling asked.

"No," he said. "A true binding would embolden our magic beyond what this realm or the next has ever witnessed. We'd be limitless, Aisling."

Limitless.

Adrenaline drummed inside Aisling's chest.

"Is this a confession of your love, barbarian lord?" Aisling asked, grasping at her venom but sounding flustered instead.

"Who said anything about love?" Lir said, and against Aisling's own volition her heart splintered. She didn't love Lir—no, she couldn't love him. He was no longer her enemy by blood but by power. Both she and Lir racing for dominion whether it be at Lofgren's Rise or elsewhere. But with these new words, with Lir's proposal of a true binding, a fork in the road was written in the stars: to either truly bind with Lir or battle him for an eternity.

Aisling's heart burned with hate for him, desperately, manically, bound to his. Because he left her in the dark, because he hunted her, because he risked everything Aisling wanted for his own motives, and now, had the nerve to try and align with her if it meant his own success. To use her. And still, her heart translated his flippancy for any affection between them as betrayal.

Aisling lit like a broken star, violet, and pulsing. Shriveling Lir's shackles of vines to ash at her feet. The collar at Aisling's neck strangling her till it ringed her neck with red.

Lir stepped back, studying her expression. Her fires forcing a distance between them. A fleck of hurt flashing across Lir's face and disappearing before Aisling knew if it was real or her imagination. His nostrils flaring at the bruising already forming around her throat thanks to Fionn's collar.

"Win this last test for me," Aisling said. "Free us from Oighir and then we'll venture our separate ways to Lofgren's Rise. And should we both survive? Only then would I consider a true binding for the benefit of emboldening my might alone."

Lir smiled, but it was joyless and wicked. Weaving a bloody rose around her hand till she held it between her fingers.

"I have no intention of ever letting you go again, *ellwyn*."

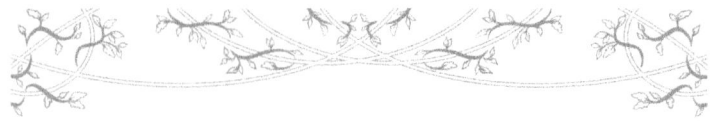

CHAPTER XXIII

DAGFIN

Dagfin wasn't familiar with Aos Sí tribes in either size or gathering. Yet, it appeared as if all Oighir stood before Fionn's castle holding their breath. Watching as Fionn and Lir stood on either side of a glass bridge connecting Oighir to its surrounding kingdom of ice before dissolving into the feywilds. A treacherous drop beneath, filled by a river of fog.

The final test had yet to be announced. This was the only challenge during which Lir was allowed to wield his magic. The finality to the son of Winter's game.

"Whether or not the opportunity presents itself, we leave tonight," Starn said. Killian, Iarbonel, Fergus, and a mostly recovered Annind nodded their heads in agreement. All save for Dagfin, too focused on Aisling standing at the front of Castle Oighir to form a coherent thought. Greum and Frigg paced behind Aisling. A great mirror looming over her: the threshold to Oighir's keep, reflecting the spectacle.

She was statuesque, clad in a sage gown and wrapped in the Roktan cloak he'd gifted her aboard the *Starling*. How she'd managed to preserve it, he knew not. Only that it lit a fire in his heart where even the Ocras couldn't.

"Ready, brother?" Fionn asked, as their audience fell silent with anticipation. "Let's begin and correct an ages-old mistake."

Lir's posture turned lethal, yet to Dagfin's surprise, the fae king drew his twin axes. Prepared to battle the son of Winter for the last test and the conclusion to Fionn's games.

"Not so fast, brother." Fionn quirked a knowing brow. Lir shifted, twirling his axe in his grip as he focused on his brother.

"Bring me Aisling," Fionn said, and at his command, Greum and Frigg nudged Aisling toward the son of Winter. Aisling didn't protest, the collar of ice glittering more brightly around her throat as though it anticipated the conclusion to the deal as much as those around it.

Now it was Dagfin's turn to pause, a pit forming in his stomach at the sight of Aisling moving toward the bridge of glass and into the crossfire.

AISLING

Aisling held her chin high—even as she passed Lir, not daring a glance in his direction despite the way his eyes studied her, counting every step that led her away from him and to Fionn at the other end of the bridge.

Fionn offered a hand to Aisling. Forearms chiming with bracelets and cuffs as Aisling placed her hand in his own and he pulled her to his side.

Lir's expression dimmed at her and Fionn's proximity, his axes twirling more quickly, more sharply between his fingers.

"The third and final test is a joust," Fionn announced. The audience rustled, whispering back and forth.

"And my opponent?" Lir asked.

Fionn stifled a chuckle, moving behind Aisling. She stiffened, skin crawling the moment his fingers grazed her shoulders and wet her gown with frost.

"Your only opponent is yourself. Your objective: to destroy my heart of ice with the tip of your joust."

Lir nodded his head. "Simple enough."

Fionn smirked. "I hope you consider this second portion just as simple." Fionn waved a hand in front of Aisling, pressing a finger between Aisling's breasts. Aisling inhaled sharply, biting down her protests as the crystal collar around her neck gripped, reacting to the flicker of *draiocht* heating alongside her anger, her outrage. Lir stepped forward, axes stilling. The veins in his forearms, in his neck, growing bolder as his eyes flicked between Fionn's hand and the collar at her throat, weighing a decision.

"Hold your ground, brother," Fionn scolded, jagged ice creeping around Aisling's torso in his anger.

At the son of Winter's touch, an ice-carved heart grew from Aisling's chest, floating just in front of her true heart. If Aisling moved, it followed, hovering a breath before her yet magicked to her being all the same.

Dread seeped beneath Aisling's bones, a new chill taking root. And by the expression on Lir's face, horror gripped him as well, swiftly evolving into undiluted anger.

"You wish for me to kill her?" Lir growled, the rumble of his voice, inspiring newfound terror in every surrounding spectator.

"The quicker your mount's gait, the fainter the prick to destroy the ice heart, brother. Break the heart and you win. Whether or not you kill your *caera* in the process, well, that's another story entirely. Of course, if you've no faith in your-self that you can win and still have a breathing bride, surren-dering is always an option." Fionn leaned closer to Aisling, kissing the backs of her ears till jewels dripped from her lobes, sprouted between her braids, and her tangled tresses. A crown of ice speared from her head like the rays of a frost-bitten sun, transforming Aisling into a queen of Oighir. The queen she'd become if left to rot here for all eternity should Lir fail the tests, imprisoned as Fionn's prize. The other alter-native, death, whether Lir succeeded or not. This, consid-ering destroying the ice heart without also impaling Aisling was impossible.

Aisling should've anticipated this; Fionn would ensure it was impossible for Lir to win. If Fionn couldn't have Aisling and the power she promised, no one could.

Aisling bit down on her tongue till she tasted blood, clenching and unclenching her fists at her sides.

"So, what say you? Will you surrender or accept the third and final test?" Fionn continued, straightening.

Lir's nostrils flared, eyes shifting between his brother and Aisling. No doubt weighing the same consequences Aisling had as well. Verdant eyes flashing with woodland tempests the whole of Fjallnorr felt until, at last, Lir sheathed his axes.

"Let's begin," Lir said, calmer than his posture implied.

Aisling couldn't see Fionn's smile from where he stood, but she could feel it tiptoeing across her nerves till her entire body shook with the cold.

An ebony stag was escorted to the bridge, six or so silver wolves nipping at its heels to herd it. It huffed, stomping atop the bridge as Fionn summoned a 'tilt' railing of stone-hard snow along the length of the bridge.

"You'll ride on the left side of my tilt. Aisling will stand at the end of the bridge to the right of said tilt. Destroy the heart with the tip of your joust and Aisling is yours, dead or alive. Fail to do so and Aisling stays here with me. Forever."

Forever.

The word struck Aisling like a punch to the gut, leaving her struggling for breath. And at the faintest sign of her *draiocht*, the collar around her throat squeezed till the edges of her vision blurred black.

Lir tore his eyes from her, shoulders taut as he appraised the stag. He brushed his palm over the beast's muzzle, soothing its restless energy after having been corralled by the wolves. Aisling too could feel its anxiety. Could feel the brush of the fae king's fingertips atop the stag's pelt as though he were stroking her own bare flesh.

"Ready, *mo Lúra*?" Fionn whispered as he guided her to her position atop the bridge.

Aisling pursed her lips, biting down every insult sprouting inside her mind. Words were a consolation for the true punishment the son of Winter would eventually face at Aisling's hands. And when the time came, Aisling wouldn't hold back.

"Don't look so vexed with me, Aisling," Fionn continued.

"Vexed isn't nearly a sufficient description, my Lord. There are far more colorful terms I had in mind."

"Before or after our kiss?"

Aisling stiffened, gently fanning the embers of her anger.

"Have I enchanted you so that a single kiss still weighs heavily on your mind even as you position me for my death?"

"Death?" Fionn feigned outrage. "Who said anything about death?"

"Lir's to break your ice heart, isn't he? The object floating just before my own. To break it would be to break my own."

Fionn laughed. "Surely you know my brother better than that, *mo Lúra*. Or is it coyness that compels you to deny the deathless longing in his eyes each time his eyes gravitate to you? How he bloodies himself failing to resist your natural enchantments? You're his obsession, *mo Lúra*."

Aisling turned away, hiding whatever emotion Fionn's words provoked.

"He hungers for power and nothing more."

"Aye, Lir doesn't know anything else. And so, he'd never let you die, much less kill you. You're the key to his ambitions, and so neither would I for what it's worth. Lir will surrender. He'll choke and the test will be lost."

Aisling blinked. So, this was how Fionn anticipated a win. One laced with humiliation on Lir's part.

"You're hoping Lir will forfeit?"

"I don't hope. I know."

Aisling scowled at Fionn, simmering with heat.

"Then perhaps you've spoken one true statement: I do know Lir better than you." Aisling planted her feet in place, steeling herself atop the bridge. "Lir would rather die than ever surrender."

Fionn made a mocking sound, but Aisling saw the bobbing of his throat and the flash of doubt. For if Fionn had misjudged Lir, he'd lose Aisling too. Aisling, his answer to correcting the history he believed illegitimate. His answer to correcting everything he believed Lir had taken from him. Not to mention, usurping his brother and Danu alike to rule the realm with Aisling at his side.

LIR

Galad handed Lir his lance. A lengthy, translucent spear, settled into a grapper hooked to his right pauldron with a belt. The stag beneath him stirred, inhaling the smell of the hunter-green needles wrapping around the lance, summoned by Lir's temper.

"I'm guessing any attempts to discourage you from going forward with this would be in vain," Galad said, tightening the saddle buckles. His blade, *Bréachta*, winking from where it hung against his back.

Lir adjusted his grip on the lance. "Your guess would be right."

"You'll kill her, Lir." The emotion in Galad's voice surprised the Sidhe king.

"And what would you have me do?" Lir bore two choices: to either trust himself enough to win this final test against all odds or forsake Aisling to Fionn's whims for the rest of eternity. Both paths risked Aisling's life but at the very least, the first option was within his control. He could end this and win everything: Fionn's test and Aisling's freedom. Or he could lose everything. The latter, unfathomable.

Galad hesitated, opening his mouth to speak but unable to find the words.

"Be quick with it," was all he said, nodding his head before turning to join the others.

Lir swallowed, clearing his throat as Peitho tossed him his antlered helmet.

Lir had jousted on plenty of occasions before but never like this. Never with the stakes being everything or nothing. His body setting flame the moment his eyes connected with Aisling's from across the bridge. Two glittering amethysts amidst a landscape of ivory watching him prepare to stake her through the heart should he make a mistake. Should he commit even the slightest of misjudgments.

She inhaled deeply, finding in herself the resolve Lir had become well acquainted with. The courage she stirred awake when it was time to come face to face with a nightmare. And like most days, that nightmare was Lir himself.

Lir tore his eyes away, unable to look at Aisling for too long. He assessed the weight of the lance in his grip, shifting the shaft till he found the perfect grip.

"On the count of three, you'll ride," Frigg snapped at the stag's hooves. Lir tipped his chin in acknowledgement, ignoring the mad beating of his pulse, the throbbing of his temples, the aching of his chest. Lir couldn't remember the last time he felt this way: immeasurably nervous. Battles, wars, duels, hunts, chases, were commonplace for Lir and hardly made him dizzy, much less twisted his heart. Yet now, Lir struggled to focus, blinking away the image of Aisling as he prepared to race for her.

"*One*," Frigg barked in Rún.

Oighir held its breath.

"*Two.*"

Lir tightened his grip.

"*Three.*"

Lir shot forward, a blur of color as he cut across the bridge. Fionn's ice heart, a radiant light hovering before Aisling.

Fionn stood to the side, beaming from ear to ear even as Lir drove forward, his lance aimed at both the ice heart, and just behind it, Aisling's own.

Lir forced himself not to glance at Aisling. To instead, focus on the tip of his spear, the gait of his mount, the distance between himself and the ice heart. Everything, all of it, unraveling as though Lir were plunging toward the earth, destined to meet his ruin.

The tip of Lir's lance was three or so heartbeats from the

ice heart. His stomach catapulting into his throat the quicker the seconds slipped through his fingers.

I summon the forest, Lir said to his *draiocht* and in response his wolf came snapping from its abyss, conjuring emerald vines, wrapping around Aisling and grappling her to the ground the precise moment the tip of his lance pierced the ice heart. It shattered, driving through and into the space Aisling once stood. Skimming her arm and spraying both Lir and the stag in her blood.

Shards of ice exploded from the impact as Lir leapt off his stag and reached for Aisling, already drowning in his overzealous vines. He tore them off her, ripping every leaf and thorn-ridden vine, unburying her even as they grew alongside the height of his desperation. His hands shaking with adrenaline. The same adrenaline propelling him onward as he ripped his own flora apart till emerald carnage surrounded them, unearthing Aisling at long last. He brought her against him as though she might vanish like the fog. Her blood and tears seeping into his leathers as she gasped for air and still, she wasn't close enough.

Perhaps it was her own adrenaline, but Aisling buried her face in the curve of his neck, startling him. The pounding of her heart against his chest, everything he'd never realized he craved. His *draiocht* brightening feverishly to the hum of her magic.

"Don't think this means I trust you now," she said, her voice ragged. Despite himself, Lir smiled, knowing that despite the humor in her voice, the sentiment was both true and reciprocated.

Lir shut his eyes.

"Never," he said into her ear, "*never* make me do that again."

But the moment, that blessed fragment of relief, evaporated the moment Fionn's clapping erupted behind them. The mass whispers of the surrounding crowd grew into a roar as they beheld Aisling and Lir, both alive. Victors of the third and final test for Aisling's freedom.

The collar around Aisling's neck, shattering.

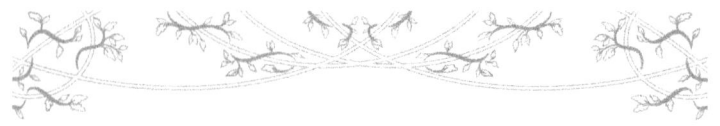

CHAPTER XXIV

AISLING

"How dare you?" Fionn stalked closer, expression warped with earnest outrage.

Aisling and Lir unfurled from their place on the floor of the bridge, gathering themselves once more.

"How dare you enter Oighir and repeat the crimes of your father?" Fionn continued. "You'll be punished for such cheating."

"Cheating?" Lir asked, his expression narrowing in response to Fionn's accusations.

"The rules were simple: destroy the ice heart frozen against Aisling—"

"The ice heart *was* destroyed despite being frozen against Aisling. Magic was allowed in the third and final test, as outlined by you. I've broken no rules."

Fionn seethed, eyes wide and cruel.

"You will pay for this."

"We had a deal, Fionn," Lir said, already drawing both his axes and stepping forward so he stood a shoulder before Aisling.

The crowd fidgeted nervously, whispering like oaks before the tempest.

Even Lir's knights leaned in closer, keen to see what was unfolding.

"Is that what you hoped for?" Lir asked. "A surrender?"

Fionn sneered. "It no longer matters, brother. You're not leaving here with Aisling, deal or not."

Lir grinned but it was wicked, heartless, and inhuman, his fangs flashing with promise.

"You always were a sore loser." Lir swiped his axes and they sparked against one another, ringing while he positioned himself to battle Fionn for escape, for freedom, for Aisling.

"Let's see how the woodland survives the permafrost." Fionn spun his greatsword as he approached Lir.

Aisling shook her head behind them both, gathering herself. She was too angry, too frustrated, too annoyed to stand still and watch. She needed to feel vengeance on her own tongue, needed to exact her revenge by her own means, and watch as Fionn begged for mercy.

Aisling stepped around Lir. The fae king hesitated so Aisling glanced in his direction, hoping he gleaned the flicker of violent need in her eyes.

Fionn blinked, his patience growing thin. His attention shifting between Lir and Aisling.

"This is between my brother and me, Aisling," Fionn said.

"Is it? Because it isn't me you've stolen, imprisoned, and brandished as a prize," Lir said, straightening at Aisling's side.

Fionn, son of Winter, frosted over with rage. White fury conjuring a blizzard that spun around their spectacle—the eye of the storm, the bridge where Lir, Aisling, and Fionn stood.

Lir moved till he stood shoulder to shoulder with Aisling, wrapping an arm around her waist to steady her against Fionn's winds. Greum rose on his hind legs, but even the bear was aware he couldn't intervene lest he contradict his lordship's command. One that was yet to be given. This considering, if Fionn were to request aid from any of his guards or Oighir, it would be his humiliation and not Lir's, as the son of Winter always intended.

"Aisling, think rationally," Fionn pleaded with her, his waist-length hair billowing in clouds of silver. "I don't want to hurt you."

Aisling focused, fingers moving at her sides, prickling with newfound heat.

"Show them how you burn, *ellwyn*." Lir spoke to Aisling and only her. His voice slipping inside her mind despite the rage of the blizzard swirling around them.

"Call upon your wolf," Lir told her. A reference Aisling understood, her eyes lighting in recognition and burning more brightly because of it.

Fionn shifted, baring his fangs as the winds increased their pace.

So, Aisling closed her eyes, hair whipping in the blizzard like a pool of bleeding ink around her head.

And when she opened her eyes once more, she was fire incarnate.

"By the blood of the Forge."

Their audience hissed, drawing blades or fleeing from the spectacle entirely, unsure whether to intervene or allow their lord to duel the flaming queen in their stead.

Aisling inhaled sharply as she summoned more fire. The sound of a spell breaking, a deal ended and met, the sound of a string being snipped, echoing throughout Fjallnorr.

Aisling held out her hand and twisted, inspired by the *draiocht* within.

A giant serpent, shaped by fire, snapping its flame-forged fangs, rose from Fionn's bridge.

Fionn's jaw went slack, eyes wide as he beheld Aisling's power anew. The serpent slithered toward him and raised its great head to peer down at its prey.

"Enough!" Fionn shouted, lifting his sword and spearing it into the floor. Ice exploded, splintering the bridge as it drove for the serpent, winter's teeth rising and jabbing at Aisling's fires. The serpent hissed, drawing back and away from the ice Fionn cast.

"Think rationally, Aisling," Fionn repeated as he approached, sword in hand. "I could give you everything and anything Lir cannot."

Aisling's expression twisted.

"You know not what I want." Aisling waved her fingers and the serpent lunged for Fionn's ice.

Aisling's work was clumsy. New. Yet it served its purpose. Fionn's glacial onslaught burst into shards of glass, forcing every Sidhe surrounding the spectacle to stagger back several steps. His sleeping spells destroyed and burned to ash.

"You crave freedom." Fionn swung his gleaming blade. From its tip, ice streaked for the serpent and wrapped around its neck.

"Power." The ice squeezed Aisling's thrashing serpent and snuffed out her fires, flame by flame. Aisling's knees weakened, the force of the *draiocht* expelling more energy than she'd anticipated.

"And purpose." Fionn swung again, this time, at Aisling's

fires. Her spells dissolved, captured by ice as Fionn defeated the distance between them, blade to Aisling's throat. Lir started forward but Aisling held out her hand, stopping him. A command that corded Lir's neck and locked his jaw. But he listened, awaiting her signal.

"You were meant to be *mine*," Fionn said.

Mine.

The word sounded different than when Lir had said it. From Fionn's lips, it was spoken with a need to *own* her, but Aisling had already been caged behind castle walls before. Had already been owned and given away.

Aisling grabbed the edge of his blade with her bare palm, pushing it from herself.

Fionn's eyes grew wide, glaring between Aisling's eyes and her hand.

Their audience stilled.

Easily. Quickly. The blade cut into her palm. Blood trailed down her arms, dying the sage of her gown crimson.

By now, Aisling was accustomed to pain. To the exact temperature of her blood as it slithered down her hands and arms. The smell of its iron and *draiocht* alike. How the torment seeped into her bones. And she relished it. Not the pain. But that she could endure it.

Aisling's body blazed. A wildfire blown into the shape of a woman. Casting Fionn off lest he burst into flames alongside her.

She watched as he collapsed backward and floundered, still clasping his greatsword, a blade sheathed in her blood. She released its edge, found its haft, and studied its fae forgery.

An exploding star, she carried Fionn's weapon the way Galad and Rian had taught her what felt like a lifetime ago.

Fionn's wintry elegance dissolved entirely, panicked and afraid as Aisling approached.

Unarmed. Defenseless. Fionn found himself trapped at the center of their ring. Aisling had already won the duel and yet, her body continued. Her thirst for this dominance, insatiable. The sins against her suddenly made more right with even this small victory.

So, when Aisling was near enough, she paused and appraised him, glaring down and into his glacial eyes.

"You were meant to be mine," Fionn repeated, this time more desperate.

"No," she said. "*I was meant to burn.*"

Aisling raised the blade above her head and swung down.

The Forge didn't spare the son of Winter's life.

A mortal prince did.

Dagfin stood before Aisling, holding her hands, the haft, the blade mid-swing. The edge of it centimeters from slicing his shoulder as her flames beaded his forehead with sweat. His flesh glowing red with her kiss of fire.

Lir bristled from behind but held his ground.

"You've already won, Aisling," he said, Roktan blue eyes searching her own.

"You fight to spare a fae lord's life?!" Aisling bit, fighting his grip.

Dagfin shook his head, brow furrowed. "I only ever fight for you, Aisling." He glanced over his shoulder at Fionn, rising to his feet. "And this is a decision you cannot undo. You'll live with his death till you meet your own."

"The *Starling*—"

"The *Starling* was desperation, survival. This—this is

anger. This is vengeance and it'll never remedy his sins against you."

For a moment, they'd fallen back in time and were once more in Tilren, running through the thoroughfare with her brothers and a baker's husband chasing after them with a rolling pin above his head. Fergus had fallen, the rolls in his pockets spilling across the cobbles. He'd glared up at Aisling, but she'd turned away, knowing Fergus's failure was a success of her own. But it was Dagfin who'd stopped. Who'd raced back, lifted Fergus, and dragged him back toward Castle Neimedh.

She met Dagfin's stare and held it. A part of her resentful for him always forcing her to acknowledge the kinder choice.

But resentment or not, it was enough.

Aisling released the blade. It clattered to the floor. The only sound until Dagfin exhaled out of relief, Aisling's fires extinguished, and the *Faerak* collected the sword, brandishing it himself so that Fionn couldn't wield it again.

"How dare you!?" Fionn straightened, ice jutting from the floors in great pillars of glass. "Try as you might, Aisling, you'll come to recognize the better choice between Lir and I, whether willingly or by force."

The world erupted into chaos.

Ice blasted from the ground, threatening to implode Oighir entirely. Sidhe raced for all and every escape, guards, bestial or fae, swarming. Arrows raining from the plucked strings of fox bows.

Aisling spun on her heel. It was time to run.

On her right, Galad, Gilrel, Peitho, and Filverel held off Fionn's guards. Lir waiting for Aisling, hand outstretched. Something desperate flaring in his eyes.

On her left, stood Dagfin and her brothers shouting Aisling and Dagfin's names, gesturing to flee with them while they still bore the opportunity, at last freed from Fionn's deal. Voices masked by the sheer volume of the discord.

"We need to leave, Lir!" Peitho screamed, unpinning herself from Greum's oppressive weight and swiping his right paw as he swung for her again. "*Now!*"

Lir's jaw tightened, never once unleashing Aisling from his regard.

"Ash," Dagfin said, unable to force himself to glance in Lir's direction.

Aisling shook her head, temples throbbing. Heartbeat pulsing in her throat.

"Go and live to be king, Fin," she said. "I'm sorry."

And a part of her was. Fionn was right about one thing: this journey wasn't fit for mortal souls. And Aisling knew, of all the crimes she'd willingly commit in exchange for what she craved, being the reason Dagfin's life ended wasn't one of them.

Aisling turned and stepped toward Lir.

The fae king wrapped his arms around her, sheltered her in the curve of his chest as he raised one of his axes and shielded them both from the reeds darting for Aisling's heart. Not a second, a moment to bid Dagfin farewell as he no doubt already raced for Starn, Iarbonel, Fergus, and Killian. Out of time.

Lir swiveled, searching for a path out of Oighir. But there was no passage, no trail, nor a way left unmarked by chaos. Even as Fionn approached from behind. Rage freezing the edges of his eyes with ice.

"The mirrors," Aisling said to Lir, pointing to the one cracked and splintered, leading into Castle Oighir.

"Fionn's most likely bespelled them, to ensure we couldn't flee regardless of the outcome of his test. It could lead straight into Oighir's dungeons," Lir said, the cord in his neck tightening.

"Fionn described it to me," Aisling said, awarding herself Lir's full attention as he searched her expression for answers, the sensation of it bone shuddering. "The mirrors harbor all the mischief and agency of the *draiocht*. Simply asking the *draiocht* for access might be enough to circumvent Fionn's orders and open the door we covet."

Lir weighed her words. "A door to where?"

Aisling bit her bottom lip, shaking her head. "I suppose we'll soon discover."

"Lir!" Galad growled, elbowing a Sidhe guard in the jaw with one arm and punching another with the pommel of his greatsword.

Fionn neared. His eyes locked on Aisling and Lir, rendering his palace to rubble with the sheer force of his temper.

So, Lir wasted not another moment, running to the mirror, Aisling's hand in his own, cutting down Sidhe after Sidhe, beast after beast. Any that threatened their path. The perfume of their blood sprayed the air and painted Fionn's landscape of ivory, red.

At last, he paused before the mirror, waiting for the others to join them. And once they had, he met Aisling's eyes.

"Hold onto me," he said, picking Aisling up and pausing a breath before the mirror. His grip impenetrable, reminding Aisling of how they'd been torn apart when Danu had sent them forward in time. Aisling wrenched her eyes shut and called upon her *draiocht*.

Fionn approached, a few paces away.

"YOU WILL NOT LEAVE!" he screamed, aiming at the mirror with his longsword.

Grant me access, Aisling spoke to the *draiocht*. *Open the door*.

The *draiocht* cackled, thrumming with an energy that drove Aisling wild. So unlike how it'd behaved over the last several weeks.

Fionn's ice struck the mirror, splintering it. The horrible crack of it echoed off the crumbling walls.

Grant me access! Aisling yelled.

The *draiocht* leaned a little closer, *Oh dear friend, you're never satisfied with where you are, are you?*

And the door opened.

"NOW!" Aisling screamed, as she, Lir, Galad, Gilrel, Peitho, and Filverel tore into the mirror just as it burst into shards.

CHAPTER XXV

AISLING

Aisling emerged, gasping for air.

Everything was ice. Cold and water. Here and there, up and down, a streak of light and shadow.

Her eyes blinked repeatedly, chin struggling to stay above the surface as she gulped down mouthful after mouthful of water.

Arms wrapped around her waist, pulling her nearer and delivering them both to a shore of river stones and verglas.

They'd traveled to a pool amidst the Fjallnorrian feywilds, pummeled at one edge by a waterfall, now frozen over by high winter's bite.

Aisling coughed up water, emptying her lungs as she rolled over. She couldn't feel her limbs, but she could see them trembling.

"Use your *draiocht, ellwyn,*" she heard Lir say, his voice sobering.

She summoned her flames and exhaled. Painful at first, her bones thawed, then her muscles, and lastly, her flesh. The *draiocht* breeding new life into her body after months asleep.

LIR

"The forest tastes her," the trees whispered in his ears. "The forest couldn't forget the texture of her magic even after we've wilted and grown gnarled with age."

Lir stood before Aisling, watching as her fires dissolved into plumes of smoke and then nothing. The smell of her intoxicating as he weighed the density of the air between them.

Lir gripped his hands into fists, white knuckled.

"Have you already forgotten everything I taught you?" he asked, despising himself for the humor in his tone. His fury struggling to break the surface. For now.

"When there is no air, no space for life, you must forge it yourself."

Indeed, Lir had taught Aisling how to breathe beneath the water while venturing through the feywilds. A lesson that proved useful when Danu had thrust her forward in time.

Lir summoned the *draiocht*, his own, a thrashing wolf snapping inside, eager to be let loose.

Vines grew from the earth, breaking through the frozen dirt and sprouting through the rocks, wrapping Aisling in their embrace. The feel of her against his magic raised the hair on his body. But it was short-lived.

Aisling burst into flame once more, scorching his vines and dissolving them to ash. She conjured a den of snakes licked by violet fire and they snapped at Lir, slithering nearer.

"Wasn't it I who advised we muzzle her?" Filverel seethed between his fangs as he, Galad, Peitho, and Gilrel, stepped forward to intervene.

"Stay back," Lir ordered and reluctantly they did, expressions taut.

"You will not shackle me," Aisling said, gesturing to the vines shriveled to ash around her feet. Currents of ink-black hair sticking to her back, her arms, her neck despite her *draiocht*. Her gown blessedly clinging to the shape of her.

Lir laughed.

"Trust it's for our safety and not your own, *ellwyn*."

He raised the vines again with the intent to bind her till she calmed. The first taste of a fully summoned *draiocht* after months without was a euphoric one. The magic of Fionn's mirrors distorting her perspective. Enough to drive the mind mad till it was fully slaked, and the magic indulged.

Aisling growled, the tension in her muscles mirrored in her flames as they grew, lashing at Lir in a whip of fire.

The Sidhe king moved lithely to the side, avoiding her strike the same moment the earth rose from beneath the ice, folding over Aisling's flames and snuffing all her might. The tree branches craned in her direction, reaching to apprehend her to no avail. She burned again, glorious and bright scalding Lir's trees as they recoiled in a collective hiss.

"I have to admit, I only half believed you when you promised to run from me after you broke free of Oighir," Lir said, padding toward her. "You're more ruthless than even I believed."

Aisling tilted her head to the side.

"You wouldn't like me quite as much if I weren't."

Lir grinned. "I like you no matter what form you take. We're made for one another. That's why you chose to align with me, to refuse an unbinding, and aid me in the tests."

"Don't flatter yourself. You were an opportunity. Nothing more," she said, casting a bolt of flame at his head.

But despite the sharp edge of her words, the soft glimmer in her eyes was wholly unconvincing.

As quick as any could blink, Lir drew one of his axes, blocking the bolt and sending it hurtling for the waterfall as he continued forward.

"So, you used me."

"Does that wound you?" Aisling mocked, conjuring another bolt and then another. Lir deflected them both, defeating the distance between them. His axe, dividing her from him.

"On the contrary, *ellwyn*, you're becoming irresistible."

Aisling burned more brightly, conjuring what remnants of her strength she could muster. Pulsing with fire toward the Sidhe king.

Lir focused, commanding an oak to grow between them. It shot from the earth, turning over soil, rocks, and ice and shoving Aisling back several steps.

Stunned, she hesitated, searching for Lir around the tree, until she turned and came face to face with the Sidhe king.

Lir grabbed her throat, pushing her against the oak, studying her as she burned, fires desperately trying and failing to puncture his fae gauntlets. And anything more, any other new talent she bore, was swiftly bled from her lungs as Lir held her throat firmly, stifling her *draiocht*.

"In truth, *ellwyn*, nothing could stop me from finding you," he said, allowing himself to drown in her violet eyes as he tilted his head down to meet her. "Not a mortal legion, not the Sidhe, not even fate could keep me from you."

Aisling's expression twisted with rage.

"In Oighir we were allies thanks to a common goal, my freedom. Outside, we're competitors once more. If you think you can prevent me from achieving my ends at the cost of the curse breaker, I'll make certain you rue the day you ever found me again."

The corners of Lir's lips curled like a fox. "Your chances of surviving and reaching Lofgren's Rise alone are not forge-blessed." He leaned closer till their lips were a mere breath apart. "Whether our goals are aligned or not, you need me."

Aisling stopped her struggling, seemingly as bespelled as he himself. She appraised him, hesitating before speaking. Her attention burned his blood the way her magic was designed to by nature. Allowing Lir a moment to look upon her fully for the first time. As they couldn't in the shadows of the alcove, the steam of Oighir's bath, or the veil of night atop Fionn's castle. The two of them lost between the folds of this realm and the Other.

She was heartbreaking. The nuances of her features, blessedly unholy. Enough to bring Lir to his knees if just for one more—

A clang of metal sounded to their right.

Lir and Aisling fell apart, searching and finding the source of their interruption.

"I'll wear your bones around my neck, *Faerak*!" Peitho screamed.

They both turned to find Peitho mid-tussle with another. But Galad, Filverel, and Gilrel all stood to the side, wringing their garments of ice water. In which case, Lir could piece together who'd leaped through the mirror alongside them, masked by chaos.

Dagfin unpinned himself from Peitho's grip, slamming her into the shore and poising a dagger beneath her chin.

Dagfin grimaced. "Enough! Before you force me to harm y—"

Peitho headbutted Dagfin. He flew backward, shoved to the ground in mid-air.

Dagfin slammed into the stones, the wind knocked from his lungs and Peitho's boot atop his chest.

Unable to stop himself, Lir's eyes drifted to Aisling. She'd already jolted upright, hair sticking to her back, her arms, her neck, watching in horror as the *Faerak* struggled without his dust.

"So, this is the great strength of a mortal *Faerak*." Peitho smirked.

"He isn't supplied with his Ocras, Peitho," Gilrel chimed, shoulder still bandaged from the second test and rifling through every one of Dagfin's pockets while he lay prone. "And judging by his complexion, not for some time."

"If you're searching for iron, it's all been confiscated by Fionn," Dagfin growled, nailed to the ground by Peitho's otherworldly strength.

"Iron, poisons, coins. Whatever piques my fancy," the pine marten huffed, finding nothing but lint and water.

"Speaking of Fionn, we must move," Galad said, already scouring the surrounding wilderness for a direction. "If it weren't for his mirror shattering, he'd already be a step behind."

"I'll be quick." Peitho drew her blade, *Luinagren*, from her back.

"No!" Aisling shouted, stepping forward.

Instinctively, Lir's fingers twitched, his body reaching for her without his consent. But he stopped himself, forcing his body still.

Peitho whipped toward Aisling, brandishing the tip of Luinagren at her instead, eyes wandering to Aisling's fists at her sides.

"This is none of your concern. The mortal prince still owes a debt to the Forge, and I intend to deliver it."

This was true. Dagfin had deceived the *draiocht*. Magic

intended to bind one *caera* to another at his and Peitho's union. A mortal trickery the Forge wouldn't soon forget. Magic given was always magic taken.

"I'm in favor of Peitho exacting her justice," Filverel said, tying his hair behind his head. "The *draiocht* isn't the only one owed a debt. Peitho, too, was cheated."

Aisling scowled, but Galad spoke first.

"The magic will take when it deems fit. It doesn't need anyone or anything to do its bidding."

Peitho seethed, baring her fangs and tightening her grip on the haft of her blade.

"Very well, then I'll make it so he begs for the *draiocht* to reap what it's due."

Peitho lifted the sword.

Dagfin cursed under his breath, searching for an escape. A way to free himself from her strength. Fionn's blade strapped to the *Faerak*'s back beneath him. So, Aisling inhaled. Just as she always did before she summoned her flames.

"Do not interrupt," the pines whispered to Lir, clicking their branches together. "It's not wise to meddle in the affairs of the Forge. The forest knows."

Lir didn't need the reminder. Yet should he do or say nothing, with what strength Aisling still harbored, she'd set them all aflame, the forest included. And although he'd enjoy nothing more than to witness the mortal prince's life reaped, when that blessed day arrived, it would be his axes cleaving the *Faerak*'s body and soul, and not another's blade.

"Release him," Lir said, ignoring the surrounding evergreens.

They each froze, his voice commanding acquiescence as he approached.

"You can't possibly—" Filverel began but was quickly silenced by Lir's glance.

"Let him flee into the feywilds. Without his Ocras, he won't survive long."

Hopefully, Lir thought to himself.

Galad, Filverel, Peitho, and Gilrel exchanged glances, but none said a word.

Peitho, grumbling under her breath, at last, complied and freed Dagfin from the stones.

He stood, his knuckles bruised and bloody where they'd collided with Peitho's face, leaving an equally angry mark on the princess of Niltaor.

"Forge be with you on your travels, *Faerak*," Gilrel said as she crossed her arms and paws.

Yet the Roktan prince didn't flee nor wilt, planting his feet in the snow instead.

"I'm coming with you," Dagfin said.

Lir bit down his annoyance, scraping his bottom lip with his fangs.

"No," Lir said, starting for the trees.

"It wasn't a question."

"Nor is it an option," Lir growled.

"Aisling ne—"

At the sound of Aisling's name on his lips, Lir paused, interrupting the *Faerak* before he could say another word.

"Every breath you withhold from what you owe is a breath you jeopardize the lives of those around you. The *draiocht* is searching, waiting, hunting, and during *Samhain*, your chances of survival are slim if none," Lir growled. "Return to your mortal haven. You've done enough, princeling."

A wise man would've obeyed the Sidhe king and taken his leave. A wise man couldn't imagine all the ways Lir could maim and artfully torture them, but the suggestion alone would set them racing.

Instead, Dagfin scoffed, knocking them all off guard. A sound that tightened the curve of Lir's shoulders and inspired unique rage.

And yet, the *Faerak* gambled his life further. "I've brought Aisling this far, what have you done, fae?"

Stilling, the forest held its breath, anticipating the Sidhe king's reaction.

Lir grinned, fangs glinting beneath a winter sun. The consequences of, at last, slaughtering the *Faerak* growing less and less potent in comparison to the unadulterated satisfaction he'd glean from bleeding him dry. Aisling already loathed Lir and so, there was little else to lose. Yet still, Aisling's presence was the *Faerak*'s last and only saving grace.

"Dagfin has made the trek to Lofgren's Rise before," Aisling interjected.

At the sound of her voice, Lir's heart leaped, violent thoughts made sober.

"You can purchase my compliance with Dagfin's life," she said. "He'll accompany us."

"I don't need your compliance, *ellwyn*."

"Yet you'll want it."

A muscle flashed across Lir's jaw, the forest groaning around them. Words made worse by she who wielded them.

"*Easca, Damh Bán,*" the trees hissed. Awaiting his inevitable fury. For Lir still loathed his not-so-mortal queen as well. Loathed her the way he despised all that bore power over him.

"Very well, princeling," Lir said, at last, cracking his neck side to side. "Let's see how long you last."

CHAPTER XXVI

LIR

The trek to Lofgren's Rise, from where they'd fallen outside Oighir, wasn't far. Lir estimated the journey would last another fortnight, unless their enemies slowed them down: rogue beasts, mortals, Sidhe, the gods... Lir ground his fangs.

Nevertheless, the Sidhe king didn't anticipate more humans than he'd already encountered attempting the journey. This considering he'd already witnessed the Aithirnian queen turn her ship around at the sight of his fae party. Lir slaughtered the majority of Bregganite soldiers who'd traveled ahead of their sovereign, attempting to ambush the Sidhe king and his knights. Their deaths, a warning to their mortal laird to journey no farther.

As for the other Sidhe sovereigns, Lir knew which of them relied on him to obtain the curse breaker and which didn't, instead depending on Fionn to deter him, too afraid to challenge Lir themselves.

For now, Aisling needed new clothing and their group an opportunity to resupply themselves. Even if that meant mortal goods.

"*What are you doing, Lir?*" Peitho asked in Rún, approaching from behind. Lir stood at the edge of a crag, overlooking a valley of frostbitten pines twinkling beneath a shuddering sun. Lofgren's Rise hunched in the distance.

"*Isn't it obvious?*" he said, glancing at her over his shoulder. "*Determining a path of travel. There's a village through these woods that will—*"

"*You know that's not what I mean.*" Peitho's expression hardened, taking a cautious step toward him. "*Oighir, Fionn, the tests. It's already gone too far. You need to end this now. Kill Aisling if you must now that you've garnered a semblance of her trust and if you cannot bring yourself to end her, wound her greatly enough that she cannot continue. Every breath she exhales is a challenge to your—to our pursuit of the curse breaker. She cannot be trusted. I've held my tongue this long but after Oighir and Fionn... you risk too much.*"

Lir ground his fangs. Doing his best to resist the ripple of his temper.

"*I'll forgive those words for the last time, Peitho,*" he said, every word colder than Fionn's ice. "*But speak them again, and I'll not be so forgiving.*"

"*You've gone mad, Lir. Whatever power your bond as caera holds over you cannot take precedence over your duty to the Sidhe.*"

"*And it never will.*"

"*Then why have we come for her?! Why do we not end her for the threat she is?!*"

"*Because I can't!*" he shouted, more loudly than he'd anticipated. Peitho startled, stepping back in fear or disgust—Lir wasn't certain. Only she did her best to mask whatever it was she felt, glancing back at the forest to see if the others had overheard.

Peitho swallowed.

"*Filverel, Galad, Gilrel, and even I will support you. Will follow you to end of this realm if we must, but we don't agree with whatever bind she holds over you.*"

"*I never asked for your opinion, Peitho,*" he bit, his patience thinning. "*I chose this path and each of you followed of your own free will. So, turn back if you like. My choices are my own.*"

Peitho's brows drew together.

"*Turn back? Is that what we mean to you? Knights who've sworn their allegiance so trivial as to dismiss on a whim?*"

"*What is it you want from me? The union between you and me was never meant to be, Peitho. We owe nothing to one another.*"

Peitho winced, eyes glassy with tears.

"*I came to you when Niltaor was in need and you swore—*"

"*I will keep my promises to the South. Niltaor will remain under the protection of Annwyn and Racat if that's what concerns you.*"

Lir and Peitho's union had been discussed long before Lir had ever met Aisling, in the hopes that Annwyn would aid Niltaor. A union Lir had almost forgotten until now.

Lir started back through the woods, brushing past Peitho without another glance. The princess glared vacantly at the valley below, seemingly on the verge of tears. Until she reached out and grabbed Lir's arm without warning, moving her mouth toward his.

Instinctually, Lir jerked back, avoiding her kiss. He tore himself from her hold, watching the red humiliation blur over her cheeks alongside her anger. And yet neither emotion rivalled Lir's frustration, his thinning patience.

"*And you and me? Is this what's become of you and me?*"

she asked, her voice thick with emotion as Lir increased the distance between them, stepping further back.

"There's nothing between you and me," he said, his voice slick. And by the twitch of Peitho's expression, as though she'd just endured a physical blow, Lir knew it was for the best.

"I don't believe you. Niltaor and Annwyn could unite the Sidhe once more, breed fear into the Unseelie once more, but it is she who undermines you! It is she who betrayed our kind, who burned me! Who threatens everything and if it weren't for you, I'd have killed Aisling thrice over by now!"

Lir tossed his right axe, and the blade flew. Spiraled toward Peitho, forcing her to duck in time to dodge the gleaming edge. Thudding into the birch behind her.

Peitho rose, eyes wide, as Lir approached, reaching over her to draw his blade back from the tree in a flurry of splinters.

"Speak her name again, and next time I won't miss."

AISLING

Even through the labyrinth of snow, the voice of a mortal town forced its way through. Churning, bleating, heaving. The teeth of its furnace grinding till smoke rose into the sky and steeped the forest in its musk.

"What mortals build a settlement in the middle of the feywilds?" Aisling asked, turning to face Galad walking beside her, covering his nose with the fae-spun wool of his hood.

But it was Lir who replied from behind.

"Those who worship it."

Aisling's brows knotted.

"Druids," Gilrel clarified.

And as though summoned, a great wall appeared between the woodland's bones.

The height of age-old oaks and made of stone, it was formidable and christened with a thick drawbridge lying over a river of sparkling black.

A weathered plaque reading "Bludhaven" hung above the drawbridge.

Yet the Aos Sí symbols, dripping from the walls in sheep's blood, drew Aisling's attention and held it. Characters in Rún mirroring many of the images etched into Lir's, Galad's, Filverel's, and Peitho's skin.

"Protection runes," Gilrel said, climbing a nearby tree to get a better look.

"Protection against the Sidhe?" Aisling asked, remembering the runes Killian had carved into Dagfin's and her brothers' flesh.

None of their group replied. The anger, the resentment, the frustration they harbored for her after she'd run from Dagfin and Peitho's union potent in the air. Tangible in the way they kept their distance, only spoke to her when necessary, and enjoyed most of their conversations in Rún. Masking what they could from her. A coldness that rivaled the surrounding landscape. None quite so painful as Galad and Gilrel's flippant disregard for her.

"No," Dagfin responded. "Protection against a beast."

The forest reacted, chittering and thrashing its limbs.

Aisling shuddered. "How do you know?"

"I've seen its likeness before," Dagfin said. "Runes painted to ward off Unseelie lest their sacrifices not appease the feywilds."

Aisling eyed the surrounding woods more closely. They

peered back at her, shifting to get a better look. More composed than they'd been outside Lir's presence. Where they once clawed for her, now they stood in the periphery, watching intently as she passed.

"We'll stay the night," Lir said, to Aisling's relief. She needed new garments, lest she traverse the feywilds and climb Lofgren's rise in no more than a soaked gown.

Peitho grimaced. "You can't possibly—"

"Make yourself useful, princeling," Lir interrupted, ignoring Peitho and gesturing to Bludhaven with a nod of his head.

Dagfin scoffed. "You intend to enter a mortal township with four fae, the not-so-mortal queen of Annwyn, and a weasel?"

Gilrel frowned. "Careful, *Faerak*, before we gift you as an offering."

But before Dagfin could reply, the air adjusted, and the pressure popped their ears. The distinct scent of pine needles and rain perfuming the air. As though the spirit of a storm had come and gone, rinsing them each in magic.

To Aisling, nothing had noticeably changed. But by the expression on Dagfin's face, Aisling knew they'd been glamoured by Lir's *draiocht*. Disguised as something other than fae.

"Problem solved," Lir said, starting for Bludhaven.

"Name yourselves," two men shouted from atop the wall's battlements, crossbows armed with iron-tipped arrows.

Dagfin approached first, the rest behind.

"Dagfin of clann Feradach and crown prince of Roktling."

The archers hesitated, lowering their crossbows as recognition dawned.

"The *Faerak*?" one of them asked, hope inflecting their northern mortal accents.

"Aye. My group and I come in search of refuge for the night," Dagfin continued and before he could say more, the drawbridge was lowering, groaning till the interior of the township was visible. A civilization overgrown by the forest despite their great wall: moss-covered wattle and daub cottages, pigs roasting over spits, the plucking of a distant fiddle, unfamiliar incense, and the churn of hundreds flooding the cobbled corridors and spilling at the seams. Mortal builds, stacked upon one another, all nestled between crisp cypresses and their roots.

A poor mortal imitation of a fae world.

"Please, please enter, Your Majesty," one of the archers said breathlessly. "Veran will be most honored to make your acquaintance."

Cautiously at first, their group crossed the drawbridge and stepped inside Bludhaven. The guards' attention lingered on those accompanying the Roktan prince.

Before them, at the center of the main thoroughfare, was a rune nailed into the flagstones. And etched on its surface read a prayer:

> I sing this song to Dark One
> Whose shadows keep me warm.
> Protect me in your woods.
> Forge a path amidst your keep
> And, while I wander,
> Spell your beasts to sleep.

Lir considered the rune for but a heartbeat, swiftly distracted by the bustling village.

These druids worshiped Lir, prayed to him, and the fae king despised them nevertheless. At best, considered them with apathy, these druids spared for their reverence and nothing more, Aisling assumed.

Aisling shook her head. Throughout her life, she was taught humans both feared and despised the mythic barbarian lord. Never could she have imagined some mortals *worshiped* him. Beseeched him for protection while traversing his forests.

The villagers whispered, heads bobbing to get a better glance at the strangers passing through. Women were leaning through their upper story windows, the smithy pausing his smelting, the beggars cursing beneath their breath, the sentinels twitching as they eyed not Lir and his knights, carefully glamoured, but Dagfin.

"It's he!" a muddy child shouted, quickly silenced by his friends. "Prince of Demons Death."

They revered Dagfin. A folk hero, brought to life through the smog of *Samhain*'s breath, bleeding across Fjallnorr at dusk. Forcing Aisling to wonder if Lir and his knights had noticed the shift in the air Dagfin inspired as well.

Aisling had known, had seen how Dagfin had changed since she'd last set eyes on him as a boy. But today, she saw the legacy of his evolution and the esteem he'd won as a result. The fame. Even as Dagfin chose to ignore their ill-masked gossip and reverence, leading four fae knights, the not-so-mortal queen of Annwyn, and a marten in disguise into the pit of their world.

But Aisling's attention was swiftly stolen by the bloody runes painted across Bludhaven, the bones hanging from rooftops like wind chimes, and the temple at the end of the thoroughfare. A colossal structure adorned with countless statues of winged Aos Sí. The statues swung their blades beside the pointed archways, plucked harps, blew flutes atop the spindly spires, and danced across the stained glass. All chiseled with such lifelike realism as though a single lingering glare could bring them to life. Crowned by the image of a stag bowing to all those who crossed its threshold.

And growing from within was a blood ash. Branches and roots breaking through the stained glass, around the galleries, and along the stone exterior, rising from the roof of the cathedral and to the grumbling clouds overhead.

Chanting roared from its inside and slithered through Bludhaven's passages, its song wholly unsettling.

"This looks as good a place as any," Gilrel said, carrying her tail so the sea of mortals didn't trample it. She gestured to one of the many inns pressed between smoking hospices.

"*Abhaile*" was written across a creaking sign just above its threshold. A fae word, Aisling conjectured.

They entered.

The roar of the town faded into the twang of the bard plucking at his lute and the drunkards singing along, washing over Aisling as she stepped onto the sticky ale-stained floorboards. Soft, golden firelight flickering beneath eight or so wooden beams, carrying the weight of what Aisling imagined were rooms for stay.

Filverel approached the bar, whispering beneath his breath to the mortal who stood behind it. Aisling studied their interaction. To Aisling, who saw beyond Lir's glamour, Filverel was a pale opal surrounded by common highland stones. Another testament to the Sidhe's glory, made blinding by the fae king standing beside her. A dark jewel inside this mortal, dusty cavity. Glittering with all the lethality she'd dreamt of over the past several months.

"You should eat," Lir said to Aisling, starting for one of the various tables spread throughout the inn's first floor. In a cobwebbed corner of *Abhaile*, the dark cloaked the one he chose.

Galad and Gilrel followed Lir while Peitho approached the bar alongside Filverel.

Aisling hung back, Dagfin a step behind, finding in himself the motivation to join Lir.

"It's dangerous to be walkin' round these parts dressed such as yourself." A man stepped between Aisling and Lir's table, bulbous eyes devouring her unapologetically. He smelled of bitter ales and body odor, boots caked in mud, and had a face marred by both an unfavorable life and indulgent drink. Poorly drawn fae markings etched beneath his skin.

Indeed, only Dagfin's Roktan cloak prevented her from being entirely bare to the ravenous winter. Whatever Sidhe blood flowed freely within her warmed her bones enough and if a faint whisper of the cold threatened to chill her, Aisling simply summoned her fires beneath her skin. Nevertheless, glamoured by Lir, these druids saw only a woman in a weathered dress and cloak, stumbling into their tavern.

"It's no concern of yours," Dagfin said from behind Aisling, his voice taut with calculated anger.

"I wasn't talkin' to ye," the man said, stepping nearer to Aisling. "I was talkin' to the lady."

Aisling simpered, the *draíocht* prickling at her fingertips.

"A choice you'll regret if you don't clear my path."

The man revealed a collection of yellowed teeth. "So the lady has fangs. Why don't you come and sit a while, I'll warm ye—"

The man's eyes went wide. The words seemingly caught in his throat. Aisling glanced over her shoulder at Dagfin, but his daggers were still sheathed. Only his shoulders hiked in anger.

The man gagged, face red and horrified. And Aisling knew. Knew before the first vines slithered from his mouth, suffocating him from the inside and crawling to the light to boast their victory. Just as Lir had done to Ciar before Dagfin and Peitho's failed union.

Lir, seemingly bored, shoved past the man to return for Aisling. The druid, knocked off balance, tumbled into a nearby table drawing the attention of the tavern.

Lir pressed his gloved hand to the small of Aisling's back, gently guiding her to their table.

Dagfin hesitated, torn between following Aisling or helping the druid. A punishable crime but, in Dagfin's eyes, not by death, Aisling knew.

"Remind me not to let you out of my sight again," Lir said, even as the man collapsed against *Abhaile*'s floor, thorny tendrils wet with mortal blood as he heaved the last of Lir's magic.

"I'm not your hunt," Aisling said, still glancing at the man over her shoulder.

"Don't look," Lir said.

"You're killing him."

"The art of the kill is often a practice of managing guilt. And after a few hundred times, it grows easy until nothing is felt at all."

"You're wicked."

"You say it like you're surprised." Lir pulled out a chair for Aisling at their table, gesturing for her to sit. "For him"— Lir tilted his head in the man's direction, his suffering drawing a crowd—"not only do I feel no guilt at all, I enjoyed it. And if you'd known what he intended, you would too."

The tavern erupted, wandering eyes drawn by the fleshy

thud of his body against the floorboards. They gasped, and some screamed, praying to the *Damh Bán*. The irony, a grisly spectacle unraveling before their eyes.

Aisling took her seat, Dagfin following shortly behind.

"Save the sanctimonious lecture, princeling," Galad said as Dagfin threw himself into a chair. But Aisling knew Dagfin wouldn't have picked this fight. Dagfin was a peacemaker, an argument-ender, and wise when it came to choosing his battles. He'd known who he'd chosen to follow for Aisling's sake. So, despite his horror or the weight of his conscience, he swallowed his vitriol and sat quietly. Arms crossed, biding his time.

A plate of what Aisling could only describe as ash clattered before her: stale bread, bland oats, and bruised fruit. She resisted the urge to gag, eyeing her plate like a death sentence. The thought—let alone the sight—of mortal foods sickened her. The memory of Fionn's fae banquets flashing across her memory.

Lir leaned back in his chair, watching her beneath hooded eyes.

"You can no longer consume mortal foods, can you?" he asked. A question that summoned Dagfin's full attention.

Aisling's nose wrinkled. "No," she confessed. "Not for some time."

With each passing day, Aisling's mortal blood ran thin till she was forced to wonder if, at some point, it would vanish entirely.

Dagfin stilled. Aisling knew he'd suspected. A part of him had known but hadn't been forced to fully confront the reality until now. Still, his posture was warm, as though he wished to comfort her. All this, despite the thickening of her enemy blood.

Filverel and Peitho threaded through the crowds still gathering around the coughing druid, and to their group.

"The last four rooms," Filverel said, holding up an array of keys made from bones. Immediately Gilrel groaned, giving voice to Aisling's frustration and the consequences Filverel's expression implied.

They'd have to share rooms.

"You fae can decide amongst yourselves," Dagfin said. "Aisling and I will take the first room."

Abhaile grew three shades darker, seemingly overcome with the deathly shadows spilled from Lir's wolfish smile.

"If you want me to kill you, princeling, just say the word."

All cleared their throats uneasily, save for Dagfin.

"Do you believe I'd let her out of my sight whilst in your presence, fae? You may be here, inspired by motivations of your own, but my intentions are Aisling's protection alone."

A muscle flashed across Lir's jaw, his eyes narrowing even as the corners of his lips curled, both ruthless and feral all at once.

"You shouldn't dwell long on my intentions with my *caera*, princeling." Lir stepped forward, the air growing hot and burning Aisling's lungs.

Galad, Peitho, Filverel, and Gilrel moved not a hair, watching as though eager for Lir to satiate his temper. The mortals, on the other hand, took notice of the tension brewing, bubbling, and squealing with heat.

"Then it's settled," Aisling piped, awarding her both their attention. "The two of you will share a room."

Lir's expression muddled, brows drawing together. Unsure whether to be horrified or furious before settling on both. Dagfin was similarly outraged.

"That way, you both can keep a keen eye on the other."

"I'll stay with *mo Lúra, Damh Bán*," Gilrel said, mercifully leaping and taking hold of one of Filverel's bone keys. "And I vow to ensure her safety." She bowed her head, placing a single paw atop her heart.

Before anyone could argue further, Aisling shoved past them both, Gilrel on her heels as she climbed the tavern stairs toward refuge.

CHAPTER XXVII

AISLING

"You cannot have them both, *mo Lúra*."

Gilrel scoured the entire chamber, thrusting aside the embroidered curtains, crawling beneath the quilted bed, digging inside the moth-infested closet, and rummaging through the drawers. Ensuring no one or no thing lurked inside their room unbeknownst to either she or Aisling.

Aisling stood by the window, glaring down at the thoroughfare below. A river of mortals, increasing the pace of their gait as the northern sun lay to rest below Lofgren's peaks. Shutters slamming shut, doors locked, and shops emptied.

Dagfin, among them, ventured into a shop of herbs, incense, and teas, speaking in whispers to a haggard-looking man as he disappeared inside. A fresh hood pulled over his head. Aisling leaned further out her window to catch a better glimpse, but the moment was fleeting and her vantage point limited.

"You straddle the line between your old life and the new. Between your princeling and the *Damh Bán*."

Aisling tangled her fingers in the curtains.

"I'm both. Both my old life and my new," Aisling replied more honestly than she'd intended. "And I cannot commit to either my mortal or fae reflection without killing the other first."

"Then perhaps you must welcome such death, *mo Lúra*." Gilrel smoothed out her furs, hopping atop the table at the center of the room and pouring herself a glass of water from the decanter. Without hesitation, she spewed whatever touched her tongue across the room. Aisling didn't need an explanation. Mortal water wasn't comparable to what the Sidhe drank: cool, freshly collected, glacial, rapid, and rainwater blessed and purified by nymphs.

"'*Mo Lúra*,'" Aisling repeated. "The last I saw you, you called me by my given name."

Gilrel straightened, gathering herself.

"And last I saw you, you were fleeing on horseback with five mortal princes. One among them, the son of the fire hand, and Galad's torturer."

Aisling flinched as though physically struck, forcing herself to meet Gilrel's eyes.

"You're angry with me, I understand. But I needed—*need* to reach Lofgren's Rise before all else who might complicate my ends. I've lived half a life. And I'll perish before I settle for such an existence for a second time. If there's even a chance my life means more than it has, I must know it."

The groaning of the tavern was deafening. Moaning as though weeping uncontrollably, bracing itself for the storm stalking in the later hours of the evening.

Gilrel didn't move. Her paws hanging motionless at her sides.

But before Aisling could say more, a knock sounded at the door, startling them both.

Gilrel unlatched the locks, peering through the needle-thin crack with the haft of her blade in one hand, prepared to be drawn. Her suspicions were seemingly assuaged by whoever stood in the corridor, for the door swung open entirely.

Galad, expressionless, stood in the doorway, a pile of clothes in his hands.

"Lir had me fetch these for *mo Lúra*." He handed the clothes over to Gilrel, deigning to glance in Aisling's direction.

"Galad—" Aisling began, his name spoken in her thoughts before finding its way onto her tongue. But the fae knight ignored her, turning and leaving without another word. The door swung shut behind him. The sound of its slap echoing painfully.

Gilrel cleared her throat, thoughts masked by the growing dark of evening. Both she and Aisling, wordlessly having agreed to forgo firelight in their chambers.

The pine marten handed Aisling the bundle of clothes. Leather pants, gloves, and boots lined with fur, a tunic, a wool vest, and a thick cloak, proper for the growing cold of Fionn's winter.

"How quickly you forget the Sidhe's role in revealing your true nature. I welcomed you—befriended you. Lir guided you. And Galad, despite the loathing of all others, believed in you. And yet you betrayed us—"

"Betrayed? It was the Aos Sí who corrupted the treaty my union symbolized, not the mortals."

"Ah yes. The Aos Sí—*your* people as queen of Annwyn and bride of the forest. You are no longer mortal, Aisling, despite how desperately you cling to those who drank the blood of half your life. And so, our betrayal of the mortals was yours as well."

Aisling bit her tongue.

"You left us, and coupled with those who've indulged in our suffering," the pine marten continued. "If you believe for a moment even your most recent sins will be forgiven so quickly, reconsider what naivety remains while you pursue something more for yourself."

Gilrel started for the door, pausing before shutting it entirely. A temple bell clanging outside the tavern and crying into the night.

"And be glad," the pine marten added, "it's our anger you face and not the edge of our blades."

DAGFIN

Dagfin was familiar with Bludhaven. The second time he'd visited this druid settlement, he'd been half blind and nearly deaf after an encounter with the bánánach Unseelie, haunting mortal settlements closer to Heill. So he'd memorized the path to this very shop by sound, smell, and the press of the gravel beneath his boots.

And over time, Dagfin had learned the way of druids. Druids were most often peaceful. They enjoyed their incense, their runes, and their prayers, often keeping to themselves, secluded from the rest of the mortal world. This, by their own design but also because humankind despised them, feared them, and kept them at an arm's length as outcasts, strangers, and, often, traitors.

But because of their proficiency with herbs, spices, potions, and draughts, druid settlements like Bludhaven were where *Faerak* Ocras was often brewed and sold on the outskirts of kingdoms in the cloak of anonymity. And Blud-haven was no different.

Dagfin threaded through the flagstone thoroughfare, slip-ping between the flood of burghers passing through. A steady susurration of village sounds, calming his spirit after weeks of wilderness. Of fae.

He needed a moment away. Not to mention every glance at Aisling since they'd entered Bludhaven broke his heart. Lir's magic transformed Aisling's appearance back to her mortal self, seemingly entirely human once more and painfully familiar. A ghost still stalking this realm with its body staggering behind.

Dagfin slipped into a ramshackle shop; those were the best sources of dust, stores in disrepair. It meant the owners, artisans, and brewers paid close attention to their craft, priori-tizing authenticity. At least, that was the trend Dagfin had met sifting through villages across the north as a *Faerak*.

Indeed, it was these mortals who spent years chipping away at Iod's mountain range in the cloak of shadow and outside its gates. Furiously harvesting the Ocras where they believed the spirit of the mountain's late queen couldn't catch them stealing.

"Here comes the Roktan prince," a man boomed from inside the dusty interior. A hearth defrosting Dagfin's weary muscles the moment he'd stepped across the scuffed thresh-old. "I didn't think I'd be seein' ye so soon."

"Neither did I."

"Are ye lookin' for more Ocras then?" he asked, scratching his beard as he appraised Dagfin more closely.

Dagfin glanced over his shoulder, nodding in response. The *Faerak* knew how pale he looked, the rings beneath his eyes, the dry grate of his voice, and his tired posture. So, he did his best to mask himself in the shadows.

The man before him, on the other hand, was robust, marked in fae runes and wore bones in his braids. The Roktan prince wasn't certain of his name, maybe Sisin... Sarragh... or Sean... Dagfin couldn't remember. At some point, every person who'd ever sold him Ocras had begun to blur together, countless to name and remember.

"You didn't finish the last of it yet, did ye?"

Dagfin ignored his question, fishing a bag of coins from his pocket before remembering all his belongings had been stripped from his person in Oighir.

"Roktling will repay you for your services," he said, hoping the man accepted the debt. And by the look on the shopkeeper's face, said hope was kindled. "A few more throwing daggers as well." This, considering those had also been stolen by Frigg and his pack of wolves. Now, all he carried was Fionn's sword, strapped to his back.

Behind the shopkeeper were shelves of bottled ointments, salves, elixirs, and remedies. Some Dagfin had made use of himself after his more dangerous *Faerak* pursuits: changeling's shroud, giant's bane, ghost scream, and fox foot. And above their heads hung iron weapons of all make and size, freshly forged at the back of the shop.

"Does Feradach know of this?" the shopkeeper pressed.

Dagfin soured at the sound of his father's name. Feradach indeed knew where Dagfin was and what he was pursuing. He'd never been dishonest with his father even if the Roktan king disapproved. And yet, perhaps, Dagfin couldn't help wondering if his father hoped his son would return with the curse breaker himself, bringing honor to their seafaring kingdom.

Nevertheless, Dagfin had never told his father the consequences of Ocras. After all, Feradach already despised all

Dagfin did as a *Faerak*. Dagfin was meant to be in Roktling, preparing to be king, studying politics and acquainting himself with the day-to-day chores of running a kingdom. So, any mention of Ocras would only worsen those tensions he already bore with his father.

"I don't mean to pry," the shopkeeper said. "I only can't continue to supply you with Ocras in good conscience if it means I'm slowly killing the heir to the Roktan throne."

"I'm not the heir," Dagfin said, too quickly. "My brother was."

The shopkeeper shifted awkwardly, sweat beading across his creased brow from the heat of the forge at the back of the shop.

"If you aren't willing to sell me anymore, I'll find it someplace else," Dagfin said, mouthwatering at the prospect of Ocras being so close yet just out of reach.

"I'll sell it to ye," the man mumbled reluctantly, reaching beneath the counter for a discreetly labeled flask. A concoction of equal parts Ocras and water. "But know, even if ye've heard it a thousand times, there's a reason not every boy with a stick in his hand and dreams of being a hero becomes a *Faerak*. Once you've tasted the Ocras it'll never let go, yer only way out is to master its allure enough to survive and no more. Otherwise, what gives ye strength to fight the beasts will kill ye before some fae ever does."

Dagfin took the bottle and turned on his heel. The man was right. He'd heard this advice a thousand times over. And yet, Dagfin not only craved more Ocras, but he also *needed* it.

"Look out for yerself," the shopkeeper urged him as the prince stepped out the door. "And watch yer back."

Dagfin inhaled winter, uncorking the bottle and taking a swig as soon as he was able.

After years of Ocras, when he was deprived, he could scarcely find the energy to walk much less fight, and Dagfin had sworn to fight until his day's death.

CHAPTER XXVIII

AISLING

A flash of Roktan blue, Aisling swept outside the tavern after nightfall.

Her cloak billowed behind her as she blazed a path through Bludhaven, head down and hood up. It was difficult for Aisling to remain indoors for long periods of time, especially when inside a mortal hospice. One where wisterias didn't drip from the ceilings, thorns didn't bite the banisters nor trace the walls. Where moss didn't hug the decanter and magpies didn't draw her a bath, filled with blossom butters and rose petals.

Not to mention, inside her *Abhaile* quarters, Aisling was left alone with her thoughts. Visions of the Lady, of Danu, of Fionn. Each and all pursuing her, nipping at her heels as she clawed for an answer to what she was. Who she was. Answers she feared she'd never find.

Aisling pushed through the crowds, shoved by those in as much of a hurry. Druids, seemingly afraid of the moon and its luminous aura. As though its pale light was poisonous to the touch, bewitched should they not find refuge before the moon sat atop its miraculous throne.

A shop billowing with incense and traced with wind-chimes, lanterns, and bundles of herbs, caught Aisling's attention. She approached it cautiously, avoiding the crush of villagers as she slowed her gait.

A woman emerged from the warm light of the shop's interior. She was perhaps a decade Aisling's senior, vibrant despite the wintertide and painted in fae runes. She tossed a blonde braid over her shoulder, crossing her arms over her woolen dress.

"Come inside, stranger," she said, pushing aside the garlands of herbs to better see Aisling. "By the light in your eyes, I can tell you're looking for something. Or someone."

Instinctively, Aisling pulled her hood closer, shrouding her features in shadow, forgetting for a moment she was still glamoured by Lir.

"I'm just passing through."

"Even so, you might find something of interest inside my shop. The choice is yours."

Aisling chewed on the inside of her cheek, considering. She had nowhere else to go and she'd draw suspicion wandering around Bludhaven's streets alone. So, Aisling nodded her head, stepping inside the woman's shop.

The shop's interior was a mess of mortar and pestles filled with crushed sugar leaves, dried pine branches, bottles of smoking incense, parchments and books, jewelry made of precious stones and bones, and a table strewn with white rocks etched with symbols in Rún.

"I saw you enter Bludhaven with the Roktan prince," the woman said, following Aisling with her pale eyes. "Are you also a *Faerak*?"

Aisling shook her head, wandering further into the shop.

"A princess perhaps? From one of the southern or eastern continents? The west?"

Aisling said nothing but the silence spoke loudly enough.

The woman's expression brightened with curiosity, stalking a few paces behind Aisling.

"Not a princess either then. We don't often have visitors in Bludhaven. Especially those who accompany princes and *Faeraks* this far north."

Aisling did her best to ignore the woman, brushing her fingers over the open tomes and studying the illustrations more closely.

Charms for forgetting, was written on one page.

Potions for love, incantations for dreams, songs for opening, and touch for memory, on the following pages.

"Those are spell books," the druid woman said, stepping beside Aisling.

"Can druids cast spells?" Aisling asked, genuinely curious. As far as Aisling was told, she was the only mortal, in either this realm or the next, known to harness and summon the *draiocht*.

"No, although some enjoy believing they can," the woman said, studying Aisling more closely. It occurred to Aisling then that perhaps her questions were common knowledge amongst mortals. Her ignorance piquing the shopkeeper's interest. Throughout her childhood, Aisling was both sheltered behind iron walls and unaware of the duplicity of the world. Of the gray that blurred whatever Aisling once believed was black and white.

"Druids harness a certain… *inspiration* from the natural world. A connectivity with the bark of a tree, the undercurrent of a river, the layers of a mountain, the shape of ice.

Nothing in comparison to the Sidhe themselves but impressive by mortal standards nonetheless."

"Then why the spell books?" Aisling asked.

"Some druids believe, with enough time, study, and strength of mind, a druid bears the potential to master such spells and even cast them at will."

"Yet even the fair folk do not *cast* spells," Aisling added. "They breathe through their magic."

"You know quite a bit about the Sidhe," the lady said, narrowing her eyes. Aisling smiled half-heartedly, eager to change the subject.

"And what of the runes on the table?" Aisling asked. The woman turned on her heel, so Aisling took the opportunity and ripped whatever page the tome was already opened at.

Touch for memory.

Aisling crumpled and pocketed the page, starting for the threshold even as the woman still spoke, distracted by the runes spread across the table.

Aisling slipped out the door and rushed across the thoroughfare, glancing over her shoulder to ensure the woman wasn't following her trail, turning in time to collide with another.

Aisling staggered back, quickly regaining her balance. Cursing her luck when she met eyes with the Sidhe king.

Lir tilted his head back, watching her. An amused smile played across his lips, quickly fading the moment he acknowledged the Roktan blue cloak she wore. Shadows taking root.

"Were you following me?" Aisling asked, face twisting in anger. She knew Lir wouldn't let her escape so easily but if he believed her compliance was anything more than self-serving, he was wrong. Aisling could flee any time she liked; she rather found her chances of reaching Lofgren's Rise more quickly higher if accompanied by a group of legendary Aos Sí. Ignoring the ache-like pain in her heart each time she was reminded Lir was real and no dream, no vision, no fireside tale alive in the periphery of one's imagination.

"You collided with me, *ellwyn*. I have more reason to believe you were following me."

Aisling snorted, "I'm in no mood for your games." She shoved past him, continuing down the thoroughfare.

"Wait," he called after her. "I have something to show you."

"At this hour?" Bludhaven's doors were slamming shut, locking, and bolting on the other side. The torrent of villagers passing by, eager to settle before the hearth for the night.

"Is there a better one?" he asked.

Aisling shook her head, searching for an excuse but finding none. The thought of returning to *Abhaile* and being alone with her thoughts sickening. While the prospect of following Lir was far more seductive than aimlessly wandering Bludhaven's alleys.

Aisling dipped her chin, a silent agreement she forced herself to make, immediately regretting it the moment Lir brightened triumphantly, already gesturing for her to follow behind him.

Lir slipped through Bludhaven like a leaf in the wind, winding through cottage, apothecary, and smithy, Aisling shortly behind.

At last, they broke through the smoking city-town and wandered into a garden still protected by the village walls.

It was dismal. Naked, sickly trees drooping over carpets of dead flowers and pale fungi. The leaves that remained had all turned gray or brown, brittle and ashen. Lost to the kiss of wintertide.

Lir wandered through regardless till he reached the

center where they grew cloaked by the twisted, rotting branches. Surrounded by statues of life-size stags and wolves chasing one another through the ruin.

"What is this place?" Aisling asked. For although it felt like a graveyard of everything green, it still chuckled with magic. The stars fell from their kingdom of black, tangling through Aisling's hair, and scraped her cheeks with their jagged edges. Real or not, Aisling wasn't certain until Lir brushed a star from his shoulder.

"Is this a dream?" Aisling asked.

"If it were, would you kiss me again?" Lir asked, circling her like a wolf padding around its prey.

"No," Aisling said, swallowing.

"Why not?"

"A kiss is prayer, dark lord. Faith-filled, spoken on one's knees and in the dead of night. Not a weapon to be wielded nor a currency for your ambition."

Fionn's kiss tore through her memory, making a hypocrite of Aisling. Yet the kiss she'd traded for an advantage in Oighir didn't feel as sacred as whatever she shared with Lir. Didn't feel as consequential, as cosmically important.

Lir tilted his head to the side, eyes glowing with the reflective sheen of beasts in the wood.

"Another reason we should share one tonight."

Aisling frowned, turning when he caught her wrist and gently pulled her back. He bent down and kissed her cheek, tasting her blood where the stars scratched her skin. Aisling froze, their proximity, his touch, burning a fire in her abdomen.

Lir's eyes flashed a headier shade of evergreen and the garden transformed. His magic given new breath with their kiss; for each time their lips met, both Aisling and Lir grew more powerful whether it be the kiss they shared when Aisling fled from Dagfin and Peitho's union yielding the forest Lir summoned, their kiss in Fionn's arena aiding Lir's victory, or his kiss now, giving new life to the garden in which they stood. Every touch, every intimate glance, inspiring their *draiocht*. A kiss paid to the *draiocht* in exchange for Lir's power.

The trees straightened, exhaling and blooming leaves like chips of emerald. Lush and radiant, they grew enormous, rising toward the night sky and bubbling over with red bulbs. Garlands of scarlet ripe apples, plump and polished. Crowding around the statues of stags and wolves until everything was lost to the sheer growth of the garden. The canopies eclipsing the moon and cloaking their underbelly in darkness. A graveyard brought back from the dead.

"Are you trying to impress me?" Aisling's eyes, wide and sparkling, drank in the sight of Lir's magic, half-worried it might vanish before she could memorize it. Pop like a soap bubble, never to be experienced again.

"Did it work?" he asked, stepping toward the nearest tree.

Aisling said not a word, but she didn't have to. Her expression spoke for itself and so she damned it. Lir beamed, dimples tracing the edges of his brilliant grin.

"Follow me," he said. He climbed up the tree, reaching down to help Aisling. She took his hand, a step behind as they navigated into the heart of the apple tree. Brambles of berries bubbling from the branches and making dense their path.

At last, they emerged where the tree's limbs spread like the hand of a giant. Its palm facing the black sky, fingers splayed. But the leaves and the apples protected them both like a secret, obscuring them from the voyeuristic stars above.

A cradle of apples, of branches braided and woven, and the light that spilled between the tree's limbs.

Lir reclined atop the heaps of fruit; his fingers stained in berry juice from their climb. Aisling inspected her own hands, red too with their influence.

"You must be starving," Lir said, his voice the sound of a twilight gale. "Had I known mortal foods no longer slaked you, I'd have provided something for you sooner."

Aisling laughed beneath her breath. "You'd grow trees simply to abate my hunger?" She gestured to the garden around them.

"I'd do anything you asked of me."

Lir plucked an apple from the piles in which they lay.

He took a bite, offering Aisling a taste next.

Aisling, when amongst the fae, found herself insatiable. She could devour cauldrons-full, if only for one more bite. Perhaps the remaining morsel of her mortal life, gasping for air.

Aisling indulged in the apple. Sickly sweet and scarlet, it shimmered, replenishing every bite the moment after she'd swallowed. The apple whole and seemingly untouched, time and time again.

Startled, Aisling gasped, dropping the apple. It rolled through the nest of branches, through the garlands, smashing onto an antler from the stag statue below.

Lir laughed, the sound of it setting flocks of silver-eyed ravens aflight in Aisling's stomach.

"Sidhe apples are endless, capable of feeding entire kingdoms. Lest they be mortal kingdoms. A human could sit below this tree for a lifetime, gorging themselves on a ruby-crisp yet never satisfied. And after decades, the tree would collect their bones, a single apple still clutched in skeletal hands, untouched. The legend of Connla is only one example of this."

Aisling reached for another, watching again and again as the magic perfected the supple edge of the apple.

Lir drew a knife from his belt, peeling another plucked apple idly.

"How is such *draiocht* harnessed? Or is it simply born?" Aisling asked, her interaction with the druid in her shop still alive and burning in her memory alongside the torn spell paper in her pocket.

Lir thought for a moment, running his fingers through his hair.

"Enchanted objects or places are designs of the gods. Usually, areas where the Forge first spilled into the universe and its power grows most potent and ancient. But enchanting an object or a place that otherwise bore no special magic, is also possible. Though these spells are more complex."

"Have you always known how to conjure such spells?" Aisling asked. By now, Aisling was familiar with how Lir bred magic on a whim. Sorcery, second nature to the Sidhe king who was half-spell himself.

"No," he said. "To breathe through the *draiocht* is one thing. A matter of emotion and forming a connection with your *draiocht*. To construct, build, create, or even manipulate through the *draiocht*, is far more complex and almost always learned. The first to do so was Niamh. A Sidhe queen to the west where rain perpetually falls. It's said, her sword, gifted by the gods, could cast spells upon wielding it: *Sarwen, the mortal reaper*."

Aisling's brows pinched.

"Why did they call it the 'mortal reaper'?"

Lir smiled despite himself. "Niamh wielded Sarwen to destroy entire fleets of mortals."

Silence brewed between them. Aisling's heart surging at the tale of Niamh and her enchanted blade. But not with loathing as she would've anticipated. With satisfaction. As though this Sidhe queen had corrected a wrong Aisling wished she could correct herself.

"Can you teach me?" Aisling asked and Lir considered her. "To cast spells," she clarified. Aisling held her breath, half anticipating him to decline. To warn her of its dangers, of its complexities, of its consequences.

Instead, Lir tossed her an apple.

"Close your eyes," he said and so Aisling did, plunging into the dark. "How familiar are you with your *draiocht*?" he asked.

"It's most often shrouded in shadow," Aisling said. "Huddled in the abyss inside. Its eyes just bright enough to peer back."

"Over time, it will live freely inside you, no longer cooped deep below. But it's feral, wild, and seeking to either be dominated or dominant. It will learn from you which role it prefers."

Aisling's *draiocht* stirred, waking from its slumber and blinking. Ancient bones clicking as it yawned and straightened.

"Try giving it a specific task. One not fueled by emotion but purpose."

"Everything I've ever asked manifests in fire."

"Aye, for whatever reason the Forge decided, that's your nature: flame. Your essence. But with enough mastery, you can bend the *draiocht* to perform outside your impulses. Like you did with our dreams unknowing."

Heat crept up the nape of Aisling's neck, but she ignored it, focusing on the *draiocht* instead.

Come alive, she ordered it, imagining the apple floating

in her palm, moving of its own accord. The *draiocht* grimaced at the details of its task, the newfound discipline she asked of it, and snarled.

"Don't stop," Lir said, as though sensing her *draiocht*'s temper.

Aisling ordered it again, constructing the complexities of the spell in her mind for the *draiocht* to follow. It snapped its jaws like a hound objecting to the guidance of its master.

"It's testing its boundaries. Seeing how far it can push you," Lir said, his voice closer than it'd been before.

Aisling tried again and the *draiocht* snapped once more, a breath from clamping its jaws around her throat. She flinched, resisting the temptation to open her eyes and break her concentration.

"Dominate it, Aisling."

Come alive! she shouted at the *draiocht*. It roared, thrashing, and lunged for her. Lir, quicker than Aisling could anticipate, grabbed her hand, his *draiocht* strengthening her as she swelled with heat and shoved the beast back with her mind. The creature flailed, hissing as it squirmed back into its cavernous abyss inside Aisling.

"Open your eyes," Lir whispered, his breath grazing her cheeks.

Aisling did as he said, meeting Lir's eyes directly before her own. Closer than he'd been before she'd begun the lesson. Her chest hitched, almost oblivious to the apple still in her hands. Unmoving.

Aisling's spirits fell.

"It didn't work."

"Don't be so sure." Lir tipped his head to his right where a blur of white flashed in Aisling's periphery. The stag and wolf statues, frozen and chasing one another beneath the apple trees, now raced through the air, winding through the branches and their garlands. Enchanted and bewitched. By Aisling.

Aisling exhaled, her lungs suddenly filled with laughter as she traced the statues' every movement while they frolicked. Yet Lir's eyes were fixed on Aisling, searching her expression for what, Aisling knew not. His breath intermingling with her own. The world buzzing, heating, a strange thump sounding in the air as though his heartbeat were the boom of a distant drum calling her to a ring of fire.

"Return with me to Annwyn and I'll show you everything. Teach you everything. The wonders of which will put the witchery of a fae apple and statues to shame. Spells limited only by the imagination, pools of moonlight, gardens that sing, mares as pale as gypsum and crowned with a single, resplendent horn."

Aisling couldn't help but grin, refusing to undermine the fantasy Lir spun with reality. Just for breath. Returning to Annwyn... Aisling frowned, stopping the thought from progressing. The backs of her eyes pricked with heat at the thought of never setting eyes on his kingdom again. And yet, how could she? Her future was tangled by both her own ends and those of others. Lir, Dagfin, her clann.

"You ask such things of me like it's simple," she said.

"It is."

"No, it's surrender."

Lir's expression grew hard, his jaw sharp.

"The mortals demanded you surrender. The Sidhe will ask you to *withstand*. Something you're uniquely capable of, Aisling. Why the Forge has fated you queen."

Aisling's heart fluttered but the feeling was swiftly interrupted.

The temple's bell-tower rang, tearing both she and Lir apart. From where they sat in the trees, it was deafening, rattling the garden till every one of Lir's flowers, roots, and garlands recoiled from the vibration.

Swiftly, the fae king moved, looking out and over Bludhaven through the thicket.

Aisling pushed aside branches, catching a glimpse as well.

A shadow skulked across the drawbridge, the sparkling black river, and through the gates.

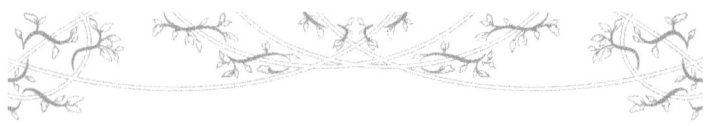

CHAPTER XXIX

AISLING

The moon cowered, shuddering behind streaks of clouds like rips in a painting. The demon skulking beneath its half-light.

An aberration built with the bones of a mare, yet more gaunt and gangly. Its slender legs creeping into Bludhaven. Pupilless eyes gilded and a foil to the pale shimmer of its mane or tail, dragging behind it like the hair of a hag. And most horrifying of all, was its grin. A crooked smile peeling unnaturally far, pausing just before where the ears should sprout but were noticeably absent.

Lir stood between the branches, high in the apple-crowded canopies. The fall from where they stood life-ending for a mortal.

"A phuka," Lir whispered, studying it as it ambled through the empty corridors of Bludhaven just visible from where they stood.

The Sidhe exchanged this name often, chronicling tales of their encounters between goblets of fae wine and song.

"So, this is the Unseelie the druids worship?" Aisling asked, joining him at his side.

"Aye," Lir said.

The phuka moved like a ghost. Head hung low, it traveled aimlessly, stopping to ogle town doors before continuing. Quiet, weightless, and gentle, it left clouds of dread in its wake. A blistering fog, scratching at Bludhaven, climbing the temple walls, and shriveling Lir's garden till it sunk into Aisling's skin.

"We should return," Lir said, seemingly unbothered by the phuka's influence.

"And what of the Unseelie?" Aisling asked, paralyzed by its image.

"What of it?" Lir held out his hand for Aisling, preparing to begin their descent.

"The mortals are sacrificing their own to it, aren't they?" Aisling asked. Indeed, she'd smelled the iron of their blood smeared across the town. The sound of human bones clicking from the thatched and shingled roofs, singing with the memory of those perished. Witnessed the townsfolk bolt their doors and drain the streets come dusk. Felt the empty clang of the temple's bell to announce a feeding when all but the moon would bear witness.

"It appears that way," Lir said, voice emotionless.

Aisling considered him, lingering atop the branches even as he waited for her.

"You bear no inclination to help them, do you?"

Lir did a double take, tempering his emotion, but Aisling caught the flash of confusion then outrage, flickering across his verdant gaze.

"Help a village of mortals?" He shook his head. "Set aside my loathing and still there's little if any reason to intervene."

"Yet it's your woodland. Your Unseelie and they're dying—"

"Ask it and it's my command. But if you're appealing to my compassion for mortal kind—if you want a hero, a knight in polished armor, return to your princeling. For a hero I'll never be."

Aisling stilled, Lir's words echoing long after they'd sounded. Spoken as though they'd lived inside his mind for far longer than he'd want her to know.

"They're surviving. This village is prospering, the hunters, the gatherers, all able to leave their mortal walls in exchange for a blood sacrifice. A deal they struck of their own free will, considering fae deals can be sealed no other way. Humans are never the victims they'd have you believe they are."

Aisling stood silent, watching the phuka glide from door to door, searching for its offering.

"Yet you can end it. Do away with more unnecessary bloodshed."

"Bloodshed is always necessary, *ellwyn*."

"That's heartless."

"It's survival," Lir said, the wind winding through his dark hair. "That Unseelie has no less right to live than any mortal. Both beast and man are nightmares incarnate: humans are simply more efficient at feigning innocence."

The night died screaming.

Aisling covered her ears till the sun rose and morning was born. The ghosts of Roktan sailors burned alive, imbuing present horrors. Of sacrifices made in the dead of night to those who forgot to paint their doors. Of those blood sacrifices whose families shoved them into the streets and left them for dead.

So, as soon as Aisling descended the tavern stairs and met Dagfin's eyes, he realized her restless night.

He moved toward her, a question in the tilt of his brows. Gilrel hadn't allowed him into her quarters but, at the very least, he'd known Lir hadn't returned to his chambers till early morning, if at all.

The familiar scent of him, of childhood memories, of summer chases, of salty seas, and adventure, wracking her chest with guilt. Dagfin felt like a home she could never return to. One she thought of often, a piece of her still living in its simpler memories.

"I purchased horses for travel," he said as they walked out *Abhaile*'s doors side by side. Today, his posture was straighter, his eyes brighter, his voice stronger. The knicks, bruises, and scratches from Oighir, gone. Vanished and replaced with vibrant, warm skin, and renewed energy.

"The rest are already prepared to leave," he said.

And as though conjured, Lir, Galad, Filverel, Peitho, and Gilrel, sat on restless horses at the center of the thoroughfare, the rest of Bludhaven not yet awake.

Lir spoke with Filverel at the front of their group, dressed again in his leather, pauldrons, and hood, yet he found her eyes at once. Drifting to Dagfin at her side.

"This one is yours," Dagfin said, leading Aisling to an ivory mare. Its coat was longer than most, hooves thickly feathered and obscured by snow-white hair.

A Tilrish highland horse, in the likeness of a mare she'd grown fond of in Castle Neimedh's stables but was never permitted to ride.

"Sorcha." Aisling smiled, remembering its name. And as though this creature bore the same spirit, it neighed, leaning into Aisling's palm as she stroked its side.

Dagfin's expression lit like Odhran's constellation, a heavy breath exhaled.

"Enough dithering," Filverel hissed from upfront. "We need to ride till evening if we wish to reach Lofgren's base by nightfall."

Dagfin lifted Aisling onto the mare with surprising ease. With enough strength to lift the entire horse if he wished. Aisling hesitated, watching as Dagfin leapt onto his own mount behind her. Lithe and agile. The gaunt Dagfin from the day prior, suffering from the consequences of Fionn's imprisonment and a trek across the north, gone. Replaced by a radiant warrior, rivaling the strength of the fae. A transition occurring overnight.

LIR

"*Blood seeps beneath the soil, drunk by our roots*," the forest whispered, still and solemn. Cursed to remember the sins committed beneath the shadow of their branches but eager to protect its beasts.

Lir wrapped the reins around his gloves. Mortal mounts weren't as quick, as obedient, as silent as Sidhe stags. But for now, they'd do.

Lir could smell the *draiocht* of *Samhain* ripening with each new day. The cologne of an approaching storm, threaded through the overcast skies in webs of light, making pregnant the clouds above. He could feel Lofgren's Rise stirring, rolling in its sleep like a bear in the distance, and preparing itself to be met. And once there, Lir would achieve, at long last, complete dominion of the mortal race, sealing their fate in the Forge. For the sins of his mother to be made permanent—etched into forever.

The gates of this godsforsaken mortal town groaned open, unveiling the wilderness beyond.

Lir was glad to be gone from this place. Made useful only for Aisling's sake: to allow her a respite before continuing their trek.

Still, the toll of their separation hung heavily on both their shoulders. Yet, close to her, he felt his *draiocht* stretching and gasping for breath after months without air. And he damned himself for it. For the desperate need of her. Every new breath, a prayer Aisling was not his damnation but his salvation. Not his destiny to repeat his mother's crimes but a forging of something new. Something powerful. Something to change the course of Danu's prophecies and the Lady's alike. His hope to weave a tapestry of their own. To not yield to fate, but to master it. To change the course of everything.

But even if she were his damnation, Lir found to his horror, he'd relish damnation if only wielded by her hands. And Lir was concerned he was already experiencing it, too bespelled to realize it. That's what Filverel and Peitho claimed.

Once all were set to leave, Lir nudged his mount onward. The feywilds stirred in anticipation of him.

"Halt!" a voice cried from behind.

A cloaked figure appeared, wrapped in linen robes and crowned by a circlet with stags' antlers on either side. A poor imitation of Lir's own crown, given to the high chief of the druids that worshiped him as well as the feywilds and their beasts. Fifteen or more followers dressed similarly and huddled around him.

Over the centuries, Lir had come across several settlements like Bludhaven. They made offerings and sacrifices, copied Sidhe runes, and christened their children with Sidhe names. All in hopes of Lir's blessing. Lir dismissed their prayers, for the only blessing he'd ever bestow upon them would be to spare their settlement his wrath when he purged this realm of mankind. Of the blood that had maimed, tortured, stolen, and burned his land, his people. Brought about by his first *caera*, Narisea's, undoing. This despite carrying his child and the heir to the greenwood throne.

Lir cringed at the memory, glaring at the druid.

"Your Majesty, crown prince of Roktling." The druid addressed Dagfin, bowing his head in greeting. The priest, a spiritual guide for the druids, nevertheless unable to see through the simplest of Lir's glamours.

"I, chief and high priest Veran, intended to request an audience with Your Majesty, not realizing you were to leave as swiftly as you arrived."

"Apologies," the *Faerak* replied. "Our business here was short-lived and our time of the essence."

"Please, Your Majesty, I only beseech you to stay until the end of *Samhain*. Our people have caught word of your heroism elsewhere, slaying the beasts that plague our kind despite our mortal tendency to ignore all that is Other. To recognize the magic of our realm as anything more than stories. It is an honorable service." The priest bowed, the bones hanging from the circlet, clacking.

"And so, I request such heroism on behalf of my people."

Lir struggled to bite his tongue. He needn't draw unnecessary attention to either himself or his knights, especially during *Samhain*, when the *draiocht* was especially mischievous and lawless. Capable of unveiling his glamour should Lir indulge in his rage.

"You worship the feywilds, the beasts, the Aos Sí. What

reason would you have for my services?" Dagfin asked, forcing Lir to wonder if the princeling was aware of the phuka wandering the streets and claiming souls yestereve or if he'd been too consumed with inhaling Ocras to notice. Enough to kill a weaker human. And if Dagfin hadn't wreaked of it, Lir would've noticed regardless. The sharp transformation from wounded mortal to gleaming *Faerak* in a handful of hours. His dependency deepening.

"All things worship out of fear, Your Majesty. We're attuned to the earth and the churning of the Forge, harboring utmost respect for all its creation." The druid paced nearer, his cloaked followers matching his movements. "But with you here, Prince of Demons Death, we bare the tools to end bloodshed until the next beast arrives, and we're forced to strike a deal we must abide by lest we starve."

"You wish me to hunt this Unseelie down?"

Peitho and Filverel both glanced at Lir, gauging his reaction.

"The phuka, Your Majesty."

Aisling considered the priest through narrowed eyes, reminding Lir of their conversation the night before and wondering if Aisling felt the inclination to help once more. Angering him further.

"There's no time," Lir growled from up ahead, meeting Dagfin's glare. "And this isn't our concern."

The druids all scowled at Lir, noticing him for the first time. Tempting Lir to strip himself of his glamour and have them fall to their knees.

"Fionn and the Lady are still nipping at our heels." Aisling spoke to the princeling, her words nearly a whisper. "We cannot wait till the end of *Samhain*."

Dagfin worked his jaw, considering. A fact which

annoyed Lir more than most things. For despite the priest's ignorance, the choice was not the princeling's.

"I cannot refuse them help," he replied to Aisling, just as low. "And if placed in my position, neither would you."

Aisling grimaced.

"You think too highly of me," she said.

"You sacrificed your life for the mortal race once before. At the expense of all you held dear. Why should today be any different?"

Aisling held Dagfin's gaze, expression unreadable. But Lir saw the conflicted curve at the edge of her lips. The frown that settled across her brow. The way her eyes slid to Lir's own, weighing the correct choice. Caught in between. And so long as Aisling was lost somewhere in the middle, Lir suffered, drowning in his own longing.

"We ride now," the Sidhe king growled, his patience spent.

Lir nudged the mount onwards, his knights following suit while Dagfin and Aisling lingered behind. A shred of doubt blooming in Lir that perhaps Aisling wouldn't follow.

Lir's horse reared, startled by a figure approaching from the feywilds.

Lir knew before he could make sense of its details the figure was mortal. A child, no older than a handful of years, racing for Bludhaven. Mud and blood alike, streaked across its blue cheeks and lips purpled by the cold. It wept as it collapsed across the drawbridge, but not a druid moved. Instead, they glared at him, whispering useless prayers to the gods. The guards at the front entrance raising their crossbows and aiming at the child.

"Be gone!" the priest shouted, fear mingling with anger and breaking his voice. "This is no home to you now, child!"

The child stuttered. Unable to use its tongue for shock or the cold, Lir couldn't tell.

The Sidhe king hesitated, his mount huffing and stomping in place.

"I said be gone!" the druid repeated, voice echoing amidst the silence.

Without thinking, Lir leapt off the horse and approached the child in one movement. He felt Bludhaven stir, their whispers scraping against the cold.

"Do not touch him!" The druid's face burned red, shaking with fury. "That child is the phuka's now. Touch him, and you will condemn us all to certain death for entertaining an escaped sacrifice! He must go back, and our payment must be paid unless his majesty slays the phuka."

Lir ignored the priest, kneeling before the child. He was just a fledgling.

Sidhe children, as rare as they might be, lived decades as children. On the other hand, and at the cost of mortal lifespans, human children lived only a handful of years from birth to adulthood. Meaning this child hadn't entered life but perhaps three years prior. Its handful of years a blink in comparison to Sidhe children. Nothing more than a bairn.

Lir reached out and held the child's cheek. Its flesh hard and waxy to the touch. Lir's loathing for the child's mortal blood cooled by the streaks of tears and the child's cooing. The fluttering of its lashes, the innocence, so akin to Sidhe bairns it almost ached.

The memories of a hungry cry echoed in his mind. Nightmares of a Sidhe bairn calling out to a mother who'd presaged its own death as Lir cradled it in his arms. Desperate to keep its small fire burning if just for a breath longer. To hear its cries for an eternity. And at the time, Lir didn't realize that despite the bairn's death after Narisea's, he'd indeed hear its cries forever. Its precise decibel finding him in a quiet room, a dreamless sleep, a still morning. The pain of every memory, a reminder he still bore a heart. That Lir had once loved and lost greatly.

"This is but one of hundreds of mortal children they've given to the phuka, *Damh Bán*," the forest whispered. "He rode the phuka far between our trees until at last, the creature stopped for its meal, and the child—clever child—escaped, screaming for its mother. But where is she now?"

Lir glanced over his shoulder at the crush of townsfolk gathering to witness the spectacle. Aisling and Dagfin stood nearest the flock of mortals. And beyond them, he could smell the mother from where he crouched. The same blood as the child intermingling with potent terror and regret.

Lir scooped the boy into his arms.

"Tell me, what do you see, *Damh Bán*?" the forest continued, groaning. "Is it possible you see what you've lost in something left living? Even if that something is a mortal child? Ahh, I see now, yes, yes, there is a child-shaped hole in your heart, *Damh Bán*. A wound that will never heal."

Lir stood before Bludhaven, sheltering the child from their judgement. A moment of confusion unspooling before Lir dropped the glamour and allowed his audience to glean his true self. The barbarian lord of Annwyn towering before them, their sacrifice in his arms.

They gasped, staggering back in shock. Veneration muddled with potent horror. The chief druid, paling, his old bones supported by the followers around him. All of Bludhaven holding its breath with no sign of release.

"I'll kill the phuka," Lir said. "And in exchange you'll not only care for and take in this child, but you'll also offer yourselves before you ever sacrifice another child again. Lest I allow the feywilds to swallow this village whole, consume you from the inside out, and spare only the young."

CHAPTER XXX

AISLING

Racat was obsidian.

Its sinuous shape tangled between two others of similar size, cut and glazed into stained glass portraits. One red and winged. The other green and three-headed, coloring the interior of the cathedral as morning light crept inside.

Aisling had never seen Racat in all its glory. Only in dreams, in darkness, beneath the boat that'd sailed her into Annwyn.

"Racat, Muirdris, and Aengus," a familiar voice sounded from behind.

Galad stood a few paces from the entrance to the temple, appraising the stained glass for himself.

From Aisling's vantage point before the altar, she could see Gilrel just outside the doors, Peitho and Filverel guarding the entrance from the now-frenzied mortals eager to set eyes on either the Sidhe or Aisling herself, Galad personally tasked to guard Aisling while Lir and Dagfin hunted the phuka. A partnership that might find the Unseelie unscathed and themselves both hunter and hunted.

"The *dragún* of power, prosperity, and immortality," Aisling conjectured.

"Respectively."

An awkward silence smoked the temple. The only respite, the druids just outside the doors, collapsed on their knees, bowing and chanting as though entranced. A worship Peitho seemed to enjoy, even if it were mortals who kissed the streets before her feet.

"You're more than welcome to guard me from outside the temple," Aisling said—for her own sake or the knight's, she wasn't certain.

"I was ordered not to let you out of my sight."

"You've disobeyed orders before," Aisling said, recalling how Galad allowed Aisling to leave her chambers in Annwyn to deliver a letter to the fire hand. A letter, that with hindsight, she wished she'd burned long before it ever flew across the Isles of Rinn Dúin.

"It isn't the same," Galad said.

"*It* isn't the same? Or *we* aren't the same?"

Galad met her eyes. Sapphires that cut into her soul and forced Aisling to feel what she'd desperately attempted to stifle: uncorrupted guilt.

"'*We?*'" Galad scoffed. "It has never been a '*we*,' *mo Lúra.* Your lips have only ever known '*I*.'"

Aisling winced.

"My decision to leave wasn't meant to either forsake or condemn our friendship."

Galad shifted at the final word.

"It hardly matters, *mo Lúra*—"

"Enough. Don't call me that after my name has been spoken from your mouth before."

Galad's expression tightened.

"Very well, *Ash*." Her name like venom on his tongue. "It

means nothing what you intended. It only matters what you did." His voice rose, slapping against the pews, the stone statues, the pillars. "You fled from my king, from Gilrel, from our *friendship*, without a glance back. Ran with he whose most forgiving crimes were my own branding. A crime I never blamed you for until that day."

Starn.

Aisling's eyes pricked with heat, but she willed not a single tear to fall. It wasn't her place to cry. The stone lodged in her throat, making impossible the task.

"I only ever meant to pursue what it is *I* am. Could you truly say, without a morsel of doubt, you'd have done any differently, Galad?"

The knight studied her, as though he wished to understand but simply couldn't. Wished to redeem her, to justify what she'd done, but found her unforgivable all the same. The pain such a realization evoked flashing across his expression. And the sight of it, enough to crush Aisling's heart and fill her chest with blood.

"We will reach Lofgren's Rise," he said. "Yet you'll find that whatever it is you were searching for—who you are, what you are, why you are—was never anything an Unseelie, a god or even the Forge could give you. It was something unraveling all around you. Something you ran from."

DAGFIN

Dagfin had always cherished winter. It heralded the death of all the rot that'd grown throughout the sun's last cycle. The death of everything unwanted.

The summer was hot and gave light to everything better

left in shadow. Was endless. Was the anniversary of his eldest brother's final words. The rightful heir to the Roktan throne.

Yet now, winter was tainted by Fionn.

Dagfin wove lithely between the trees, the Ocras more potent than it'd ever felt before. Near the brink of collapse, his body was suddenly renewed.

The Roktan prince spun his daggers between his fingers, half eyeing his surroundings for the phuka and half expecting the fae king to appear out of nowhere, swinging his axes.

It was Dagfin who'd been tasked to hunt the phuka and the fae king who'd bore a change of heart; for Aisling or himself, the *Faerak* was uncertain. Only that he'd cursed it, wishing to face the phuka alone rather than align himself with Lir. And mercifully, they'd wordlessly agreed to venture their separate ways the moment their boots stepped foot outside Bludhaven's threshold.

Dagfin had never caught or slayed a phuka before. Yet, by the looks of the clumsy trail it left in its wake, the *Faerak* knew it'd be a straightforward hunt. Hoofprints in the frozen dirt, broken branches from a heavier gait, lazy lines in the snow—its tail dragging behind it. And most disturbing of all, children's clothing torn and left billowing on tree branches, tiny shoes discarded atop piles of leaves, and blood, both fresh and old, splattered across a landscape of ivory.

So, it came as no surprise when Dagfin set eyes on the creature curled beside the edge of a steep drop.

It looked no different than a pale stallion. Magnificent in the light of a fair winter's star, innocently sleeping. And had the phuka's trail not led the *Faerak* directly to the cliff's edge, Dagfin would've second-guessed himself.

The phuka startled awake, searching its surroundings.

Dagfin crouched between the trees, more silent than the

chittering birches or the splintering ice. Steadying his breath and drawing Fionn's longsword.

One flick of the wrist and the task would be done with.

The phuka stood, tossing its glittering, moon-white mane. Dagfin hesitated.

It made no sound, yet the *Faerak* heard its lullaby. The soft humming of a woman emanating from its magical luster.

Unlike the murúch, the sound itself didn't spell him. Only the question of how a creature so resplendent could commit such sins.

Dagfin shook his head. The distraction, he knew, was intentional. The sign of a beast designed to convey innocence so children might follow it into the feywilds of their own accord.

Quick as lightning, Dagfin defeated the distance between himself and the phuka, raising Fionn's blade to sink into the beast's side. The blade plunged the same moment an axe flew across the expanse, both striking the Unseelie with a fleshy thud. The phuka reared, eyes glazing back, its lullaby dissolving into an otherworldly scream as blood as black as tar stained its coat and pooled by its hooves. Collapsing against the edge of the cliff.

Lir appeared from the trees, swinging the other axe in his free hand.

"You're free to return now, princeling," the fae king said, eyes focused on the Unseelie's corpse, transformed into something else entirely. A gaunt, spindly-looking creature whose hair was thin and gray, its mouth pulled to the knobs where its ears should be. A haggard, grotesque beast that gave name to the evil it committed.

"I'm not leaving without the creature's head."

The fae king fixed his eyes on the *Faerak*.

"The phuka is mine."

"Yet felled by my sword."

Lir's expression sparkled, darkly amused.

"If you did anything, it was notify the phuka of your presence. You're fortunate my axe found its throat to commit true damage, worthy of slaying it."

Lir bent over the beast, wrenching the edge of his blade from the leaking wound. He lifted it above his head, prepared to sever the phuka's head.

Dagfin reacted, shifting and unsheathing Fionn's blade from the body of the phuka and toward Lir's axe.

The arc of the blade whistled. Its tip knocking the axe from Lir's hand and scraping the back of his palm as a result.

Lir hissed, fae blood sizzling after the kiss of the blade's edge.

"Very well, princeling; I'd be lying if I said I hadn't hoped to return with two heads instead of one."

Lir threw his left axe. The weapon spun, wicked fast and straight. And had Dagfin been but an average mortal, it would've been a mere flash of color, finding his throat before he'd borne the time to react. But Dagfin stepped to his right, avoiding the strike by a mere hair's length. The axe striking the birch behind him with an angry judder.

"How much Ocras did you take, princeling?" The fae king collected his second axe. He adjusted his grip and tossed it.

Dagfin moved, and the second axe sunk into another tree.

"Perhaps the better question is, how many days must bleed before you can't survive lest you consume your Ocras?"

Dagfin wasn't surprised Lir knew the limitations of Ocras. That for mortals, magic never gave but always took. And ever since he'd narrowly escaped Peitho's blade at their union, the Ocras had become irresistible. The only means of surviving. For without the dust, his muscles ached, his head throbbed, his skin paled, and his bones became brittle. On the cusp of death lest he inhale the Ocras once more—both a surety of more time as well as the reaper of it. A cruel mischief Dagfin found the magic enjoyed. Found satisfaction in both the mortals' denial yet thirst for it at whatever cost.

"Enough to ensure Aisling cleaves from you." Dagfin swung Fionn's blade, once, twice, three times. Yet each one ricocheted off the face of Lir's blades, artfully and easily blocked. Sparks flying and blades ringing each time they connected.

"So, the Lady and Fionn gain a new ally."

Dagfin frowned. "My motives are for Aisling and Aisling alone. I align with no one else."

Lir's shoulders tensed and the wind heightened. The birches lurching, grabbing for the *Faerak* and forcing Dagfin to strike at their branches. They recoiled like snakes, lashing at him repeatedly. The *Faerak* making ribbons of their wood.

Nevertheless, it was not enough. Lir approached, shoving Fionn's blade to the side. Dagfin recovered lithely, striking again, but the fae king was too quick, his branches latching around the *Faerak*'s ankles, as Lir drove his axe for Dagfin's heart.

Dagfin slammed his right fist and the butt of his sword into the fae king's jaw. Lir, impossibly feline, didn't stagger but stepped to the side, bottom lip bloodied by the sword's pommel.

He grinned, licking his own blood off his lips.

Patience thinned.

A sure sign of defeat for Dagfin, as the whole forest twisted, grabbing Dagfin and shoving him onto the ground and on his back. The wind knocked from his lungs.

Lir plucked one of his axes from the nearest birch,

crouching over Dagfin as he'd done the phuka, and positioning the axe's edge beneath Dagfin's chin.

Dagfin laughed beneath his breath, still recovering what little he had left of it.

"That took longer than expected," he said, wrists chafed by the grip of the forest around him. "The great, mythic barbarian lord of the fae, stalled by a mortal."

Lir considered him, head tilting to the side, but said nothing. Only rage and fury and something else entirely, brewing in the nuances of his expression, knocking Dagfin off guard.

Envy.

"So, what took you so long?" Dagfin pushed.

"What fun would your death be if not first relished?"

The trees tightened their grip, slithering around his legs, his torso, his arms, and even his throat. Threatening to bury him alive.

"Do you relish, or do you hesitate?"

Lir pushed the blade till it conjured a bead of Dagfin's blood.

"You won't kill me," Dagfin said, despite the bone-white of Lir's knuckles on the haft of the axe.

"I wouldn't be so certain, princeling."

"To kill me would be to lose Aisling."

Lir's expression narrowed. Dagfin had noticed that Aisling's name on his tongue inspired unmatched rage in the fae king, so he said it often.

"You and I both know forgiveness isn't among Aisling's virtues," Dagfin continued. "And despite whatever fated cord your gods claim knots between you, Aisling's future isn't guaranteed yours."

Dagfin gambled his life with those words: this he knew. And yet, Lir didn't flinch. Didn't move nor scarcely breathe. The inhuman edge of his glare made more severe.

"I think of your death often, princeling. And one day it'll be dealt richly by my axe, I swear it to the Forge." His voice thrummed through the forest, weaving his vow into the roots of the earth. "Aisling's future isn't guaranteed mine, perhaps," he forced out. "A part of her still clings to her past. And to you."

"You believe me a burden."

"I believe you a hero. A slave to your desires; among them, proving to your mortal clanns and tuaths that your purpose isn't to rule atop a throne but in the shadows, vanquishing the demons that hunt your kind. Including myself."

Dagfin despised that the fae king was, in part, correct. Had accurately measured even a fragment of the *Faerak's* motivations. Yet, it was both the fear and the nausea the Roktan throne inspired that compelled Dagfin to reject it. For to sit upon it, to claim it, was to inherit the ghost of his sibling.

"A fact for which you envy," the Roktan prince said instead. "If only for Aisling to admire you instead of despise you; you, the villain of her people."

Lir grimaced, his scowl deepening.

"You misread me."

"That's why you chose to hunt the phuka, wasn't it? To prove to Aisling you aren't the demon she believes you to be."

Lir ground his teeth, jaw flexing at his words. Seemingly wishing to speak but thinking better of it.

But by the hesitation, the thoughts visibly blooming behind the fae king's glare, the Roktan prince knew his assumptions were wrong. He'd indeed misread the fae king.

To Lir, the phuka had nothing to do with Aisling, at least not directly. So, was it somehow possible the fae king bore sympathy for a mortal child?

Lir focused.

"The eve of prophecy is swiftly approaching, and Aisling will be forced to make a choice: to forge a future or revive the past. And that choice will be hers alone."

Lir lifted his axe from Dagfin's neck and uncurled from his crouch. The forest released him, groaning as though protesting their lord's final verdict. Dagfin gathered to his feet. The Ocras healing the aching in his limbs, his muscles, and his bones.

"What makes you so confident?" Dagfin asked, crossing his arms as Lir returned to the phuka.

"You're a hero, princeling. But a good heart is only ever appealing until you're forced to make a choice between what's right and her."

This time, Dagfin didn't interrupt Lir as he lifted his axe. As he severed the phuka's head, the feywilds memorizing the sound of its flesh ripping and bones splitting, bound to repeat it to those who wandered too far within their keep.

CHAPTER XXXI

AISLING

Galad tore through the village with Aisling atop Sorcha, every Bludhaven hand reaching for both she and Lir's knights. A sea of druids seeking to pull them beneath the surface.

"*Skalla*," they chanted. A word wielded against Aisling since the moment it'd been spoken. Today, it lacked its usual poison.

"Save us," they sang, louder and louder, eager to kiss her boots, her legs, the pelt of the mount that guided her to Bludhaven's threshold. If only to glean a morsel of her magic.

In the eyes of mortals elsewhere, Aisling was a traitor. But to the druids, Aisling was hope. A sign that perhaps mortals could take back what was taken from them so long ago. To undo the crimes of the Sidhe.

They worshiped her. And Aisling found she relished it.

Despite the hordes, Galad encouraged Sorcha onward till at last they broke through the mobs and raced across the drawbridge, Peitho, Filverel, and Gilrel shortly behind.

Lir stood waiting at the entrance, wet with blood and the

head of the phuka draped over his shoulder. Dagfin to his left, mercifully still alive.

Aisling exhaled in relief, watching as Lir tossed the head of the phuka at Veran's feet.

A beast slayed until the next woke to haunt them.

Just as it had in Annwyn, the feywilds of Fjallnorr came alive the deeper and further they traveled. Pearl pines speared into the misty veiled clouds above, as large and sharp as Oighir's highest towers. Boulders and rock faces slept like bears atop a carpet of crystallized leaves while caves huffed clouds of fog into the forest's corridors. A realm of whispers, of music, of shadows and light that moved in the periphery only to disappear as swiftly as they'd arrived. Indeed, *Samhain* was as tangible to smell as it was to taste. An odor of winter spices—anise, buttered nutmeg, cloves, and tea cardamom—and the taste of ice on the tongue. Of slick glacial waters and burning wood.

Aisling rode Sorcha alone at the center of their procession. Lir and Filverel rode at the front, Galad last, and Peitho, Gilrel, and Dagfin at the center, surrounding Aisling. Galad humming melodies Aisling remembered from her time traveling alongside Lir's knights in Annwyn: "Niamh's Crown of Rain", the "Memory of Tir Na Gog", and the "Sidhe Knight's Oath".

"Another northern song and the Forge might reap my spirit," Peitho said, wrinkling her nose at Galad. If it weren't for Peitho's sun-bright mane, her gilded eyes, or her richly bronzed skin, Aisling would've forgotten she hailed from the southern Sidhe kingdom of Niltaor.

Ever since Aisling introduced to their fae world, Peitho had lived in Annwyn, having traveled there with every intention of handfasting Lir on account of inter-political strife between the Aos Sí. Conflict Aisling was growing to understand after her time with Fionn.

"By all means, grace us with a southern lament, Peitho." Galad raised a brow. "We all know how well you sing."

Peitho rolled her eyes. "Princesses are the muses of song. Never the composers themselves."

"Tell us of Niltaor then," Aisling piped, knowing the risks of speaking directly to Peitho but speaking, nevertheless. There was a time Aisling feared, or at the very least, trod with caution while in Peitho's presence. Now, their dynamic had flipped. Peitho never freed Aisling from her regard, often sneering, often cursing, often flinching when in her presence. Wishing to serve Lir out of honor or interest, and in so doing, forced to be near she who'd scarred her with flame and, in Peitho's eyes, stolen Lir.

"I'd never waste my breath telling you of its glory." Peitho tossed a strand of honeyed hair over her left pauldron, intentionally or not, reminding Aisling of the lesions across that side of her face.

"*Easca,*" Lir hissed from upfront.

Peitho shifted, wrapping her wrists in the mount's reins.

"Go on, Peitho," Filverel chimed. "If Aisling is to be the true queen of Annwyn, this is the sort of education she needs." And while the words were not explicitly cruel, Lir's advisor bore an unnatural talent for steeping all and everything he spoke to Aisling with undiluted malice.

At the words, 'queen of Annwyn,' Dagfin held his breath but said nothing. The Roktan prince bore enough wisdom to know a verbal fight with Filverel, or any of these Sidhe knights for that matter, was not worth the battle. A wisdom Aisling was, once again, grateful for.

"Niltaor was an obelisk of gold, whittled into a kingdom of everlasting sunset."

The crunch of the horses' hooves on earthen twigs echoed into the surrounding forest. As though every holly, pine, and cypress, hung to each of Peitho's words. Seemingly as invested in her tale as the beating hearts around her.

"Was?" Aisling asked.

Peitho swallowed her snide remark.

"It was glorious *before* the Wild Hunt," she said. "Centuries of competition, of war, of battle, and a resolution that left Niltaor with nothing but destruction. My people left to rebuild the year the conflict between Sidhe and mortals began. And so, Niltaor never recovered."

Aisling bit the inside of her cheek.

Peitho's desire to marry Lir wasn't only borne out of personal interest, but survival. A need to bind Niltaor with Annwyn, the only Sidhe kingdom in possession of a *dragún*, Racat. A union that could've seen the long last renaissance of Niltaor. Until, that is, Aisling became involved. Chosen to wed Lir for the sake of all the Sidhe and mortals alike. Given preference over any single kingdom.

"Was Niltaor ever in possession of a *dragún*?" Aisling asked.

Each Sidhe knight perked up, appraising Aisling, seemingly surprised she knew that detail of their history.

"No," Galad said from behind. "But legend says Muirdris, the *dragún* of prosperity, sought refuge in the dunes of the south, near the shores of Shuilan. Many have sought it, but the landscape that far south shifts, moves, dances, swallowing whosoever dares venture through its keep. Even the Sidhe. And so Muirdris is still lost."

"And Aengus?" Aisling asked.

"Aengus hasn't been seen since Lugh speared its third

head during the finality of the Wild Hunt," Gilrel said. "It devoured half his kingdom before fleeing, showering those still alive in its blood. Those fortunate few are said to bear unnaturally long lifespans even by Sidhe standards."

Aisling considered, pulling her hood over her head as the trees trembled, sprinkling their procession with snow.

"So how was Ina able to capture Racat? The strongest of the three?"

Once more, the fae knights exchanged glances. All save for Lir, eyes pinned to the trail up ahead.

"She made a deal."

"Do you know what happens after death, Aisling?"

Aisling rose from where she lay in the Lady's thicket of stars, plucking them like gems from their branches as she spoke.

"The Aos Sí and their believers sail into the Otherworld," the Lady continued. "While the mortals simply vanish into oblivion. An everlasting dark. But what about those who exist somewhere in between?"

Aisling steeled herself, straightening and lifting her chin so she met the Lady's eyes unafraid.

"We live long enough that it remains a mystery," Aisling said, gritting her teeth as the starry branches brushed her cheeks lovingly.

"We?"

"There will be others like me," Aisling said. "A kind to call my own."

The Lady laughed, the decibel of it threatening to shatter every star in an explosion of shimmering shards like glass.

"So says the lonely. The rejected. The outlander. Not

quite human, not quite fae. Destined to be alone so you cling to a fae king who gives you a sense of purpose. Makes you feel powerful in his desire and praise. Who's turned his loathing into obsession, stripping the power the hatred of others has ever held over you."

"You speak as though you have any authority over the matter."

"I am the Lady of Fate."

"You are the slave of fate. Cursed to weave its threads but never to create them. Bound by fate's Forge-given law."

The Lady's smile fell. "And yet, still I have seen your end, Aisling." She approached, a pathway like galaxies lighting her every step. "You perish in a world of your own making. Of fire, of war, of chaos. Collapse before your throne of antlers. An axe in your heart."

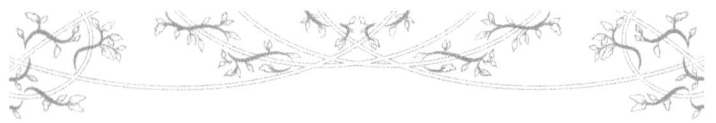

CHAPTER XXXII

AISLING

The forest was bleeding.

Sap oozed down its bark, freezing before it ever kissed the snow.

Aisling lay awake, listening to its pining. To the wind, the crackling of the fire, and the skittering of beasts prowling in the dark.

"You need to rest, Ash," Dagfin whispered, startling Aisling from her thoughts. The same words the Roktan prince had spoken a thousand times, but always inside an iron embrace, mortal castles, and bastions, lest the wet-nurses discover them awake while the moon still reigned.

Aisling opened her mouth to speak but thought better of it, piquing Dagfin's interest.

"I used to avoid the nightmares as well," he said, understanding despite Aisling's silence.

"You're braver than I."

"It isn't courage. It's a hardening of the heart. A refusal to feel if it means feeling afraid."

Aisling shook her head.

"You're too good, Fin. You cannot understand what it means to be haunted by innocent lives taken and to despise it not out of guilt but anger. Anger that it still bears any power over me at all."

Dagfin rolled onto his back, glaring up at the canopies above. The rest of the Sidhe slept around them with the exception of Galad and Lir, pacing the periphery of their camp for the first half of the night. Then, Filverel and Peitho would eventually take their place until the sun rose, grinning at dawn.

"You speak of the men aboard the *Starling*."

Aisling didn't respond. There was no succinct method to explain every sin she'd ever committed and those she was destined to deal. To describe the chokehold prophecy bore over her.

"The Lady speaks of untold desolation in my future."

"She's wrong."

"Is she?"

Dagfin hesitated.

"The night before your union, I offered to run away with you. Do you remember?" he asked, turning to meet her eyes. His own, the soft churning of a starlit sea.

Aisling nodded her head.

"We still can. We can cleave ourselves from the narratives of all that is fae."

Aisling's heart splintered, wishing he'd never spoken the words that Aisling knew he considered often.

"I will not run from those who seek my defeat."

"You consider it a surrender, but it is anything but. It's a victory, Aisling. To rid yourself of the power they hold over you and charter a life of your own."

"And charter I shall, after I bring them to their knees."

"At what cost?"

Aisling locked eyes with the Roktan prince. She'd weighed the cost time and time again and still she found herself wanting. Thirsting. Needing, what it is she craved. And so, she would pay it and relish the conquest.

"You're meant to be king, Fin."

"Damn my throne," he said. "It isn't mine and was never meant to be."

"Your brother would've wanted you to rule, Fin. He never would've wanted this for you—throwing your future away to accompany me on this forge-forsaken quest—"

"He would've wanted me to pursue what it is I love."

Dagfin's expression broke, the edge of his jaw sharp and his lips taut with emotion. As though the words had slipped from between his lips and found their way between both he and Aisling.

"*Who* I love."

Aisling paled.

The final word as tangible as though it were alive and breathing between them, wrist-deep in their chests and twisting their hearts.

"You've changed in ways I can't understand," he continued. "But that doesn't and never could diminish what it is I feel for you. Rage for you. And if power, vengeance, supremacy is what you need to at last prove to your clann, the fae, this realm, and the next that you aren't the pawn they once believed, then so be it. We could rule Roktling if you wanted, side by side. As it should've been."

Aisling blinked, hot tears streaming down her cheeks.

"You were born to make the world a better place, Fin. To protect as you've done for me all my life. Even now." Aisling couldn't swallow, nearly choking on the stone in her throat. "I, Fin, was born to change. To reap it, to make it, to herald it. For better," she said. "Or for worse."

Dagfin shook his head. Deep sea tempests swelling behind his lashes.

"This isn't your journey, and I should've never let you accompany me. If you care for me at all, then return to Roktling. Honor Feradach and accept the crown before it's forced upon you."

The *Faerak* scowled, his anger and sorrow rising. The sleeping Sidhe around them stirring in the commotion. As for Galad and Lir, Aisling only prayed they weren't within earshot.

"It's because I care for you that I'm here at all."

"I'm not your destiny, Fin. Our lives have forked. You will be honored, and I will be feared."

"You are *great*, Aisling. Capable of both great good and great evil. I'm not naive to the forces that wage war within you. But a battle is a battle because it's meant to be fought. So, fight for it, Aisling. Fight to be good. Fight for what's right in place of those who have no strength to do so themselves," Dagfin reached out and held her hand, as they'd done as children when the tales of fair folk became too frightening. "For every mortal village pillaged, every forest burned, every death committed in vain. Because above all, Aisling, I believe in you. In the heart that sacrificed everything for her race. A heart I'd die for again and again, if it meant fighting by your side."

Aisling squeezed his hand, memorizing its pulse.

Dagfin loved a woman who'd died before she ever set foot in fae land. Her body burned and her ashes buried in a circle of fire. Offered by those she'd loved.

"You will accompany me to Lofgren's Rise. You will discover what it is I seek alongside me: this much I owe you," Aisling said, biting down tears. "And then you will go home."

LIR

"*Turn around,*" the trees hissed.

Lir measured them, peering further into their depths. Weighing the density of the *draiocht* as it built, spell by spell till even Lir's ears popped beneath its pressure. A consequence of *Samhain* or something else entirely, the Sidhe king had yet to decide.

"Turn around," the trees repeated, "the forest here is not your own."

The mount beneath Lir agreed, nodding its head forward in warning. Its heart beating swiftly.

Lir cursed, raising his hand to stop the others following shortly behind.

"*What is it?*" Filverel asked in Rún, suddenly more attune to the shift in the air. Peitho's hand drifted to the haft of her weapon, quickly interrupted by the subtle shake of Galad's head. A gesture the princeling noticed as well. So long as Danu believed them ignorant of her ploys, they bore the advantage.

The stench of forge-old rot rose like the fog.

"By the Forge," Gilrel whispered a silent prayer as black sap bled from the birches like tears of ink. And the forest shifted to black.

"Danu," Lir said.

Once identified for what it was, Lir could taste the poison of her influence as it spread through Fjallnorr's northernmost woods. The envy, the resentment, the anger mushrooming till every pine, every stone, every river, and every beast of the feywild was touched by its mold.

The only path to Lofgren's Rise was through Danu's

legions of traitors. Made obvious by the eyes of her dryads peering from behind their obsidian bark, the beetles that skittered between their branches, and the ice that made moist their wooden flesh. Like spiders on a web, salivating, believing Lir to be entering their trap, ignorant of their ready pincers.

Lir encouraged his mount, his knights shortly behind, choosing to ignore the warnings of those still loyal trees in favor of continuing onwards. Into Danu's waiting embrace.

"Bring Aisling's mare beside my own," Lir ordered Filverel.

His advisor obeyed without complaint.

Aisling found Lir's eyes but said nothing. So, Lir was left to hope Aisling sensed it too. Knew that the blood black of the surrounding woodland was no longer under Lir's control, but Danu's herself. And knowing the empress, whatever Lir coveted most would be what she sought to destroy.

And had Lir not heard the rapid beat of the dryads around him, the anxiety of the robins still bold enough to peer from their canopies, or the energy drumming through the mud, the ambush would've come without warning.

The trees bent backwards, reeling before crashing into the earth. The world shook, knocking the mares off balance in a violent, screeching explosion.

Lir dove for Aisling, shoving her off the beast before it crushed her. They flew to the earth, torn apart and a few paces from the other.

The Sidhe leapt lithely from their mounts, rolling and finding their footing. Even the princeling, turning to find the dryads in their tree forms growing thorns, stretching larger, tangling between one another only to hurl themselves into the earth in a thunderous burst of dirt, splintered branches, and blade-sharp ice. Stakes that jutted at Aisling, flame swathed fists digging their nails into the dirt in anticipation of the pain.

Lir turned ashen. Dread prickling the hair at his nape.

He cursed, sprinting for Aisling where she lay and crushing her beneath him.

Aisling wrenched her eyes shut as Lir hid her, covering her body with his own. Her breath against his ear scalding and quick, the fluttering of her heart pulsing against his own and stressing the intangible cord between them. The intensity of it alone near capable of blinding him to the pain of the ice and wood flying from the mayhem and staking Lir's back instead of Aisling.

Lir roared, the sensation somehow worse than an iron blade.

Six or so wooden stakes shimmied between his armor and slid into his back. Scarlet leaking from his wounds and dripping onto Aisling beneath him.

"Lir," she breathed, violet eyes searching his own with horror. Feeling with her palms the warmth of his blood as he sheltered her.

"Lir," she said again, this time more desperate. The Sidhe king struggled to answer as he uncurled, kneeling before her as every sliver of traitorous tree slid between his muscles and took root. Centimeters, perhaps inches from his heart.

Aisling reached her arms around him as if to embrace him, instead, unsheathing the stakes from his back. The pain euphoric when dealt by her hands. The smell of her so near, unbridling his power and renewing what was lost when apart.

His knights drew their swords, allowing Aisling the gruesome duty of drawing each stake from his back as they slipped through the mayhem like blood-bent shadows. A line of defense until the job was done.

"Lir," she said again, after the last stake was removed. Already his body healing, made new when so near to her own. But time was fleeting.

They stood, swiftly dodging another tree as it pummeled into the earth, racing after the others. The world titling beneath the pressure of the onslaught.

"Aisling!" Dagfin screamed, still waiting—always waiting for her.

Lir cursed beneath his breath again, drawing his axe and severing a branch that whipped at them, splitting and writhing in the dirt as it fell. His movement slower than he was accustomed to, a sharp pain slithering through the flesh around his spine.

"Hurry!" Gilrel shouted, leaping from flailing branch to flailing branch, splitting its spindly claws till the dryads hissed, lurching in pain. Filverel, Galad, and Peitho soaking the earth in its sap. Their blades glinting despite the density of the canopies above, the showering of stones, roots, and soil. A choir of ripping, of groaning, of crunching as the discord ensued.

Aisling cast flame after flame, tearing through the trees and sizzling them to ash. Her violet eyes glimmering more brightly, dark hair fanning as she spun from one target to the next, the edge of her lips bent with determination.

Lir gritted his teeth through the pain, slicing through Danu's legion. As though needles of undiluted iron buried beneath his flesh where the dryad's stakes had penetrated his flesh. The torment, all-consuming as their party battled through the dryad's ambush, until the world seemingly ended with a rock face.

A river poured over its edge but was frozen by winter's will. A sparkling veil draped over and between the body of a colossal, obsidian ash. As though the giant once showered beneath the waterfall's sheets, now bejeweled by its ice.

The ash twisted and the ice cracked. The body of a woman taking shape, blinking arachnids, thorns, and vermin. Peeling from its bark and shuddering with life.

Danu.

"Go on, *Damh Bán*," Danu said, her voice thrumming through the earth and echoing through her corridors of black. "Bend the knee to the true sovereign of the greenwood."

Danu twisted one rotting hand wrapped in a gauntlet of thorns.

And at the gesture, blinding pain consumed Lir.

The agony of the dryad's stakes, heightened, iron in his blood, his bones, his *draiocht*, eager to slowly devour him morsel by morsel from the inside out.

Lir collapsed onto his knees, grinding his fangs against his teeth, if only to brace against the pain.

"You've poisoned him," Filverel realized, longsword dripping with sap at his side. Expression lit with desperate outrage.

"A combination of mortal hemlock and burning nettle, also known as *Neantóg*," Danu chuckled to herself. "A brew that mimics the effects of iron when exposed to Seelie. The *Damh Bán* should feel as if iron tangles through his muscles and between every nerve. And at my command, it will spread, seeping beneath his bones, having taken root the moment it plunged beneath his armor."

Neantóg.

One of the poisons Fionn had used in his second test.

Her rage abounding, Aisling reacted and summoned flames of amethyst.

They grew from the earth, hot and wild, barreling toward Danu.

The empress shifted her attention, lifting several behemoth roots and slamming them against Aisling's *draiocht*.
The flames flattened, suffocated beneath the dirt.

"You'll have your turn as well, little beast."

Aisling seethed. Both Galad and Dagfin moving more
closely behind her should she try again.

Danu slid her attention back to the Sidhe king.

And at Danu's smile, Lir screamed. The poison growing
teeth and slithering around his heart.

Aisling reached for him. Without hesitation, Galad
grabbed her arm and held her back. Danu hissed something
Lir couldn't understand. His ears ringing, stomach twisting as
Danu moved again and Lir felt her intentions before the
hemlock and nettle obeyed.

She forced Lir's wings from his back. Wrenching them
one by one from their hiding place in some *draiocht*-made
cavern till they draped over his shoulders in a cloak of silver.
Resplendent, shimmering, and capturing whatever light it
reflected.

The forest stilled, his knights cursed, and the world
beheld his Iod ancestry sparkling across his shoulders.
Opalescent and dug from his body without his consent.
Among the most gruesome, dishonorable crimes committed
against any winged Sidhe.

Danu's dryads lifted Lir with their branches and hung
him by his wings mid-air. Aisling screamed; Galad held her
in place while Filverel, Peitho, Gilrel, and even Dagfin
swiveled, searching for an escape. A solution. But so long as
Danu's poison coursed through Lir, she was his to do with as
she liked, lest it be a quick death.

"Rise, greenwood and the feywilds! Come and see your
king in all his glory!"

Lir felt the edges of his wings pull and scrape against the

dryad's branches. Tears, punctures, rips, capable of being remedied slowly, if at all.

Wings to the fae were a vulnerability. A weakness and rarely, if ever, brandished lest they needed to take flight. But Danu knew this well. Savored the spectacle she'd created of Lir's pain, his humiliation, finding his weakness and using it against him. A symbol of all the vices he'd inherited from Ina, considering only those Sidhe with blood from Iod bore wings.

Lir's knights, Aisling, and Dagfin backed into a circle below him. For in Lir's periphery, he knew who'd come.

Bipedal bears, foxes, rabbits, wolves, and badgers appeared from the hollows, their dens, their nests. Pixies, phantoms, ghouls, goblins, hounds, changelings, bánánach, among others, crept around the dryads to glean their king hung by his wings, frozen by pain. All those creatures who'd sided with Danu after his union with Aisling, now aligned with the empress's efforts to usurp Lir, too frightened to show their faces until she'd proved her supremacy. Until Lir hung prone and unable to punish their treason. An audience of traitors come to scavenge their victory.

And had Lir bore the health, he would've disemboweled them each, nailing their skulls to pikes around Annwyn. The pain only rivaled by his wrath. His *draiocht* shredding the walls of its abyss, clawing to be set free so it might make blood and bones of Danu and her legions.

"Let it be known that the lineage of the original twelve Sidhe sovereigns will end, first with Lir, then his brother. The Unseelie need not be ruled by the fae lest our needs, our hungers be sacrificed in exchange for mortal acquiescence once more. A revolution that drips here but ripples throughout the realm," Danu shouted, *Samhain* dissolving her words till they bled from the forest to the Other. "From this day onward, the feywilds belong to the Unseelie, the beasts beneath oak's shadow, and none other!"

The beasts, the fiends, the creatures of midnight hours and woodland secrets, banged their fists against the earth, hollered, howled, barked, and squealed, growing more frenzied by the heartbeat.

Danu grinned and the trees obeyed.

They pulled Lir's wings and ripped them from his back.

AISLING

Aisling screamed, Lir's agony her own, coursing through the intangible thread between them and sinking its teeth into her soul.

Galad tightened his grip, arms wrapped around her waist as she struggled against him.

"He will rot, slowly dying as the poison seeps more deeply," Danu said, voice bubbling with glee as dirt spilled from the corners of her lips. Salivating over her conquest. "And let the forest witness his death. Bury his body beneath its soil and return his corpse to the Forge, ashamed of his betrayal—his alliance with those who felled us, hunted us, burned us. Let the Other mock him as he enters their shadows broken. His only salvation, the fire, the fae rebuke."

Lir lay in the snow, fangs bared as he desperately battled the misery. Left to collapse, his wings discarded at either side of him. Muscles taut and runed fingers gripping the earth. The pain pulsing through, shadowing the sorrow of Danu's dismemberment. The grief, the anguish, smoking his periphery as he fought to remain alive.

Aisling turned to face Danu. Their eyes met and the hordes of beasts and Unseelie hushed.

"And his last memory of the mortal realm? His bride, the fire hand's daughter, the bane of our realm, dethroned with violence."

Lir struggled to fight, reaching for Aisling despite the pain.

Galad, at last, released Aisling, raising his blade the moment Danu's dryads swung for the not-so-mortal queen. His sword split their wood in half, sap spewing. Yet it wasn't enough. Not for Aisling.

Aisling summoned the *draiocht*. Violet fire roared awake, seizing their branches, both severed and intact, and bled their limbs to ash.

More drove toward her, wielding their twigs, their vines, their roots like whips.

Aisling, swiftly, focused the *draiocht*, allowing it to slip from its abyss and rise through her, lurching and casting its fire till Aisling was forced to hold her breath a heartbeat longer than the last. Fires taking hold of the dryads and burning them alive. Their screams bloodying the air they each breathed.

Danu fumed, slamming her fists into the earth and tilting the axis on which they each stood.

"You know not the way the forest lives, little beast!" she screamed, swarms of beetles, of flies, of ants, pouring from her pale white eyes. "No matter how hard you try, your iron bones, your mortal flesh, will never fully burn. You do not belong and never shall you. You will rot having served your purpose and brought the *Damh Bán* to his knees."

Aisling's fists blazed, her gut lit with wildfire when she glanced at Lir, the suffering worsening. All because he'd sheltered her, protected her from Danu's dryads. Taken the onslaught upon himself.

She should suffer, the *draiocht* whispered. She manipulates. She deceives. But she does not hold power over us.

Aisling could ignite the whole of the forest around them as she'd done the *Starling*. Could burn every last beast and Unseelie that'd celebrated Lir's torment. That prayed for her own.

Yet Dagfin's voice echoed in her mind, "*Fight to be good.*"

She exchanged glances with the Roktan prince. He stood to her left, frustrated, furious, confused. Thrown into the center of fae conflict he bore no stake in other than Aisling's role in it.

Perhaps there was a path to salvation that wasn't as ruthless. A path Dagfin would recognize if placed in her position.

Danu laughed. "What do you say, little beast?"

The forest writhed, lashing at Aisling. Lir explained this to Aisling before. The forest didn't concede to good or evil. It conceded to power. And it would concede to Aisling.

"Kneel," Aisling said.

Aisling inhaled, trapping the *draiocht* inside her chest. She'd done the same in Nemed's tent before Dagfin and Peitho's union, except this time, it was purposeful.

She unleashed the *draiocht*, allowed it to grow, to swell, to explode from her lungs and rise, coaxed by her hunger. And this time, fire was not a serpent but a colossal *dragún*. A sinuous demon roaring into existence, crackling, morphing, shifting in licks of flame.

Racat.

The shape and spirit of her *draiocht* come to, at long last, unveil itself.

Danu's pale eyes widened, her legions fleeing from

whence they came, and her dryads, recoiling, pulling at their roots, unbinding themselves from the earth.

But before any could speak, before they could run far, Aisling allowed Racat to ravage Danu's legions.

A beast of flame clawing between the trees, flaying every creature alive, the smell of their hides, their furs, their fear smoking the air, stoked by the dryad trees crackling with heat.

At last, the *dragún* flew toward Danu, the empress, who recoiled, drawing back into her tree form and burying herself inside the cave hollowed behind the waterfall of ice from which she'd emerged.

Aisling compelled the *draiocht* to find her. Slithering and disappearing inside the cave as the realm burned and Aisling memorized their howls for mercy. Writhing, bent over, kneeling on the ground.

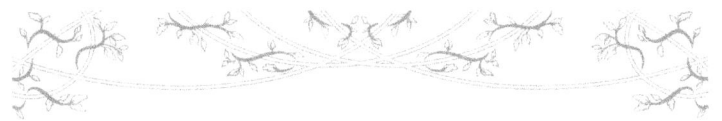

CHAPTER XXXIII

LIR

The tears spilt between his lips were not his own.

They were hers. Even now, in slow death, the bond between them renewed his soul. Coaxing his eyes open despite his suffering.

"Something must be done," Galad said.

"The poison has taken hold," Filverel replied, barely a whisper. "It cannot kill him. Not fully. Only iron or fire will."

Peitho gaped. "You can't possibly mean—"

"If it will end his misery," Gilrel said, voice shaking as she staked her blade into the earth beside him and bowed her head, "then perhaps it is the only solution."

Beside him lay his wings. Bloodied at the appendages. The absence of them left him cold. The last vestige of his mother. Grief, a fathomless hole inside his chest, cannibalizing him from the inside out.

"No." Peitho shook her head. "How dare you all give up so easily? Surrender to Danu, her legions, and forsake your king?!"

"Surrender?" Filverel narrowed his eyes, "You believe

this the easy path? The flippant choice that spares us?! If there was a way, I'd risk it no matter the cost to either myself or anyone else here for that matter."

Lir desperately tried to scream, to move, to open his eyes and fight for his life. He'd endure an eternity of pain to live another day. He was forever, destined for more than a death by Danu's trickery.

"She's right," Galad said, expressionless, still stunned, staring at Lir's wings. "We can't do this."

"And what then? We let him suffer?!" Filverel yelled, voice breaking mid-sentence—unable to separate his grief from anger.

Lir wasn't certain how long the silence lasted. The stillness after death and, now, before it. The few birches, pearl pines, and silver spruces still loyal to him and untouched by Aisling's rage, wept. Arching their wooden spines in the swelling, in the absence of the nuthatch melodies, the gale's blow, winter's sun veiled by clouds in mourning.

"You're panicking," Galad said, eyes drifting from Peitho to Filverel.

"What other options do we have?" the advisor said, his voice stripped as though he'd been shouting for the last several days.

"An elixir, an herb, a potion, a draught, a spell, a curse," Gilrel offered, listing them without taking a breath.

"We don't have that sort of time!" Filverel shouted.

"We'll make the time," Gilrel bit back.

Galad shook his head. *"His only salvation, the fire the fae rebuke."* Words Danu had spoken, silencing them each.

All shifted, finally drawing their attention to Aisling.

∾

AISLING

"She'll kill him!" Peitho screamed. "We can't possibly trust her with this."

"She's his *caera*, Peitho," Gilrel said, the word "*caera*" slapping Peitho in the face. "And the only one capable of wielding the fire necessary to destroy the poison."

"She is by every definition his bane. His undoing. The ill-omen of the fae!" Peitho continued, as though Aisling weren't kneeled beside Lir as she spoke.

"You saw the form her *draiocht* took," Filverel said. "Somehow, impossibly, she summoned her flames and in so doing, summoned Racat in the image of her flames. That must mean something."

"But what?" Galad asked, the only calm one among them.

"She's been chosen, selected, or forged by either Ina or Racat."

Aisling's face twisted, her mind whipping violently from thought to thought. Her soul expanding and swelling with the extreme form of so many emotions.

"Perhaps she isn't the enemy, the mortal weapon we once believed," Galad said. He turned to Aisling, a soft gesture inherent in his gaze. As though, in this moment, he wanted to believe she wasn't the traitor they'd witnessed at Dagfin and Peitho's wedding. Wanted to believe she could still be an ally.

"If her *draiocht* manifested itself in the shape of Racat, it implies her destiny is with the fae. With the greenwood." Galad exchanged glances with the rest of Lir's knights. And at the words, Dagfin turned away. "So, give her an opportunity to prove it."

They glared at Aisling, hatefully, intensely. A look that

dissolved into hope when the silence became unbearable. Lir still clutched by otherworldly pain.

Aisling inhaled.

"You perish in a world of your own making. An axe in your heart."

The Lady's words crept into Aisling's mind, spoken on a loop until Aisling knew their cadence by heart.

This was not Lir's death day. He would live to kill Aisling: this much was prophesized.

And if it was possible to change prophecy, Aisling's choice here and now would speak of it. It wasn't revealed when or why Lir would be Aisling's end. Only that he would be. A mere fragment of the portrait drawn by the Lady.

One day, Aisling and Lir's positions would be reversed.

Aisling turned to his knights.

They each beheld her in silence.

Dagfin, however, avoided Aisling's eyes entirely. Head bent and eyes red.

In that moment, Aisling wished she bore the strength, the will, the courage to kill the fae king. Desperately tried to convince herself she could. That with so much blood on her hands already, another meant nothing at all. That *he* meant nothing at all. Especially he, the enemy of mortals, her own deceiver. He, who not only threatened her goals in the curse breaker's name, but was also the reaper of her end.

And yet, Aisling was physically unable. Her body paralyzed, her heart thrashing inside her chest, stomach churning. Not only could she not stomach it, but she also found her soul would shatter. Not because of a bond or fate or prophecy. Something else. Something ravening, chaotic, and bonded to her.

Aisling bent over Lir.

She ran her fingers through his hair, watching as he

leaned into her touch, still overcome with torment. She brushed her lips against his ear.

"Do you trust me?" she whispered.

The corners of his lips curled despite himself. "No," he managed.

The sound of his voice sweetening her hate. Her loathing an addiction if inspired by him.

Aisling pressed a palm to his chest and closed her eyes.

I wish to summon you, she spoke to the *draiocht*, watching as it stirred inside its abyss, angry it'd been woken after its recent battle.

I wish to summon you, Racat, dragon of power. The form her *draiocht* took, living within her since her union with Lir, perhaps even before, unbeknownst to herself. A magic unnamed until now.

The basilisk moved, popping its primeval bones and creeping into the light.

Enough to burn whatever poison threads through the fae king and no more, Aisling added.

Racat growled, rattling the interior of his lair.

You will kill him, it said.

This isn't the end the Lady prophesied for him. He will not die, Aisling replied.

And you believe her? Have you considered it was all a deception? A trickery to ensure you unbind yourself from the fae king by slaying him yourself?

Aisling had already weighed this possibility. The Lady bore no motivation to speak the truth especially if it conflicted with her own goals. And so, what Racat suggested was likely.

I've made my choice, Aisling said, focusing her magic like Lir taught her and opening her eyes.

Embers bloomed from her fingertips.

Peitho sprung for her.

"Wait!" Filverel shouted, grappling the princess of Niltaor. "Let her do this."

Had Aisling been aware of her surroundings, she would've been baffled alongside the rest. Filverel, who'd abhorred and distrusted Aisling since her union with Lir, desperate enough to let Aisling attempt to save Lir's life.

Aisling burned all which had no place in Lir's body. Finding the poison with her *draiocht* and devouring it. Precise magic carved by unsteady hands.

"*It's feral, wild, seeking to either be dominated or dominant. It will learn from you which role it prefers.*"

Aisling rehearsed Lir's lesson from the apple tree in her mind. Her temples pulsing with pain in her concentration. Hardening herself against the *draiocht* wrinkling its muzzle and snarling.

Lir bared his teeth, finding her wrist and gripping it till Aisling believed he might crush it. Turn her bones to dust, as the fire seeped beneath the skin and traveled. Weaving, knotting, folding, tangling inside. Reviving the fae king. The remaining forest thrashing around them, monk's moss, clovers, fresh mounds of emerald growing from where he lay, spreading, and transforming Fionn's winter into everlasting green. The woodland exhaling in relief as the northern gale danced and new trees sprouted from the earth, spreading their branches like limbs, yawning and stretching after centuries of sleep.

The poison squirmed, leaping from his body and bleeding into Aisling's own, crawling up her arm and scalding her bones.

Aisling screamed, releasing her hand and falling backward. An angry scar wrapped through her fingers and up her forearm. The poison burned, leaving its mark regardless on she who expelled it.

You didn't think such precise magic came without a cost, did you? Racat chuckled.

Aisling stood waist deep in a river: water gargled by this northern land. It ran from one side of Fjallnorr to the other. A corridor the Ashild had dug into the earth.

It was cool, speckled in fallen leaves and lined with precious stones made more vibrant by the life Lir's healing inspired.

Aisling dipped her arm in the waters. It burned still, scarlet and blistering. The rest of her wounds from Danu's ambush paling in comparison.

"Starn and I used to spar in rivers like this," Dagfin said, appearing from the surrounding forest to lean against a boulder nestled beside the river. "Before the mortal sovereigns chose to build their walls. The song of running water veiled our ruckus and washed our cuts before supper."

"That was another life," Aisling said, surprised Dagfin spoke with her. Since their last conversation around the fire, the *Faerak* had been reluctant to glance in her direction or exchange more than a handful of words. His coldness was a punch to the gut, but Aisling didn't push him. She knew he needed time to process the forking of their lives. A truth that'd been breaking Aisling's heart since it first took root.

"Aye, back before we knew what true battle was. What it meant to harm another much less kill them."

Aisling swallowed. The smell, the sound, the emptiness Aisling had felt when she'd slaughtered all who'd stood with Danu slipping into her mind.

"I don't regret what I did," she said, meeting the *Faerak*'s eyes. "It was necessary. A means of survival."

The image of every beast kneeling in flame flashed across her mind's eye.

Dagfin weighed his thoughts, brow pinched and arms crossed.

"I've killed countless Unseelie in my lifetime, Aisling. I'm hardly one to judge."

"Yet you do judge." And Aisling didn't blame him for it.

Dagfin's brows drew together, furrowing his expression.

"It's more so that I don't understand," he said. "I kill to protect the innocent. You kill for power." He hesitated. "And for *him*."

Aisling looked away. Mortal minds weren't weaved with the capacity to understand survival in the same manner the wild understood. As for his mention of Lir... Aisling couldn't think of it now, afraid to touch the *Faerak*'s implication.

A passing gale sifted through her hair. One of the few sounds amidst the quiet. Dagfin's anger finally breaking through.

"Whatever binds the two of you, Aisling, undo it. Before it costs you your soul."

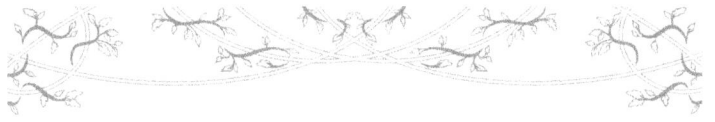

CHAPTER XXXIV

AISLING

Time didn't burden the feywilds.

After endless days and sparkling nights, Aisling wasn't certain how long they'd traveled. Only that they did so in silence. Still stunned from their encounter with Danu. The fae king a shadow of his former self, haunted by his mutilation. Haunted by the absence of what he'd carried for centuries, careful of its vulnerability. Wings now torn and left to freeze in Fionn's ice.

He ignored her. Aisling wasn't certain why. Only that Lir disappeared for hours between the trees, refusing to be accompanied or respond, to be near, to speak with anyone save the forest itself. So, Aisling allowed him his time to grieve. To understand both the sadness and the anger.

Aisling tossed in her sleep, avoiding another encounter with the Lady to little avail. A plane the Lady accessed easily, warping Aisling's dreams into nightmares and prophecies.

The rest of the Sidhe slept in a circle beside her. All of them, beneath the shelter of a cave. Dagfin an arm's length away, still clutching a dagger even as he slept. Lir and Gilrel were on night watch, threading through the forest for any enemies that dared lay siege so soon after their last onslaught.

Racat hadn't found Danu after she'd escaped. The dragon, a question in all their minds, grief and shock the only barrier preventing any to speak of the form Aisling's *draiocht* had taken and interrogate her for it. Although she knew, by the look in Filverel's eyes, the questions were coming. Questions that haunted Aisling and answers her *draiocht* hid each time she confronted the beast with her queries. Mastery of magic, in its essence, was the dominion of beasts, Aisling was realizing. A balance between control and power; to either leash your *draiocht*, let it ravage freely, or find some alternative in between.

Nevertheless, Danu hid. Her roots shriveling, knotting, and slithering into the cave where she'd fled. Gathering her legions in another part of the continent, Aisling assumed. Lying in wait to finish what she'd begun.

But despite Aisling's fires, Danu hadn't entirely lost.

The empress had managed to best Lir, the most powerful Sidhe lord, because she'd taken advantage of his weakness: Aisling herself. Had Lir not sheltered Aisling from the poisoned roots and shards that staked his back, he never would've fallen prey to her schemes. It was Aisling and the protection he'd allotted her that'd ultimately been his downfall. A sacrifice that went against his very nature.

One half of Aisling grew sick with guilt. The other half convinced herself Lir's actions were self-serving. Protecting the host that amplified his power and nothing more.

And yet, despite their escape, Danu had taken, and would continue to take, from Aisling's mind. Plaguing her dreams, alongside the Lady, with the caustic screams of Aisling's victims. The brutality of her slaughter dissolving the anger Aisling wielded so readily into unfamiliar sadness. Rage, anger, fury made Aisling feel strong. On the brim of spilling over with power. Sadness, on the other hand, made her feel weak and helpless. A memory of her human self. Her dreams flooded by midnight tears till she sprung awake screaming and sobbing in a cold sweat.

"Ash," Lir's voice sounded in the night. Aisling whipped her head to the forest's lip, finding Lir's eyes reflecting the light of the moon amidst the dark. Lir emerged from the surrounding pines. He studied her closely and before Aisling could wipe away her tears, he was kneeling beside her. His proximity stirring the forest and enveloping them in wisps of cypress needles and sweet saps from the midnight gale he inspired.

Aisling made to push him away. To hide her tears. But Lir pulled her close, his long legs on either side of her, his arms holding her waist against his torso.

Too stunned to move, Aisling held her breath, the sensation of his arms burning through her garments and knotting her stomach.

Aisling glanced up and into his eyes. Flecked with a sorrow of their own, they softened, exploring the red sheen of her eyes still glazed with the memory of her nightmares. Aisling had never seen him like this. Looking as sad as she felt, his embrace warm and... almost kind. And then it occurred to Aisling that Lir had never seen her so unguarded either. That Aisling had never wept in sorrow before him, only in anger. That Aisling had never cried out in fear in his presence. That Aisling had never let Lir witness when she felt fully vulnerable. Fully as fragile as she did in the night, when she was powerless against the guilt that racked her.

Upon the realization, Aisling thrust her walls up once

more and, afraid he might pity her, she placed a hand against his chest to push him away. He caught her wrist.

"It was a nightmare and nothing more," she said.

"You're afraid," he conjectured, his voice deep and vibrating through her core. Aisling said nothing but her silence was answer enough. "So long as I'm near, neither Danu nor the Lady nor Fionn will ever harm you." At last, his voice was laced with familiar bloodthirst.

Aisling shook her head. "That's not what frightens me."

Lir searched her expression for the answers he sought.

"Then what? Tell me and I'll take it all away."

Aisling fixed her eyes on his own. Unsure what to think of his words. Afraid to let herself believe he, the dark barbarian lord of the greenwood, might care for her. Might *want* Aisling independently of the power she promised.

"I'm afraid of myself," she said, surprising herself the moment the words fell from her lips. "I'm afraid of what I'm becoming."

Lir's eyes narrowed, shaking his head as though in disbelief.

"You're becoming who you were always born to be."

"And who is that?" Aisling asked, both to herself and Lir. "I still hear their voices, their screams. Whether it be on the *Starling* or Danu's legions. My hands are stained with their blood. Irredeemably burdened by the lives I've reaped." The words forced out more tears, reddening the apples of Aisling's cheeks and the tip of her nose.

Without hesitation, Lir's grip tightened. And the comfort, the *rightness* of his embrace, shook Aisling with her cries. She wet his leathers with her sobs, allowing herself this weakness. This vulnerability against the beat of his wicked heart. Because such a heart understood her own. Understood the evils she'd now committed in a way few others ever could.

For who understood and accepted the curve of one's shadow better than the darkness himself?

"Change is painful, *ellwyn*; the oaks mourn their leaves come autumn, the night bleeds into sunset, and the wolf cries at the blood moon. But there is meaning in the suffering."

The wind wove through both their hair, whispering in a language Aisling couldn't understand. Bracing itself against the groans of thunder up above and the approaching storm. Droplets, slipping through the canopies and sliding down Aisling's face alongside her tears.

She only needed a breath. A few minutes to sort through her thoughts before she pulled away, cooled by the rain. Yet his touch muddled her mind, an intense intimacy blooming between them as his words, his hands, his heart pounding against her ear became all consuming.

Aisling moved to pull away but met his eyes instead. A mistake for, this time, they captured her, bespelled her with their sage magic. Nuanced and pining as he leaned closer the same moment Aisling did. His expression shadowed, eyes drifting to her lips. Both of them, closing their eyes as they defeated the last remaining distance.

Yet their lips never met, the movement interrupted by Aisling's arm knocking into Lir's axes, strapped against his back.

Immediately, Lir pulled away, jerking free of their embrace. Expression shuttering with a flash of betrayal.

They both unfurled from their position on the ground. Their pocket of peace, destroyed. A thin veil of rain, separating one from the other.

"Never," he said, "touch my axe again. Are we clear?"

Aisling had wielded Lir's axes once before. At the *Snaidhm* where she'd beheaded the trow at his command. Hardly able to lift it, much less slay the beast that'd hunted her. Now, its blades twinkled as though glazed with tears themselves.

Aisling frowned, still orienting herself from the sudden shift in his temper. Wiping away the last of her tears with the sleeve of her leathers.

"Afraid I'll wield them against you?"

"Would you?" he asked.

"If necessary."

"You almost wound me, *ellwyn*."

"Perhaps I should try harder then."

Lir's expression brightened, flashing with amusement. The first time since Danu's encounter his eyes flickered with light.

"What do you know of these axes?"

"Gifted by the gods, they've spilt mortal blood for centuries."

"Aye, imbued with primeval *draiocht*."

"Is that why you never let them out of your sight?"

Lir considered her, the sensation of his undivided attention chilling.

"Together their name is Hiraeth, the Heart of Annwyn."

Aisling repeated the name in her mind, familiarizing herself with its nuances. *Hiraeth, the Heart of Annwyn.* "What does that mean?"

"To destroy either Annwyn or Hiraeth would be to destroy the other," Lir said. Aisling appraised his axes anew, glimmering with life. Their blades were black, as though chiseled and sculpted from onyx and engraved with fae runes. The haft was wooden and wrapped in leafy vines that moved, slithered, at times braiding themselves around Lir's forearms while he fought.

Aisling arched a brow. "Why would you entrust with me such information?"

"You're the queen of Annwyn. You should know."

Aisling bit her bottom lip, wondering if this was Lir's way of exchanging her vulnerable tears with a vulnerability of his own.

"Filverel would seethe if he knew you'd divulged anything of the sort with me."

Lir shrugged. "Maybe I think it's attractive when we play with fire."

Aisling's stomach dipped. The fact she was alone with the fae king, suddenly more electric. The others soundly asleep beneath the blanket of stars above.

He stepped closer.

"Careful." Aisling held out her hand, her fingertips holding back his chest from coming any nearer. "I might start to believe you're flirting with me."

"Who says I'm not?"

Lir moved nearer still. His hair dripping with rain as it fell over them with more force. Speckling his otherworldly features as it had in her dream.

Lir was toying with her, his manipulation clear, intentionally balancing on a knife's edge of affection. His abrupt shift from kind and vulnerable to sharp and wolfish made Aisling certain of it. Anything to convince Aisling to truly bind with him if it meant complete sovereignty. An archaic sort of magic that left all but a fortunate few bloodied and scarred. But Aisling could wield such manipulation just well.

"If you were flirting with me, you would've taken me by now." Aisling moved closer, steeling herself. Spelling her every movement with the seductive tilt she'd studied in her encounter with the merrow. And to her surprise, Lir's arrogance flickered, his expression flashing with surprise, before his eyes darkened and his throat bobbed, studying his opponent anew. His fangs lengthened, balancing a bead of rain at their tip.

"Or are you too afraid?" Aisling asked. "Afraid you're no longer in control?"

A muscle flashed across Lir's jaw.

Aisling moved to touch his shoulder, but Lir stepped away, just out of reach.

"You shouldn't taunt me, *ellwyn*. It's a game you won't win."

"Who says you're the only one who seeks the power our binding will yield?" Aisling asked, her voice as silky as wine and as thick as cream.

"Is that why you're doing this?" he asked, his voice rougher than Aisling had ever heard it. "The power?"

Aisling despised herself for hesitating. For taking more than a breath to respond.

"What else is there?" She repeated the sentiment he'd spoken in Fionn's castle. And for a moment, Aisling thought she saw a glimmer of disappointment in Lir's eyes hidden deep within and carefully veiled.

"But if you're not ready to truly bind, there's always Fionn—"

Lir moved toward her, quicker than Aisling could blink. Forehead to forehead as he glared down at her.

"Never," he growled, his voice dangerously deep, "threaten that again."

Aisling resisted the urge to wilt, grinding her teeth and leveling her scowl.

"Why the change of heart?" Aisling asked. "At Peitho and Dagfin's union, you were forge-bent on either killing me or protecting me. So, what's changed?"

Lir closed his eyes, battling something Aisling didn't understand. His face contorting with frustration, anger, and boundless yearning. Enough to spill past his walls and poison Aisling's resolve.

Lir bared his teeth. "A piece of whatever sanity still bloomed in my bones was ripped the moment I thought I'd lost you and burned entirely when you left me."

Aisling willed the fluttering of her heart to stop. The rhythm of Lir's heart pounding, maddening.

"Without one another," Lir said, "we're half of our true potential. Made obvious by our months apart."

Lir cupped her neck with his bare fingers, sliding his hand up and into her hair. Chills ran down Aisling's spine, vanishing the words on her tongue. Burning her lips where his hand moved, finding her jaw and pressing his thumb against her bottom lip. Mercilessly, his eyes grazed her mouth.

"Maybe you need me more than I need you," Aisling said. "Maybe you bare your fangs now, but you still mourn the loss of your wings. What Danu took from you."

Lir wrenched his eyes shut.

"Danu will pay for what she's done," Lir said.

"Aye, she will, by either you or I but she'll pay all the same."

Lir searched her face, but whether he found whatever he searched for, Aisling wasn't certain.

"Let me see your scars," Aisling said, her voice lowering.

Lir hesitated. This demand was a risk. To, for a breath, lay down their serrated words, their blades, their enemy masks, and allow Aisling a glimpse beneath his armor. As she'd done for him.

Lir clenched his jaw, the sharp edge of it slick with rain. And just when Aisling believed he'd leave her there, standing in the storm to wallow in his grief as he'd done the past several days, he pulled off his leathers, his tunic, his pauldron, his hood, till nothing except for his axes and their bandolier were trapped against his bare chest. An abdomen chiseled, lean, and etched in fae markings.

Painfully, she swallowed the stone in her throat, daring herself not to stray from his gaze, even as he unsheathed his axes and turned, displaying his scars in all their glory.

Fair folk flesh healed rapidly. Miraculously. But these were the scars of deep, lifelong wounds that could never heal entirely. Angry, jagged, deep, and fresh, they tore into his shoulder blades as though blunt knives had clumsily dug out Lir's wings. The memory of his pain and Aisling's fires, lacing every stroke. The image of it, a tale better left forgotten.

Before Aisling could think better of it, she reached for him, that familiar sadness she'd felt upon waking, reigniting and pressing the backs of her eyes with heat. Her fingertips traced each scar, and the moment they touched his back, Lir flinched. Shoulders shuddering the longer she trailed every angle. And yet, Aisling felt as though she were already on borrowed time, Lir capable of snapping at her like a wolf protects its wounds.

"Thank you," Lir said instead. "For sparing my life."

Aisling opened her mouth to speak but stopped short. He didn't need to thank her. There was no reality where Aisling would've let him die. The decision already forged in her bones and in her heart.

CHAPTER XXXV

DAGFIN

For each day the Ocras dwindled, Dagfin found the north grew colder. The wilderness harsher. He'd bought enough Ocras from Bludhaven to last the rest of the journey lest he endure severe injury. In which case, Dagfin only harbored what was necessary to heal himself and no more. But it was his appetite that truly plagued him. The desperate need to remind his tongue of its taste.

Dagfin stood at the mountain's edge peering into the valley that lay between it and another ridge. Lofgren's Rise was another half day's journey, and so, they'd chosen to rest while still able.

Gilrel stood with Aisling at a river's shoreline at the center of the valley, instructing Aisling on the best form and technique for wielding a blade. At first, she began the lesson with the marten's sword. Something small, weightless. Then they offered her Galad's weapon—a wicked sharp longsword forged with gleaming metals and cast so its edge curved.

Aisling performed better than she ever had in Tilren. She'd been miserable at their lessons, often chastised for her

lack of skill. Starn, Iarbonel, Fergus, and Annind conde-
scending her for her weakness. But Dagfin never understood
their scorn. Aisling was powerful before she ever inherited
magic. She was fearless in the face of nightmares, of authority, of those who told her she couldn't do whatever she liked.
She was quick-witted and cunning. And she was hungry for a
throne Dagfin never bore the courage to seize himself.
Indeed, while Dagfin ran from the Roktan crown, Aisling
pursued a crown of her own making. And yet, Dagfin was the
hero the north heralded as Prince of Demons Death. Aisling,
a traitorous thief and witch.

Dagfin couldn't deny the shadows he'd witnessed,
seeping beneath her skin like veins filled with tar while she
burned the *Starling*'s crew. It was survival. A means of
preserving their own lives. *A necessary means to an end*,
Dagfin repeated till he exhausted himself. And how she
slayed Danu's Unseelie but a few nights prior, winning a
battle hundreds of mortal men had fought before her and
lost... Aisling simply bore the ability to win. She'd done what
Dagfin's own father would have done to protect his people.
Aisling was just more powerful. Still, Dagfin found it unsettled him. Made him fear for her soul. For whatever this
binding between her and the fae king was becoming. The
urge to rip it apart if it meant rescuing her, more reasonable
by the hour.

No, she was brave and would stop at nothing, even in the
face of pain, of danger, of conflict. Whether it be Nemed's
wrath as children or the gods' now. She could fight the fae
king's influence.

"Sulking doesn't befit you," a feminine voice sounded
from behind.

Dagfin shifted, doing his best to conceal his surprise. The
fae were silent, stealthy, and weightless upon the forest floor.

Peitho stood a few paces away, approaching as lithe as a cat. Her blade sheathed at her back. Hands empty. Seemingly uninterested in physical conflict with the *Faerak*. Still, he held his breath when near her. When she walked too close to Aisling, eyeing the twitch of Peitho's fingers. Memorizing where she hid her blade whilst she slept.

"I'm keeping watch, lest there be another ambush."

"Ah, is that it?" Peitho said. "Do you normally keep watch by glaring solely at a dark-haired maiden?"

Dagfin cleared his throat, crossing his arms.

"Tell me, fleshling, why are you here?"

"I already told you. I'm keeping watch."

"No," she said. "Why have you journeyed this far with her?"

"I could ask the same of you," Dagfin replied.

Peitho squinted but nodded her head in understanding. She tipped her chin at the river where Lir and Galad emerged, having bathed away the blood, dirt, smoke, and snow from the past several days. They approached the shore, Lir finding Aisling's eyes as he exited. And as it always did each time Dagfin witnessed these exchanges, his heart sunk. The way their eyes connected across an expanse or when nearby. The way the world paused whenever they did so, holding its breath.

"It appears we both find ourselves unrequited," Peitho said, her voice as broken as Dagfin felt. "It's an unfortunate thing to find yourself on the periphery of a legend. The tales won't speak of us. Only them," she said, jealousy a Cornelian shade of orange behind her lashes.

"And yet you risk your life, aiding the one who rejected you."

"And you she." Peitho frowned, leaning against a nearby birch.

"Aisling hasn't rejected me." Dagfin knew Aisling felt for him at least a semblance of what he felt for her. He witnessed it time and time again, in her touch, her care, her wandering glances. And when everything was said and done. When Aisling found whatever she craved at Lofgren's rise, Dagfin would wait a lifetime for Aisling to recognize the *rightness* of their pairing. That she made him brave and he made her good.

Peitho ignored him. "My only hope is that Lir finds himself at odds with his not-so-mortal queen in their pursuit of the curse breaker and whatever else lies at this godsforsaken summit. And if that's the case, Lir will act accordingly. For Annwyn."

"Are you certain of that?" Dagfin challenged.

"I've known Lir for centuries and if I know anything about him, it's that Lir is motivated by two things: Annwyn and his fear of repeating his mother's mistakes."

"Motivation is only so potent until combined with a *want*," Dagfin said. "What does Lir want?"

Peitho paused, thinking to herself and recognition dawning.

Aisling swung the blade by the shoreline, her hands suddenly overcome with rare violets. She smiled, glancing over her shoulder at Lir, still dressing himself, and grinning at his mischief. His sorrow the past several days eclipsed by his renewed, easy arrogance. This despite the angry scars scratched beside his shoulder blades.

"Hope is a damnable thing," Dagfin said. "For it is almost always false."

∽

AISLING

> Welcome are those of breath,
> My children, pardoned by death.
> Enter and find in my keep a sanctuary
> For all those whose blood runs faerie.

A colossal arch stood before them. The entrance to Lofgren's Rise.

Aisling wasn't certain what she'd expected, but it certainly hadn't been a behemoth of a fae city, interlaced with the highest, snow-capped mountains in Fjallnorr. A threshold presaged by giant statues in the image of winged Aos Sí, holding the scroll of entrance before them as well as a mighty cauldron.

"This is Iod," Aisling said breathlessly. All this time, Lofgren's Rise was inside Iod. Aisling shook her head, weighing the importance of the ground she trod. A kingdom lost to both a curse and time. One that presaged her own birth and that of all humankind. A place of legends, of myths, of songs sung around campfires, and hummed at dawn. All before her, whittled into stone giants and forsaken by a ruinous love.

The group approached cautiously.

"Aye, this is Iod," Lir replied, glancing inside the cauldron. "And it appears we weren't the first to arrive."

"There's already been an offering?" Filverel asked, seeing for himself.

"Offering?" Aisling asked.

"Sidhe blood," Filverel replied, appraising the already opened gate to the city.

"'*For all those whose blood runs fairie*,'" Aisling repeated. "Only the Aos Sí may enter."

"Another fae sovereign?" Dagfin suggested, twirling his knives between his fingers.

"Fionn," Gilrel growled in conjecture, hopping atop the brim of the cauldron.

"No," Lir said. "I'd know the stench of his blood as part of it flows freely in my own veins. This is someone else. None I recognize."

"Lofgren's Rise is heavily guarded," Dagfin said, reminding Aisling he'd come before but never made it to the peak. "Whoever's gone first has done us a favor. They'll trip every alarm before we do."

"Now that you mention it, how did you enter last, princeling?" Gilrel asked, crossing her paws.

"*Faeraks* often carry fae blood in vials for masking our mortal scent. Last time I was here, I made use of those supplies."

Gilrel softened her posture, but by the glimmer in her beady, black eyes, Aisling knew she still harbored suspicion.

The rest of their group stepped closer to the gate while Aisling lingered behind. Swiftly, she reached inside her pocket and found the parchment she'd stolen from the spell book in Bludhaven's druid shop.

Touch for Memory:
> Speak the following enchantment and touch
> the desired object to relive its every memory.

Cuillhnigh ar rach hud
> *a kheap tú go ndearla tú dearkad.*

Aisling memorized the words, quickly slipping the parchment back into her pocket the moment Filverel glanced back at her. And once he looked away, Aisling closed her eyes and hoped, gripping the cauldron and repeating the incantation beneath her breath while the others appraised the threshold into Iod. She felt the *draiocht* rise and breathe, but this time it was different. It was soft, guided, and molded by the words of the incantation instead of her own will. A spell. The *draiocht* straining against this new practice in discipline, one she'd attempted in the apple tree with Lir, the second in an effort to heal Lir, and the third now.

The *draiocht* snarled, nipping at Aisling as she spoke the incantation more loudly in her mind. Racat grimaced, resisting, until Aisling hissed in return, scolding the creature and demanding its obedience.

And it worked.

But the triumph was short-lived, eclipsed by the flashing of the cauldron's memory: days of wintertide forced a shiver from Aisling's body, the sensation of a bird's talons gripping the lip of the cauldron, digging into Aisling's temples, the memory of silence, of the stirring of the surrounding wood until at last, a memory that mattered appeared.

Starn, Iarbonel, Fergus, Annind, and Killian, stood around the cauldron. One by one they painted their palms in the blood of the fae, whose throat was slit at their feet, and dripped a single droplet into the cauldron. And once the last drop was spilt, they continued into Iod, lugging the body of the fae soldier by their ankles.

Aisling snapped back into the present time. She exhaled a laugh, quickly recovering before joining the others. A handful of seconds she'd been gone, maybe more, but it'd felt like much longer whilst inside the spell. And if Aisling could wield spells such as this, what else could she wield other than fire?

Aisling would indulge in such possibilities later. For now, her attention was focused on her brother.

Starn. One couldn't enter Iod lest they bore fae blood, so her brother had found a way to circumvent Ina's law by slaying a member of the Sidhe. A knight from Oighir, Aisling conjectured by the forgery of his armor. Starn, her brothers, and Killian desperate for a disguise.

Aisling cleared her throat.

"My brother has already been here," Aisling said and the rest of the fae and Dagfin gritted their teeth or shifted. Perhaps having assumed but not been certain. Lir looked at Aisling over his shoulder where he stood nearest to Iod's arch, eyes drifting to her hand still leaning against the cauldron.

"He'll die before he reaches Lofgren's peak," Filverel said.

"He's desperate enough not to," Dagfin said. "That's how they've made it this far."

Indeed, Aisling's brothers and Killian claimed they were returning home as soon as they'd escaped Oighir. But now that Aisling thought of it, her brothers' plans had been designed with Annind's health in mind and so, once Fionn had remedied him back to health to gain Aisling's favor, there was no longer reason to return to Tilren.

Aisling cursed beneath her breath. She should've anticipated this but with everything unravelling so swiftly around her, she'd forgotten about her clann entirely. Glad to be rid of them.

Aisling shook her head.

"May I borrow a blade?" she asked. Galad did a double take, searching her eyes.

He handed Aisling a dagger from his bandolier and

watched as she sliced her palm. The smell of her blood affording her the rest of their party's attention.

"For the *Faerak*?" Galad asked as Aisling let her blood drip into the cauldron. Dagfin flicked his eyes away, understanding that it was the half of Aisling's blood that ran fae that allowed him entry.

"Aye," Aisling replied.

"We'll see if it works," Galad said, collecting his dagger.

"And if it doesn't?"

Galad hesitated, avoiding looking at the *Faerak*.

"Just as with his union with Peitho, the *draiocht* doesn't take kindly to being deceived."

Aisling's heart stuttered. Glaring at the trail of blood scraped across the dusty, snow-ridden floors and into Iod's winding halls.

Iod was breathtaking.

An endless city carved from the mountains and dusted in snow, divided by a slender valley parting the rise before it connected overtop once more. An arch in and of itself riddled with staircases, terraces, turrets, and battlements, and warmed by floating lanterns of fae light. Snowy owls perched and flapping their wings on every ledge. Carvings and statues of winged Sidhe dancing, battling, soaring. And where the staircases didn't lead, still homes, arcades, shops, and village levels cut into the highest layers of stone, spindly towers suspended in the air by magic alone—reached only by those who could fly and no other.

All of it, abandoned and preserved despite the millennia that passed since Ina had forsaken her kingdom.

A land of ghosts and curses, casting whispers into the wind as their group walked inside.

Aisling was struck with the sensation she wasn't meant to be there. That whatever remained of her mortal blood fought with every morsel of its will to flee in the opposite direction. Aisling glanced at Dagfin. The *Faerak* rolled his shoulders, seemingly as affected as Aisling was.

Lir drifted to where Aisling walked, unsheathing his axes.

It was deathly quiet. Not a sound except for the howling of the gale as it purled through Iod's corridors.

"*Which direction do we travel first?*" Peitho asked in Rún, her radiance a contrast to the pale landscape around her. As though she too, didn't belong.

Iod was a labyrinth of rocky corridors, staircases that broke off, tunnels, caves, and artfully carved reliefs. Winter flowers and garlands of pine needles draped and clinging to every landing, every arch, every ornamental buttress as the city loomed around and above them.

"Lofgren's Rise is the tallest peak in Iod," Lir said, gesturing to the tip of the kingdom's arch.

Aisling squinted, glaring up and into the nebulous sky where Lofgren's Rise slept.

"Do you remember how to get there?" Filverel asked, staring up and into the distance.

"I spent little time here as a child," Lir said, brow furrowing. Aisling wasn't certain what feelings his mother's kingdom aroused in him. Sadness, grief, anger. Only that it disturbed the fae king. His temper short and his mouth bent cruelly.

"Nor I," Galad added. He, another subject of the greenwood, born with Iod ancestry.

"We'll follow the trail of blood," Filverel said. "And hope the *Faerak* is right."

"Let's get this over with." Lir led their group down the valley.

They each held their breath, and none spoke. Their thoughts ricocheting off the emptiness of Iod as they wandered through.

Aisling could almost hear the laughter that once spun through these pebbled corridors, filling these shops. The smell of gingerbreads, hazelnut pastries, sugarplum jellies, and cranberry ciders. The sound of their sleigh bells, lutes, and trumpets, and the taste of their *draiocht*. Like frostbite and perilous highland trails. How the air would've been crowded with fluttering winged fae. Their mirth, their life, vanished. All gone, corrupted, and forsaken by Ina for her *caera*. A foolish mistake that cost her everything. Standing in Iod now, the weight of such a mistake was made obvious.

And if the ghost of Iod's past wasn't enough, Aisling felt as though she were being watched. Studied as she entered. Every owl, glaring at her with their bulbous eyes till her skin crawled.

The trail of blood ended beside a staircase that barreled into the side of the mountain.

Above the staircase, letters were etched in Rún. So Gilrel translated for both Aisling and Dagfin.

> Enter here only the invited.
> The chosen, the mighty, and the knighted.
> Otherwise, pay by breath,
> the lasting coin of death.

Their attention wandered to a hand of stone, protruding from the wall beside the threshold.

"Ina enjoyed her riddles, it appears." Filverel read the

passage a few more times, disassembling each sentence word by word, syllable by syllable.

"This is ridiculous." Peitho rushed to the entrance, prepared to dive into the darkness. Her hand slipped past the entryway first, snatching a bloodcurdling scream from her lips. And when she drew back her hand, it was skeletal; phantom white, the flesh stripped from her fingers and shriveled to dust, slowly returning to normal the longer she stayed away from the threshold. Horror marked her features until her hand, at last, bore no signs of the death-given bones it had just donned.

"I suppose we haven't an invitation after all," Gilrel said, grabbing Peitho's hand and studying it up close.

"From whom?" Dagfin asked.

"Ina." Aisling moved forward, tracing the stone hand with her fingertips.

"Careful," Galad said, moving beside her as if to take her hand away. Before he could, Aisling's fingertips lit like matches, sparked by the magic of the mountain.

"Remember the doorknob in Annwyn?" Aisling asked the knight. "The whittled hand each and every visitor must clasp to make its acquaintance? This is no different. Only now, we meet the mountain itself. Lofgren's Rise will determine if Ina has invited us or not."

At Aisling's words, they each peered through the threshold.

Darkness veiled its full passage, but Aisling could nevertheless see its path spin upwards into the heart of god-forged rock.

Aisling folded her hand into the stone's grasp.

The mountain heaved in and out, as though gasping for breath. Its every expire low, thick, and timbersome, vibrating with magic lingering from the beginning of time. With rain pelting its jagged back, trees growing over its boulders, and stars bending lower to lick its peaks. This giant annealed by the Forge and the gods themselves, weary after centuries of hoarding Iod's abandoned kingdom.

Fire ignited around Aisling's knuckles, wove across the stone hand's wrist, and spilled into the interlace tracing the door. Every stroke and groove filled with flame, lighting the entryway in violet fire.

"Wait," Dagfin and Lir said in unison, but Aisling was already stepping through the threshold. She crossed, unharmed, and purpled by the glow of her flames.

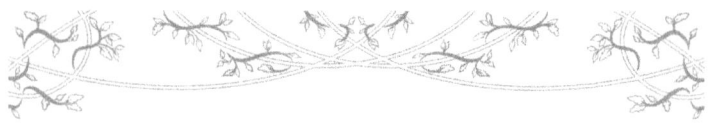

CHAPTER XXXVI

AISLING

One by one they traveled up and into the dark.

Aisling cupped her hands together and bloomed the *draiocht*. A bud of fire that fluttered into individual flames like rose petals, catching the mountain's sighs and lighting their path as it floated through their party.

"Impossible. Ina's been dead for centuries, how could she have invited her?" Filverel asked, glancing at Aisling over his shoulder.

"Her *draiocht* takes the form of Racat. Is it really so outlandish to believe she's been foreseen by Ina herself?" Gilrel argued, eyes narrowed as she led their party up the mountain.

"You needn't speak of me as though I'm not here," Aisling said. "Perhaps the entrance responded to magic and spells alone."

"Then it would've allowed Peitho in," Galad replied. "Her lungs alike breathe with magic, as do all the Sidhe."

Aisling's brow furrowed. When she'd first arrived in Annwyn, a snake had guided her to a hidden chamber. One adorned with a large fountain and the image of an owl, watching her as she appraised it. Her first invitation, Aisling was now realizing. A chill crept up her spine at the thought.

Lir avoided Aisling's eyes, preferring to stare into the dark instead. He knew something, but Aisling wasn't certain what. Only that no matter the situation, she could depend on Lir to harbor his secrets.

Aisling swatted the questions away lest her anxiety worsen. Everything she'd ever wanted rested at the tip of Lofgren's Rise. Just within reach, yet Aisling couldn't help feeling like it were somehow farther away than it'd ever been.

At last, they arrived at a landing that spilled into a wide corridor. One that belonged inside a magnificent fae castle, dressed in banners of ivory and embroidered with three-eyed owls. Fae light hung from the beams overhead in quilts of white clover, illuminating the velvet carpets, the vases spilling over with prickly poinsettias and holly. Ceilings distantly high, knotted with ribbons, wind chimes, and dripping with dark jewels mined from within the mountains, Aisling assumed.

And just before them, at the center of the corridor was a mighty threshold made of wood. Carvings of thorny wreaths, interlace, and one slender dragon adorned the door, vibrating with the sound of music on the other side.

"It's a trap," Filverel said, drawing his sword from his back. "No one goes near the door."

The advisor approached slowly, weighing the possibilities of what lay beyond. It sounded like a celebration. One of wild music, of swishing gowns, and uninhibited laughter.

"The corridors aren't predictable," Dagfin said. "They shift and change direction, leading further into the mountain until it's near impossible to find one's way back."

"What's your alternative then, princeling?" Gilrel leapt atop Filverel's shoulder.

"The mountain is divided in two," Dagfin said. "The left side is trickery. The right side is riddled with beasts. At least, that's what I pieced together last I was here."

"And why were you here, princeling?" Peitho asked, arching a brow.

"*Faerak* business."

"Care to share?" Galad pried.

Dagfin grew taut, glaring at the fae through shadowed eyes. Each day he grew weaker, Aisling could tell. His Ocras lessened by the hour as he consumed more than he ought to. And despite standing in Iod now, where Ocras was harvested from the stone, Aisling didn't know how or if it were possible for one *Faerak* to reap the Ocras alone. So, Aisling was left to hope Dagfin knew what he was doing. And selfishly, Aisling needed him to indulge in the Ocras lest he perish. Lest he be another mortal caught in the crossfire.

"Is there another way?" Aisling interjected. "Or do you know what lies on the other side of this door?"

Dagfin shook his head. "Last I was here, I chose the corridors instead of this threshold. The music persisted even then, meaning—"

"It's an enchantment," Filverel conjectured.

"Not all enchantments are bad." Peitho shrugged.

"And what of the corridors?" Galad asked.

"As I said, most are deceptive, but it isn't impossible to navigate them. Based on the landscape of the rest of the mountain, however, the ballroom should be the quickest route to the top. Almost a direct path."

Aisling eyed the trail of blood. It traveled down the right-hand side corridor and into darkness. Starn was being sloppy. A sign of desperation.

"We'll divide ourselves," Aisling said. "Half can follow Starn's trail of blood through the corridors, a guide despite the labyrinth. The rest will venture through this threshold in case the corridors are a deception. If either or both of us are successful, this doubles our chances of reaching the top of Lofgren's Rise before anyone else."

"Is it wise to divide ourselves against unknown enemies?" Peitho asked, appraising the reaction of the rest of their party. "We have no idea what else lies here, much less who. Our chances of survival are slim when apart."

"Peitho's right," Galad said. "There's no guarantee we'll find one another again considering we lack communication whilst inside this keep. If anyone were to grow lost or…" The rest of his sentiment died in the air between them. The perils of their quest made tangible and bitter on their tongues.

"Not one of us was ignorant to the risks involved when entering Iod," Aisling said. "Whatever our motivation, we came to reach Lofgren's Rise before any others, not to dawdle in fear."

Aisling could taste what she'd coveted for so long. It was close. All the answers she needed were right here, beating like fae drums. She couldn't—*wouldn't*—slow her pace now. Wouldn't let the frivolities of fear keep her from losing what was just within reach to the ambitions of another.

"Your impatience blinds—"

"Enough," Lir interrupted. "Your queen has spoken."

His tone commanded silence. Filverel swallowed his rebuttal, bowing his head at Aisling. And at the gesture, Aisling's stomach fluttered. As though his acquiescence was born from more than just his respect for Lir but his respect for Aisling as well. Yet, it wasn't possible. Filverel despised and distrusted Aisling more than most, yet the glister of recognition in his opalescent orbs spoke a different sentiment entirely. One Aisling hadn't been prepared to receive.

"How should we divide ourselves then?" Gilrel asked, brushing dust off her pauldrons.

"The princeling knows these corridors best," Galad said. "Gilrel and Peitho will follow him through."

"I go where Aisling goes," Dagfin said. Immediately, Lir's posture tightened.

"You'll go where she commands you to go," Lir said.

Yet Aisling didn't protest. In truth, Aisling didn't want Dagfin to leave her sight whilst inside Iod's keep. The whole of their relationship lived thus far, Dagfin had protected Aisling. From the other children, from her father and tutors, and from herself. Now it was Aisling's turn. She wasn't certain how much Ocras Dagfin had left, and she wasn't willing to risk it. So long as he was near, Aisling would know he was alright.

"Then you'll accompany me through these doors, alongside Galad and Lir," she said, the music growing louder on the other side.

"He's mortal, *mo Lúra*," Galad said, forcing himself to meet her eyes. "An enchantment could deal... fatal consequences on any who lack fae blood whilst inside Iod."

"Regardless," Filverel continued. "We need him to navigate through the corridors."

Aisling studied the trail of blood till it disappeared into the hallway's abyss. Aisling bit her bottom lip, weighing the choice. Caught between her impatience and her anxiety for the *Faerak*.

"Aisling and Lir are the most powerful among us," Gilrel said. "Let us venture through the corridors with Filverel and Galad as well. Especially if the princeling is correct and this path boasts more physical means of guarding whatever lies atop Lofgren's Rise."

Dagfin shook his head, a cord wrapping around his neck.

"Lead the others through the corridors, princeling," Lir said to Dagfin, drawing one of his axes. "You can rest assured I won't keep my eyes off her."

Dagfin's nostrils flared but already the group was dividing itself, those chosen to accompany Dagfin through the corridors drawing their weapons and starting down the tunnels.

The *Faerak* hesitated but Aisling knew Dagfin couldn't forsake even the Sidhe to wander unguided when he alone knew the way.

So, reluctantly, Dagfin tore himself from Aisling.

Aisling caught his hand. She felt Lir shift behind her, the gesture catching his eye.

Dagfin appraised her, eyes at once softening despite the rigidity of his lips.

"Be careful," she whispered. "And don't do anything too heroic."

Dagfin curled his fingers around hers. "If I didn't, they wouldn't sing ballads about me."

The *Faerak* bent his head and kissed Aisling on the cheek, bathing Aisling in his cologne of crisp waves, starry nights, and sea-faring adventure. In his warmth. In iron and fire. In home.

Dagfin's mouth lingered by her cheek for a breath too long, at last, pulling away and searching her expression. Hopeful for what he might find. Aisling wasn't certain if he was pleased with whatever he'd gleaned or disappointed. Stormy eyes awash with emotion.

He untangled his fingers from Aisling's and started into the dark.

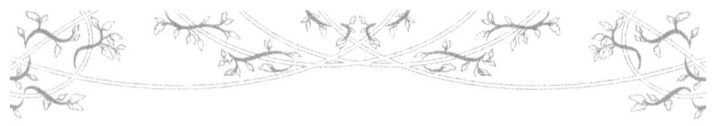

CHAPTER XXXVII

AISLING

The door shook with laughter.

Music like a Tilrish reel thrummed beneath their feet. Yet its tune was distorted, made more alive, as though every note of the fiddle, the flute, the tambourine, and the harp were the blood of Iod, coursing through its corridors like veins till the heart of it pumped rapturous melodies from the door just beyond.

Its sound was familiar. Not only because it was fae but rather because every inflection, note, and melody was reminiscent of another time.

"That sounds like—"

"A *Snaidhm,*" Lir replied. The festival's name was a spell, showering Aisling in memories. A *Snaidhm* was the celebration of a consummation between two *caeras* intended to bless the coming of an heir. Last Aisling had attended a *Snaidhm*, it had been her own. The evening she'd both committed her first kill and encountered a Cú Scáth Lir swiftly slayed. Yet the festival had been in vain, celebrating a consummation that'd never occurred.

"Is it possible Iod isn't abandoned?" Aisling asked, for who else would be partaking in such merriment on the other side? This, considering an enchantment of these proportions would require someone capable of mass magic. And the only beings capable of *draiocht* in that magnitude were fae sovereigns, some Unseelie, and the gods themselves.

"It's not possible," Lir said, his expression still thrashing with the fury of a woodland storm after Aisling's interaction with Dagfin. But still, there was more. As though the fae king was experiencing a persistent memory, forcing itself to be remembered.

The threshold's owl carvings peered more closely as Aisling and Lir approached.

"This isn't an enchantment," Lir continued, placing his palm against the door.

"*Samhain* spirits," Aisling gauged. "Are they not a threat?"

"Not typically," Lir replied. "The spirits of *Samhain* are fae-pardoned and allowed to exist in the Other. They bear no ties to this realm, nor do they wish to. They're chaotic in nature, interested only in entertainment and mischief but this close to Lofgren's Rise and so potent... yes, they could be a threat."

Aisling swallowed. Whoever celebrated on the other side of that door was indeed powerful. Pulsing with the *draiocht* and rattling the whole of Iod.

"They'll recognize us 'non-spirits' the moment we step through those doors." Lir cracked his neck, bending it side to side before turning to face Aisling.

He closed his eyes and when he opened them, Aisling could smell the essence of his glamour. Of pine needles, rain-steeped earth, and crisp leaves.

Lir's leathers had vanished entirely in exchange for a

loose-fitted, unbuttoned blouse that unveiled the length of his chiseled abdomen. Trousers belted indecently low while a gold leaf, embroidered jacket held the weight of a pauldron and scaly chainmail shimmering down his left arm. Rose gold chains like thorny vines wrapped around his throat. The complement to the small hoops in his left ear.

Aisling, against her own volition, traced his fae markings with her eyes, creeping up the hard, muscled angles of his abdomen. Her attention inspired a dimpled grin from the fae king that could've undone Aisling if she'd lingered a moment longer than necessary. Heat bleeding behind her cheeks as she broke eye contact.

Aisling looked down at herself, discovering a floor length, form-fitting gown of sensual violet. Silk folds, sparkling spider's lace, and secret-thin panels of sheer chiffon hugged her curves like simmering cauldron teas. The neckline dipped dangerously low, exposing the rapid pace of Aisling's every breath. Parts of her abdomen, hips, and arms made vulnerable and exposed to Iod's chill thanks to the sheer panels that sparkled with dew. Droplets scattered across her skirts and jeweled the bluebells braided through her undone hair; their hue, dipped in the memory of amethysts.

Lir's expression flashed with something unholy, marveling with wicked satisfaction at the gown he'd sewn in his mind then glamoured onto Aisling. A dress fit for a royal *Snaidhm*. So she resisted the urge to burn, her toes curling.

"This will disguise us well enough," Lir said, adjusting the rings magicked onto his fingers.

"And what of my mortal scent? Whatever remains of my mortality, the spirits will identify the moment I step through those doors."

Lir frowned, glancing at the door.

"By now, it's barely recognizable," he said. "Although, you're partially correct. Even a sliver would be enough for the spirits to recognize. And my blood will only mask yours to an extent lest you travel directly beside me the whole way through."

Aisling swallowed, ignoring the fluttering of her stomach as Lir stepped nearer.

"Stay close to me," he said. "And never leave my side."

Aisling opened her mouth to speak, but before she could manage a word the door creaked ajar, pushed open by a phantom hand. A ribbon of light spilling into the stone corridor.

An invitation.

Music colored the air in decadent golds, rich emeralds, royal blues, hungry reds, and lush lavenders. The smell and taste of fae buttered rolls, sweet cakes, gelatins, roasted pig, and freshly plucked apples marinated in syrup and baked in artfully kneaded dough, hung in the air.

Aisling squinted, bracing herself against the contrast. The lip of icy highland corridor, a cliff's edge to the revelry that took place before her. A glittering, rib-vaulted chamber of glowing roses puckering from garlands that coiled around great ashes, sprouting from the marbled floors, dappled in leaves and petals, and winding to the ceilings. Every branch draped with bluebells, wisterias, bushes of bone's breath and Connemara poppies, cocooning the room in their embrace. A gathering blessed by showers of flowers, braided branches, and ripe fruit begging to be plucked.

Aisling inhaled, brushed by a rogue firefly slipping through the threshold they'd opened. One of hundreds, floating lazily between winged dancers. Countless of them, twirling, spinning, leaping to the drums, the flutes, the fiddles, laughing.

"Care to dance?" Lir asked. Aisling whipped her head in his direction. He offered her his hand, fangs shimmering where his lips curled like a wolf.

Aisling shook her head, her tongue suddenly thick. "It isn't worth of the risk."

Lir's smile broadened. "To walk would risk discovery."

"You mean to say they haven't noticed us yet?" Aisling asked, as a gathering of toads crowned by hoops of daisies leapt to the rhythm, hand in hand with mice. The mice's paws full of soft cheeses stolen from the banquet table.

Bears lounged at the base of trees, the roots of the mightiest oaks their throne, as they huffed on pipes beside giggling phantom nymphs, brushing one another's hair.

"The veil between here and the Other is thin thanks to *Samhain* but not torn entirely. To disrupt a procession of spirits would award us their full attention. And such attention is never recommended."

Aisling stepped toward him so Lir bowed his head in invitation as the badger, the tortoise, and the fox adjusted their instruments and flipped their sheet music, preparing to begin another song.

"Whatever you do," he whispered, "don't stop dancing whilst the music plays."

Aisling slipped her hand into his, the contact scalding. So, Lir pulled her close, wrapping his other hand around her waist till they stood chest to chest. The thump of his heart accelerating beside her own.

Aisling tipped her head entirely up, finding his verdant gaze.

"Is this necessary?" Aisling frowned.

"Depends," he said. "Would you rather be disemboweled

by the fangs of millennia-old spirits? Or stay this close to me?" Lir's lips split into a hot-blooded grin.

Already, the spirits' attention was wandering toward them, raising a brow at the stillness of their legs.

"Both bear unfathomable consequences."

"I'm flattered."

"That wasn't a compliment," Aisling bit, but Lir was already plunging them both into the crush of spirits.

The flowers hanging above their heads danced, nodding their bulbs to the music. Sprites bathed and leapt between the punch bowls. And the billowing smoke puffed from the bears' pipes traveled above and through the flying dancers in countless characters. Three of the six were wispy *dragúns*.

Racat, Muirdris, and Aengus.

Among the others were an owl, a stag, a badger, a fox, and a white bear.

Animals symbolic of the fae monarchies across the mortal realm. Aisling knew many of them but not all.

Ina, the queen of Iod, the owl. Bres, the king of Annwyn, the stag. Delbaeth, king of Oighir, the white bear.

"They narrate the Wild Hunt," Lir said, spinning in pace with the music. "The twelve Sidhe kingdoms battling for Racat, Muirdris, and Aengus. Each desperate for either power, prosperity, or immortality."

Aisling had seen this tale portrayed in smoke before. Around a campfire after hers and Lir's union, told by Rian. But never had she seen the part of the story where Ina was besotted with Delbaeth, Fionn's father. A story Fionn mentioned; perhaps this particular chapter was often excluded when chronicled in Annwyn.

The smoke moved to the rhythm of the melody,

increasing its speed as the beat rose in tempo. The owl not lunging for Racat with the intent to hunt, but rather twirling around it, finding a pattern of flight till they flew together. Both the stag and the white bear, chasing shortly behind.

"Did Ina learn before or after Delbaeth her *caera* was Bres?" Aisling asked, watching as the stag and the bear battled one another, growing dizzy with every furthering step.

Lir hesitated. "Before."

Aisling twirled in a circle, clasping hands with a spirit before the dance returned her to Lir. This spirit appeared like any other fae, though made of forest fog and dappled in mist. A bygone glint in its opalescent eyes that forced a shudder from Aisling's bones.

"She despised my father at first," the fae king continued. "Intended to wed Delbaeth instead."

"A union that would've left one or the other dead considering they weren't *caera*. Bres and Ina were."

Lir nodded his head. "In the Old Age, there was no mention of *caeras*. Ina and Bres were the first. So, there would be no way of knowing until some years later when magic reared its head at an un-fated union."

"Then Fionn was spared the loss of a father as a result of Ina's change of heart."

"An inevitability delayed only by a handful of days," Lir said. "Delbaeth, believing both Ina and her victory during the Wild Hunt—Racat—to be rightfully his, sieged war on Ina and Bres the day they were to be handfasted atop Lofgren's Rise. And so, Ina unleashed Racat, slumbering atop her mountain in the Linn of Wanting, and burned Delbaeth alive as well as his legions."

A drunken toad bumped into Aisling's knee, almost

knocking her off balance. So as the toad leapt away, Lir sprouted a root from the floor, tripping the little beast.

"Your questions, are they born of interest for Racat or Fionn's motives?"

"Both," Aisling answered honestly. "Why is it that my *draiocht* is manifested by Racat? A question worsened by the involvement of the Winter Court. Delbaeth felt cheated for having lost Ina and, by default Racat, and now his son wishes to truly bind with me? It takes no stretch of the imagination to realize Fionn is under the impression Racat and I are in some way, one. Binding with me, a form of achieving what his father never could and avenging Delbaeth's death. And if his beliefs are true, *why*? What reason is there for my *draiocht* taking Racat's shape?"

Aisling spun, facing Lir. His expression taut with rage.

"Fionn wished to truly bind with you?" he repeated, woodland storms brewing behind his dark lashes. Made electric by the flecks of fae light reflected in his eyes. Aisling was aware Lir had known Fionn wished to unbind he and Aisling. But there'd been no mention of a true binding between Aisling and Fionn whilst in Lir's presence.

Aisling didn't need to respond. The truth hung in the air between them.

"Aye," Lir forced himself to continue, his voice nearly a growl. "Fionn believes not only Racat to be rightfully Delbaeth's, but that he is the rightful heir to the *dragún*. You see, Fionn was born of both Delbaeth and Ina before Bres ever became involved. Yet, Ina chose to bequeath Racat to Annwyn and to me. In which case, not only did Ina kill his father, but Ina also circumvented her firstborn's inheritance for my sake. And so, Fionn is of the opinion that everything I am, and have, is his. Including you."

Aisling stepped to the side, another spirit taking her hand

and dipping her. And as soon as their clasp unlatched, Lir found her, catching her and bringing her back to him. Chest to chest, forced to gaze up and into his eyes.

The music heated. The beating of animal skins growing louder. The pipe smoke thickening.

"How long must we dance like this?" Aisling asked, more breathless than she anticipated.

"Till we reach the other threshold."

The other end of the ballroom was still a lengthy distance away. Their pace slow and gradual as they danced from line to line. And at the far wall, another door materialized behind the folds of ballooning gowns and sparkling armor.

"We could race for it," Aisling said, impatient.

"Not unless you wish to disrupt their dance and tear the veil. The two of us against a legion of war-bred spirits."

Aisling swallowed, reminded of the weapons that hung from their wispy belts, the fangs glistening behind parted lips, and the savage sparkle that grew more hollow, hungrier by the moment.

Lir slid his hands to her waist, pressing her closer. The tips of his fingers grazing her bare thigh where the slit of her dress parted.

Aisling hesitated.

"What are you doing?" she breathed, the air suddenly stifling, her palm instinctively finding his chest and holding him at bay.

"Dancing," he whispered, the fire in his breath sending chills down Aisling's spine.

Aisling forced herself to look around. Indeed, the pace of the song had grown slower, headier, as the celebration dissolved into something more primal. Losing the elegance and grace-like patterns of the earlier dance for something far more savage.

Aisling dithered, fighting Lir's enchantment cast only by touch. By the gale soft brush of his fingers against her bare skin, the sensation of his abdomen flush against her own, moving to the rhythm of the song. The caress of his every breath against her throat as he bent his head beside her neck. Afraid she couldn't find her way out of his spells if she dared enter one.

You will perish in a world of your own making. An axe in your heart.

"Dance, *ellwyn*," he said against her ear. The eyes of countless spirits wandering back to Aisling as she stalled. Their ancient expressions studying Aisling for the first time. Nostrils flaring at whatever scent Lir's own couldn't mask.

At last, Aisling wrapped her arms around Lir's neck, moving against his body. This was the closest they'd ever been with one another without the intent to slit the other's throat. Yet, this was a duel all the same. A dare with mortal stakes. So, Aisling didn't look up at his expression, but she could feel the easy arrogance of his smile. One inspired by bloody victories and ruthless triumphs. His hands finding her waist and pressing her closer still. Till she could feel every hard edge of his body, his forge-blessed muscle, smell the forest as though doused in its incense.

"Prophecy says we'll destroy this realm," Aisling said, enveloped by the smell of him. "Centuries of war, ruin, and death. This realm will crumble."

She wasn't certain why she said it. Only that every touch, every meeting of the eyes, every breath they shared was cursed by the omen. Compelled Aisling to remember if only to dissuade her from ever touching him a second time, a third time, a fourth. To sever the thread between them.

Lir tangled his fingers through her hair, breathing against her neck, breaking away only to tip her chin toward him.

"So be it," he said.

Aisling shivered, fully bespelled by his verdant eyes as they drowned in her own. Unapologetically, they flicked to her mouth.

"What is there to rule if everything becomes ash?" she asked, as he traced the length of her arm with one hand, finding her own and tangling his fingers between hers. The press of his palm against her own excruciating.

Then, once more, his hands found her thighs, but this time, his grip deepened. His touch possessive. The torture made unbearable as they continued to spin to the music.

He ignored her question in favor of another.

"Would you believe me if I told you I wanted more?" he purred against her ear.

Aisling ran her fingers down his arms, exploring the contours of his shoulders, his biceps, his forearms as they, in response, tensed and flexed to clutch her more tightly. No doubt bruising what mortal flesh remained. Yet she didn't care. She'd craved this, and wondered what Lir felt like against her own bare flesh. What it would feel like for him to want her, even if this were all pretend. A means to deceive ghosts and their ravenous appetites but nothing more.

"I'd be a fool to believe anything you said."

"You're well aware I can't lie."

"So, you've mastered trickery."

He smiled, flashing his fangs. "Ask me what lies I would tell if I could."

The fae king twirled Aisling, stopping her so her back faced him, finding her waist and bringing her flush against him once more. Her spine against his abdomen.

Lir found the slits in her dress and slipped his hands underneath, sliding his palms to the round curve of her hips.

Elegant fingers pressing against her skin, the sensation coursing through her muscles and dizzying the mind.

Aisling inhaled sharply, leaning the back of her head against his shoulder. An invitation for him to slowly graze her neck with his fangs. The pulse in his throat, beating against her own with increased need.

"Very well," she said, her voice thick with wanting. "What lies would you tell if you could?"

Against her own volition, Aisling pressed her backside against him and moved. Lir let loose a noise Aisling could only describe as half exhale, half growl, his heart thrashing against her shoulder blades. The music, the spirits, the surrounding realm churning, bubbling in a forge that revolved around Aisling and Lir as they danced. As their thread pulled, groaning, and fraying with desire.

Lir reached through her arms from where he stood behind her, grazing the naked flesh where her neckline began with the back of his knuckles—intentionally or not, Aisling couldn't tell.

He grabbed her throat, then her jaw, turning her head so she could see the darkening of his eyes as they bled black with yearning.

"I'd lie and say I care nothing for you," he said. "I'd tell you I want nothing to do with you. That I pray you stay as far from me as this realm could take you. I'd lie and say I wish I never thought of you. That you didn't possess my every waking thought."

Lir's hands traveled further, finding the inside of her thighs as she danced against him. Pressing the tips of his fingers into the soft flesh between her legs, just beneath her apex, as though forcing himself to stop short. As though begging whatever will remained to shackle his need. His every movement more protective than the last as the spirits celebrated around them, closing in. Splashed them both in fae wine and petals from the hanging branches above. The smoke purling into Aisling's lungs till the chamber burned in a soft gold as they shifted, moved, glided through the hall in a mess of limbs, of wetted fangs, of hot pulses, and reckless whispers.

He released her legs, moved his hands up till one pressed her lower abdomen, moving her hips back so her backside shifted against the hardness of him. Aisling inhaled sharply. So, Lir slid his free hand and held her throat gently, turning her head so it faced him.

"Whatever it is you truly covet, Lir: power, vengeance, both at once," Aisling said. "Our binding will risk it all. Would be a damnation."

Lir leaned forward, as though to kiss her. To taste her lips but forced himself short.

"For a kiss," Lir said, "I'd damn the world."

"I thought you said you couldn't lie."

"I can't."

The music broke and the sea of spirits cheered, clapping their hands. And in the abrupt shift, Lir and Aisling broke apart.

Aisling, flushed, adjusted her dress, forcing herself to stand on weak knees. Lir also composed himself, posture shifting back into the barbarian lord of the fae before her eyes. As though their dance had been nothing more than the work of the love potions Aisling and the Tilrish children would brew with spices and champagne they'd stolen from their family's banquets.

Aisling couldn't deny the sight of his walls building once more stung. Needled into her chest. Everything, her gown, her pinned hair, the festival, she and Lir, were just a phantom, bursting into mist at the insinuation of a passing breeze. Just pretend.

Yet it was for the best, Aisling knew, no matter how painful. For caring for the fae king was a death sentence—a promise of heartbreak.

But Aisling didn't have the luxury of time to dwell on her own feelings or lack thereof. Her attention was swiftly diverted by the jeering of the spirits around her. Fists in the air, a storm of petals descending from the vaulted ceilings, punctuated by butterflies of all size and color.

A spirit couple stood at the top of an imperial staircase.

They were miraculous, shifting in the light, their edges bleeding like mist. The female smiled at the male. The dimples framing her pearlescent beam, familiar. Her beauty familiar, feline, and resplendently lovely, clad in a dress made entirely from the wind and accented with highland mist. Spirals of silver hair spilling down her back, and beneath her headdress, a crown that sprouted two snowy owl wings from both temples, partially covered by a red veil.

Beside her, the male worshiped her with a mere glance. He was breathtaking as well, sage green eyes crinkled by the force of his smile. Brushing aside his shoulder-length dark hair to reveal a pair of twin axes at his back.

Hiraeth.

Aisling paused, whipping her attention to Lir.

The fae king was entranced, ceasing all movement. His lips parted open and eyes glazed the longer he forgot to blink.

Aisling herself felt as though her stomach were in her throat. Recognition dawning.

This was Ina and Bres, their spirits reliving their *Snaidhm* for all eternity.

Aisling wasn't certain if Lir was enraged or overjoyed, heart aching or filled with sorrow. Only that he froze, watching his parents with undiluted attention. But Aisling and Lir couldn't remain here, for already the spirits' attention was sliding to them despite the dance having ended. Lingering would only result in their death.

Mercifully, both Ina and Bres waved at the ballroom of spirits, vanishing through the threshold on the other side of the room.

"We must keep moving," Aisling said, her voice as soft as she was capable. She reached out and touched the back of his arm, bracing herself for his temper, his fangs, his flippant disregard for her feelings.

Instead, he found her eyes and Aisling was dumbstruck at the sight of them. His father's orbs awash with grief. All of it, left for Aisling to behold.

CHAPTER XXXVIII

AISLING

Stepping into Iod's corridor was like waking from a dream. One Aisling found she clung to, despising herself for the tumbling of her stomach each time she dared glance in the fae king's direction after their dance. The silver-eyed ravens that usually let loose within her gut, maddened and riled by the celebrations of *Samhain*.

Yet as they wandered further through Ina's castle, the murals against the walls turned green with emeralds, depicting the forest. A viridescence that spread like swarms of beetles into the heart of the fae queen's keep. As though her love for Lir's father, Bres, had devoured her soul and bloodied her home with the gore of their binding.

Aisling approached a steepled door at the end of a dark, cobwebbed corridor, its fae light dim and wilted after a millennium. She sensed no witchery, no darkness on the other side. Heard nor tasted anything suspicious. So, Aisling pulled a ring lodged between the snarling teeth of a knocker in the image of Racat.

"Wait—" Lir piped but it was too late. The threshold slid open, releasing a cloud of age-old dust as it yawned awake.

Immediately, Lir moved in front of Aisling, shielding her from whatever might lie on the other side. The air this deep into the mountain was bone-chilling.

The room was cast in shadow. Still, Aisling could make sense of the darkness.

Two wispy figures laughed, raced, and opened the door on the other side.

Ina and Bres.

Lir's bottom lip bled where his fang punctured it, aware their trail was marked by his mother and father's ghostly footsteps. Ina and Bres, a pace ahead of both Aisling and Lir as they navigated to the top of Lofgren's Rise.

The threshold behind them closed of its own accord. Creaking shut as the roses in the room flickered to life, illuminating a chamber cast in ice. Of the colossal statue of a maiden with two owl wings crowning either side of her head. Both eyes veiled by a supple cloak that spilled down her body and to her feet in great folds across the marble floors. Both palms extended before her and facing the mirrored ceilings, as though in eternal prayer. All bejeweled by the sparkling trove of winter's keep.

Aisling now knew Ina's appearance well enough to recognize her, even if etched in stone.

Yet Aisling's attention was drawn to the ice. The frost coating every morsel of the room.

Realization dawned on Aisling; a curse hissed past her lips as the great body of a bear peeled forth from the shadows.

Greum rose on his hind legs, hurling himself at Aisling to pin her against the ground. Without hesitation, Aisling produced a bolt of fire, burning through the beast's fur as it roared in pain. In the same heartbeat, a leaf-ridden root shot forth from the frozen trees surrounding them, wrapping around Greum's mighty neck and slamming him into the floor.

Aisling spun on her heel, meeting Lir's eyes as she made to run to him. His forest green eyes flashing with panic the moment something or someone wrapped their hand around Aisling's wrist and held her in place.

Aisling turned, finding, to her horror, Fionn towering above her, exploring her with a gaze frosted by northern winds.

"I've missed you, *mo Lúra*," he said in a voice made of velvet, pulling her closer by the wrist. Aisling summoned her flames again but this time, her *draiocht* was met not with fear, but amusement. Fionn blew on her fist full of fire, and like a match, it extinguished, smoking. Her magic, gasping for breath the moment he clasped a collar around her throat.

Not again, Aisling screamed inside her mind.

Dread iced each of Aisling's bones as she desperately clawed at Fionn's jewels to no avail. Aisling tried over and over again, grinding her teeth, but the more she scavenged her abyss for Racat, her *draiocht*, she found it cold. Colder than it'd ever been inside Oighir. This collar somehow more powerful than the one that'd sealed Lir and Fionn's deal in Oighir. The walls of her darkest corners glazed over with ice and made sharp with icicles like blades.

Please, she pleaded with her *draiocht*.

I cannot, Racat groaned in frustration, *this Sidhe lord wields powers beyond his making. This is the Lady's doing.*

"Don't look so surprised, *mo Lúra*," Fionn purred, leaning toward her. "Surely you knew I'd come for you."

≈

LIR

"Release her," Lir growled from behind, his voice filling the chamber. The vines he'd wrapped around Greum's neck, tightening like a noose even as the beast squirmed for breath.

"Are you threatening me, little brother?" Fionn laughed, and at its sound the room grew colder. Every mirror possessed by Fionn's winter till they each splintered down the center. Verglas cutting across the marble floors and slithering around Lir's vines, freezing and shattering his hold over Greum.

The bear gasped for breath, lumbering onto its paws. Fionn held up a hand, commanding Greum to stand his ground and allow Fionn this battle alone.

Lir squinted, resisting the urge to behead his brother with the mere flick of his wrist and the trajectory of his axe.

"So protective over what was never yours to begin with," Fionn continued, doing his best to provoke Lir while he bore the upper hand. Aisling was swathed in smoke, draining her energy to conjure fire. Mischief on Fionn's part, Lir already knew. He could taste the work of the Lady in his brother's *draiocht* as it stalked up the walls. Of bloody stars, a shear's edge, or a spider's web.

"What makes you think we haven't already truly bonded?" Lir said, padding nearer.

"So, you did?" Fionn asked, gathering Aisling in his arms. Lir felt his stomach drop, but he held back, refusing to give Fionn the satisfaction.

Aisling shoved against him, unable to best a Sidhe king in matters of brute strength alone.

"Tell me then, what was it like?" Fionn continued, face brightening the moment he'd spoken. Reading the hesitation flickering across Lir's expression regardless of his attempts to mask it. "Did she scream? Did she squirm like she is now—"

Lir threw one half of Hiraeth.

It hurled through the chamber, thirsty for the blood between Fionn's eyes. Disappointed when Fionn raised a hand, freezing Lir's blade mid-air and shoving it across the room with venom. The axe slapped against the wall before clattering against the ground.

Fionn laughed. "You think you can fool me? I can smell the unsatiated want on the both of you. Can taste everything *unmet* between the two of you." Fionn bowed his head to smell the sweat beading at Aisling's throat despite the cold.

Lir went rigid, rivaling the rage evolving into wrath within.

"Lir—" Aisling warned, but Lir couldn't hear her above the storm of gore in his mind.

"Touch her," Lir said, deathly slow, "and I'll serve every last mortal a chalice of your blood as they bow before both her and I. Your head piked before our dais."

"I'm afraid you're envisioning both mine and Aisling's future."

"Never speak her name again," Lir warned a final time, his fangs scraping against his tongue.

"Or what?" Fionn grinned as Aisling's smoke thickened, her efforts to breathe her *draiocht,* stifled at once.

"Release me!" she hissed, the anger, the desperation in her voice staking Lir through the chest.

"Into the prison of another? My brother keeps you all the same," Fionn said.

Aisling hesitated, violet eyes flashing with something Lir didn't have time to explore.

Fionn pulled Aisling's hair away from her face so her

shoulders, her throat, her neckline, were all exposed as he tipped her face to his, mouth moving nearer to her own.

Lir felt the realm snap.

He exploded the chamber with great oaks and vines and roots, reaching for his brother as the statue of their mother, overcome with both forest and ice, cleaved at the center.

For the first time, Fionn's smug arrogance collapsed, swiftly recovering as he froze every branch, every root, every growth, but it was already too late.

Amidst the mayhem, Lir tossed his second axe, finding Fionn's wrist and slicing it clean off.

The son of Winter screamed, releasing Aisling so he could clutch his bloodied limb. Greum roared, chasing after Aisling. It was futile. Lir's willows shielded her from the bear, collapsing over the beast even as Aisling reached for him.

Lir forced himself to turn away. She couldn't stay. Not when Fionn had meddled with her *draiocht* at the aid of the Lady, his collar winking at Lir the moment it'd been placed around Aisling's neck.

"Who amplifies your power?!" Fionn seethed at Lir, desperately trying to gather himself despite his severed hand. "What cursed creature favors you to share their strength?!"

Indeed, no Seelie nor Unseelie, no mortal nor beast, was made to wield enough power to grow an ash, a yew, an oak, an alder, much less a forest. But Lir found Aisling's proximity, her smell, her taste, inspired unique strength within him. Brightened his *draiocht* and fed it new life. His sheer proximity to Aisling during the dance through the spirit's *Snaidhm*, enough to embolden his power for sorcery such as this.

"You think this is power?" Lir asked Fionn as he drew

closer. "Then imagine what'll become of you if you so much as glance at my *caera* again."

Fionn grimaced, maddened by his brother's warning.

"You know good and well that if I can't have it, I want it all the more," Fionn said, unsheathing a new weapon from his back with the one hand still intact. A spear.

"Take it as a commandment from your sovereign then. High lord of all Sidhe and the rightful heir to Racat." Lir smiled an easy grin, relishing Fionn's reaction. "Come now, brother, where's your decorum? You're intended to bow."

The forest around them, growing from the inside of Ina's chamber, continued to break through Fionn's ice, delivering Lir's axes into his waiting palms. Lir twirled them between his fingers as he approached.

"You think I'd ever bow to you?! Only should my body rot beneath the earth would you ever catch my crown below yours!" Fionn's face warped with anger, wrist dripping at his side.

Lir stilled his axes, readying himself for combat.

"So be it."

Lir was a violent star, the arc of his axe a gleaming blur of metal as it swung for his elder brother.

Fionn parried the strike, raising his spear vertically. The clang of their weapons rung throughout the chamber, echoing off the icy walls and vibrating through Lir's trees.

"You should've stayed in Oighir, brother." Lir shoved Fionn a few paces back, spinning his right axe as he prepared for his next attack. Fionn was a talented fighter, having been trained by Ina herself the moment he'd bore the capacity to lift a sword in preparation for the Wild Hunt. Nevertheless, her lessons were short-lived, coming to an abrupt halt after her untimely death. Leaving Fionn's talents, alone in bitter winter, to rust. Not even the mortals of Fjallnorr dared venture into the snow ridden feywilds of Fionn's permafrost. A surety of death to all those who didn't worship the Sidhe.

Fionn's movements were, thus, slower and less agile than Lir remembered. His severed hand and the loss of blood, doing him no favors. His only saving grace against Lir, whatever the Lady had lent him.

"And let you condemn both Seelie and Unseelie on account of your ignorance?!"

Lir scoffed. "You always were so self-righteous."

"This is no game, Lir. Both the Lady and Danu have foreseen the destruction you'll yield should you truly bind with Aisling. Destined to reap the same mistakes as our mother."

Like veins, needle thin cracks crawled up the statue of Ina at the center of the chamber.

"And do you also believe the Sidhe will lose this war to the mortals? That the Sidhe will be forced behind the veil while humanity plagues the Earth?" Lir deigned to dwell on Danu's vision for long. It hardly mattered. Whatever the empress of the dryads believed was written in the stars could be slashed and bloodied till it no longer spoke the same truth. Stars could be changed, and fate bent to his will. For every vision, every prophecy, every omen by either the Lady or Danu was wrought with ulterior motives. With lies and deception and trickery.

"I believe you aren't the Sidhe to change such prophecies," Fionn said, thrusting the edge of his blade at Lir's abdomen. Lir feinted left, leaping back, and slicing through the shoulder Fionn had left exposed, patient to wield more damage at the right moment.

"Your mind has grown muddled," Fionn continued.

"You've lost sight of both Seelie and Unseelie and everything Other. This isn't what Ina would've wanted."

Lir blocked Fionn's lunge, shoving the edge of his spear to the floor with the lip of his axe. Circling him like a wolf skulking around its prey.

"Damn Ina!" Lir shouted, expression bridling with heat as the image of her spirit and Bres's flashed across his mind's eye without his consent. "Ina deserved everything. Committed a sin she deserved to answer for. And if you ask me"—Lir swiped at Fionn, drawing blood from across his cheek bone—"the gods should've damned her then and there. Ended her life as well as the legacy of Iod. Instead, they punished the rest of the Sidhe for her crimes alone, breeding the mortals that would burn our villages, our forests, torture our own. All in the name of my father, who died regardless."

Fionn winced. "And yet you race to repeat her sins."

"I race to *correct* them," Lir seethed.

Fionn's ice rose from the ground like giant thorns, immediately shattered by Lir's axes. "Mine and Aisling's binding will be successful, will bring the mortals to their knees, and undo anything and everything our mother committed."

Fionn laughed, the room clicking as his frost creeped over every surface. He swung his spear, ice exploding from the tip and trapping Lir's boots against the ground. The surrounding roots bursting through Fionn's shackles, in time for Lir to raise his axes and shield himself against Fionn's swing. The spear shimmered, its metal bleeding verglas and binding everything it touched with the cold. The statue of Ina weeping crystals from the edges of her stony eyes.

Lir shoved Fionn off, artfully striking twice in the same breath, summoning blood from both Fionn's arms and legs.

Fionn braced the pain, leaning on his back leg before

lunging forward with his great sword, the room speared through with monoliths of ice.

Lir weaved through the madness, lost in the labyrinth while Fionn hid amidst the discord. Leaving Lir to pray a faithless prayer that Aisling had fled when she'd bore the opportunity to escape.

"She will be your undoing, brother," Fionn called through the freeze. "The Lady has foreseen it."

Lir moved swiftly, silently navigating till he found his unassuming brother once more. Biding his time.

"I prefer the visions the Lady has seen of my victories, of my sovereignty, of my—"

"Kin?" Fionn interjected, voice echoing through the labyrinth of ice he'd summoned. "Do you care for Aisling at all? Or has this all been some correction of the past? A way for you to undo our mother's crimes, perhaps, but to also erase whatever grief Narisea and your child's death cursed you with?"

Lir continued moving, afraid that should he stop, his mind might register Fionn's words. The sound of Narisea's name, a damnable curse, tossing Lir back in time. A time better left forgotten along with whatever love he'd ever felt.

"That's it, isn't it?" Fionn pressed. "You'll use Aisling for your own completion and then what?"

Lir shook his head, grinding his fangs against his teeth. Fionn's voice growing louder and closer.

"Then her purpose will be fulfilled, ended by my axe." Lir forced the words out, physically pained by the sentiment that'd once been common sense. Before he'd ever met Aisling. Before he'd been forced to realize she was his counterpart. For no matter how greatly the sun despises the night, the moon carries its torch till morning. Life to fire. Magic to iron. Green to violet.

"That's odd," Fionn said, his voice directly behind Lir. The fae king swiveled, coming face to face with his brother. Fionn jabbed his spear, avoided by Lir, yet not quickly enough. The tip of his spear scraped across Lir's shoulder, summoning blood. "Because I seem to remember the Lady telling me a similar tale. One where both Aisling and you are coated in one another's blood. An axe in her heart and a flaming dagger in yours."

Lir cursed beneath his breath, parrying and striking with his axe. Fionn stepped lithely back, narrowly dodging the attack. Doing his best to mask the terror, the fear, the horror of Fionn's words. That it was possible the Lady had foreseen a future where Aisling and Lir were one another's end should they truly bind. Destined to destroy the realm then leave it, death gleaned by the other.

Lir shook his head. No. It was all a lie. A manipulation to breed doubt.

"What allegiance do you bear to the Lady?" Lir sneered, stalking toward his brother as the son of Winter backed away.

"Common goals. Common enemies. Ultimately, to spare both this realm and Aisling from *you*."

Lir allowed his rage to build. Fanning the embers of his fury so his *draiocht* might breathe more thickly.

"You're right to spare the world but not from me. Aisling will wreak ruin in her wake if met with the full force of her power."

"'The full force of her power,'" Fionn corrected, "*influenced* by you. There is still time for her to choose the correct path. To be good."

Lir laughed but it was humorless. "All these years trapped at the edge of the north has made you sound so... *human*."

Fionn lifted his spear above his head, striking Lir with

ice. The frost seeped into his bones, freezing him from the inside until Lir broke through the sheets in an explosion of translucent needles. His magic was powerful, emboldened by the Lady and still, not enough.

"You will die with a dagger in your heart," Fionn repeated. "A blade wrapped in flames of violet. And she, an axe in her heart."

Lir defeated the distance between himself and his brother, slashing with wicked ability. His axes grazed Fionn's ears, his cheekbones, his throat as his brother desperately moved to avoid the onslaught.

"It has been foreseen. It has been written in the stars. And it cannot be outrun."

Lir felt the madness overtake him. The frustration. The fury. The aching of his heart as the cord between him and Aisling jerked and flooded him with emotion.

Fionn caught Lir's axe, freezing it with ice and twisting. Lir flipped and slammed against the crumbled floors, beneath the shadow of their mother's statue. Ice creeped over Lir, imprisoning his wrists, hard as Forge-cast stone. Lir struggled against their grip, finding the Lady's aid growing more formidable the longer Fionn battled.

Fionn raised his blade above his head, prepared to deal the final blow. And yet he hesitated.

Fionn ripped open Lir's jacket, exposing the scars where his wings had once been sheltered away.

"So, it's true," Fionn said, eyes wide and glazed with tears. A shimmer of sadistic triumph in his opalescent eyes. "Danu ripped them from your back."

Lir dug his nails into the debris beneath him, the black of his most shadowed depths chomping, clawing at the walls within to, at long last, slake their thirst. To sink their teeth into Fionn's death.

"So it is: you never deserved our mother's wings." Fionn pressed his boot on Lir's back. "Enjoy the Other, brother. I welcome your haunting so you might overhear your *caera*'s screams during hers and my true binding."

Whatever humanity, starved and forgotten inside Lir, broke.

Burst into madness as he tore the ice from his wrists and the feywilds erupted from inside the castle, devouring all and everything in its wake. Thrusting Fionn off Lir and into chaos. A chamber of groaning alders and rowans, heaving, stretching, thrashing against the vaulted ceiling for escape. Crushing all and everything in its sight with the snap of their spindly, gruesome limbs and thorns.

Lir searched for Fionn, unable to find him or Greum through the growing thicket.

The fae king cursed beneath his breath, turning on his heel to throw himself through the following threshold. A threshold where he found Aisling's violet eyes, wrought with emotion.

CHAPTER XXXIX

AISLING

The cold of Fionn's chamber betrayed the warmth of the following hall.

A chapel of some sort, wrapped in the mosaic of Racat and blurred by the incense purling to the glass ceilings up above, warning of the night to come. An altar at the foot of the room, protected by the image of an owl, wings outstretched.

Aisling moved first, near racing down the center aisle. She needed to reach Lofgren's peak before she dissolved into madness. Her heart ripping in two with every bloody beat.

"Aisling, wait—" Lir called after her, but Aisling despised the sound of his voice. Its every seductive lilt, the depth of its timber, how it thrummed through her core. How it made her, even for a breath, justify what Lir had confessed to Fionn.

"Then her purpose will be fulfilled, ended by my axe."

Lir couldn't lie. And so, his words rang true and straight, threading the lines of fate into a tapestry of her death.

"Aisling." Lir caught Aisling's wrist spinning her toward him. Aisling summoned her *draiocht* but found it still swathed in smoke. The *dragún* inside manically trying to defrost whatever bitter winter Fionn and the Lady had blown into Aisling's heart. The collar around her neck strangling her.

"Aisling," he said again, searching her eyes, his own ringed with dark circles. The sharp edge of his jaw lined in cuts and his arm still bleeding from the clash with his brother.

"Never speak my name again!" she shouted, shoving him back. Embarrassed by the height of her anger, by the intensity of her emotion.

Lir had never claimed to be anything other than her enemy. An ally at times. Someone bound by the Forge. But never a friend, never a lover—Aisling shook her head, stopping the thoughts from progressing and swirling inside her head. Yet the betrayal was as potent as if they were lovers. As if they didn't despise one another.

Lir grabbed her wrist, moving closer still, backing her against the far wall and beneath the marble owl frozen midflight. Their heads curtained by the creature's wings.

"You're angry," he said, tightening his grip. "Yet you should know everything I spoke was—"

"The truth for you cannot tell a lie? Or can you?" Aisling seethed. "Which is it, Lir? What sort of liar are you?"

"I never pretended to care for you," he said, spearing Aisling in the heart. Her stomach rising into her throat and lodging itself like a stone she couldn't swallow. Cheeks blistering with heat.

"No," she said. "Yet you promised me an alliance, an allegiance at least. The power, the position you knew I hungered for, you used it against me—the crimes of my clann against me, my newfound *draiocht*, my need to reach Lofgren's Rise. Everything you've manipulated to your benefit."

Lir bared his teeth, the tips of his canines sparkling. Shoulders hiked with tension. As though he himself wasn't certain which mask to don. Which lie to speak to either Aisling or himself.

"You *are* my benefit," he said, every word as cold as the grave.

"I am a means to your end!" Aisling screamed, moving to push him. but he caught her instead, wrapping an arm around her waist to prevent her from striking again.

"No," he said, hardly a whisper, his lips a hair width from her own. "You are my nightmare." He pressed his forehead against her own. "My torment, my inevitable ruin." His breath was heavy, muscles tightening, eyes burning through her lips as he studied their every nuance with a hunger that inspired the feline glimmer in his verdant gaze. "And my unholy obsession."

Aisling forced herself to swallow, to meet Lir's eyes, to claw through the hurt that ravaged her chest and laid waste to her lungs.

"I'd ask which it is: obsession or manipulation?" Aisling steeled herself against the thrashing of her heart. "Yet I'd never receive a clear answer void of trickery."

The corners of Lir's lips curled despite himself. "I don't have a clear answer, *ellwyn*."

Aisling turned her head to the side.

"I can't accept that," she said. Aisling moved out of his arms and pressed her palms against the far wall. As though no distance was enough to separate them.

Lir opened his mouth to speak but was stopped short by the runes that burned into the wall behind Aisling, carving out a door.

Lir stepped back, appraising it anew, eyes wide with wonder.

"How did you open this?" Lir asked, eyes darting between the glowing runes and Aisling's hands at her sides.

Aisling shook her head. She didn't know. Hadn't known it was a door to begin with.

"What does it say?" Aisling asked.

Lir fixed his eyes on her and her alone.

"By the blood of the Forge, I vow to you the first cut of my heart, the first taste of my blood, and the last words from my lips."

LIR

Wedding vows marked the passage into the following chamber.

A bedroom the spirits of his mother and father brushed through, slipping through to the staircase that wound further up Lofgren's Rise, hand in hand. Wrought with rich quilts, flickering candles, a canopied bed draped with ivory pelts. The air thin and frigid.

Lir fought the urge to chase them. To dive into his parents' shadows and let them see him, eye to eye. Their presence made possible, made visible by the thinning of the veil at *Samhain*.

Yet the sight of the room kept him still. Kept him glaring at a small, hand-crafted bassinet designed for a child. The screams of his late bairn echoing inside his mind, as though his and Narisea's child squirmed inside this bed. Reached for him. Made him believe, even for a second, he still bore a heart.

Against his own volition, Lir approached the bassinet. His body moving of its own accord. Mercifully, it was empty.

A bed Ina and Bres had prepared for Lir once he was born. And yet, he stood above it, forcing himself to endure the haunting of his most visceral loss.

"Lir," Aisling said, tearing his reverie. She was still angry with him, the tone in her voice a ghost of what it'd been just outside the door she'd magicked open. Another invitation on behalf of his mother. As though Aisling were just as entitled to Iod as he was.

Lir ripped his eyes away, fearing Aisling had seen even an ember of what he felt. That he'd felt out of control, unable to prevent Narisea's death, his son's, Aisling's. That he'd felt useless, helpless to find Aisling when he believed her dead at the bottom of the gorge then lost and running from him. Unable to protect her. Unable to instill obedience so no kingdom laid outside his hand. Be it Seelie or Unseelie. Unable to stop Danu from ripping the wings from his back.

He prayed daily that he might never be powerless again. Never lose control. Never watch everything he cared for slip through his fingertips, unable to do anything but witness his own tragedy unfold. The last breath of his child slip past its small lips. He'd burn the world if he must. Rule every morsel of it if it meant never being powerless again.

He cleared his throat, walking past Aisling to the staircase beyond.

"We have to keep moving," he said.

"Lir, you don't have to—"

"I do," he said, harsher than expected. "There are greater things at stake. We have to keep moving."

"If that's what you wish, then so be it," she said. "But if this is an effort to conceal from me what happened in your past, trust I know it already."

Lir did a double take. His heart thrashing inside his chest.

"I know you lost your first *caera* to childbirth and along

with her, your child," Aisling said, her voice gentle, soothing the flaring of Lir's temper. But to hear the tale told aloud, at least part of it, pained Lir more than just the memory of it.

"Not to childbirth," Lir said, the words spilling from his lips, coaxed by the spell of her. "Narisea was attacked by mortals hunting around Annwyn. They stalked through the trees in pursuit of legends, of myths, of tales spoken around flames, and found one. Narisea was humming by a river that bled into Annwyn's gorge when she was surrounded by mortals. Ten or so Tilrish soldiers, chaining her with iron till she rendered helpless. Then..." Lir stopped short, closing his eyes as though he couldn't finish the story. Nevertheless, Aisling was clever enough to piece it together. "So, she died in childbirth but not because of it. My child passing soon after despite our efforts."

Lir clenched his jaw, cursing every word. Wishing it were nothing more than a story. Wishing it was all a lie.

Aisling stood still, her every breath thick as she processed Lir's story. She was still angry with him, and yet, she'd listened. Heard what Lir had never spoken aloud before. Never dreamed of saying aloud lest the words be tortured and knifed from his throat. Yet here he was, freely giving it to her. She, the only creature in the world he enjoyed having power over him.

"We'll find vengeance then," Aisling said at last, meeting his eyes. Sinful, violet eyes flashing with dark magic that seeped beneath Lir's flesh and crept up the nape of his neck. "We'll make them rue the day they ever entered our Sidhe forest."

A muscle flashed across Lir's jaw, realizing fully in that moment, that Fionn, the Lady, and Danu were all right. Aisling would be his undoing. For no creature, no curse, no spell, made Lir feel more vulnerable and powerless than Aisling, and yet, he relished it.

AISLING

From atop the staircase, Lir and Aisling stepped into a giant, cylindrical room.

It spun to the top of Lofgren's Rise where a moonstone staircase blazed the path upwards. A trail of blood climbing every step.

Aisling's breath caught, a cloud of mist winding into the frozen highland air. Everything, all of it, was so close. The answers she'd craved, within arm's reach.

Aisling started forward until Lir caught her arm.

"Wait," he said, studying the dew-dappled webs draped across the chamber. As though the gods themselves had pulled dreams from their ears and cast them here, forgotten in sheets of shimmering ivory.

"This is—" Aisling began, swiftly cut off by another voice. Something small yet mighty.

"The neccakaid."

Gilrel, Peitho, Galad, Filverel, and Dagfin stood at the other end of the corridor, having appeared from another shadowed entrance. They were covered in red scrapes, bruised, and caked in both sweat and dirt.

Immediately, Aisling met Dagfin's eyes. His expression brightened at the sight of her then dimmed when he noticed the collar around her throat. Before she could think differently, Aisling's feet carried her to him. Relief, a wave crashing over her that he was still alive and well.

"Aisling," Lir warned, drawing one of his axes. Lir's voice

held Aisling back, forcing her beating heart to stutter. The rest of the Sidhe unsheathed their weapons as well, glaring up at the surrounding webs. At the dark crevices, caves, and nooks that tunneled deeper into the mountain.

Dagfin nodded his head in her direction, a silent agreement for her to stay put as he unlatched his daggers from his bandolier.

"Are the neccakaid guarding this final path?" Aisling asked, bumping into Lir as she stepped back.

"It's possible they're dormant after so many years. Unbothered by any save for the spirits," Lir said, running his fingers through his hair so it hung away from his eyes. "It's also possible they lie in wait. We won't know for certain until we climb our way to the top."

Aisling's tongue turned to ash. The neccakaid, as described by Gilrel, were behemoth arachnids and cave dwellers. Chaotic Unseelie bearing vast appetites, as well as the slayers of Gilrel's sister, Nuala, during her efforts to save a mortal child.

And as though her sister's death were replaying before her beady eyes, Gilrel's expression grew taut, grasping at her steel lest the emotion flood past and drown her entirely. Ears laid back and pressed against her head as she stepped forward first. A tiny form amidst the vast landscape of web, precious stone, and highland frost.

Aisling's heart ached for the pine marten. And whether Gilrel was still angry with her or not, Aisling hardly cared. So, she started after her, ignoring the others' caution.

They met at the center of the chamber. A pillar of light illuminating them both.

"Should you plan to run once more," Gilrel said, "now would be the time."

Aisling absorbed the impact of her words, lowering onto her knees so they were eye to eye.

"From now on, the only direction I care to run is toward the fire. Preferably, with those half as wicked by my side." Aisling swore it to Lir, to Gilrel, to the Sidhe, and to the Forge. Carved it into her heart till it rung into eternity.

Aisling wasn't certain if the pine marten believed her or not. Only that Gilrel blinked, searching Aisling's expression before, at last, exhaling.

"Half as wicked?" the pine marten grinned. "Let today be a test of our wickedness then."

Aisling both mirrored her smile and nodded her head in agreement. The rest of their party joining them as they began their ascent to the tip of Lofgren's Rise and through the neccakaid's den.

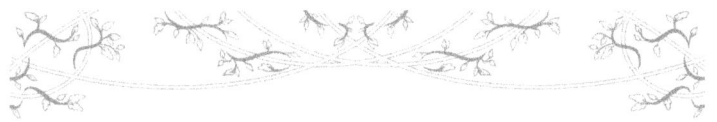

CHAPTER XL

AISLING

"Glad to see you alive," Aisling whispered to Dagfin as they climbed the staircase upwards. Lir and Galad traveled at the front of their procession while Peitho trailed behind. The rest trekked at the center.

Aisling's words felt criminally insufficient to the relief she'd experienced spotting him across the chamber. Dagfin was a flicker of warmth, of home.

Aisling wanted to embrace him, to hold him close or, at the very least, hold his hand. But she denied herself this comfort, knowing the pain it would inflict.

"You have no idea how often I've thought the same of you. Even when we were children. And yet, my concerns weren't in vain: you encountered Fionn didn't you?" Dagfin said, his brows furrowing the longer he considered the collar at her throat.

Aisling nodded her head. "He's being aided by the Lady, but I can't imagine he survived after his encounter with Lir."

"If he were dead that collar would've shattered by now."

Aisling touched the sparkling jewels absent mindedly.

"I'll tear it off like the last. Everything will be fine, Fin. Just like we always find a way back to one another."

Dagfin didn't seem convinced, yet, despite himself, he smiled.

"It's not too late to turn around."

"Are you asking me to run away with you again?" Aisling asked in jest, yet the words sounded more sober than she'd intended. A part of her, screaming to run away with him now. To turn and flee and never think of the past again.

"The offer always stands," Dagfin said, meeting her eyes. He ran a hand through his soft brown hair, moving closer till their shoulders brushed.

Aisling cleared her throat, physically unable to process the pain, the hope, the confusion a single glance of his inspired. Not now. Not when she was so close.

"Starn is already at the top," she said, diverting the conversation as they drew nearer to the peak. It was barely a whisper. Loud enough for only Dagfin to hear. But the sound of her eldest brother's name rang back and forth inside Aisling's mind.

"I knew he'd come but never realized he'd make it this far. When he left in Oighir, I assumed he'd be startled home. But it's clear now: Starn would never return to Tilren lest he'd obtained what he wanted for Nemed or died trying, using some dead fae to weave his path through Ina's defenses undetected as a mortal."

Dagfin's brow furrowed but he nodded his head.

"Have you told your fae?"

Aisling despised the way "*your fae*" sounded on his lips. Immediately glancing at the fae king at the head of their procession, Hiraeth in hand. But she opened her mouth to respond regardless, swiftly interrupted by a bead of moisture plopping onto the center of her forehead.

Aisling stopped in her tracks, glaring upward.

"What is it?" Peitho asked, halting a step beneath her own.

"Ssshh," Aisling said gently, stilling the rest of their party with her voice. Her heart thudding inside her chest, loud enough for all Fjallnorr to hear as she wiped the bead away. A thick syrup.

Both the Sidhe and Dagfin followed Aisling's line of sight, finding to their horror a single, glittering thread, vibrating above their heads. As though plucked and left to thrum.

Gilrel clenched her jaw, whiskers trembling with anticipation.

The silence swelled into a crescendo; the hiss and click of a body moving inside the nearest cavity of Iod, skulking closer, giggling and salivating. At first one and then many. Thousands, creeping to the mouths of their dwellings.

Aisling paled, realizing alongside the others, they were surrounded. Watched by a trove of reflecting eyes, peering back from the dark.

LIR

Before death reaped a soul, the air always tasted of smoke. And the moments after, stained the tongue with ash. With unlived nights and unspoken words.

Before a slaughter, the sun dimmed. Too ashamed by the blood rage to peer past its veil of clouds. But the moon always looked. Always beheld the shadows' devilry.

And so, as Lir readied his axes, he gave fair warning to

the pale, dying winter sun, studying the neccakaid's every step as they crept from their nests.

"*Damh Bán*," they hissed in Rún, bubbling over with laughter. "*We spin and we spin and we spin, century after century after century. And yet, the tapestry always weaves the same.*"

"*You weave for the Lady,*" he replied. "*And she lacks creativity.*"

"*We weave for the gods,* Damh Bán*, and so does the Lady. Nevertheless, your threads are exceptionally complex.*"

"*So, I've heard.*"

"*Turn back now,*" they said, creeping into the light. Giant, snow-white creatures, whose spindly legs clicked against Iod's stone. "*This is your last opportunity to forgo whatever it is you covet in exchange for a future. Lest this day be your last.*"

Lir, instinctively, searched for Aisling in his periphery. Daring not to turn his head lest they glean his priorities. The eight bulbous eyes of the nearest neccakaid studying the flashing edges of Hiraeth.

"Are you willing to spill your blood for the Lady?" Lir asked, stepping closer. The neccakaid hesitated, half retreating into their hollows.

"*Tis not for the Lady, Damh Bán,*" another chittered, "*but for the sake of both Seelie and Unseelie alike.*"

"*I'm wounded.*" Lir feigned offense.

"*The neccakaid are left with little choice but to align ourselves with both the Lady and Danu: those who fear their visions more so than you. You served the Unseelie well, Damh Bán, until you made the ill-fated choice to bind yourself to a mortal whore and forsake us.*"

Lir wished the neccakaid hadn't spoken those words. There was another path that could've been trodden. One that bore no violence. Now, Lir was forced to gut every last beast till they gargled their apology through lungs filled with scarlet.

"Lir—" Filverel started, swiftly cut off by the slash of Lir's axe. In a blink, Lir was before the neccakaid, the blade slicing through its head with a hideous screech, splattering their crystal webs in gore.

"By the Forge," Galad cursed, glaring up and around them as every neccakaid descended upon their small group.

Lir only grinned, gathering his axe from the carnage and launching toward another. It rose on its hind legs, spear-tipped legs jutting for him as he faced the foul underbelly. He cut through it easily, pivoting to lunge for another, casting its white string. Lir sliced through the thread, tossing his left axe so it plunged into one of many beady eyes, swiftly dodging the onslaught of three more beasts as they descended upon him. Summoning roots from the stone that impaled their thick bodies and tossed them down the chamber till they smacked against the furthest most floors.

"*I remember you*," Lir heard a creature say through the mayhem, focusing on Gilrel, blade already decorated with Unseelie blood.

"*No, no, this one's slightly different.*"

"*How can you tell?*"

"*I ate the last, bone by bone. I know every meal by heart.*"

Lir cut down five more, axes warm and guzzling death.

"And so shall you know the edge of my sword by heart," Gilrel screamed, leaping atop the largest of them and running her blade through the top of its head. The others shot their webs, torn apart by Gilrel's swift swing. But there were too many. The final web wrapped around Gilrel's blade, cleaving it from her paw. The neccakaid smiled as it threw the blade down, clattering onto the marble floors distantly below.

Gilrel's expression furrowed, balling her hands into fists as six more neccakaid approached. They reeled, standing on their hind legs and filling their fangs with venom.

Lir cut through three more Unseelie charging toward him. And the first free second he bore, he drew a dagger from his belt and flicked it at the neccakaid on the precipice of striking. The beast felled, its corpse offering Gilrel the blade as though served on a silver platter.

Gilrel nodded at Lir, gathering the blade and cutting through each neccakaid. She, a flurry of wicked vengeance as she made ribbons of those who wove threads.

"Ash!"

Lir spun, stomach plummeting the moment he heard the *Faerak*'s voice. The sound of her name pronounced with such desperation, stilling his heart.

AISLING

Aisling reached for the *draiocht* endlessly, screaming at Racat, her magic, whoever it may be skulking in the abyss, to rise. To breathe through her. To light the entire chamber on fire. Yet all she found was silence. Fionn and the Lady's magic having snuffed whatever power she harbored. Leaving Aisling as she was before she'd ever met the fae king, stepped foot into Annwyn, or defended herself against the fomorians. Without magic. Mortal.

The rest of their party blazed through the Unseelie by blade or strength, decorating the chamber with grisly remains and ear-splitting screeches. Peitho cleaved a neccakaid in two, Filverel plucked their legs from their bodies with the tip of his sword, and Galad danced through their hordes, piles of carrion left in his wake. Dagfin, on the other hand, stood beside Aisling, tearing down any and all Unseelie that approached her.

It'd all occurred so fast. Their swarms descended with wild abandon. Lir was surrounded by the majority of their nest, rising from the piles to spare Gilrel in her moment of need.

And Aisling was useless. Racing up the staircase with Dagfin by her side. Unable to aid their efforts even as the fiftieth? The hundredth? Aisling wasn't certain, only that this neccakaid finally broke through Dagfin's strike and pinned him to the stone.

They were so close. The dusky light of Lofgren's peak blinding and an arm's reach away, blasting into the chamber from a large, steepled threshold.

Aisling panicked, smoking without her flames. So, she ran for Dagfin, unsure what to do only that she'd do something. Anything. Sprinting when her body suddenly fell onto its knees, white-hot pain spreading from her shoulder and into her chest.

The threshold a pace away. Everything and all she'd pursued, so close.

"Ash!" Dagfin screamed, appraising her shoulder with horror-filled eyes. But the sound was distant and muffled, eclipsed by the ringing in her ears.

Aisling followed his line of sight, finding the tip of a neccakaid's leg speared through her shoulder and slippery with her blood.

It wasn't as painful as Aisling would've assumed, but she knew, even now, the lack of pain was most likely shock or adrenaline. Perhaps both, thrumming through her veins.

"Aisling!" Dagfin screamed.

DAGFIN

Dagfin nearly lost Fionn's sword, digging it through the throat of the neccakaid atop him. He shoved the beast off, racing to where Aisling kneeled.

But Lir was already there, slicing the creature behind her in half and falling to his knees before her.

Dagfin despised himself for the jealousy he felt even now. Seeing for himself how the fae king's expression was possessed. Riddled in panic, in despair, in anger, and fury, each emotion burning a fire in his eyes as he cupped her face with one of his blood-soaked hands, then her waist, bringing her against him.

"Hold still," he whispered in her ear, just loud enough for Dagfin to glean, reaching around her with his free hand and tearing out the neccakaid's leg.

Dagfin despised the sight of him touching her. Always protective and possessive as though she were the fae king's. As though Lir had known her soul for an eternity and breathed every last breath in anticipation of touching her again. And it was so vastly unfair. As though the true life Dagfin had lived with Aisling was stolen from him. Everything he'd ever hoped for, given to another. No, not given, ripped from his hands by the fae before him.

Aisling screamed into Lir's shoulder. Tears spilling and staining his already red-steeped leathers. Lir held her more tightly, running a hand through her hair and bringing her head into the curve of his neck.

"She needs a healer—she needs away from here," Dagfin

said, the body of the neccakaid that'd pinned him left mutilated behind him.

"Her fae blood will combat the venom," Lir said. Yet Dagfin couldn't see past the pool of blood beneath her, soaking through the dress she wore. As children, Dagfin had mended more than his fair share of Aisling's cuts, bruises, and even broken fingers or toes. But this... this was gore. This was violence. This ripped his heart from his chest. The sight of so much blood loss puddling beneath her, unbearable.

"I can take her to the druid's village. If I run, I can make it. The neccakaid are distracted, I'll slip past—"

"There's no way out," Lir growled.

"I'll make a way out!"

Lir made to scoop Aisling into his arms, but she resisted.

"I can walk." The words slipped through her gritted teeth.

Lir ignored her. "Don't make me fight you, *ellwyn*."

He lifted Aisling, carrying her in his arms as he started through the threshold and toward Lofgren's Rise, Galad, Peitho, Filverel, and Gilrel still battling the army of neccakaid below them. A grisly muddle of blades, of screaming, of hissing, of the plucking of webs, and the penetrating of flesh. The darkest crevices of the Other somehow alive and well in their realm. Unseelie nightmares protecting Lofgren's Rise.

"You'll kill her if you continue," Dagfin growled, grabbing Lir's arm to prevent him from traveling any further, his breath heavy from having little to no Ocras left. The flask at his hip emptied after the last corridor they'd traversed to reach here.

They stood in the doorway, on the precipice of emerging at the utmost peak of Lofgren's Rise.

"No," Aisling mumbled, speaking through the pain. Dagfin bristled with frustration.

"If you care for her at all, you won't do this," Dagfin pleaded. "Let me take her back."

There was a flicker of reason in the fae king's eyes. A measure of hesitation as he weighed an impossible choice. But Dagfin knew as well as any that the fae king had just as much motivation for reaching the peak of Lofgren's Rise as Aisling did.

"Going forward, she'll die," Dagfin pressed.

"And she'll die if you turn back now! You think the neccakaid won't try to finish what they've begun? That you, surviving on the last doses of Ocras, could race her back to a druid village in time?" Lir said, jerking his arm out of Dagfin's grip and shoving past the Roktan prince. "She's safest with me. With magic that can do for her what you cannot."

Dagfin absorbed the blow, electric storms pulsing inside.

The *Faerak* drew two daggers.

"Don't make me do whatever it takes to stop you," he said, blind with rage.

The fae king turned slowly, appraising Dagfin's daggers in his hands.

"I can't return now, Fin," Aisling said, squirming out of the fae king's grip till she settled on her own two feet. The gesture stiffened the fae king, his body sharp as she leaned against the threshold. "I'm so close."

"I won't let you die, Aisling," Dagfin said, spinning his daggers between his fingers. All he needed was to take her away. To save her body and soul from the nightmare the fae king was delivering for her. He could spare her and end the fae king.

"Don't do this, Fin," she pleaded, eyes wet with unfallen tears.

But the bleeding wound from her shoulder tore something apart in Dagfin he couldn't quite describe. Fionn's collar around her throat once more... Dagfin couldn't let this proceed any farther. More than being king, more than being a son, a brother, a friend, Dagfin felt he'd failed in his duty to protect her. It was the only duty he'd ever cared to honor. And so, he couldn't—wouldn't let this carry on any further.

"I love you, Ash," he said, words spoken into eternity. For he'd eternally loved her and known it all his life. Had forsaken her, wronged her, not been enough for her that entire life and he could be now. Could be what she needed but didn't want.

"Dagfin, this is a death wish," she said.

"I can't die," he said. "I haven't kissed you again."

Again.

Lir shifted, posture morphing into something lethal. Something that struck fear into both realms and gods. The forest beyond tossed violently to the thunder that groaned up above, flashing in splinters of light.

Dagfin's words alone were enough to provoke the fae king into a battle. Lir's eyes were riddled with jealous hate, till Dagfin only saw blood rage in his sage orbs.

"Stop this," Aisling said, now swathed in smoke from failed attempts to summon her *draiocht*. Teeth bared as she leaned against the threshold.

Lir stepped past Aisling, axes in hand, a few steps above Dagfin on the stairwell.

"Very well, princeling," he said. "Let's end this."

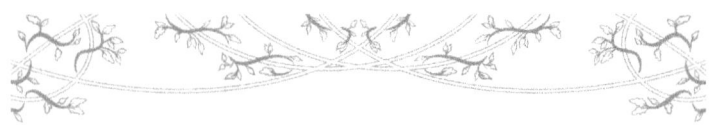

CHAPTER XLI

AISLING

Roktan blades were forged with undiluted iron. Heated in fire and cooled by the tears of the Ashild. Dagfin had cast every blade that lined his bandolier. Another excuse to avoid his princely duties to play the part of hero, perhaps, but somewhere along the way, he'd stopped pretending and become one.

The tip of his blade grazed Lir's cheekbone. The fae king dodged the attack nimbly yet, still, it grazed his flesh, carving an angry, thin red scar along his right eye.

Lir laughed, the sound of it freezing the marrow in Aisling's bones.

"Relish whatever you're feeling now," he said, "because you won't ever feel it again."

Lir swung his axe, forcing Dagfin to stagger back and collapse against the stone entirely on the second swing. The *Faerak* rolled to the side as Lir slammed his axe into the stone.

"Enough!" Aisling screamed, watching as Dagfin leapt to his feet, a sliver from Lir's axe as he aimed for his throat, feinting left before throwing another dagger, then another. Lir raised his axe, deflecting each one artfully before raising his blade and thrusting down. Dagfin spun, grabbing his last dagger and jabbing it at Lir's ribs.

The fae king moved lithely, knocking the blade from the *Faerak*'s hand with the butt of his axe.

Aisling's chest hollowed, mind spinning. Two halves of her heart, of her soul, battling one another with the intent to end the other. Whichever outcome, bound to kill Aisling if her wounds didn't first.

"Please," she said, screaming at the *draiocht* inside. Quiet, gone, forsaking her to watch their exchange. She staggered toward them, bleeding across the stone.

"Care to forfeit?" Lir said. "I'll make your death swift."

"Not quite. I've always wondered what it'd be like to kill a fae with my bare hands."

So, with no weapons left, Dagfin charged the fae king, tackling him into the light and onto Lofgren's Rise.

Aisling sucked in a breath and held it. From this vantage point, they stood atop the world if the world were a freezing, bone-white realm of twinkling evergreens and rock giants asleep in the shape of mighty mountains. A great, shimmering lake of pure silver nestled at the center, veiled like a bride in thick clouds beading with moisture. The first drip of the Forge onto the earth.

Lir and Dagfin spilled onto Lofgren's peak, a tussle of fleshy sounds as Lir punched Dagfin in the jaw with his fist still wrapped around his axe. They fell apart, but not for long. Dagfin had pilfered a blade from Lir's belt, raising it and swiping for Lir's throat.

"You'll ruin her!" Dagfin yelled, his voice echoing through all Fjallnorr. "You and your selfish, primal need for power will corrupt Aisling until there's no going back."

"You act as if Aisling doesn't have a choice in the matter. You see, princeling, with me, Aisling is free to be who she's always been: wild and powerful beyond measure."

"You force her destiny! You shape it as you like!" Dagfin lunged for Lir, grazing his jawline with the tip of his blade.

"I seem to remember you being at our union, watching as you traded her to the Sidhe. Complicit in the sins of your kind when it came to forcing Aisling into anything."

Dagfin ground his teeth, rage abounding, attacking faster than Aisling could make sense of their tussle.

Lir parried, growling as he elbowed the *Faerak* in the face. A blow Dagfin endured, jaw red and lip bleeding as he swiped for the fae king again.

Quicker, the fae king stepped to the side kicking the *Faerak* in the chest and shoving him onto his back with his boot. An axe to his throat.

"No!" Aisling screamed, the respite allowing Aisling to, at last, approach from behind, holding out a hand to the fae king as though he were a wolf in the woods, just as capable of stalking away as he was devouring her body and soul.

"Please," she begged him. Aisling had sworn to never submit to the fae king. To never forfeit even a morsel of her power. But in this moment, she didn't care. She only saw Dagfin's throat growing slick with blood as Lir pressed harder.

"I will *never* forgive you!" Aisling screamed, knowing the fae king wouldn't care but saying it regardless. Lir cared for one thing only and that was power. Anything that threatened it would meet its end swiftly thereafter.

Lir, at last, tore his eyes from the *Faerak* to meet Aisling's own. The same unholy, inhuman sheen she'd witnessed when he'd killed the Cú Scáth, when he'd slaughtered the fomorians, when he'd turned on humankind, when he'd cut through the neccakaid. Each and every time, assuring death.

"If you and I are to be," Lir said, his words rougher than Aisling expected, "then he cannot live, Aisling. You know it as well."

"Then kill him," Aisling cried. "And in so doing, you kill a piece of me as well."

Lir flinched, as though it were Aisling with an axe to his throat. Eyes flecked with anguish and horror alike.

An eternity passed while the clouds whispered among them. While the silver lake reflected their exchange in mocking. It was always meant to end like this. A hero and a villain at odds. A hunter and a beast, battling for survival. Yet, Aisling needed both. Couldn't live without the other.

"You must end this, Aisling," Dagfin said, straining beneath Lir's axe. "You must choose. Here and now, pick your destiny."

Aisling's chest hitched. Her ears rang. Her vision blurred. Either from loss of blood or the converging of her fate, spinning, weaving, braiding before her eyes and waiting for the last word of the spell to be spoken and sealed.

Aisling shook her head, her body going numb the longer she stared at both Dagfin and Lir, awaiting her decision.

Aisling looked into Dagfin's eyes. The Ashild staring back and warming her soul with summery, salt waters. With stars they'd watched shoot across the sky as children, making secret promises to one another they'd never been given the chance to keep. Stolen, ripped, torn from their hands at hers and Lir's union.

"I love you, Dagfin," Aisling said, her voice broken.

Dagfin froze and Lir's expression shuttered. The words, brittle, true, and pure. "But, I choose Lir."

Aisling forced herself to witness the agony in Dagfin's

expression. The image of a soul ripping in two. Lir didn't move, didn't react, still as a windless wood. The realm holding its breath as her words seeped into the fabric of fate, magic taking root and fizzing in the air till all smelled of forge fires, of forgotten prophecies, and vows made from the heart.

At last, Lir released his hold.

The fae king uncurled from his position and let go of Dagfin.

Dagfin stood, panting, eyes ringed with red, having used the last of his Ocras.

Aisling exhaled, relieved enough to weep until no tears were left. Instead, she picked up her feet, fighting through the pain to embrace Dagfin.

She wrapped her arms around him, tangling her fingers in his jacket.

He held her, salty tears wetting the crown of her head as he did his best to avoid her neccakaid injury, still soaking her dress through.

"I can't lose you," was all he said. As though she hadn't chosen Lir instead. "Tell me you'll be alright."

Aisling nodded her head. "I'm always alright. Even now."

Indeed, the pain came in waves, always worst after she'd desperately clawed for her *draiocht* to no avail. But Aisling could ignore it, for they'd reached Lofgren's Rise. They'd made it, all together. Reached what she'd longed for ever since she'd heard its name spoken. Trodden through the feywilds, survived despite the cold, been freed from Fionn's keep, endured the druids, struck fear in Danu, navigated through Iod.

Everything was right here. After all this time.

They'd done it.

"Aisling," the Roktan prince said but it wasn't out of relief. It was spoken in warning. Dagfin shoved Aisling to the side so hard, she slapped against the floor. And when she rose, she at once wished she never had.

A gaping wound ran from one side of Dagfin's body to the other. Lir's axe bloodied on the floor behind the *Faerak*.

Dagfin reached for Aisling, collapsing into her arms as she dove for him. Struggling to process. To understand. It'd all happened so fast. He was alive, he was standing, he was pushing Aisling and now the light in his eyes was fading, Aisling was covered in both her own and his blood. A hole in his chest.

"No, no, no, no," Aisling said, out loud or in her mind she couldn't tell. Only that it echoed again and again, her heart imploding inside.

"No."

"Ash," Dagfin said, his stormy blue eyes dimming.

"No."

"It's alright," he repeated, lifting his hand to cup her cheek. Still warm, calloused, the touch of home. "We'll find each other again. Follow Odhran's constellation."

Aisling went numb. She couldn't feel her hands, her legs, her arms. Couldn't feel her body as the light faded from his eyes and then extinguished entirely.

Aisling would kill Lir.

And if her magic never returned, she'd find a way with her bare hands.

Aisling lay Dagfin's head onto the ground, slipping Lir's dagger from the *Faerak*'s grip. Tears streaming down her face as she stood and turned on the fae king.

"HOW COULD YOU?!" Aisling screamed, voice breaking mid-sentence.

He stood still. Expressionless as she ran for him, making

to stab him in the heart. He moved swiftly to the side, dodging her onslaught. But she followed his every step, lunging again and again, breathless, lungs burning but unable to interrupt her impulse. Her every pore, smoking where her *draiocht* wouldn't light.

"Stop, Aisling," he said softly.

"I'll never stop!" she screamed. "Not until you're dead!"

"Clear your mind, Aisling," he said, catching her wrist and watching her with a hollowed, anguished expression as she clawed at his chest, pressing the dagger closer to his heart. His eyes torn and cracked with depthless sorrow as she struggled against him. Finding her other wrist and holding it. Keeping her in place as she wept. As she screamed. As she shattered before his eyes.

"Please," he begged her.

But Aisling couldn't. Couldn't find her way out of these woods. Not this time. Not when every tree, every stone, every river, every shadow scratched at her soul and ripped her bloody with endless torment. As though her heart were being devoured whole. The only thing more powerful than her despair, anger.

"Would it help?" Lir asked, even softer this time.

Aisling didn't know what he was asking, still straining against his grip.

"Would it help if you hurt me?" he asked again and this time Aisling understood.

She met his eyes and that was answer enough.

Lir released her wrist. The dagger plunged into him.

Aisling held her breath, eyes wide with shock as she glared at the dagger fully submerged in his shoulder, just above his heart. The fleshy sensation thrumming through Aisling's hand. A small groan slipping between his teeth as he clenched his jaw.

Lir didn't flinch, didn't look away from her even as his blood dripped down his front. Instead, he brought her closer, holding her against him, hand still wrapped around the hilt of the dagger.

Aisling was too stunned to move, warmed by his blood as it seeped into her gown. Glaring past his shoulder into the endless oblivion of the north. Winter, a chill in comparison to the cold she felt inside. The emptiness that grew with each passing breath. Silent, until she heard the footsteps.

Slow, heavy boots behind her.

Lir held her tighter, already aware of who'd approached.

"Well done, Sister," Starn said. "You did what few mortals have ever been capable of: stabbing a fae king. Had I known killing Dagfin would yield such results, I would have done it sooner."

CHAPTER XLII

AISLING

Aisling spun, and the realm spun alongside her.

Starn, Iarbonel, Fergus, Annind, and Killian stood a few paces from Dagfin's body. Lir's bloodied axe at their feet.

Slowly, her eldest brother bent to retrieve it. Every muscle in Lir's body tightening at the sight. So, without another thought, vines grew from the stone and snatched it from the Tilrish Prince's fingers, returning it to its rightful master as Lir plucked Aisling's dagger from his shoulder.

"Your tricks are less impressive now that I have my own." Starn smirked, sliding his hands into his pockets as though unfazed. "On a whim, I can wrench that axe from your hand once more and beckon it into my own. As I've already done." Starn's eyes darted to Dagfin's body.

Aisling shook her head, understanding but wishing desperately not to. It wasn't possible. It wasn't feasible that Starn could wield any *draiocht* at all. Could snatch Lir's axe from his hand and hurl it through Dagfin's chest by the will of his mind alone. Only Aisling, born a mortal, was capable of such sorcery.

"Although, I must admit, I made a mistake," Starn continued. "I'd intended to kill you, Sister."

That was why Dagfin had shoved Aisling aside. Had spared her from the onslaught, taking the death himself. One last form of self-sacrifice. A debt paid for his crimes against her when she'd been traded to the fae. A debt paid to the *draiocht* after fleeing his union with Peitho.

Aisling's legs grew numb. Her face drained of blood as she processed everything. As her vision clouded with smoke intended to be fire.

"Touch her and I'll have your heart in my fist before you can flinch," Lir growled from behind Aisling, Fjallnorr's forests, whipping in the distance at the sound of his rage.

Yet Starn smiled, amused.

"The Lady said you'd make things difficult."

"The Lady?" Aisling repeated, every word broken from a throat stripped raw.

"Aye, it appears magic and mortals are not so at odds after all." Starn raised his hands, his iron sword unsheathing from his belt as though drawn by a phantom hand. "You see, the Lady and mankind's goals align: we both want you dead."

"Starn—" Iarbonel warned, face streaked with tears, but one glance from their eldest brother and he quieted.

Aisling balled her hands into fists at her sides. Planting her feet against the stone.

"Are you so afraid of me?" Aisling asked, tilting her head to the side. Gathering every inch of her sorrow, of her despair, of her endless anguish into rage, into wrath, into fury. Into vengeance.

Starn laughed. "Afraid of *you*? You're a mistake, Sister, just as capable of setting yourself on fire as the world. In fact, I've come to realize, it never should've been you who happened upon this magic." Starn grinned at his floating blade. "Rather I. Power was meant for sons, for men who lead battles, for kings. Not princesses traded to the fae."

Aisling narrowed her eyes and smiled through the tears.

"So, this is what it's come to? Begging the Lady for magic so that you might obtain the curse breaker and steal whatever she's lent you?"

Starn shook his head. "No begging necessary. The Lady rather hates the two of you."

"Tell me, how long till those 'tricks' wear off, brother? Till you can no longer pretend to be me?"

Starn bristled, rolling back his shoulders.

"The only thing I wish to glean from you is the power that should've rightfully been mine. Should've been Father's."

"You always were such an insufferable child. Always begging for Nemed's approval, even at the cost of your own soul. That's why you're here, convincing yourself this is for your own benefit and not another task he's set for you to prove yourself. One you'll never quite live up to. So, was it he or you who made the deal with the Lady?"

Starn hesitated, opening his mouth to speak but stopping short. An answer in and of itself. Aisling had assumed as much. Nemed had orchestrated all this, Starn nothing more than his puppet goaded by the fire hand on lies Starn was somehow a cherished part of his plan. No, Starn as well as all of Nemed's children were pieces to be slid across a chessboard. Not one spared from his ambition.

"Either way, Sister, your adventure ends today." Starn commanded his blade, pointing in Aisling's direction. Lir stepped beside Aisling, white-knuckled on Hiraeth.

"Listen to him, Aisling. Concede and we can spare your life," Iarbonel said. "It's better this way."

"Fergus, remove his body," Starn commanded their brother, jerking his chin in Dagfin's direction.

"Don't touch him!" Aisling growled without thinking, taking another step forward. Fergus flinched, unaware Aisling couldn't wield her *draiocht* since her most recent encounter with Fionn.

"Don't look at me like that, Sister," Starn said in mocking. "Dagfin was living on borrowed time as it was. The Ocras was eating him alive from the inside out and even if he'd lived to return to Roktling, he would've been hung as a traitor."

Aisling ground her teeth.

"You killed a brother," she said. "All of you. You killed him in cold blood."

Killian's brows furrowed, unable to look down at Dagfin's body. Fergus, Iarbonel, and Annind exchanged glances, desperately clinging to the guise of indifference Starn had mastered. A glimmer of guilt creeping into the edge of the high prince's mouth, the posture of his shoulders, the tension in his arms.

"The moment you wed your fae king, you died, Aisling. And the moment Dagfin chose to follow you from Oighir is the moment he died to me as well."

I wish to summon the fire, Aisling asked the *draiocht*. Fionn's collar choking her, but she didn't care.

Starn stepped forward, his floating blade following his direction.

"Dagfin never should've followed you," he continued. "He was meant to be king. To rule alongside myself and the other mortal sovereigns. To lead mankind into greatness. Instead, he let you manipulate him and plague his mind until he bent at your will. Until he followed you down a path that offered no escape for him. And you *let* him."

Starn licked his lips, crouching down beside Dagfin's body. He brushed the backside of his knuckles against Dagfin's cheek. A gesture that awakened something in Aisling.

"You are selfish, Aisling. Pathetic. Weak. And wholly undeserving."

Aisling's veins ignited.

I wish to summon the fire, she shouted internally at the *draiocht*. The collar blocking her lungs.

Starn unfurled from his crouch. "It wasn't I that killed him, Aisling. It was you."

I SUMMON THE FIRE.

Aisling's eyes lit with violet flame, Fionn's collar shattering at the force of her strength alone, and from the silver lake, a beast appeared.

A *dragún*.

Forged in a cauldron of boiling night sky, Racat lifted his head, the crown of horns spiraling from its temples, a foil to its silky, obsidian mane, billowing in the highland wind.

Starn, Iarbonel, Fergus, Annind, and Killian staggered back, faces slack with terror. The *Faerak*'s hands instinctively reaching for the crossbow on his back.

Lir cursed beneath his breath, eyes gone wide at the sight of his *dragún* outside Annwyn. Not a dragon of fire as it'd been before Danu. A flesh and blood beast, glittering before them with all the majesty of the Other.

"We come for the curse breaker!" Starn shouted. "By order of the Lady!"

Racat moved closer to the shore, fixing his eyes on Aisling's brothers and Killian. His shimmering scales sparkling amidst the fog.

"High prince," Racat said, his voice an ancient, primeval song. "You've owned what you covet all your life only to now take it with a knife?"

"*Owned what you covet.*" Aisling's eyes glazed over, her mind elsewhere.

Iarbonel, Fergus, Annind, and Killian drew their weapons.

"Enough riddles," Fergus shouted. "Give us what we want so we may go in peace."

Lir shook his head, not understanding. Racat was the fae king's dragon and had found a home in Annwyn thanks to Ina. How was it possible the curse breaker they all sought was hoarded by the dragon of power all this time?

"You speak of peace, yet you threaten war," Racat said.

Aisling and Lir exchanged glances, turning to search her brothers' and Killian's expressions. The *dragún*'s ominous words seeping into both their bones.

"Your armies thread through Fjallnorr prepared to destroy and burn everything in your mortal wake."

Aisling raced to the edge of Lofgren's peak, peering over the ledge.

Dread sunk its dull teeth into her gut.

Thousands, if not millions, of soldiers approached Iod, donning the armor of those left from every northern mortal court. Aithirn, Kinbreggan, Roktling, and Tilren. Their iron contaminating the feywild opiate.

"Then be threatened," Starn continued. "And give us the curse breaker."

Aisling's stomach fluttered.

"*Owned what you covet.*" Recognition dawned on Aisling. It was her. She was what Nemed wanted, Starn, her brothers, the mortal realm. "*Owned what you covet, so you might take it with a knife?*" Owned, controlled by her own clann only so they might wrench what she's worth to them with a magic blade gifted by the Lady.

Aisling's mind spun. Ears buzzing.

The world suddenly brighter.

Aisling was the curse breaker. The means to either end Ina's curse and revive mankind to their previous glory or to ensure the curse was never broken. Ina's punishment forever sealed even if at the cost of mortal ambition.

It wasn't possible. Aisling didn't understand and yet she did. Felt justified never having fit inside an iron keep, in a mortal den, in a magicless, purposeless life. She was wild. Forged not to sit at banquets nor wade silently through life as pawn. She was rather forged to race through forests barefoot, to dance in the night, to roar alongside the beasts of yore.

"Give us the curse breaker!" Starn repeated, jutting his blade forward.

"She stands before you," Aisling said, at last.

The *dragún* shook its mane, casting itself in a layer of violet fire that mirrored the flames enveloping Aisling.

Lir's feline gaze focused fully on Aisling, dark hair windswept by her magic. The others shielded their eyes from the blinding, violet light.

"To claim the curse breaker, you must defeat Ina's greatest weapon and seize its heart." Racat lowered himself, so his great head hovered at Aisling's side. "Ina's sorceress."

"Godsforsaken Forge," Lir hissed, searching Aisling's expression licked by fire. His axes hanging at his sides. Staring at Aisling as though she were a dream. A vision. A memory cast into eternity and far from him. His opportunity to spite the fire hand and all of humankind, to prevent Danu's prophecy from ever being fulfilled, standing before him. A single death away.

The cost: the heart of his own *caera*.

"Go on," Aisling said, her flames burning brighter. Heart hammering inside her chest, fulfilled by magic's decadent satisfaction. "See if you can take what it is you want."

Lir shook his head, eyes glazed and wet. Ringed in red and harrowed. Yet slowly, so slowly, he lifted his axes. Aisling's heart splintering. A part of her, a part she'd shoved into its cobwebbed corner again and again, that hoped he'd choose her above his need for power, for vengeance, for blood, died the moment he raised his axe.

But it was Starn who attacked first, shouting as he unleashed his floating blade.

The iron sword darted through the air, spearing for Aisling's head.

Without another thought, Aisling lifted her hand and wrapped it in flame, holding it mid-air with wrath, with loathing, with impatience.

"Did you really think you could borrow some spell? Some flimsy means of magic and best me?" Aisling bared her teeth, spinning Starn's blade and pointing it back at her brother.

Starn swallowed, staggering back alongside Killian and her brothers.

"I *let* you make it this far. *Allowed* you to stand before me now so you might face the full fury of my strength. A strength you caged, shackled, and starved." Aisling seethed.

Killian released six quarrels. So, Aisling flung Starn's blade to the side and burned every last bolt till they shriveled to ash atop Iod.

"Mortals were not made for magic." She approached them. "Humans lack vision, a cognizance for the world. You breed a desire to control that which was never yours to command."

Aisling summoned a ring of fire, trapping the tip of

Lofgren's Rise in amethyst walls. Lir watched her, as though transfixed by some unspoken spell.

"You stand here before me by my design. I could bring you to your knees atop the stone that made your kind."

"Your kind?!" Fergus shouted. "You're mortal, Aisling. Don't let the fae king convince you otherwise."

Aisling laughed, a sound serrated with a cruelty she understood.

"No, our brother is right. I died a first death the night you traded me to the fae," Aisling's eyes flickered to Dagfin's body. Limp and unmoving. The sight of him burning her fires brighter. "And a second death when you killed Dagfin, blighting whatever shred of humanity I still bore."

Aisling lifted her hands, veins pulsing with fire, as she glared at her eldest brother.

"No, no!" Iarbonel shouted, "Dagfin never would've wanted this for you!"

"*You are great, Aisling. Capable of both great good and great evil. I'm not naive to the forces that wage war within you. But a battle is a battle because it's meant to be fought. So, fight for it, Aisling. Fight to be good.*" Dagfin may have been dead, but his words were alive and beating in her mind.

Aisling wrenched her eyes shut.

"*Fight to be good.*"

Aisling lowered her hand, flames dimming. Her heart beating a pace slower. Aisling was prepared to kill her brothers, yet it was Dagfin's words that held her back. His way of protecting her soul, even in death, should she make a decision she could never return from.

"AISLING!" Lir shouted and before she could blink, Starn's sword was running through her gut.

Aisling was numb, casting a bolt of fire that wrapped

around Starn and inspired blood-curdling screams. Racat roared, diving for her brothers, lost without their magic sword, now staked through Aisling. A wound to accompany her others.

Lir was by her side in an instant, wrapped in smoke from her dying fire. The sound of her brothers' boots fleeing, echoing in the northern wind as Lir held her against him. The Lady's magic potent in the air as she sheltered Starn's escape.

The fae king roared. A sound so terrible, the forest recoiled, bled black, and quivered. Screaming so loud, Aisling thought the veil might, at long last, shatter.

"Breathe, Aisling," Lir said, voice strained and rough. "Breathe through the *draiocht*. The blood will stop. Just breathe."

Gilrel, Galad, and Peitho arrived from below, gasping for breath. They gaped at Racat, at Aisling and Lir, eyes as wide as the northern moon at *Samhain*'s peak. Beholding the remnants of everything that'd occurred, including Dagfin's body.

"Their armies are approaching," Gilrel said, kneeling down to hold Aisling's hand. Galad looked away, unable to bear the sight of Aisling impaled by an iron blade.

"We can't stay any longer," Galad mumbled. "The mortal fleets are approaching."

"Did you obtain the curse breaker?" Filverel asked.

"Breathe, Aisling," was all Lir said again and again. "Breathe, Aisling. Breathe."

But Aisling didn't feel short of breath. Didn't feel pain.

She felt madness.

Inhaling.

And exhaling.

A ripple of fire blasted from where she lay atop Lofgren's peak and ravaged the whole of the north. A ripple of unbridled wildfire, scorching the earth and felling every last mortal till nothing remained but their iron armor, scorned by the fires once spread by their torches.

CHAPTER XLIII

AISLING

Galad pulled the blade from Aisling's body.

Aisling gasped for breath, clutching her already healing wounds kissed by Racat.

Lir held her tightly enough to crush her, Aisling felt at times. Holding her against him where they lay atop Lofgren's peak.

"Ina was a favored child. Blessed not once but twice by the gods. First with her sight and then with a weapon. One that was hidden away for a millennium, asleep and waiting: a soul," Racat said to them, his voice imbuing the cloudburst that showered them all. That pelted over the spirits of Ina and Bres, knee-deep in the silver lake whispering in one another's ears. A promise of ruinous, devastating love. One that persisted despite its potential for ruin. One that hadn't managed to change the stars Ina had foreseen.

"Ina was patient, biding her time, dipping her hand into the future and burying her weapon inside a mortal keep. For what better place to hide a treasure than the den of a thief? Knowing that when the time came to wield it, it would be awoken by the blood of her son. Fate did not choose these two as *caera*. The bond between weapon and son made them so. The first act of snipping fate's noose."

Here, at this silver linn, Ina made the deal with Racat. And so, it would be at this linn that Racat revealed himself once more. Rose from the shadows and unveiled Aisling's prophecy on the peak that vibrated with the Forge's witchery. She would confront her destiny in the place it began.

Lir held Aisling's jaw, brushing her cheek with his thumb as he closed his eyes and pressed his forehead to hers.

Galad, Peitho, Gilrel, and Filverel silent. Soaked in carnage and rainwater alike.

"During the Wild Hunt, Ina found me in the Linn of Wanting but did not attempt to shackle me as had the rest. Instead, she made a deal. She, nor any of her heirs, would ever own me. Instead, we'd be bound together. Equals. I blessed Iod and Annwyn with power, and in exchange, she bound me with her weapon. Emboldening my might as well as her weapon's. Linked for an eternity, I am the *draiocht* you summon inside. I am the magic that breathes inside your lungs. And I am your power, curse breaker. You, the remedy Ina knew could rectify her sins, gifted by the gods in trickery: to force Ina's son to kill his *caera* in order to achieve his ends and undo his mother's curse. And yet, you and I together, we will live so long as the moon ascends come dusk. Forged and intended by Ina to commit the second act of snipping fate's noose: destroying the mortals before they destroy us and uniting both realms: the Otherworld and this mortal plane.

"Aisling you will be the guardian of realms. The faerie to protect the spirit world from the iron of mortals. Together, the next step is to win the gods' favor."

Peitho and Galad lifted Dagfin's body and placed him at the lake's shore.

Aisling mustered what strength she still bore, kneeled before him, and placed his head in her lap.

She kissed him. One last kiss. A promise to follow Odhran's constellation, praying he'd found a home in the Other. That one day she'd meet him there.

And although she wept till she thought her heart was punctured and bleeding saltwater, she was also angry. So damnably angry that Dagfin had perished atop a mountain of the very Ocras that'd almost killed him, his own iron finding him first. That as Aisling cradled his face, forcing herself to push him into the silver lake so that magic might take what it was owed, she hated the *draiocht* and everything it'd already claimed. His body buried in Racat's oblivion alongside what was left of Aisling's humanity.

"The choice is yours, Aisling. You and I may forge a path for ourselves, unbinding from the fae king once and for all. Or, we may align with the dark lord. Regardless, we are bound together, dear friend. All that's left is a choice so that you and I will rule this realm till kingdom come. Together, we'll enter the Otherworld and join the Other and this realm into one. Ours."

The evening burned slowly. Patiently indulging the revelry of Annwyn below till Aisling believed the sun might never rise. That the fae would dance till their feet bled, the world would never seize its spinning, the wine would endlessly spill, and the *Snaidhm* all Annwyn celebrated would scream into oblivion.

It was Tyr's, one of Lir's knights, *Snaidhm*, in celebration of his recent union. One bound and sealed after Aisling, Lir, and his knights had returned from Lofgren's Rise, boots covered in both ice and soot.

"You should join them," a voice sounded beside her, laced in fae wine.

Galad approached, wearing little save for trousers and an unlaced shirt. Every last Sidhe rune glistening in sweat and reflected by the fae light, idly floating through the *Snaidhm*. "If they knew you'd come, they'd feast in your honor."

Aisling scoffed, crossing her arms. They stood at the edge of the forest, glaring through the last trees before shadow gave way to glowing festival.

"They'd curse me as thief once more. Demand my death so the threat of the curse breaker is no longer. Even if it would cost them Racat."

"Not anymore," Galad said. "You destroyed seven mortal fleets at Lofgren's Ri—"

"I know what I did," Aisling bit, unable to hear the words spoken out loud. Not yet. Perhaps not ever if it helped her forget what'd happened to Dagfin. She could still pretend Dagfin was alive elsewhere. Had run off as he'd always dreamed and made a new life for himself.

"The Sidhe won't forget what you've done so easily, no matter how badly *you* might try to. And with Racat bound to you, they cannot demand your death. Without Racat, Annwyn is made vulnerable to the mortals and Unseelie alike. To Danu. You, Aisling, are the weapon the Sidhe *need*. That they want. And that's a cause worth forgiving all else."

"And you," Aisling asked, turning to meet the knight's sapphire eyes. "Have you forgiven me?"

Galad stepped away, never once unlatching her from his gaze. His dark hair brushed by the midnight breeze.

"Come and partake in the festivities," he said, ignoring

her question as he walked away. "Lir will be searching for you."

And as though summoned, the fae king materialized between the folds of fae dancers. Miraculous, brilliant, twisting Aisling's heart at the sight of him. Both rage and something else stirring inside her gut, near making her ill.

He wore only a jacket, his bare abdomen exposed and teasing the eye. The axes he never parted with crossed at his back. Chains like thorns wrapped around his throat, ringed fingers, and several hoops in one of his pointed ears. But his charcoal-lined eyes met Aisling's across the path, pulling at the intangible cord between them. His left eye marked by a thin red scar. A memory of Dagfin and how the magic indeed took what it was owed.

Aisling turned away.

She couldn't face Lir. Not without losing what composure she still harbored.

Lir hadn't killed Dagfin, yet for an endless moment she'd believed he had. And the desire to kill him, to punish him for his betrayal was real until that moment, at last, ended. Replaced by another. One where Starn had slayed Dagfin instead, with Lir's axe and the magic the Lady had lent him to kill Aisling. In so doing, ending a prophecy for the Lady and empowering humankind for Starn.

She'd kill her brother. Ensure he felt every morsel of pain before at last meeting his end. And Aisling wouldn't rest until said end was dealt by her hand. At one point, she'd feared her brothers died escaping Lofgren's Rise. That she hadn't killed them when she'd bore the chance and another had stolen the opportunity. But a strange sort of glee filled her lungs when she felt his heart beating further north. A signal from the *draiocht*, a whisper, a calling of blood and clann that could never die, screaming at Aisling that Starn, her brothers, and her father were still alive. No doubt thanks to the intervention of the Lady, aiding their escape. An unintentional gift to Aisling, for now, she couldn't help but look forward to the day she'd relish the gore of their deaths.

As for Fionn, Aisling doubted he'd died. Winter froze Fjallnorr into solid ice with his living rage, biding his time till he found her or Lir again.

Aisling's eyes burned as she darted into the woods. Her vision blurred by tears as she mounted Saoirse, the stag Lir had gifted her after their union. And they raced through the trees, the forest where she'd been hunted by the Cú Scáth, where she'd summoned her flames for the first time, where she'd been confronted with her tuath's lies. Where she'd found a sense of belonging at long last.

And she screamed.

Yelled until her lungs were stripped. Until the trees whipped madly on a windless night. Mourning Aisling's second death.

Yet even when Aisling scarcely bore the breath to weep, she kept racing, flying through Annwyn's corridors and toward Lir's castle.

Aisling didn't know where she was going. Only that she couldn't stop moving. Couldn't hesitate lest the grief inside catch up to her, pin her to the earth and devour her, body and soul.

The bear sentinels opened the doors for Aisling as she tore through Castle Annwyn, unknowing where any staircase led save for her bedchamber. But she couldn't retreat there. A den of restless thoughts, of memories, of silence where everything that'd occurred atop Lofgren's Rise would be given space to be remembered. So, she let Saoirse guide her through a castle that was meant to be Aisling's own. She, a queen of the Sidhe and yet she knew not her own castle. Was despised by her subjects. Wanted dead by her *caera*. And loathed even by her blood. Alone and lost, in a world of her own making. The answers she'd coveted hadn't been what she'd wanted. Galad had been right. The answers she craved were not answers that could be given to her. They were moments yet to unfold. Choices, memories, experiences happening all around her, making her who, why, and what she was to become. Be it for better or worse.

Saoirse burst through two mighty doors and into a great hall.

A room of stained glass portraits, of cross-vaulted ceilings supported by eight colossal ash trees, winding their branches to the ceiling and veiling the murals painted above. Ivy clinging to every surface, made brilliant by the precious gems and stones clipped and cut into the walls, the floors, the pillars, and the arcade. A world made by fae hands and fae hands alone. Where a colossal tree sprouted at the end of the hall, a throne made from its roots and crowned by mighty antlers.

Aisling dismounted Saoirse.

This was Lir's throne room. Images of Bres were depicted in the mosaics, in the sculptures, his dedication to Ina made tangible in the hundreds of owls that flew amidst the canopies, hooting at Aisling's arrival.

Aisling approached the throne, her every footstep echoing amidst the silence.

There was magic here, ripe and thick. Pressing down upon her head as though submerged beneath several layers of the ocean.

This is ours, Racat—the shape of her *draiocht*—said inside her. *We will rule everything.*

Aisling traced the arms of the throne with the tips of her

fingers and what *draiocht* lurked here thrummed through her. Every hair on her body stood to attention.

Once the throne of her enemy, the nightmare muse of blood-soaked legends. Now, the throne she craved. Wanted, and would no longer feel guilty for desiring.

Desire stoked all power. Desire made her limitless. Made everything she'd ever wanted within grasp if she wanted it enough to take it.

Aisling paused, allowing the magic to flow through her. Until she heard him at the threshold.

Lir wanted her to know he was there, otherwise, Aisling never would've gleaned the soft press of his boots atop the marble floors. Like a wolf pads across the forest floor.

She turned, meeting his eyes, overtaken as she'd been at the *Snaidhm*.

"I wish to be alone," she said, forcing the words as calm and resolute as she could manage. But they broke regardless, exposing the emotion inherent within.

"You've avoided me since we departed Iod," he said, slipping his hands into his pockets as he approached, stopping only when they stood at opposing ends of the hall.

"It was intentional."

"I gleaned that."

"Then be gone."

A muscle flickered across Lir's jaw, his sage eyes growing shadows.

"I want to know how you're healing."

Against her own volition, Aisling glanced down at her abdomen. She'd healed almost fully from Starn's iron blade but the considerable amount of blood she'd lost had taken its toll. For the next several weeks, her body would be recovering, harnessing back its strength.

"In time, there'll scarcely be a scar. That's what Gilrel tells me."

Lir's shoulders slackened, taking another silent step forward.

"What happened at Lofgren's Rise—"

"If you've come seeking my gratitude for sparing my life in place of seizing the curse breaker before you knew I was bound to your *dragún*, then look no further," Aisling bit. "You'll find no such thanks here."

Lir shook his head, brows drawing together in either anger or sadness, Aisling couldn't tell. Only that the emotion traveled deep within him, rising to the surface.

"You think that's why I've come?"

"Why have you come?" Aisling said, turning to face him fully. "Why do you insist on haunting me?"

"Haunting *you*?" Lir's expression contorted, eyes flecked with torment. "The image of you, the sound of you, the smell of you, wakes me in the night and its possession does not falter in daylight. I've tried to rid myself of your spells time and time again, to cut them from my heart by blade of iron if I must and *still* you sink your fangs into my soul." Every word sharp with frustration, with anger, chilling Aisling's blood.

"Your name stalks my thoughts even in battle," he continued, the room growing darker. "Whilst my name on your lips is a curse I cannot banish, cannot break, cannot muster the strength to wish it gone. Instead, I need it. Need you and I despise you for it."

Aisling blinked, damning the tears that fell down her cheeks as he continued to approach. Defeating the distance between them.

"And so, there is no trust between us," Aisling said, louder than she'd anticipated.

"But there can be." Lir walked up the steps of the dais, nearing both the throne and Aisling.

Aisling shook her head, "We were born enemies, discovered *caera*, and we will eventually die by one another's hand."

"Because fate has chosen for us?"

"Because fate has deemed it so! Because I will perish with an axe in my heart!"

Quicker than Aisling could blink, Lir drew his right axe from his back.

Instinctively, Aisling's fists lit with flame. She took a single step forward.

"Take my axe then," he said, offering the blade where she stood several steps above him atop the dais.

Aisling opened her mouth to speak but no words left her lips. Speechless, she glared at the twinkling axe, considering it the way she had the night of their union.

"None but the fae king wield Hiraeth," Aisling said, summarizing what she'd been told of the fae king's weapons. Twin blades that were akin to limbs, forged for his hands alone, and the embodiment of Annwyn itself. Capable of crumbling the fae king's world if destroyed. Blades Aisling had never seen Lir without. Even as he slept.

"It's yours," Lir said, his fangs reflecting the violet of her fires. "Yours to wield. Yours to destroy. Yours to burn. As am I."

Aisling's heart stuttered, her stomach twisting. Eyes glazed over with tears and red from exhaustion.

Slowly, Aisling raised her hand, wrapping her violet fingers around the axe.

The axe hissed, as though it bore a soul, writhing, squirming beneath the heat of her *draiocht*. Swiftly, Aisling extinguished her fires, allowing the pure body of the weapon to flow through her. Ancient, primordial, and cast in the Forge, gifted by the gods to Bres himself, Aisling felt the life breath of the forest. Rain seeping through canopies, leaves falling to the earth, beasts skulking inside their shadows. Every groan and growl and roar the woodland sang, danced when it believed no one was watching.

And it was glorious.

Lir ascended till he stood atop the dais, forcing Aisling to look up and into his eyes. A window into the arcane woodland that surrounded them and grew through Castle Annwyn. The portrait of every leaf, every grisly hunt, every riverbed, alive and breathing from the green of his eyes.

"You describe control. That isn't love," Aisling said.

"No, love is loss. Love is human. Be you mortal, be you fae, be you something in between, what I feel for you is something more. Something everlasting." He bared his fangs. "I only ask you never uncurse me. Never fail to haunt me," he said, holding her chin between his knuckle and thumb. "Never cease to possess me."

Lir dipped his head, pressing his mouth to Aisling's.

His kiss was deep, full, dizzying to Aisling's mind as she allowed the pain to meld with her pleasure. Allowed the grief, her mourning, her torment to slip into whatever witchery the fae king bled into every touch of his lips. He, the taste of magic, of fae wine, and smoke in the woods. Fangs scraping against her lips the harder he kissed her, as though he'd begun and couldn't pull himself back, up, and out of whatever oblivion they'd fallen into by allowing themselves this one kiss.

Aisling wasn't certain when Lir's axe fell onto the ground. When he laced his fingers through her hair, cupping the back of her head as he leaned further into her. Aisling knew it was wrong. Knew it was forbidden. The Lady's prophecy echoing again and again in her mind. Whether it be the doom of the world or her own damnation, dealt by the edge of Lir's axe. Every droplet of her blood screaming in protest each time he touched her let alone tasted her. Let alone tore open her chest and devoured her heart, savoring every bite like the beast Aisling once feared. Yet she couldn't help but hope for a night filled with nightmares. Yearned for him, her body tightening, heating as he kissed her more deeply, as though in question. His lashes brushing against her cheeks.

"You will perish in a world of your own making. An axe in your heart."

Aisling pushed him away, straightening an arm between them. A fathomless distance, slackening the intangible cord.

Lir growled, flushed, pressing his lips into a straight line, appraising her. The green of his eyes shadowed with endless yearning.

So, Aisling pushed him farther and toward his throne.

Lir hesitated, confusion riddling his otherworldly expression. Till he reclined in his seat and Aisling moved atop him, straddling the fae king.

Lir shuddered. His expression shifting, darkening a shade deeper than the depths of the Forge. The curve of his lips prickling every nerve in Aisling's body as his body hardened against her. Eyes sparkling as though lost in an enchantment of his own making.

His hands wrapped around her waist and brought her flush against himself. Eliciting a growl as bestial as the wolf starved all its life. His flesh hot, heart thudding against the runes carved over his chest. So, he held her jaw and brought her lips back to his, insatiable for another taste. His tongue slipping between her lips, lingering to taste the supple curve before entering entirely. An invitation for his hands to possessively wrap around her neck, reach for her waist, and bring her closer.

Aisling's abdomen was set aflame. Not by the *draiocht*, but something else entirely. Something more ancient; the sheen of a midnight sky, the cadence of a whisper, the juice of a freshly bitten berry. The cord between them agonizing as it frayed, grew taught, and pulled.

Aisling ran her fingers through Lir's hair, panting against his lips when they broke apart, swiftly finding one another's lips once more, sharing every breath lest the world rupture.

Lir grabbed Aisling's hips, gripping them and pressing her harder against himself. Soaking the pulsing length of him hidden beneath his trousers, firm beneath her and aching enough to make him groan something deep and wicked in Rún.

Aisling tore off his jacket, needing to feel the cords in his arms as he moved her hips against him. Guided her into a rhythmic grinding that elicited something unholy in them both. Made Aisling fear she might literally ignite with flame and burn the whole of the world at the cost of whatever boundless pleasure the feeling of herself against him inspired.

She clawed at his back, felt the scars where his wings were torn, and he allowed it. Moaned at the press of her fingertips against his scars and moved her faster against him.

"Together, if you truly bond with the Sidhe King, you will breed desolation and ruin."

Lir kissed Aisling's neck, no longer slow but hungry. Licking her windpipe where once she feared he might rip it from her, grazing her collar bone with his tongue, growling at the curve of her breasts as he slipped her hemline into his mouth and tugged with his fangs, tearing a sliver. But that one sliver was enough to rip her bodice entirely apart, exposing the thin chemise beneath.

Lir's eyes lit with the light sinners extinguished, burning with dark desire. His hands forsaking her hips to move on their own, so that he might hold her. First her ribs, thumbs slipping beneath her breasts. Patiently, the edge of his fingers finding the apex of each breast and brushing them. Aisling arched into his touch. Just a graze at first. Enough to drive Aisling mad and plunge Lir's expression into abysmal dark at the sign of her pleasure. At the sound of her pleasure, the feel of it as she moved harder against him.

"Aisling," he growled, closing his eyes the more she pressed.

"Should I stop?" she asked, the corners of her lips curling as she traced the veins in his forearms with her fingertips.

"Gods no," he begged, standing easily, carrying her with him and setting her knees atop the throne, her back to him. He dipped his head beside her own, finding her lips then her neck, his hands slipping beneath the hem of her chemise and trailing upwards. At last, his hands surrounded her bare breasts, forcing a gasp from Aisling's lips. Lir grinned against her cheek. The hardness of him pressed against her backside.

Lir cursed beneath his breath, the throne room over-flowing with swiftly growing flora.

"But if we continue—"

"So be it," Aisling said against his lips. Words that inspired a shudder from the fae king, rippling through his every muscle as he brought her closer to him.

"Together," he said, "you and I will bring this world to its knees."

He entered her. Thrusting lightly at first, torturously slow, then deeply, throwing his head back the moment Aisling reached for the head of the throne and gripped it till her fingertips might bruise. With each stroke, the realm churned, shifted, as Aisling and Lir ripped the tapestry of fate apart and pinned their own stars to the sky.

"You're mine," he whispered, against her spine. Fangs scraping down her back. Voice ragged and rough with yearning. As though this wasn't enough, as though a lifetime of this wasn't enough, and he needed more of her. Of them.

"And I am yours."

Aisling bit down on her bottom lip, drawing blood.

He filled her, moving painfully slow, swelling inside and blinding the sorceress to anything but *this*. But the feel of his soul as it wrapped around her own, tangling itself with hers till they could scarcely tell one from the other, was euphoric. Couldn't make the two apart as they wove, as they laced, as they threaded together, becoming one.

As the cord that'd bound them, at last, ripped apart, again and again with every thrust. With every movement. Binding something new. Becoming something new. Becoming one. And truly bound.

CHAPTER XLIV

AISLING

"You know not what you've done, Aisling," the Lady hissed inside Aisling's mind as she stepped a pace away from her balcony, sheltered by the canopies of the greenwood. Beyond and below, Annwyn stood waiting, watching, listening to Lir as he spoke from Castle Annwyn's grand balcony.

"You've damned this realm and now the gods will wake with fury."

"Then let them wake," Aisling replied inside her mind.

Peitho stepped into Aisling's quarters just as Aisling was to leave. Peitho wore a Cornelian gown flocked by sun-bright beetles that crawled across the folds of her skirts. Her endless tresses were shrouded in a hood of the same fiery hues, shadowing her burn scars. A stark contrast from the leathers she'd worn over the past several weeks trekking to Lofgren's Rise.

Slowly, Aisling stood from her vanity and Gilrel's magpies took flight, releasing her braids once they'd woven them artfully together.

"I should've announced my intentions to visit you earlier," the Niltorian princess said, balling her hands into fists at her sides.

"You should have."

Peitho hesitated at the tone of Aisling's voice. The princess had made it clear time and time again she was no friend to Aisling and so her presence, here and now, wouldn't be met without hostility. Especially today.

"I've brought you a gift."

Aisling's fingers twitched at her sides, eyes narrowing as Peitho reached into her jewel-encrusted belt and unsheathed a sword. She bowed her head, holding the hilt in the palm of one hand and the tip of its blade in the other. An offering.

Aisling approached cautiously, studying the blade. It was magnificent. A slick, black blade polished to perfection, etched in fae runes that dissolved as the eye traveled toward the onyx cross guard, wrapped in the coil of a serpent. Its gaping mouth hoarding a bundle of amethysts between its fangs.

"It's a tradition in Niltaor to gift a princess a blade on the day she's to become queen."

"I became queen long ago."

Peitho raised her head, meeting Aisling's gaze. "Not like today."

They shared a moment of silence. A strange assessment of the other. As though both were anticipating a betrayal.

"I received my first blade from my father when I was crowned princess. *Luinagren.* My second will come when I become queen of Niltaor." Peitho smiled despite herself, the corners of her eyes crinkling in a surprisingly soft expression. "I could hardly carry Luinagren at the time. My cousins laughed at me, amused when my guard steadied my arm to keep it from shaking. So, I trained until I no longer shook.

Until the blade became a second limb I could no longer do without."

Aisling took another step forward and wrapped her fingers around the hilt. Peitho released the blade and stepped back, folding her hands behind her back.

The blade was heavy, causing Aisling's arms to shake even now in adulthood and with the *draiocht* running through her veins.

"I chose this blade for its finesse," Peitho said, appraising the coupling of Aisling and the sword. To the Aos Sí, a wielder bonds with their blade, the first meeting more important than any other. "It's forged with adamant, lighter than most metals yet powerful all the same. Its tip, as sharp and biting as the most lethal venoms."

Aisling held the blade like Galad and Rian had taught her, swinging it once. The movement was awkward and the muscles in both her abdomen and arms strained.

Peitho tilted her head to the side, and Aisling braced herself for the princess's ridicule.

"May I?" Peitho asked instead, gesturing to the sword.

Aisling swallowed but nodded her head, handing the weapon to Peitho.

"You hold it like a male," she said, showing Aisling how she gripped the hilt. "Your body moves differently to them and requires a more elegant approach."

"Galad and Rian were my instructors."

"That explains it," Peitho said. "They're fine warriors but they know little of what it takes to be a swordswoman. I can teach you."

"Teach me?" Aisling nearly scoffed, watching as Peitho effortlessly spun the blade between her fingers.

"Don't look so surprised. If you're to be the queen of

Annwyn, an ally to Niltaor, I couldn't let you embarrass our kingdoms with your clumsy jabbing."

Peitho tossed the blade back to Aisling and mercifully she caught it, bracing herself for the weight of it.

"What will you name it?"

Aisling's brows pinched, considering.

"I'd never thought to name a blade."

"Every Sidhe queen names her blade. It's a part of the tethering of souls."

There is power in names. Even the mortals knew that.

Aisling closed her eyes.

"Sarwen."

Peitho did a double take, eyes widening. "*Sarwen, the mortal reaper.*"

Galad stepped by Aisling's side, her personal guard now, waiting to escort her onto the balcony and join Lir's side.

She wore a gown of scorpion black, hugging her body until it spilled from her hips like liquid metal. A slit rose to her hip, showcasing the lace-up heels Gilrel's magpies had tied around her calves and thighs. Hair loose and wild, interspersed with braided strands glistering with onyx beads.

Peitho, Filverel, Gilrel, and the rest of Lir's knights stood waiting behind him, silent with their heads bowed or looking over the audience. An endless crowd of those whose ears drew to a point, whose fangs were sharp, those with wings and those without, bipedal beasts of all shape and form.

"From now on," Lir continued, "you are subjects of both myself and your queen: Aisling, the Sidhe queen of Annwyn, host of the *Dragún*, Curse Breaker, and sorceress."

Aisling paled at the sound of her titles, stomach plummeting. So Galad nudged her, encouraging her forward.

Lir met her eyes. He didn't say a word, but he didn't need to. His posture encouraged her forward, brows drawing together.

Aisling forced herself to swallow, inhaling deeply before taking the plunge and stepping into the light of the balcony.

There was silence. The inevitable pause before Aisling was to face the wrath, the fury, the hatred of any who beheld her whether it be mortal, fae, or Unseelie. A thick quiet that unnerved Aisling.

And so, such silence happened today, dense and persistent. A quiet that vegetated in the northern air until it broke. Until the hordes of fae before her erupted into applause. Screaming from their lungs, chanting her name, singing her praise. Leaping, smiling, tossing their fists into the air. Fae taking flight with admiration. A sea of veneration. Of worship.

Aisling's expression evolved into a grin. One that ached as it grew larger, unable to be stifled the louder the audience grew. The more restless their cries. This was all she'd ever craved. Purpose, power. A world that gave her what her own blood never did: appreciation. Thanks for the sacrifice she'd made in their name. Acknowledgement for everything she'd done. Respect and welcoming. And here it was, among her enemy. Now her home.

Gilrel approached at her side, her magpies fluttering around Aisling's head at the pine marten's command. One by one, the magpies collected an antlered crown and held it above Aisling's head. The counterpart to Lir's own. A brilliant headdress fit for the sovereigns of the greenwood.

The magpies set the crown atop her head, and Annwyn erupted.

"Slayer of man!" they chanted, again and again and again.

Lir watched her, a grin reflected in his expression. More breathtaking than anything Aisling had ever seen before. And that's why Aisling believed the Lady took it away, replaced by the image of a fleeting vision:

Aisling and Lir stood in the rain, steeped in both water and blood. Aisling swayed, brushed by a large wind and nearly knocked over. An axe in her chest, eyes swiftly dimming as the light fled from her violet orbs. Lir was crying, screaming something so terrible the Forge trembled. Yet Aisling couldn't make it out. Couldn't see past the dagger in his heart still lit with violet flame as he fell to his knees, clawing for Aisling, already lying on her back. Till his screams dissolved, washed away by the tempest as their heartbeats slowed to a halt in unison.

AFTER

LIR

Aisling and Lir raced on stagback through the feywilds surrounding Annwyn.

They were supposed to be in the throne room, meeting with Filverel, Galad, and the rest of Lir's knights. Instead, they'd foregone their responsibilities in favor of racing through a woodland storm. The trees bubbling over with plums, peaches, and lemons. Roses wrapping around their trunks and Connemara poppies blooming wherever their stag's hooves met the ground. Indeed, Aisling and Lir's *draiocht* was insurmountable when together once they'd truly bonded. Wherever Lir went, whenever their eyes met, violets would blossom, and the world grew a few degrees hotter.

At last, Lir's stag caught up with Aisling's own.

He dove for her, knocking her off the stag and into a glen of brownie moss and cherry-red toadstools. Their stags continued to run into the surrounding woodland with their momentum.

"You cheated," Aisling said as he pinned her arms above her head.

"So did you."

He paused, gazing at a bundle of flowers on Aisling's righthand side.

"*Ellwyn*," he said. Aisling considered the flowers more closely: violet yet almost translucent, blooming from the earth from glass-like stems and peppered through the thickest patches of grass. "A legendary flower that has no native ground, it once bloomed in Annwyn every spring for several decades until it disappeared. The Sidhe searched for it, longed for it, wondered if it would ever return."

Lir kissed her palms, tracing over the scars she'd suffered saving him from Danu's poison. Whisper-light kisses deepening as he pressed his thigh between her legs and released her wrists so she could tangle her fingers through his hair. Lir slid his hands beneath her gown and gripped her hips. The veins in his forearms flexing the harder he held her atop the bed of *ellwyn*.

"We should return. The others are waiting for us—" Aisling broke off, inhaling sharply as he pressed his thigh more firmly between her legs.

"They can continue to wait," he growled against her jaw. The forest thickened around them till walls were made of Lir's thorns, ivy, and blood-red roses. Eyes no longer green but black with wanting.

Lightning splintered across the skies, interrupting them.

Lir straightened, wicking the hair from his eyes when he spotted it: a pool that wasn't there moments before.

Both he and Aisling stood from the earth, bracing against the cloudburst, nearing the pool with caution. It glittered knowingly, blooming *ellwyn* and deepening till the center was a black eye glaring back. Lir's expression narrowed, drawing both halves of Hiraeth from his back. They'd both seen this pool before in Aisling's dreams.

"The forest is changing," the trees whispered, every word spoken as though they were peering over their shoulders. "Danu spreads her rot through your land, the Lady sits before her loom in wait, and the mortals are recovering for vengeance. But more so than anyone or anything, the Otherworld is shifting. The veil between here and there hasn't thickened despite the end of *Samhain*. Someone is opening gateways. The forest feels it. The forest knows it. The forest screams each time a door is opened to the Other."

"What is it?" Aisling asked.

Lir tilted his head back. "A gateway." And at the word, the pool rippled, hundreds of voices whispering incoherently. As though the entire Other peered back from its depths, feeding their thoughts through the water.

"A door to the afterlife," Aisling conjectured, her expression hardening, growing suddenly distant.

"Aye, the spirit realm where the gods sleep and the Forge rests," Lir said, sifting through the surrounding woodland with his eyes. "*Tir fo Thuinn*: the land beneath the water."

"Racat celebrates this pool," Aisling said. "He wishes to tether the two realms: our realm and that of the Other."

Lir ground his jaw. Racat's motivations were laced with greed: a common dragon hoarded gold but Racat hoarded power. Wanted it more than even Lir himself and would stop at nothing before he achieved it. And so, it came as no surprise that Racat wanted the entirety of the Other as well. Wanted Aisling to become the guardian of the gateway to the spirit world. Complete sovereignty achievable through Aisling. She, born of both realms. Yet the prospect unnerved Lir. The Otherworld was a land of dreams, of saturated magic, of gods, and monsters.

"What Racat demands is no easy feat."

"But it's possible?" Aisling asked, eyes glittering with hope. "We could venture into the Other?"

Lir hesitated before at last speaking. "Aye, but only with an invitation. One you've already received."

Aisling's expression lit with recognition. "The fountain inside Castle Annwyn with the statue of Ina's owl."

Lir nodded his head, impressed she'd made the connection so readily. Lir hadn't known Aisling for more than a handful of days when he'd discovered her in his mother's chamber. The fountain was a gateway to the Otherworld where the Sidhe were originally cast before the gods cleaved the world into two realms. Ina made use of its magic, harnessing her *draiocht* to peer into the future just as Danu used her pools in the Isle of Mirrors and how Fionn travelled through his mirrors. It was dangerous and forbidden witchery to all those unfamiliar with its limits. If wielded incorrectly, one could grow lost in the void between realms, the mind maddened by its reflection, or the heart split by the magic. And when Lir had found the door unlocked and Aisling inside... he half wondered if she weren't a changeling, another mockery of the gods sent to destroy one of the last semblances of Ina's legacy. Other than Fionn of course. But the question remained: all this time, was it Ina opening doors for Aisling? Or the gods themselves?

"If we decide to cross into the Other, it's Ina's fountain we must enter. To trust this pool or anything else the forest whispers from now on... is unwise." Indeed, Lir could smell Danu's influence. Could hear the mushrooms, the disease, the insects growing, swarming, spreading, the longer Danu amassed her legions of traitors. Not even his own woodland was to be trusted until Danu was killed. And this pool would be no different.

"To rule over the Other would be to usurp the gods?" Aisling asked.

"Not quite," Lir said. "To rule over the Other would be to gain the gods' favor."

Aisling swallowed. "And how might we do that?"

Lir hooked Hiraeth onto his back. "We do them a favor."

Aisling bit her bottom lip. Lir saw the desire stirring around her iris, her mind already sorting through her next steps. An ambition that quickened his heart and forced him to keep his hands to himself lest he never stop touching her, wanting her.

At last, Aisling spun on her heel, breaking the spell she held over Lir as she started for Castle Annwyn. Resolved to enter the Other at any and all costs. And despite the risks, Lir knew this was the only way to ensure a victory against the Lady, Danu, Fionn, and the mortals. With the entirety of the Other, with their true binding, with Racat, no war would be waged without a death wish from their adversaries first.

Yet as Lir made to follow Aisling through the trees, he was stopped short by a single voice breaking through the rest, calling after his *caera* from the pool. A sound that rippled through his bones and chilled his flesh.

"*Aisling,*" it sang from the sparkling shadows of the after-life. "*Come find me.*"

PRONUNCIATION GUIDE

The pronunciation of words inspired or derived from Celtic folklore can be tricky for those who aren't familiar, and are often pronounced in unexpected ways. Some words, I've adjusted to fit Aisling and her fantasy world so they aren't quite how tradition would have it. Nevertheless, feel free to reference this pronunciation guide as you read on!

Abhaile: ahb-HAIL

Aisling: ASH-ling

Annind: AH-neend

Annwyn: ON-win

Aos Sí: EES-shee

Bludhaven: blood-hay-ven

Caera: kai-ruh

Cú Scáth: coo-SKATH

Dagfin: DAG-fin

Damh Bán: dom-bahn

Dragún: dra-GOON

Draiocht: dree-OUT

Ellén Trechend: ell-AHN trekh-end

Ellwyn: ell-win

Fear gorta: FAR-gorta

Filverel: phil-VER-ell

Fionn: FEE-on

Fjallnorr: fi-YALL-norr

Galad: GA-lad

Gilrel: gill-rell

Greum: groom

Heill: hayll

Iarbonel: YAR-boh-nell

Iod: EE-odd

Lir: leer

Luinagren: LOO-ween-NAH-gren

Mo Lúra: moh LOO-rah

Murúch: moo-ROOK

Neccakaid: NEKA-kayd

Nemed: NEH-med

Niltaor: NIL-tower

Ocras: OH-krus

Oighir: EYE-yehr

Peitho: PAY-tho

Rinn Dúin: rinn-DOON

Rún: roon

Samhain: saa-win

Sarwen: SAR-wen

Snaidhm: snay-dim

GLOSSARY

Aengus – the dragon of immortality.

Aisling – the only mortal princess in all the Isles of Rinn Dúin made queen of the Sidhe and Annwyn by her marriage to Lir, and later known as the not-so-mortal queen after she discovers her magic.

Annind – one of the four princes of Tilren and Aisling's brother.

Bludhaven – a druid village in the forests of Fjallnorr.

Bres – one of the twelve original Sidhe sovereigns and the Sidhe king of the greenwood. Ina's *caera* and Lir's father.

Caera – two souls fated by the Forge.

Curse Breaker – the remedy to Ina's sins and the curse she condemned Iod to, breeding all of humankind. Capable of restoring the long lifespans, strength, and magic to the mortals.

Cu Scáth – an Unseelie shadow hound.

Dagfin – the crown prince of Roktling and its seafaring kingdom, trained as a *Faerak* and both Aisling's childhood best friend as well as her once intended before her marriage to Lir.

Danu – empress of the dryads.

Draiocht – the sentient embodiment of magic represented as a beast unique to its caster and lurking inside one's own abyss.

Druids – humans who bear a unique sensitivity to the natural world, magic, and an admiration for the Sidhe, some going so far as to worship them.

Fear gorta – Unseelie that rots in the earth, rising when it smells living flesh and blood.

Fergus – one of the four princes of Tilren and Aisling's brother.

Filverel – Lir's Sidhe court advisor and knight.

Fionn – The son of Winter and Sidhe king of Winter, son to one of the original twelve Sidhe sovereigns, Delbaeth, and Lir's brother.

Fomorians – chaotic Unseelie, orcish and rot personified, were the first to reject Lir's sovereignty over the feywilds.

Forge – the cosmic brew from which the gods made the two realms: the Otherworld and the mortal realm.

Galad – Lir's first knight and a descendant of both Annwyn and Iod.

Glamour – a spell designed to disguise and bend the appearance of someone or something to whims of its caster.

Heill – the capital of Fjallnorr.

Iarbonel – the second eldest prince of Tilren and Aisling's brother.

Ina – one of the twelve original Sidhe sovereigns and the queen of the mountain kingdom Iod. Bres's *caera* and Lir's mother, gifted visions of the future by the gods before she and Iod were cursed and condemned to mortality.

Lady of Fate – the weaver of stars and destiny.

Lir – the Sidhe king of the greenwood and ruler of Annwyn, also known as the most powerful fae king in this realm or the next and the *Damh Ban*, meaning white stag.

Lofgren's Rise – a peak in the Fjallnorrian north legend says hoards the curse breaker and the answers Aisling seeks.

Muirdris – the dragon of prosperity.

Murúch – Unseelie who lure sailors to their death in the open sea by either drowning or turning their flesh to stone.

Narisea – Lir's first *caera* who passed tragically several centuries before Aisling and Lir's union.

Neccakaid – chaotic Unseelie in the form of giant arachnids.

Nemed – the fire hand of the North and the high king of all the Isles of Rinn Dúin. Lir's nemesis and Aisling's father.

Niamh – the Sidhe queen of rain and wielder of the original Sarwen.

Niltaor – a southern Sidhe kingdom and Peitho's homeland.

Odhran – a legendary Sidhe hero who held up the weight of the night for eternity.

Otherworld – the spiritual world and/or afterlife in Celtic mythology.

Peitho – southern Sidhe princess of Niltaor and Lir's intended before he was promised to Aisling.

Phuka – an Unseelie who steals children and masks itself as a beautiful mare.

Racat – the dragon of power.

Samhain – the festival the Sidhe celebrate when the veil between the Other realm and their own is thinner than any other time during the year.

Sarwen – also known as the mortal slayer, Niamh's legendary blade.

Starn – the crown prince of Tilren and all the Isles of Rinn Dúin. Aisling's eldest brother.

Trow – an Unseelie subspecies of troll.

True Binding – a consummation of two souls that weaves their power together.

Wild Hunt – the hunt for the dragons of immortality, prosperity, and power: Aengus, Muirdris, and Racat that yielded a centuries-long war between the Sidhe kingdoms.

A LETTER FROM ASHLEY

Dear reader,

Thank you for choosing to read *The Savage Queen*. Writing the sequel to this series was a different experience from writing the first. With *The Savage Queen*, it was not only the excitement of embarking upon a new journey that breathed life into the lungs of these pages, but also the feeling of returning somewhere familiar: a home that exists only in memory, in the mind, and in the heart. Therefore, it was important as I wrote these characters, their stories, and their world that the story plunge more deeply and thoroughly into the lore, the universe, and the magic than before, grabbing the reader's hand and racing straight into the best kind of dangers—dark forests, bygone beasts, and fated romances. And so, if you enjoyed *The Savage Queen*, and want to keep up to date with all my latest releases, just sign up at the following link. Your email address will never be shared and you can unsubscribe at any time.

www.secondskybooks.com/ashley-metzler

Hearing my readers' voices has been one of the most invaluable experiences of being an author. It is a gift to be able to share my stories with you all and I treasure your thoughts, opinions, and feedback. Whether it be a book thrown across the room in frustration, a cover shut tight in anticipation, a page torn and taped to the wall, or a discussion with fellow readers, I'll never tire of hearing your experiences. Reviews are always appreciated and might help *The Savage Queen* discover new readers to steal into the feywilds.

If you feel inspired to do so, stay in touch on my social media or my website.

With love,

Ashley Metzler

X

www.aejurgens.com

 instagram.com/aejurgensauthor
goodreads.com/aejurgens

PUBLISHING TEAM

Turning a manuscript into a book requires the efforts of many people. The publishing team at Bookouture would like to acknowledge everyone who contributed to this publication.

Audio
Alba Proko
Sinead O'Connor
Melissa Tran

Commercial
Lauren Morrissette
Hannah Richmond
Imogen Allport

Cover design
BRoseDesignz

Data and analysis
Mark Alder
Mohamed Bussuri

Editorial
Jack Renninson
Melissa Tran